HOW
TO CATCH
A SINFUL
MARQUESS

❧

AMY ROSE BENNETT

JOVE
New York

A JOVE BOOK
Published by Berkley
An imprint of Penguin Random House LLC
penguinrandomhouse.com

Copyright © 2020 by Amy Rose Bennett
Excerpt from *How to Catch a Wicked Viscount* copyright © 2019 by Amy Rose Bennett
Penguin Random House supports copyright. Copyright fuels creativity, encourages
diverse voices, promotes free speech, and creates a vibrant culture. Thank you for buying
an authorized edition of this book and for complying with copyright laws by not
reproducing, scanning, or distributing any part of it in any form without permission.
You are supporting writers and allowing Penguin Random House to continue to
publish books for every reader.

A JOVE BOOK, BERKLEY, and the BERKLEY & B colophon
are registered trademarks of Penguin Random House LLC.

ISBN: 9781984803962

First Edition: August 2020

Printed in the United States of America
1 3 5 7 9 10 8 6 4 2

Cover art by Aleta Rafton
Cover design by Judith Lagerman
Book design by George Towne

*To my wonderful husband, my soul mate
and best friend, Richard.
I love you, always and forever.*

CHAPTER 1

Town might be quiet at the moment, but the *Beau Monde Mirror* will endeavor to keep our readership abreast of all the latest tonnish on-dits.

If there's a scandal brewing—an illicit affair, an elopement, or anyone high in the instep puts a foot wrong—you can be sure we'll let the proverbial cat out of the bag first.

The Beau Monde Mirror: The Society Page

16 Grosvenor Square, Mayfair

September 14, 1818

If it weren't for Lady Charlotte Hastings's troublesome tortoiseshell cat, Olivia de Vere would not be in such a mortifying predicament right now.

Of course, if Charlie were actually here at this very moment (as opposed to being miles away at her father's country estate in Gloucestershire), she would surely tell Olivia that her current situation—straddling the six-foot-high, ivy-clad wall adjoining the Marquess of Sleat's back garden as she made a futile attempt to coax said cat from the branches of a towering beech tree—was an "opportunity," not a disaster waiting to happen.

Olivia shot a quick glance at the back of her guardians' rather grand town house. Or, to be more precise, *her* town house, considering the rent was drawn from her very own inheritance money, currently held "in trust." When she ascertained no one was watching her, she permitted herself a tiny sigh of relief. If Uncle Reginald or Aunt Edith caught her committing such an indecorous act, or her cousins Prudence and Patience, or, even worse, her warden-cum-lady's-maid, Bagshaw . . . Olivia shuddered. There would be the devil to pay, that much was certain.

Ever since she'd been expelled from Mrs. Rathbone's Academy for Young Ladies of Good Character three years ago for decidedly unladylike conduct—along with the other three members of the Society for Enlightened Young Women, Sophie, Arabella, and Charlie—she'd been mired in disgrace and labeled a social pariah. A "disreputable debutante," according to scurrilous gossip rags like the *Beau Monde Mirror*.

She really couldn't afford to court disaster again.

But it seemed that was exactly what she was doing.

Her gaze flitted to Lord Sleat's town house. Now, if the forbidding yet altogether fascinating marquess happened to discover what she was up to . . . Olivia shivered again. While she longed to make the man's acquaintance, this was *not* a prudent way to go about it by any means.

As Lord Sleat was a good friend of Lord Malverne—Sophie's husband and Charlie's older brother—Olivia had it on good authority that the Scottish marquess was considered to be a very eligible bachelor indeed. Of course, Lord Sleat also had a well-earned reputation for being one of London's worst rakehells. A serial seducer of women.

However, Olivia was certain the marquess wouldn't even spare her a passing glance at this particular moment in time. With her skirts and petticoats rucked up about her knees, her silk stockings torn and smeared with something mucky and green—moss, perhaps—she looked an absolute fright. Not only that, but what she was doing certainly bordered on trespassing.

If Lord Sleat *did* see her, he'd be well within his rights to summon the Bow Street Runners.

But what could she do? She absolutely had to rescue her

dear friend's beloved pet. If Peridot fell or escaped into the mews . . . Visions of the cat darting between carriages and horses' hooves or being stalked by a lascivious tomcat filled Olivia's mind's eye, and her whole body trembled like the dark green leaves above her head.

Despite Olivia's edict to the servants that Peridot should not be let out unless accompanied, the cat had somehow slipped into the garden on her own. When Olivia looked up from the pages of *Northanger Abbey*—she'd been reading in her bedchamber after dinner—and spied Peridot leaping from the wall into the tree, her heart had taken flight like a panicked bird.

And now here she was, her heart fluttering wildly, her belly tumbling with fear, and her head spinning with dizziness whenever she looked down. How inconvenient that she'd belatedly discovered she was terrified of heights. Olivia huffed out a breath to blow a stray lock of hair away from her face. She daren't let go of the brick wall lest she fall. She'd already lost one of her shoes; in the process of clambering onto her precarious perch, her pink silk slipper slid off her foot and landed in a dense, rather prickly looking bank of rosebushes guarding the perimeter of Lord Sleat's garden.

On her side of the wall, the stone bench she'd climbed upon looked far away indeed. And part of the ivy-choked latticework she'd used as a makeshift ladder had already cracked ominously beneath her weight. But she really couldn't afford to panic about how she'd get down. First of all, she had to reach that blasted cat, and quickly. The light was fading fast, and it wouldn't be long before her presence was missed.

Olivia drew a bracing breath. "P-P-Peridot." Her stammer was little more than a ragged whisper. "Here, p-puss, puss. There's a good k-kitty now." Knees trembling, heart pounding, she forced herself to inch forward along the wall so she could peer up into the beech canopy.

There. Directly above her on a sturdy branch, but just out of reach, sat Peridot, her black, white, and tan fur barely visible in the shadows. The cat's fluffy tail twitched when Olivia called her again. A disdainful gesture if she'd ever seen one.

Little minx. If Olivia survived this foolhardy escapade, she was going to pack Peridot into her basket and send her back to Berkeley Square posthaste. Let the Hastings House staff deal with their young mistress's cat. Charlie meant well when she'd suggested in her last letter that Olivia might like to look after Peridot for a few weeks until Charlie returned to London in the first week of October. On the surface, her friend's reasoning was sound: a pet would provide Olivia with congenial company, affection, and a source of amusement—three things that were sorely lacking in her life.

Ignoring the scrape of the brickwork along the tender flesh of her inner thighs, Olivia crept forward again. And then the hem of her muslin gown snagged on something, and she winced at the sound of fabric tearing.

Damn, damn, and double damn again.

How on earth was she going to explain the damage to Bagshaw? She'd be sure to tattle to Aunt Edith, who'd tell Uncle Reginald.

And then she'd be punished.

But at least Peridot will be safe—

"Ahem."

The low, unmistakable sound of an adult male clearing his throat made Olivia simultaneously jump and squeak with fright.

Oh, no. No, no, no. Her heart plummeting like a dislodged stone, Olivia's gaze whipped down to collide with that of a man's. But not just any man.

It was the Marquess of Sleat. The very object of her girlish infatuation.

The subject of all her silly, romantical dreams.

In the flesh.

And what flesh it was. Well over six feet of muscular, broad-shouldered, square-jawed man glowered up at her.

Her grip tightened on the wall. Her pulse stuttered, and

heat flared in her cheeks. *Mortified* didn't even begin to describe how she felt.

Horrified would be closer to the mark. Definitely shaken and utterly speechless.

She'd never seen Lord Sleat this close up before. Indeed, she'd only ever glimpsed him at a distance as he quit his town house before striding off down Grosvenor Square or climbing into his coach. And there'd been that one occasion when he lounged on the stone-flagged terrace overlooking this very garden. In the summer gloaming, she'd spied the glowing tip of his cheroot cigar and the flash of amber liquid—perhaps whisky—as the light of the setting sun glanced off his raised glass.

Charlie had once described him as being the epitome of a Highland warrior crossed with a pirate. As Olivia continued to gawp in awkward dismay at the marquess, she decided her friend's assessment was quite accurate. A thick sweep of sable hair falling across his brow partially obscured a jagged scar and the black leather patch covering his left eye socket. His other eye, the iris a dark storm-cloud gray, pinned her with a hard, distinctly sardonic stare.

"Two thoughts spring to mind." Lord Sleat's baritone voice and Scots burr coalesced into a rich, deep rumble, which Olivia swore she could feel vibrate through her body like a roll of distant thunder. "First of all, what the devil are you doing? And secondly, how the hell did a wee lassie like you get up there?"

One dark eyebrow arched as he waited for Olivia to respond, and for a moment, she wondered if she'd misjudged the marquess's mood; she swore she glimpsed a quicksilver flash of humor in his gaze.

Amused or not, he still expected her to answer. She swallowed to moisten her dry-as-a-desert mouth. To undo the knots from her perpetually tangled tongue. "I . . . I . . ." She screwed her eyes shut as she attempted to wrest a coherent sentence loose. "I . . . my f-f-friend's c-cat is . . ." Lifting a trembling hand, she pointed at the branches overhead.

"Peri . . . P-Peridot . . ." Her mouth twisted with frustration. "Sh-sh-she's s-s-stuck . . . She's stuck up there."

As Lord Sleat crossed his arms over his wide chest, the fabric of his navy blue jacket pulled tight across the impressive swell of bunched biceps muscles beneath. "You're trying to rescue your friend's cat." Judging by his flat tone and skeptical frown, the marquess clearly doubted the veracity of her statement.

Nevertheless, Olivia nodded. "Y-yes."

He took several steps closer to the wall, and his gaze shifted to the beech tree. "Are you sure she's stuck?" He squinted up into the gently waving branches. "It's been my experience that cats can generally look after them—"

At that precise moment, Peridot elegantly sprang from her leafy hidey-hole and landed on the wall. With another contemptuous flick of her tail, she then leapt to the ground, alighting right beside Lord Sleat's shiny black Hessians.

Olivia's jaw dropped. She'd never seen a cat perform such a daring feat with such alacrity. She suddenly felt like the biggest fool in Christendom.

To make matters worse, Peridot began to purr and blatantly rub her body all over the marquess's boots. Her tail twined between his legs, as though she were claiming possession of this man.

Charlie's cat wasn't a little minx at all. She was a brazen minx.

Lord Sleat bent low and scooped Peridot into his arms. The cat's purring grew louder, and when the marquess stroked her beneath the chin with one long finger, she closed her bright green eyes and rubbed her fluffy cheek against his paisley satin waistcoat as if she were in the throes of ecstasy.

Good Lord, what a hussy of a cat.

As Olivia scowled down at Peridot, Lord Sleat spoke. "Well, all's well that ends well, it would seem . . . except for the fact you are still stuck on my wall, Miss . . ." He cocked an eyebrow again.

Olivia drew a steadying breath in order to control her

stammer. It wasn't usually this pronounced. However, the stress of trying to retrieve Peridot, combined with her newly discovered fear of heights and coming face-to-face with an overwhelmingly masculine marquess whom she'd been secretly daydreaming about for several months—all of these things were wreaking havoc on her equilibrium. Not to mention the fact that Lord Sleat's attention had drifted to her bared lower leg and slipperless foot. It seemed Peridot wasn't the only one being brazen. But Lord Sleat was a rake after all.

Her face aflame, Olivia at last summoned her voice. "Oh . . . Oliv . . . liv . . ."

"Lavinia?" supplied Lord Sleat as his gaze met hers again.

Olivia only just suppressed a sigh. She supposed the marquess was only trying to be helpful by supplying the rest of her name . . . even if he'd got it wrong.

But what was the point in trying to correct him or additionally provide her surname so he could address her as Miss de Vere, as decorum dictated? Despite the fact that they were neighbors, it was highly unlikely that she'd ever have such a close and personal encounter with this man again. Not unless her martinet of an uncle and equally exacting aunt could be persuaded to let her attend any ton social events.

Charlie, Sophie, and Arabella might try to matchmake when they all returned to town next month, but Olivia suspected it would all come to naught. So she simply smiled and nodded her agreement. Lavinia would do.

"Well, Miss Lavinia," continued the marquess. A crooked smile tugged at the corner of his wide mouth. "Would you like me to help you down?"

This time, Olivia did manage to find her voice. "Oh, yes, p-please, Lord Sleat. I'd be m-most grateful."

He promptly deposited Peridot on the lawn. "You know who I am?" he said as he straightened and pushed his way into the evil-looking rosebushes bordering the wall. His snug-fitting buckskin breeches and Hessians clearly provided his legs with adequate protection, as he seemed oblivious to the thorns.

Olivia nodded. "Of course, my lord. D-doesn't everyone in London know you?"

He flashed a wolfish grin as he reached toward her. His large hands settled about her waist, holding her steady. "It seems my reputation precedes me, Miss Lavinia. Now, if you'd be so kind as to swing your other leg over to this side. That's it. And hold on to my shoulders. Ready? Because here we go."

Before Olivia could even draw another breath, the marquess's grip tightened on her middle, and she suddenly found herself suspended in the air. In the next instant, he made a deft turn and lowered her to the ground in a long, slow, effortless slide, her body grazing the length of his. She was acutely aware of his body's heat. Its granitelike hardness. The power of his arms and the shifting contours of his mountainous shoulders beneath her hands. By the time her feet touched the grass, she was more than a little breathless and her pulse was racing so fast, she felt giddy.

To combat the wave of dizziness, she closed her eyes, her hands lingering about the marquess's neck. Given that his hands remained about her waist, he didn't seem in any hurry to relinquish his hold either.

Thick silky hair brushed the backs of her fingers. His distinctive masculine scent—a potent mix of leather, musk, and exotic spices—teased her senses, and for one mad moment, she contemplated pressing her face against his shirt-front, just so she could get closer to him.

No wonder Peridot had looked so beatific in his arms. He smelled divine.

"Are you all right, Miss Lavinia?" Lord Sleat's voice was no longer a gruff rumble, but low and soft, like a lion's gentle purr.

Olivia forced herself to open her eyes and take a step back. How fanciful she was becoming. Not to mention shameless. She might already have a sullied reputation in the eyes of her family and polite society, but she really shouldn't risk making it worse. "Y-yes. I'm quite f-fine," she stammered. Her cheeks bloomed with heat at the thought that the marquess might think she'd actually swooned in his arms.

Lord Sleat frowned down at her. "Not quite, lass," he said, plucking her pink slipper from a nearby rosebush. Then, before she knew what he was about, he knelt on the grass, and like the prince in a fairy tale, he slid her slipper onto her foot. His touch seemed to sear through the silk of her stocking to the flesh beneath, making her shiver with awareness. He looked up at her, his mouth curving in a decidedly rakish smile as he relinquished her ankle. "Now everything's just right."

Olivia swallowed, and her blush deepened. "Th-thank you." Was the marquess deliberately trying to make her swoon again? Because if he was, he was very close to succeeding.

She really should go.

Something tugged the back of her muslin gown, and when she glanced down, it was to discover Peridot had pounced on the torn flounce trailing from her hem. Naughty puss. She picked up the cat and bobbed a quick curtsy. "My lord, I thank you again for your . . . for your assistance. But it's time P-Peridot and I bid you adieu."

He inclined his head. "Of course." He gestured toward the terrace and the open French doors. The shadows had lengthened, and candles and lamps glowed warmly in the elegant drawing room beyond. "Let me escort you out."

Olivia froze. "Oh." She shook her head. "I d-don't think . . . Is there by any ch-chance another way? A gate leading to the m-mews? I don't mean to cause offense, but as you are a b-bachelor, and I am . . ." She lifted her chin. "And I am unchaperoned, it m-might invite unwanted attention if I leave via your front door." Good Lord, if her aunt and uncle's priggish butler, Mr. Finch, caught sight of her leaving Sleat House, she'd be done for.

Lord Sleat nodded. "Ah yes, you are absolutely right. A discreet exit would be wise. Come." He began walking with long, sure strides toward the end of the garden, and Olivia had to rush to keep up. "Let me show you something."

He stopped before a narrow gap in a waist-high box-wood hedge. Ivy cascaded over the top of the wall like a tumbling, verdant waterfall. "See here." With a sweep of his arm, Lord Sleat roughly pushed aside the heavy green curtain. "There's actually a secret gate connecting these two gardens, but it hasn't been used in years."

Peering into the shadowed recess, Olivia blinked in surprise. "My goodness." Sure enough, a small door of weathered gray wood had been neatly concealed in the brickwork. Ivy, moss, and lichen had crept their way over the paneling, and the ornate, wrought iron hinges were rusted with age.

Lord Sleat tugged at some of the ivy tendrils curling around the bolt. "I believe one of my wicked forebears had it installed so that he and his mistress—who resided next door—could conduct their clandestine affair more easily." Lord Sleat flashed a grin over his shoulder. "Shocking, I know. Especially considering the lady in question was married."

Oh.

The marquess jostled the bolt, and with a begrudging, wince-inducing grate, it slid back. Then, after delivering a small kick with his booted foot, he pushed the gate open on protesting hinges.

"There we are," Lord Sleat said with a gentlemanly bow. "I trust this serves your needs."

"Yes, it d-does. Most adequately." Transferring Peridot to one arm, Olivia held her torn skirt with her other hand and dipped into another small curtsy. "Thank you again, my lord. For everything."

"The pleasure has been all mine, I assure you." He caught her hand and brushed a kiss over the back of her fingers, making Olivia blush to the roots of her hair. "And just in case you ever need to rescue Peridot again"—he winked—"I'll leave the gate unlocked."

Olivia inclined her head. "You're too kind."

He laughed, and mischief glinted in his eye. "You

wouldn't say that if you really knew me, lass." Leaning closer, he added in a seductive, velvet-soft voice, "I'm afraid wickedness runs in the family, so you'd best leave before a sinful scoundrel like me is tempted to ruin more than your reputation. Farewell, my lovely Lavinia."

Goodness. She couldn't quite believe a man like Lord Sleat was flirting with tangle-tongued, quiet-as-a-church-mouse Olivia de Vere. She muttered a stammered farewell in return, then ducked through the small gateway and the curtain of ivy on the other side. When she emerged into the garden, she heard the door scrape shut. And her heart fell at the thought that she might never see her mysterious marquess again.

With a heavy sigh, she rounded a small knot of rose-bushes and made her way back to the house with Peridot in her arms. No, she wouldn't let disappointment weigh her down. Because even if Bagshaw tore strips off her, and her aunt and uncle locked her away in her room for the next week, she would not regret a single thing.

She'd finally met Lord Sleat, and he was everything she'd imagined him to be—ruggedly handsome and rogu-ish, yet essentially a gentleman. A small smile played at the corners of her mouth. The memory of their fleeting yet thoroughly stimulating encounter would sustain her for many a long, lonely night to come, of that she was certain.

However, all her pleasant musings about Lord Sleat fled when she gained the upper gallery leading to the bedcham-bers. To avoid her aunt, uncle, and cousins, she'd given the drawing room and library a wide berth. Indeed, she didn't encounter anyone besides a pair of housemaids lighting the last of the upstairs lamps . . . until she reached her room.

No sooner had she turned the brass handle than another door a bit farther along clicked open. And then a voice she both dreaded and loathed floated down the hall like a ma-levolent spirit.

"O-liv-liv-livia . . ." The singsong taunt, the mocking tone, was all too familiar. "How are you, my sweet little c-c-cuz?"

Damn, blast, and drat. Olivia opened her bedroom door
and pushed Peridot inside before turning around to face her
cousin Felix de Vere. The veritable bane of her existence.

The man her aunt and uncle wanted her to marry to keep
her fortune within the de Vere family forever.

When pigs fly. Tamping down her dislike and dismay as
best she could, Olivia pasted a neutral expression on her
face as she forced herself to meet Felix's frost blue gaze. He
swaggered toward her in his perfectly tailored, ton-buck
attire—purchased with her inheritance money, no doubt—
then propped a shoulder against the beveled oak doorjamb.
He was so close, crowding her in, attempting to intimidate
her, she could smell the brandy on his breath. See the glints
of gold in his evening beard.

For a man who was five-and-twenty, he was as imma-
ture as a playground bully. Not to mention as vain as a
peacock.

"You, you've returned f-from abroad," she stated as
smoothly as she could. Considering her pulse was skitter-
ing around like a panicked field mouse about to be set upon
by a weasel, she was surprised she could make her mouth
work at all.

Felix smirked as he tossed a thick wave of tawny hair
out of his eyes. "Clearly. But you haven't answered my
question." His insolent gaze traveled down her body, and
then he laughed. "Good God, Livvie, you look like you've
been tupped. Torn skirts. Flushed cheeks. Disheveled hair."
To emphasize his point, he plucked an ivy leaf from the top
of her head and crushed it between his long fingers before
dropping it on the Turkish runner. "What have you been
up to?"

Olivia's face grew hotter. Despite her best efforts to look
him in the eye, her gaze slipped to his elaborately styled
ivory cravat. "If you m-must know, I was rescuing my
friend's c-cat from a tree. In the back g-garden."

"Rescuing a cat?" he scoffed, crossing one booted ankle
over the other. "You must be joking."

Olivia lifted her chin. "Of course I'm n-not. It belongs

to Lady Charlotte Hastings, Lord Westhampton's daughter and the Marchioness of Chelmsford's n-niece. She's away at the moment and—"

Felix raised his hand. "Enough. I don't care who owns it or why you're looking after it. Just make sure it doesn't get under my feet, or I'll snap its scrawny neck." He clicked his fingers with a loud snap. "Like that." Leaning closer, he lowered his voice. "You know I will, c-c-cuz."

Olivia swallowed, and her hands curled into fists. She didn't doubt him for a minute. She'd seen Felix kick Uncle Reginald's hunting dogs when he thought no one was looking. Cruelty ran through his veins, of that she was certain. "You really are de-de-de—"

Before she could complete the word *despicable*, he gave a snort of laughter and chucked her under the chin. "Delightful. Yes, I know. Good night, c-c-cuz. Dream of me, won't you?" He dipped his head and whispered in her ear, "Now that I'm back, you know it won't be long until you're mine."

With that, he pushed away from the door and strolled back down the hall, humming an indistinct but jaunty tune.

Alone in her room, Olivia gently scooped Peridot off the damask-covered window seat and into her lap.

"Don't worry, puss. I won't let Felix hurt you," she murmured. Peridot purred as Olivia ran her fingers through the cat's soft-as-silk fur. Tears of despair burned Olivia's eyes.

What on earth was she going to do?

Aunt Edith and Uncle Reginald had been dropping not-so-subtle hints for at least a year that the day would come when she would have to marry, and that the natural—actually, the only real—choice she had for a husband was Felix. Who else would want to marry a wicked hussy who'd been caught red-handed smoking cigars and swilling spirits while poring over shockingly lewd books and pictures at a young ladies' academy?

After Olivia had been expelled from Mrs. Rathbone's school, and the scandal had spread far and wide, her aunt and uncle had been so appalled and ashamed of her, she was denied any sort of real Season for three years running. And so had Prudence and Patience, much to their unrelenting chagrin.

Olivia sensed their resentment every time she walked into the room. The way they excluded her from conversations. Openly sniggered whenever she tripped over her words, which was often. She'd been relegated to the role of "poor, put-upon companion," at the beck and call of her cousins and her aunt to perform the most menial, mundane tasks. Always overlooked, and frequently banished from their company when they grew tired of her presence.

Even then there was little reprieve, given she also had to contend with the constant scrutiny of the dour and pernickety Miss Agnes Bagshaw. While she'd ostensibly been employed as a lady's maid for Patience and Prudence, the woman seemed to spend an inordinate amount of time monitoring Olivia's activities and snitching to Aunt Edith if Olivia happened to "step out-of-bounds." Ruining a gown as she'd just done would be enough to ensure she was confined to her room for at least a day with only the simplest of fare for meals.

There were times when Olivia felt as though the lowliest maid in her uncle and aunt's household was afforded more respect and consideration. Things would have been so different if her parents were still alive . . .

Unbidden tears welled in Olivia's eyes. They'd both been killed in a terrible carriage accident five years ago, and she missed their loving presence keenly. Indeed, it was a constant ache in her heart. She hated thinking about that day and all the might-have-beens. It hurt far too much.

Besides, dwelling on the past wouldn't help her now.

Olivia emitted a despondent sigh and put Peridot aside. She really should change out of her torn gown and into her night rail. And then she'd attempt to remove the stains from her silk stockings before Bagshaw discovered the damage. She hadn't any salt, but with any luck, soap, warm water, and a small soft brush would do the trick.

Settling on the low chair before her cherrywood dressing

table, Olivia took down her hair. She couldn't bear her melancholy reflection in the looking glass, so she dropped her gaze to the small pile of pins growing in front of her.

Things could be worse, she told herself. At least she had real friends in the world who did care for her. Unfortunately, the number of occasions she'd been allowed to socialize with Charlie, Sophie, and Arabella since the academy incident had been few and far between. A mere handful of rare, treasured moments that she held safe in her heart like all the precious mementos in her keepsake box.

A small, sad smile curved Olivia's lips. Perhaps she should keep a section of her gown's torn flounce as a special reminder of her encounter with Lord Sleat. She'd much rather marry a noble, considerate man like him.

A vivid memory of a glowing Sophie and her handsome, besotted bridegroom, Lord Malverne, suddenly entered her mind's eye. In June, Lady Chelmsford had persuaded Aunt Edith and Uncle Reginald to let Olivia attend Sophie's wedding at Lord Malverne's lovely country estate in Gloucestershire. Lady Chelmsford, who'd acted as her chaperone, had promised to procure Almack's vouchers for Prudence and Patience next Season if her aunt and uncle agreed to the arrangement. It was the perfect enticement; Aunt Edith hadn't been able to resist.

Sadly, Lord Sleat hadn't been at the wedding. Nor had Arabella; she'd been in Switzerland, where she met and married Gabriel, Lord Langdale. By all accounts, both she and Lord Langdale were deliriously in love. Just like Sophie and her adoring viscount.

Olivia began to ruthlessly braid her brown hair. It would not be like that with Felix. He despised her, and it was abundantly clear he only wanted her for one thing—her fortune. Marriage to him would be intolerable. But it had been easy to brush it all aside—his odious presence and her aunt and uncle's insidious hints—when Felix was away at university, and more recently, when he'd embarked on a Grand Tour of the Continent this summer.

But now he was back . . . Olivia shuddered and gazed at

her own reflection, her pale face pinched with worry, her dark eyes solemn. No one should have to marry against his or her will.

But what if Uncle Reginald and Aunt Edith do try to force you to marry Felix, Olivia de Vere? What will you do then?

The terrifying answer was: she really had no idea.

CHAPTER 2

❧

There have been varying reports that a banshee was
let loose in Grosvenor Square late on September 15
or thereabouts . . .

The Beau Monde Mirror: The Society Page

Sleat House, Grosvenor Square

September 15, 1818

God's blood, he needed a drink.

Hamish ground his teeth together with gravel-
crushing force as he sloshed whisky into a crystal tumbler.
It didn't matter that the walnut longcase clock in the corner
of his library proclaimed the hour to be three o'clock in the
afternoon. When faced with a fresh family crisis of this
magnitude, he found that strong liquor was the only remedy
that would at least partially dampen the angry fire raging
through his veins. The anxiety churning in his belly.

Crossing back to his carved oak desk with his drink, he
snatched up the letter the courier had delivered not ten minutes ago. Lord Angus MacQueen, his younger brother, had
been quite clear. Their nineteen-year-old sister, Isobel, had
apparently been planning to run off with Angus's tutor, a
young man who also happened to be the local minister's
brother. Hamish had to give it to Brodie MacDonald; the
young man had balls. But not for much longer.

Hamish's mouth twisted with a sardonic grin. Not when he was done with him.

No, there wasn't a single doubt in Hamish's mind that he must return to his ancestral home, Muircliff Castle on the Isle of Skye, at once. Never mind that he'd been there three months ago, when everything had been quite fine. Mother had been well—well, as well as could be expected. And Isobel had seemed content enough.

However, he'd clearly been so preoccupied with battling his own demons, he failed to notice the tutor sniffing around his sister like a randy dog. And beneath his own roof!

A muscle pulsed in Hamish's jaw. God, how he hated Muircliff, that great pile of rocks overlooking the cold, crashing sea. He didn't want to go back. Hadn't planned to go back until Christmastide. *But needs must when the devil drives, hey, MacQueen?*

Hamish drained his whisky and then replenished it. So much for his plans to have dinner at White's with Max Devereux, the Duke of Exmoor, followed by an evening of gambling and then sampling the feminine delights on offer for the right price at the Pandora Club. Drinking and fucking half the night away were the only things guaranteed to help him sleep. If only they kept his nightmares at bay . . .

Christ. Hamish closed his eyes and pinched the bridge of his nose. A headache had begun to throb in his temple. He fervently wished he could forget. So many things.

He tossed back his second whisky in one long, smooth swallow, relishing the burn of the fiery liquid in his throat. He'd leave later tonight. According to Angus, Isobel was inconsolable that Brodie had been summarily dismissed and banned from setting foot in Muircliff Castle ever again. Indeed, she'd locked herself in her room and was refusing to see anyone or to eat anything substantial. The lad, only seventeen, had done well to avert a full-blown crisis and scandal. But it was ultimately Hamish's responsibility to protect the family. He really couldn't afford to delay his departure until the morrow—

The muffled sound of a child's keening cry filtered through the closed library door.

What the deuce? Hamish's eyebrows slammed together, and he cocked his head, listening. Surely he wasn't *that* foxed that he was beginning to hear things . . .

The distraught sobs grew louder, more intense. And then there was a knock on the library door. "My lord . . ."

With a growl, Hamish strode across the room and threw the door open, revealing MacAlister, his craggy-faced, silver-haired butler.

"What's all this caterwauling . . ." Hamish demanded, but his voice trailed away when his gaze skipped past a white-faced MacAlister and landed on Daniels, a strapping young footman standing a few feet behind him. And in Daniels's arms was a child. A young girl, to be exact, clinging to Daniels's liveried coat like it was a lifeline as she bawled her eyes out. Her toffee brown hair clustered in damp, matted ringlets about her flushed, chubby face. When she caught sight of Hamish's frightful countenance, the pitch and volume of her cries increased.

Jesus Christ and all his saints. Hamish had a premonition his headache was about to turn into a monumental megrim.

"My lord," began the butler again. He had to raise his voice to be heard over the ear-splitting wails. "It seems . . . It seems this child has been abandoned on your front doorstep."

"What do you mean, abandoned?"

"I'm afraid I mean exactly that, my lord. Abandoned with naught but a bundle of clothes tied up in a blanket and this . . ." MacAlister held out a crumpled, stained piece of paper. "This note that was attached to her pinafore explains it all. I didn't mean to look, my lord, but it was unsealed, and I needed to ascertain whether this was a matter that merited your concern . . . My sincerest apologies if I've overstepped—"

Hamish waved away his apology as he took the sheet and crossed to his desk. "Take the bairn out to the terrace,

Daniels," he said, gesturing toward the French doors. "Our ears will be happier for it."

"Her name is Tilda, my lord," offered MacAlister, hovering in the library doorway.

"I see," remarked Hamish grimly as he propped his hip on the edge of the desk and ran his gaze over the neatly written script. A woman's handwriting, perhaps.

> *My dearest Lord Sleat,*
>
> *I hope you can forgive me, but I fear I have run out of options and you are my last hope. You see, my little Tilda is your daughter, too, and as I am without material means and can no longer provide a safe home for her, I entrust her to your care. I know you are kindhearted and will do right by her.*
>
> > *A desperate, heartbroken, and destitute mother.*
> > *A woman you used to know.*

What the bloody hell? Hamish's gaze shot to the terrace, where Daniels jiggled the inconsolable Tilda—he assumed it was short for Matilda—on his hip while making ineffectual shushing noises. This squawking scrap of a child was his by-blow?

Surely not . . . He considered the child again, looking for any similarity in their features—any clue at all that might confirm Tilda was his—but he was at a complete loss. All he saw was a wee bairn with light brown curls, blue gray eyes, and a red, tearstained face. She looked nothing like him. But then, what little girl would resemble a hulking, battle-scarred Highlander?

She must take after her mother, he decided. Hamish was always so careful whenever he swived a woman, using whatever means necessary to prevent conception as well as protecting himself from god-awful diseases like the pox. Frowning, he racked his brains, trying to think who the anonymous author of this letter might be. Who the mother of this child might be.

Tilda couldn't have been much older than three, if she was a day. He'd had so many women over the years—polished courtesans, tonnish widows and wives, and whores. Obviously, wee Tilda had been conceived four, at a pinch five, years ago, possibly just before he'd joined Wellington's army. Then again, it was quite possible the bairn wasn't even his.

Hamish's frown deepened as he perused the note once more. The woman had addressed him in a familiar fashion. *My dearest. Kindhearted* . . . He snorted at that. *A woman you used to know.* Clearly in the biblical sense.

Damn it all. It could be anyone.

Hamish scratched his tightly clenched jaw as his gaze returned to Tilda. Daniels was now sitting on the terrace stairs, bouncing her on his knee. The man must have some experience caring for bairns, as he seemed to have a knack for it. Was it his imagination, or had Tilda's crying abated a little? He could only hope. When in town, Hamish kept a largely masculine household. As the housekeeper, Mrs. Foster, was currently away caring for a sick family member for an extended period, the few maids-of-all-work had been let go. So Daniels would have to do.

Hamish beckoned MacAlister farther into the room. "Did you, or whoever discovered this child, see anyone in the street who might have been the child's mother? Did you question any of the passersby?"

The butler nodded. "Aye, indeed, my lord. Daniels heard her crying, but when he went to investigate, the wee lassie was all by herself. He alerted me, and after I read the note, I went out into the square, but no one that I questioned had anything useful to impart."

Hamish shook his head. He couldn't believe this woman would just leave her child on his doorstep, alone and beside herself with terror. She must have been somewhere close by, watching and waiting to see if Tilda would be taken in.

Sleat House was in Grosvenor Square in the middle of Mayfair, for God's sake. This wasn't St. Giles, or Whitechapel, or Seven Dials, where motherless waifs could be found around every other corner.

After issuing orders to MacAlister to conduct another search for Tilda's mother in and around the square, Hamish picked up his empty whisky glass, then put it down again with a resigned sigh. Drinking wouldn't help, no matter how much he craved another dram. Duty was pulling him in two opposite directions. For the sake of his sister, he needed to quit London and return to Skye without delay, but how on earth could he do that now that he'd been saddled with a child who may or may not be his?

There was no denying it: today was turning out to be one of the most frustrating, if not altogether impossible, days of Hamish's life.

16 Grosvenor Square, Mayfair

"Explain yourself, Olivia de Vere. How could you have been so careless as to ruin not only your stockings but an expensive day gown of the finest Indian muslin?" demanded Aunt Edith. Reclining against the plump satin cushions of her favorite settee like a matronly Queen of Sheba, she subjected Olivia to a narrow-eyed, glacial stare. "Bagshaw tells me that the tears are irreparable and there are grass stains in the fabric. Grass stains! I can't even begin to think what you were up to."

"Something unladylike, no doubt," murmured Prudence, reaching for an elaborately iced petit four off the afternoon tea plate of fine bone china. She popped it into her mouth, and her jaw worked furiously as she chewed it with relish.

"Yes," agreed Patience, tossing her perfectly styled honey blond ringlets. Her blue eyes gleamed with pernicious glee. "I really don't know why Mama and Papa bother to buy you anything fashionable. It's not as if you go anywhere."

Aunt Edith sniffed and adjusted the fall of her cashmere

shawl. "I'm beginning to think that if you can't look after the nice things your uncle and I purchase for you, Olivia, you should jolly well go without. Well, have you nothing to say for yourself, gel?"

Olivia tamped down the urge to retort that if her aunt or cousins stopped sniping, she might be able to get a word in.

She opened her mouth to speak, but then Prudence cut in. "She probably hasn't, Mama." Her cousin fiddled with the lace on the edge of her sleeve with her sticky fingers as if to emphasize that she could wear fine things and make them mucky with impunity. "Nothing worth listening to, at any rate."

Olivia drew a deep breath, praying for patience. "I . . . I was attempting to rescue Lady Charlotte's c-cat—" she began, but then Aunt Edith waved a dismissive hand.

"I'm in no mood to hear your incoherent attempt to produce a pitiful excuse," she returned in a waspish tone. "As punishment, you shall be confined to your room for the rest of the afternoon and evening with only bone broth and bread for dinner. And keep that horrid cat in there with you. I'm sure she makes me sneeze."

Peridot had disappeared.

Twilight was rapidly descending, and Olivia couldn't find the cat anywhere in her bedchamber, the upstairs gallery, or indeed any of the rooms she could access on the upper floors. After checking every possible nook and cranny for the last half hour, *frantic* didn't even begin to describe how she felt.

If her search downstairs proved fruitless, Olivia determined she must also venture outside even though a dreary mizzle now veiled the back garden. It was not the sort of weather a cat would brave voluntarily, but nevertheless, Olivia would be remiss not to look farther afield.

Fastening a serviceable cloak of dark blue wool around her shoulders, she hurried from her room. She couldn't bear to think that anything terrible had happened to Peridot, especially if she'd crossed paths with Felix. If her horrid cousin had harmed one hair on Charlie's cat's head . . . A thought robbing mix of resentment and fear suddenly flared inside Olivia, and she stumbled on the sweeping stairs leading to the main hall. Placing a trembling hand on the smooth oak bannister, she paused and attempted to control her rapid breathing, to quiet her panicked thoughts. She wouldn't be able to search anywhere, if she fell down the stairs and did herself an injury.

As her breathing calmed and her racing pulse slowed, Olivia became aware of how remarkably still and quiet the house was. Nearly all the servants were at dinner— Bagshaw and Mr. Finch included—and her uncle, aunt, Prudence, and Patience had gone to see some melodrama or other at the Royal Coburg Theatre.

But not Olivia.

Not that she really minded all that much. There could be worse fates than lounging in her window seat as she read all about Miss Catherine Morland's adventures in Northanger Abbey with a purring Peridot by her side.

Well, at least Peridot had still been with her when one of the maids arrived with Olivia's dinner tray. It wasn't until she'd finished her bone broth that she'd noticed the sneaky puss had yet again absconded from the room. As much as she enjoyed Peridot's company, she would send the cat back to Hastings House as soon as she found her. For her own sanity and Peridot's safety, she had to.

Crossing the parquetry floor of the main hall with rushed steps, Olivia headed toward the drawing room, quietly calling the cat's name. The French doors led out to the terrace—

The murmur of voices followed by a low male chuckle floated across the hall.

Felix. Oh no.

Olivia recognized his horrid, mocking laugh immediately. And he was in the drawing room with someone else. Another gentleman, by the sound of it. She halted, torn between her need to find Peridot and the overwhelming desire to avoid her cousin.

Should she question him about whether he'd seen the cat? She didn't want to, but if he'd done something to Peridot, she was certain he wouldn't hesitate to gloat about it. He was an arrogant braggart after all.

But then again, there were other places to look.

She ducked down another hall. The door to her uncle's private study was ajar, and all was silent now save for the uneven tattoo of her heartbeat in her ears.

Perhaps Peridot had slipped into the study. "Here, puss, puss," she called softly as she pushed through the door into the apparently deserted room. "Here, P-Peridot."

The soft glow of several lamps and the fire illuminated her uncle's mahogany desk, a large glass-fronted bookcase, a pair of leather wingback chairs, and a window seat flanked by crimson velvet curtains.

But there was no sign of Peridot.

Olivia sighed. Of course, the cat might be hiding. She crossed the Persian rug to look beneath the huge desk. And then she paused, frowning. The green leather blotter was a mess, strewn with papers, which was . . . odd. Her uncle was quite particular about neatness. One might even say his standards were exacting. Olivia hoped Peridot hadn't been in here and jumped upon the desk, but given the uncharacteristic chaos, she suspected the cat had.

She began to hastily gather the documents together to stack them in a neat pile when the heading on the topmost sheet leapt out at her.

BIRCHMORE HOUSE—GENTLEMEN'S CLUB
SOHO SQUARE
Bill for services rendered . . .

And then, as she read further, Olivia gasped in horror. *What on earth?* Never in her wildest dreams had she imagined that her uncle would visit a brothel, let alone take part in such bizarre-sounding and no doubt lurid activities. She could guess what a session of "birching" might entail, however the other "services" listed were quite beyond her.

But no . . . it wasn't Uncle Reginald who'd been a customer at the bawdy house. It was Felix. And last night he'd apparently racked up a whopping bill of two hundred pounds for— Olivia shuddered and dropped the page. She didn't want to read any more.

A glance at some of the other papers—all bills— revealed Felix's account at a Bond Street tailor was in arrears for another massive sum. There was an invoice from George Hoby, boot maker, in the amount of—

"Once we're done here, Thackery, what say we pay a visit to Madam Birchmore's establishment again before attending the cockfights in Seven Dials? Or that new gaming hell in Covent Garden everyone keeps talking about. We can't set foot in the Pigeon Hole again until I pay off that cursed vowel—"

Oh, God, Felix was coming! If he knew she'd been going through his personal papers . . .

Olivia tossed the bills onto the blotter and then bolted for the window seat. She prayed that the partially drawn curtains would hide her sufficiently—if she tried to close them, Felix might hear the rattle of the brass curtain rings or see the sway of the fabric.

Olivia curled up in the darkest corner of the shadowy alcove and held her breath as Felix entered with his companion. Through the narrow gap in the curtains she caught a glimpse of her cousin as he deposited himself in her uncle's chair before taking a large swig from a glass containing a deep-ruby-hued liquid—probably her uncle's prized port.

The other gentleman spoke. "Now if you'd just sign this banknote for three hundred pounds, de Vere. And then these two for one hundred and fifty apiece . . . It will be easier to hide withdrawals of smaller amounts from my father."

Felix picked up a quill and dipped the nib in the inkwell. "It's been several months since I forged my dear papa's signature, but I trust this will do, Thackery," he said as he signed the notes with a flourish. "I also trust your father's eyesight is just as poor."

The other man—presumably the junior Thackery—emitted a short snort. "Yes, it certainly is. Believe me, the old sod won't notice anything's amiss with your cousin's account because I'll adjust the bank statement he receives too. Exactly like last time."

Olivia couldn't suppress a startled intake of breath. Thackery! Of Norton, Lyle, and Thackery, the law firm? Because Mr. George Thackery was the trustee managing her inheritance. Only, it sounded as though his son and Felix were embezzling money from her account.

How . . . how dare they!

Anger and fear churned about inside Olivia, making her dizzy. There was such a loud buzzing in her ears, she had to close her eyes. As soon as her uncle returned from the theater, she would seek him out and tell—

The curtain was suddenly yanked open, and Olivia yelped.

Felix was staring down at her. And his face was contorted with rage.

"What the fuck are you doing, invading my father's private study?" His voice was a low, savage growl. His blue eyes blazed with fury. "You're supposed to be in your room."

Olivia swallowed, opened her mouth, and then shut it again. Her lips, her tongue, her mind wouldn't work.

"Christ." Felix roughly grabbed her by the upper arm, hauling her out from the window seat. Pushing her against the oak-panelcd wall, he then called over his shoulder to the bespectacled gentleman who was in the process of gathering up the scattered papers on the blotter and shoving them into a leather folio. "Leave us, Giles," he barked. "I'll meet you at Birchmore's in an hour."

Olivia shook her head. "N-n-n-no. I . . . I w-want him to—"

But Giles Thackery had already gone, closing the door behind him.

Ice-cold fear slid its fingers down her spine as Felix's other hand closed like a vise around the base of her throat. "Now listen here. You will not breathe a word of what you just saw or heard. To. Anyone." He pressed against her windpipe, and for one terrifying moment, Olivia thought he was going to choke her. His port-laced breath gusted across her face. "And if you do," he continued in a silky yet thoroughly menacing tone, "I will hurt you in ways you cannot even begin to imagine." His gaze skewered hers. "Do I make myself clear, c-c-cuz?"

Olivia forced herself to speak. "Y-you're stealing my m-money. Right out from under your f-father's nose and my trustee's. And if that isn't bad enough, you're w-wasting it all on entirely dissolute pursuits . . . at horrid gaming hells and b-brothels. It's not right. In fact, it's indecent." She swallowed and somehow hardened her gaze even though her heart was hammering erratically against her ribs. "I won't m-marry you. I w-won't."

Felix gave a derisive snort. "Well, I don't particularly want to marry you, either, Livvie. Of course I could do away with you right now—no one really cares about you after all. But that would mean Father would inherit, and then I'd have to wait for him to fall off his perch, which probably won't be anytime soon. So yes"—he leaned in so close, his nose almost touched hers—"I'm willing to saddle myself with an inarticulate, second-rate piece of baggage like you in order to get my hands on your indecently large fortune. As soon as we're wed, dearest Papa and the trustee will sign everything over to me, and then I can do as I please. As long as you stay silent . . ." His gaze narrowed, and he pressed his fingers into her throat again. "But you haven't agreed to do that yet, Livvie. What's it to be?"

Olivia forced herself to nod. "I won't breathe a word," she rasped. "I promise."

"Good girl." Felix stroked her cheek, then released her from his vicious hold. "Now get out before I change my mind about *not* wringing your scrawny little neck."

Her hands shook so violently, Olivia could barely grasp the door handle as she yanked it open. And then she fled down the corridor, into the main hall, and thence into the drawing room. She didn't stop until she was in the back garden, sheltering beneath the beech tree.

Oh God, oh God, oh God.

Olivia wrapped her arms around herself as nausea roiled. She couldn't stop trembling. The misty rain was a chill touch on her face and bare hands, but it was nothing compared to the icy terror gripping her heart.

Felix, the man she was expected to marry, had threatened to do her unspeakable physical harm if she revealed to her uncle what she'd learned. Indeed, her cousin's secret was a grenade that could end her at any moment. Because what if Felix changed his mind and decided he *couldn't* trust her to keep silent before they wed?

Another frisson of fear skated down Olivia's spine, raising gooseflesh as his terrible words echoed in her mind: *I will hurt you in ways you cannot even begin to imagine . . .*

If Olivia thought she was in an insufferable situation before, after tonight, she was in dire peril. If she and Felix became man and wife, she was absolutely certain he would squander her entire fortune in the pursuit of Lord knew what sorts of depraved activities, without a second thought. And how could she lie with an innately cruel man who not only threatened her, but habitually frequented houses of ill repute? Arabella had warned her about terrible diseases like the pox.

Her life would be a waking nightmare.

She couldn't stay here. She *wouldn't* marry Felix.

But what could she do? She had well-connected friends, but everyone was away on their country estates, and despite her vast wealth, she was virtually penniless. Her uncle controlled all the purse strings. She didn't even have enough coins to her name to hire a hackney.

Dare she steal into her aunt's rooms and search for jewelry that she could sell? But that would take time and a great deal of subterfuge. Sneaking out of the house and finding a pawnshop seemed like an impossible feat. It might take days to arrange.

And she wanted to leave now. Tonight.

Would that Charlie or Lady Chelmsford were here. Or Sophie and Arabella.

But even then, would they be able to protect her? She was only twenty, and as Uncle Reginald was her appointed legal guardian, he effectively controlled every aspect of her life. Even if she sought sanctuary with one of her friends, the courts would surely rule that she had to return to his care. She'd loved her father with all her heart, but he'd clearly been remiss in appointing his brother Reginald as her guardian.

She needed a place to hide, but she had nowhere to go.

Despair stole the air from Olivia's lungs. There really wasn't anything she could do.

A bullying gust of wind caught at her skirts and cloak and blew icy needles of rain into her face. Standing about in a dark, rain-swept garden wasn't going to help. Besides, she needed to find Peridot.

She followed the gravel path to the end of the garden, all the while calling Peridot's name, but the cat didn't emerge.

Had she decided to explore the environs of Sleat House again?

At least she wouldn't have to scale a wall to gain access to Lord Sleat's garden this time. Olivia glanced back at her own house; light spilled from various windows, but she couldn't see anyone. Thank goodness Bagshaw was still at dinner. Olivia estimated that she had at least another half hour up her sleeve.

After she'd pushed aside the curtain of dripping ivy, Olivia felt for the gate's iron handle and tugged. To her surprise, it swung open quite easily. Perhaps Lord Sleat had asked his gardener to oil the hinges.

Picking up her skirts, she rushed across the damp lawn through the rain, heading toward the soft golden glow of candle and firelight emanating from the drawing room's

French doors. Peridot didn't respond to her calls. The panic that had been drowned by fear for her own safety returned full force. She prayed with all her heart that Peridot was all right.

Although it was bordering on improper, it certainly wouldn't hurt to question Lord Sleat—if he was in, of course. She trusted he wouldn't mind the intrusion. Failing that, his staff might be able to lend assistance.

Once Olivia gained the terrace, she could clearly see the sumptuously decorated drawing room, as the curtains hadn't been drawn.

All the beautifully carved oak chairs were upholstered in silk damask or dark brown leather. The floor was carpeted with a fine Turkish rug, and a gilt clock and Derbyshire Spar vases graced the veined marble mantelpiece. But not a single thing caught her attention as much as the unexpected tableau of domestic bliss by the fireside. For there, upon a wine-colored sofa, sat Lord Sleat and a sleeping child—a girl with spun-sugar curls and rosy cheeks.

And resting on the girl's lap, looking as content as could be, was Peridot.

Even though giddy relief whooshed through Olivia, she couldn't help but mutter a curse. "Little minx."

CHAPTER 3

෨෨

> O, what a tangled web we weave
> When first we practice to deceive!
> *Walter Scott, Esq.*, Marmion: A Tale of
> Flodden Field

Sleat House, Grosvenor Square

Hamish's shoulders rose and fell on a heavy sigh. Praise be to God for the next-door neighbor's curious cat.

Wee Tilda had been well-nigh inconsolable for hours . . . until the tortoiseshell puss wandered onto the terrace as evening fell. As soon as the girl laid eyes on Peridot—at least Hamish thought that was the cat's name—her distraught sobs had quickly turned into sniffles. Indeed, her tears all but dried up when the cat sidled up to her and rubbed its cheek against the child's chubby forearm. In fact, Tilda had been so comforted by the simple presence of the animal, she eventually fell asleep beside him on one of the drawing room sofas.

To say that Hamish was grateful would have been an understatement. Leaning back against the sofa's cushions, he studied Tilda's bright cap of curls; in the light of the drawing room fire, they shone like the amber brown stones at the bottom of a sunlit burn.

Was she really his daughter?

He had no bloody idea. He'd been going over the list of women he'd bedded four or five years ago, but it was a fruitless, frustrating exercise; there were far too many to count. And it was hard to think when suffering from a megrim. The pain persisted, but like Tilda's crying, it, too, had abated to a dull ache rather than a thought-robbing throb.

What hadn't abated was his indecision about what to do: stay in London to hunt down Tilda's financially distressed mother, or return to Skye to deal with a heartbroken Isobel and her brazen, entirely unsuitable suitor. Aside from the fact that Isobel was apparently prostrate with grief, Hamish couldn't be entirely certain that Master Brodie MacDonald—an unscrupulous fortune hunter, no doubt—wouldn't strike again. Angus had done an admirable job warding off disaster, *this* time. But Hamish was the head of the family, and looking out for Isobel's welfare was his responsibility.

Perhaps he could bundle both Tilda and Peridot into a carriage with one of the maids-of-all-work that his housekeeper had previously hired, and cart them all off to Muircliff as a stopgap measure. Except Peridot didn't belong to him, and he had no idea if any of the maids would actually make a suitable nurse—to him, they'd all seemed a trifle coarse. He needed someone with a gentle manner. A compassionate, kind soul who could ease the distress of this poor, abandoned child—

The French doors rattled. No, it wasn't a rattle. It was a light tapping sound.

Hamish's gaze swung to the doorway and he frowned ... until he saw who it was, and the corner of his mouth kicked into a smile. The thoroughly charming, delightfully artless young woman from next door stood on his terrace.

Damn. His frown returned. She'd come to fetch her cat.

When Tilda awoke and discovered Peridot had gone, she'd be sure to bring the house down with her cries.

It just wouldn't do.

Rising carefully from the sofa so he wouldn't disturb Tilda, he then crossed the Turkish rug to admit Miss Lavinia, the lass with the doe brown eyes and shy yet disarming smile. She hadn't shared her last name with him, but when

Hamish had made an idle inquiry over breakfast about who resided next door, MacAlister had informed him that the very wealthy de Vere family was currently renting the neighboring town house. She might be a "Miss de Vere," but he shouldn't make assumptions.

"Do come in, Miss Lavinia," he said in a low voice. The beguiling violet scent he'd noticed yesterday when he'd lifted her from the wall wafted around him, tempting him to sweep the comely lass into his arms again. But he didn't, simply adding like a gormless lad with nothing pithy to say, "It's rather a miserable night to be out, wouldn't you agree?"

She nodded and stepped into the room. "Yes, m-my lord," she said softly, her volume matching his. When she took in his informal state of attire—leather slippers, loose linen trousers, an open-necked cambric shirt, and blue silk banyan—she blushed, and her gaze flitted to the sofa. "My s-sincerest apologies for the intrusion, b-but it seems my cat has developed a terrible tendency to roam and has invaded your home yet again."

"Aye, she has indeed." Hamish's appreciative gaze drifted over her. Her rich brown hair was damp, hanging in limp ringlets about her pale face and slender shoulders, and beneath her dark blue woolen cloak, her sodden muslin skirts had molded to her generously curved hips and long, slender thighs . . .

Good God, those thighs. To think he'd had his hands about her slim waist and neat ankle yesterday too. Hamish swallowed and dragged his attention upward to her pretty face again. He could at least pretend to be a gentleman. "It seems you've been out in the rain too long, lass. Would you like to take a seat before the fire? I could ring for tea . . ."

If he could get her to stay long enough, he might be able to persuade her to let him keep the cat, at least until morning.

To his disappointment, the girl shook her head. Her expression grew wary. "I thank you for your kind offer, my lord. But I will be missed if I d-don't return soon."

Was it his imagination, or had a shadow of apprehension passed across the lass's face? Of course, she could just be concerned about being here, alone and unchaperoned with a hardened rakehell. She'd admitted yesterday that she'd heard of him. Which wasn't surprising. His name appeared in the *Beau Monde Mirror* and other gossip rags often enough. Her reputation would be ruined if word got out that she'd been alone with him, especially at night in his own home.

But he needed that cat. For Tilda's sake.

For his own sanity.

"Of course," he said. "I understand perfectly. However . . ." He sighed. He had to convince Lavinia to leave Peridot here. But how? If she was a member of the de Vere fold, offering her money would be useless. So what would a wealthy young woman like her truly want? What did she need? Could he simply appeal to her better nature? Her compassionate heart?

Beg her to take pity on him?

As he turned over several options in his mind, a whimper and then a high-pitched, wince-inducing wail shattered the silence.

Hell and damnation, Tilda had woken up. Unsurprisingly, the fluffy ball of feline fur in Tilda's lap transformed into a tan, black, and white streak; the cat shot to the floor before disappearing beneath the sofa.

Hamish closed his eyes and mentally muttered several curses that would definitely fall into the category of "not for the ears of young ladies or children."

"Oh, dear," murmured Lavinia. "The poor mite. Is . . . is she unwell?"

"No." Hamish sighed. "It's . . . the situation is rather complicated."

"I see." Lavinia's frown deepened. "Is there anything I can do to help?"

Making the same sort of hushing noises his footman had, Hamish approached the couch and reached for Tilda, but she shrank away from him, clinging to the back of the sofa. The howling intensified along with his increasing sense of inadequacy. "Perhaps if you could coax your cat out. The wee one seems to like her."

Lavinia dropped to her hands and knees. By the time she'd managed to retrieve Peridot, Tilda had buried her face in a pile of cushions, resisting any and all of Hamish's ineffectual attempts to offer comfort. He didn't doubt for a minute that his facial scars, eye patch, and brutish size terrified the "poor mite," as Lavinia had so aptly called her. Though for a "poor mite," she certainly had a decent set of lungs.

Lavinia sat on the sofa beside the distraught child, Peridot in her arms. Now that Tilda's cries were somewhat muffled, the cat seemed calm enough. "What is her name, if you d-don't mind my asking, my lord?"

"Tilda," he replied. "I don't know her last name."

Lavinia blushed and dropped her gaze from his, and he wondered if it was because she hadn't shared her last name with him either. She would be well aware of the breach in etiquette. Curiosity nipped. Why hadn't she divulged it?

But he had enough to contend with at the moment. After all, it really wasn't any business of his if she'd decided not to reveal too much about herself.

Lavinia reached out a hand and placed it on the child's back. "Tilda," she called gently. "The puss is back. If you'd like to hold her again, you'll have to sit up."

Thankfully, Tilda's crying began to ebb once more. Hamish retreated to the fireside, just out of her line of vision, and watched with more than a little bit of awe as Tilda wiped her nose on her sleeve and then held out her arms for Peridot.

When the cat was safely installed on her lap, Lavinia sent a glance in his direction. "Do . . . do you have a kerchief, my lord?"

"Of course." He approached the sofa cautiously and held it out to the lass.

"Perhaps you should ring for tea after all," she said softly with a small smile as she took the square of linen.

"And warm milk and b-buttered toast." Turning to the child, she added, "Would you like that, Tilda?"

Tilda sniffed, then nodded. And Hamish nearly fell over.

Good heavens, the woman was a miracle worker. The whole time Tilda had been here, the child hadn't responded to a single question. When Lavinia asked her if she'd like to wipe her eyes and blow her nose with the kerchief, again the child nodded.

At least Tilda could understand simple questions, even if she hadn't spoken yet.

Hamish rang for a footman, and after he'd issued a request for tea and a supper tray, he turned back to discover Tilda was whispering something in Lavinia's ear.

Lavinia caught his gaze. "My lord . . . it seems we might need to . . ." A furious blush washed over her face as she continued in a low voice, "We need to attend to the call of nature. It's rather urgent."

"Oh . . . of course." Good Lord, why hadn't he thought of that? He gave her brief directions on how to reach the newly installed water closet at the back of the house.

When Lavinia returned, Tilda's hand in hers, the tea things, toast, and crumpets were laid out upon a low table before the sofa. After passing a glass of warm milk and a honeyed crumpet to Tilda, Lavinia removed her cloak, then dispensed tea for Hamish and herself with swift efficiency.

Even Peridot was provided with a saucer of milk.

Hamish claimed a leather wing chair by Lavinia's end of the sofa. Tilda studied him warily with her large blue gray eyes as she nibbled on her crumpet. At least she hadn't burst into tears again. If the child felt comfortable enough to speak to Lavinia, perhaps she would answer certain questions. Could Tilda provide her mother's name? Or where she'd been living? How old she was?

Any information, even a scrap, might prove useful in helping him to reunite mother and child. And then he could depart for Skye.

When Tilda had finished her crumpet and milk, and Peridot was back on her lap, Hamish beckoned Lavinia to the fireside. "I have a confession to make," he murmured. "One that might shock you. So I hope I can count on your discretion."

Lavinia nodded. Her brown eyes were solemn. "Of course, Lord Sleat."

Hamish held her gaze. It was an effort not to get distracted by the way the firelight illuminated mahogany strands in the thick, tumbling mass of her hair. "You see, Tilda was left on my doorstep this afternoon with a note—apparently written by the child's mother—that stated she is my daughter. But I have no idea who the woman is. Or if she's even telling the truth."

Lavinia's eyes widened, and her hand rose to her throat. "Oh . . . oh, my g-goodness. That's . . . that's dreadful. Not that you m-might be her father . . ." A fiery blush stormed across Lavinia's face, and her gaze skipped away from his. "I mean p-poor Tilda. No wonder she's so distraught."

"Aye. But your presence, and Peridot's, has made a world of difference. I wondered . . ." He drew a steadying breath. "I wondered if you might consider granting me a favor." He paused. "Two, in fact."

"Perhaps . . ." Her attention drifted to the clock on the mantelpiece, just behind his left shoulder. "I don't wish to sound curmudgeonly, but it depends on what you have in mind. I'll . . . I'll be missed if I'm away for too much longer."

Hamish nodded. "Well, my first request is the simplest. Would you consider leaving Peridot here tonight? I think the cat eases Tilda's distress."

Lavinia's elegant brows dipped into a frown. "As I m-mentioned yesterday, she isn't my c-cat, exactly. I've been looking after her for . . . for a dear friend. But I don't see any harm in it."

Hamish smiled. "Excellent. Which leads me to my second request. Would you consider staying here—"

"Oh." Another bright crimson blush stained Lavinia's

smooth-as-cream cheeks as she stammered, "Oh, I d-don't think that would be appro-appropriate, my lord."

Hamish had to bite his cheek to suppress a grin. "Och, lass. I know I have a wicked reputation, but you are not—" He'd been going to say that although she was as pretty as could be with an eminently desirable figure, she wasn't really the type of woman he'd pursue. She was far too young and inexperienced. A chit practically out of the schoolroom. But he didn't wish to cause offense, so he simply said, "I do not wish to harm yours. Rather, I hoped that you wouldn't mind staying a wee bit longer to ask Tilda a few more questions. She seems quite taken with you, whereas I . . ." He gestured at his ruined face. "She probably thinks I'm some sort of terrible ogre. If I could glean a tidbit or two about her mother, or where they live, I might be able to help her. And there's no way to confirm Tilda is actually my child unless I speak with the woman."

Lavinia nodded. "Of course, my lord. I'll do my very best."

L *ord Sleat has a child?*
    Born out of wedlock?
To say Olivia was taken aback would have been an understatement. Charlie certainly hadn't known about that when she'd compiled a list of eligible bachelors—most of whom were rakehells—at the beginning of this year's Season. She'd reasoned—and Arabella, Sophie, and Olivia had agreed—that rakes might be the only men in England willing to take any of them to wife given their considerably besmirched reputations following the "academy incident."

Although, it seemed Lord Sleat was also rattled to learn he might be a father. After he'd shown Olivia the letter penned by Tilda's mother, she returned to the sofa and took one of Tilda's small hands—still sticky with honey—in hers. This would not be easy, talking to the child about her mother. It would undoubtedly upset her. But it had to be done.

"Tilda . . ." she began hesitantly. "I have to ask you a few questions. About what happened today. When you were left here with Lord Sleat." She nodded in the marquess's direction. He stood at a distance, by the fire with a glass of whisky in hand, watching the exchange intently. "Would that be all right?"

The child nodded. "Mama left me," she whispered. Tears brimmed in her eyes and slipped onto her cheeks.

Olivia smiled and gave her hand a gentle squeeze. "Yes, your mama did. Do you . . . can you tell me her name? What do others call her?"

Tilda frowned. "She's Mama."

"Yes, that's what *you* call her. But she has another name. I'm Oliv . . . Lavinia. And this is Peridot." Olivia stroked the cat's head. "And your name is Tilda. So, what is your mama's other name? The one other grown-ups call her."

More tears fell, and Tilda's bottom lip trembled. "I don't know. She's Mama. Just Mama."

"That's perfectly all right if you don't know, Tilda." Olivia smoothed a soft brown curl away from the child's tearstained cheek. "But perhaps you could tell me where you and your mama live? Do you know the address?"

Tilda nodded. "Yes. London," she said solemnly.

"Yes, we are in London, but London is a very big place. Can you tell me the name of the street you live on, or is there something nearby like a church, or a park, or a market that you know of?"

But Tilda shook her head again. "London."

"Well, maybe you could tell me how old you are. I'm twenty years old. Almost twenty-one, in fact. And you are . . ."

Tilda dropped her gaze, and her bottom lip wobbled ominously again.

"Maybe we could count with our fingers . . . Are you this many?" Olivia held up four fingers and counted out the number, but Tilda shook her head. She responded in the same way when Olivia showed her three, then five fingers.

Olivia looked helplessly back at Lord Sleat, and he

shrugged a shoulder. "Do not worry," he mouthed. "You've done well."

There was a gentle tug on Olivia's sleeve. "What is it, Tilda?"

The little girl beckoned her closer, and when Olivia bent low, Tilda whispered in her ear, "Is the beast who lives in this castle really my papa?"

"Honestly, I'm not sure," murmured Olivia. "But in any case, Lord Sleat isn't really a beast, and you mustn't be afraid of him. He's really a kind, handsome gentleman who's simply been in an accident. That's why he wears an eye patch. And you can trust him. Your mama wouldn't leave you with someone she didn't trust."

Tears welled in Tilda's large blue gray eyes once more. "I want to go home."

"I know, dear child. I know." Olivia stroked Tilda's wild mop of silky curls. "We'll find your mama."

She prayed that would be the case.

Tilda snuggled against her side, and when Olivia glanced down, she could see the child's eyelids had begun to droop. Lord Sleat continued to sip his whisky as he stared into the dancing flames in the grate. The firelight played over his handsome profile: his tousled sable hair masking the worst of his scars, the strong line of his nose, the sculpted contours of his jaw shaded by dark stubble. Charlie had once mentioned the marquess lost the sight in his left eye during the Battle of Waterloo. Such an injury to his face would have been agonizing, if not life-threatening. Olivia's heart clenched to think Lord Sleat had endured such pain.

He might be a rakehell, but beneath his roguish exterior, she sensed he was a good man.

Someone she, too, could trust.

For a moment, Olivia allowed herself to pretend that the marquess wasn't just her rakish neighbor, but her husband, and the child and the cat sleeping at her side belonged to her too. That she was in love, and safe, and adored just like Sophie and Arabella, and before that, her own mother.

That everything was perfect.

The mantel clock gently chimed the hour, eight o'clock, and pulled Olivia from her musings. She'd been here far too long.

Mr. Finch and Bagshaw could very well be scouring the streets by now.

She'd be locked up in her room for a week. With Felix only a few doors away from her . . .

Olivia shivered, recalling those fraught, terrifying moments when he'd pressed his hand to her throat. The threats he'd made. She didn't want to return home, but she must. At least Peridot would be safe tonight. And in the morning, she could ask someone from Lord Sleat's staff to take the cat back to Berkeley Square, just as she'd planned.

She dropped a kiss on Tilda's forehead—the child had succumbed to exhaustion and had fallen asleep—then carefully rose to her feet and retrieved her damp cloak from the back of the sofa. "I'm afraid I must go, Lord Sl—"

She broke off at a soft knock on the drawing room's wood-paneled doors.

The marquess frowned and put his whisky glass down on the mantel. "If you'll excuse me just a moment . . ." Rather than calling out—Olivia supposed he didn't wish to disturb Tilda—he crossed the room in swift strides and admitted an older, gray-haired man who had the look of a servant about him. The butler, perhaps.

"What is it, MacAlister?" murmured Lord Sleat.

The older man kept his voice low too. "Mr. Burke is still awaiting your orders, my lord. About whether you wish to leave tonight. Unfortunately, he's discovered one of the horses from the four-in-hand team is lame, so he'll need to organize a replacement. And that may take an hour or two."

Lord Sleat glanced back at Tilda. "Tell Burke I probably won't be leaving until midmorning, so he has plenty of time. I'll have to send word to my man of affairs about employing an inquiry agent to search for the wee one's mother. And I'll need to find a suitable nursemaid. I won't be able to manage Tilda on my own, especially on the road to Skye."

"Of course, my lord." The butler rested his gaze on Olivia for a moment before he returned his attention to his master. "It's a pity Mrs. Foster is away at the moment, otherwise she would have been able to help."

"Aye."

The butler departed, and when Lord Sleat returned to the fireside, Olivia's mind was ablaze with a mad, mad thought. Indeed, the idea was so wild, she was almost certain she wouldn't be able to put it into words, let alone execute it.

But she had to try.

Her future happiness—perhaps her very life—might depend upon it.

"Lord Sleat . . ." she said carefully, approaching him as if he were indeed the beast Tilda imagined him to be. "I . . . I didn't mean to eavesdrop on your c-conversation just now. B-but it seems you are in need of a nursemaid for Tilda. And . . . and I would like to offer my services."

The marquess frowned. "I'm intrigued. Do you have any experience with this sort of thing?"

Olivia swallowed. She couldn't lie. Not about that, at least. "N-no. But I like children. Very much. Indeed, I've always wanted a family of my own one day. And even though I have a terrible sta . . ." She forced herself to say the hated word that had forever defined her. "Sta-stammer, I can certainly attest to the fact that I'm well educated. And patient. I can sew and sing lullabies—"

Lord Sleat held up his hand, and the gold-and-ruby signet ring he wore upon his little finger winked at her. "Forgive me for interrupting, but won't you be missed? You're one of the de Vere chits, aren't you? I can't imagine someone from your privileged background would be content to work—let alone be permitted to work—as a nursemaid. Indeed, your family might have something to say about it. I'm certain they'd be none too pleased."

Oh, no. How silly of her not to realize he'd know at least something about his neighbors. But did he know anything of significance related to her? After all, he'd accepted that her name was Lavinia . . .

She hated lying—indeed, she was woeful at maintaining any type of subterfuge—but in this instance, she had to.

Olivia swallowed to moisten her dry mouth. "My lord, I am but a p-poor, orphaned relation of the family. A dis . . . distant cousin, employed as a lowly companion for the de Vere chits, as you c-called them. I have no great fondness for anyone in that household, and I can assure you, they have no regard for me and will not miss my company. At all. Indeed, I have been longing to find another situation for some time, and I can promise you that I will serve you and young Tilda well."

Lord Sleat studied her with a narrowed gaze over the rim of his glass before he swallowed the rest of his whisky. Did he believe her? Her sincerity and enthusiasm certainly weren't feigned. And most of what she'd said wasn't a lie.

She prayed God would forgive her for the rest.

"Miss Lavinia," he began, then grimaced. "I don't even know your last name. I assume it's de Vere . . ."

"N-no." She would be safer if she chose another name. One that sounded completely different from de Vere. Something less distinctive. Something nondescript. Like the shade of her hair and her eyes. Lavinia Brown, perhaps?

No. She was about to do something wild and adventurous like a heroine in a book. She could come up with a more interesting name than Brown. "My last n-name is M-Morland," she said as the heroine of *Northanger Abbey*, Catherine Morland, sprang into her mind. "I'm Miss Lavinia Morland."

"Well, Miss Lavinia Morland." Lord Sleat put his glass down on the mantel. His gray eye flashed with a considering light. "If you are certain your family won't object, I will accept your offer. But . . . be warned. My home on the Isle of Skye is a long, long way from London—over six hundred miles, in fact—and it will take many days to get there. The trip will not be easy, by any means. In fact, it will be quite arduous. My business at home is urgent, so not only do I intend to set a rapid pace, once we reach Skye, we will need to ride on horseback. The roads, if one can even call them that, are not fit for coaches. Are you prepared for that?"

She nodded. Even though the prospect sounded daunting indeed, she'd travel a thousand miles in a carriage and spend days on end in the saddle rather than live in fear of Felix. "Yes, my lord. I ride quite well."

He inclined his head. "Excellent. As I won't be spending half my day looking for a nursemaid, I won't need to delay my departure. We'll leave before daybreak, at six o'clock. I'll send one of my footmen around for your luggage."

"Oh . . . oh that won't be necessary," she said quickly. The last thing she needed was one of the marquess's liveried servants turning up on her aunt and uncle's doorstep at the crack of dawn. They would never let her leave. "I shall be able to manage my own valise. I daresay it would be far simpler if I just meet you here."

Lord Sleat's mouth twitched. "I daresay."

Panic fluttered inside Olivia's belly. Was he already suspicious of her circumstances? Who she really was? He had good reason to be. But she couldn't worry about that now. Not when escape was within her reach.

"I . . . I do have one small favor to ask of you though."

Lord Sleat raised a dark eyebrow. "And what might that be?"

"I do not feel comfortable leaving Peridot with my family. She is not their responsibility. And as much as Tilda derives comfort from her presence, I do not think it would be wise to transport a cat all the way to Skye. So I would humbly ask that one of your servants returns Peridot to her owner's residence in B-Berkeley Square in the morning. There are staff there who will care for her."

Lord Sleat slapped his hand on the mantel in the manner of an auctioneer. "Done."

"Thank you."

With a lantern in hand to light the way, the marquess escorted her onto the terrace and to the back of the garden.

The rain had stopped, but a chill wind tossed the branches of the trees and whipped Olivia's hair into her eyes.

When they arrived at the hidden gate, Lord Sleat paused. The flickering light from the lantern gave his face a strange, saturnine cast. "Before I bid you adieu, Miss Morland, there's one last thing I need to mention."

"Yes . . ." Olivia held her breath as she waited for him to continue. She prayed he wasn't having second thoughts.

The wind tossed his dark hair, lifting it to reveal more of the angry scar on his brow. "We didn't discuss your wages."

"Oh . . ." Olivia's pulse quickened. She hadn't even thought about that. And she truly had no idea what a lower servant like a nursemaid would expect to be paid. "Wh-whatever you decide, I'm sure it will be fair."

"I'm happy to pay you a good deal more than what you've been hitherto earning as a companion."

"Oh . . . as a member of the family, I don't receive a wage. So there's really no need—"

"Of course there is." He caught her hand and gave it a gentle squeeze. "Never underestimate your true worth, Miss Morland. So think on it, and name your price in the morning."

Olivia nodded. "I will, my lord."

"Good." He released her hand and parted the curtain of ivy. "Now go before it starts raining again."

"Yes, my lord. And good night to you."

"Good night to you, too, Miss Morland."

By the time Olivia reached her room without incident, her whole body was thrumming with excitement and terror.

She was running away.

Tomorrow morning, she would be free.

If she could manage to stay hidden until she turned twenty-one, then she would no longer be subjected to her uncle's tyranny. She would be an adult in the eyes of the law, even if she wouldn't gain control of her inheritance money for four more years. Or she wed and her husband was awarded that power. But it would be to a man of her choosing. A love match.

Not Felix.

She threw her cloak over the back of her bedside chair, then proceeded to unlace her damp half boots. She had so many things to get done before her aunt, uncle, Prudence, and Patience came home. Or Bagshaw walked in.

She would need to take the bare essentials with her, and that included shoes. If she set her boots before the fire, the leather would be dry by morning. Then she'd only need to pack one pair of kid slippers. A few wool gowns—it would be far cooler up north. Several chemises and petticoats. A spare set of stays and her flannel night rail. Of course, she'd also have to write to her friends about what she'd done so they'd know she was safe. But that could wait until she was well on her way to Scotland.

Should she leave a note for Uncle Reginald and Aunt Edith? At least she could mention that they weren't to worry about her, even if she didn't reveal anything else—

Her door flew open, and Agnes Bagshaw marched into the room.

"And just where have you been, Miss Olivia de Vere?" she demanded. She planted her bony hands on her even bonier hips as her ire-filled gaze raked over Olivia. "Up to no good by the looks of you," she added without waiting for an answer. "I've been searching for you for the best part of a half hour. Just wait till I tell Mrs. de Vere that you absconded from your room."

Olivia tugged off her boots and placed them by the hearth. Ordinarily she'd try to placate Bagshaw. But not tonight. Consequences no longer mattered because by morning she'd be gone.

"I had to take P-Peridot into the back garden." She straightened and pushed a stray lock of hair away from her eyes. "And then I took her to the cellar. Lady Charlotte says she's a good m-mouser." It was the only vaguely plausible reason she could think of to explain Peridot's absence.

Bagshaw shut the door, then crossed her wiry arms over her flat chest. Her coal black eyes narrowed with suspicion, then darted about the room. "Is that so? If that's the case, where is she now?"

Olivia picked up the poker and stirred the fire. Good Lord, she wished the woman would leave so she could get on with packing. "She's still down there, enjoying herself, I suspect. I think it's rather c-cruel to keep a cat locked up in one room all day, don't you?"

Her gaze met the serving woman's, and Olivia read undiluted antipathy in her expression. There was no mistaking Olivia's meaning. The question was, would Bagshaw give her a box about the ears now, or slip her a vicious pinch later when she wasn't expecting it?

Keeping the poker in her hand, Olivia raised her chin and attempted to stare down the lady's maid. For once, it was Bagshaw who was the first to look away.

When Olivia crossed to her dressing table and began to pull the pins from her hair, Bagshaw watched. Her thin lips had flattened into an uncompromising line. "Make sure you ask before you take that cat anywhere next time," she sniped. "And make no mistake, I'll be reporting your transgression to Mrs. de Vere, first thing in the morning."

Olivia continued to take down her hair. "Of course. It would be remiss of you not to," she said in a deceptively mild voice.

Bagshaw pointed a finger that was as spare as a chicken's wishbone in her direction. "You watch your tone, young missy. I'll have none of your cheek. I've a good mind to take the key and lock you in."

Panic sparked, but Olivia refused to yield to this heady feeling of having the upper hand for once. "I don't think Lady Charlotte Hastings, or her father, the Earl of Westhampton, would be pleased to hear Peridot was trapped in a chill cellar all night," she said, catching Bagshaw's gaze in the mirror. "Unless you'd like to fetch her. You can tell me how many mice she managed to catch."

Bagshaw's abject dislike of rodents was only marginally

stronger than her dislike for Olivia. As Olivia expected, disgust flashed in the maid's eyes. "Just be quick about it. I expect you to be back in your room before the master and mistress return home."

"Of course," said Olivia. She picked up her brush. "We wouldn't want to get into any trouble now, would we?"

The slamming of her bedroom door was Bagshaw's only response.

CHAPTER 4

No one who had ever seen Catherine Morland in her infancy, would have supposed her born to be an heroine.

Jane Austen, Northanger Abbey

16 Grosvenor Square, Mayfair

September 16, 1818

Olivia was so abuzz with nervous excitement, she didn't sleep a wink. She couldn't afford to. Slipping out of the house undetected, under the cover of darkness, was a crucial part of her plan's success.

After Bagshaw's abrupt departure, Olivia had locked the door from the inside—not only to prevent Bagshaw from bursting in while she packed but for her own physical safety. She didn't trust Felix in the slightest, and if he decided he couldn't trust her to stay silent about the fact that he was embezzling her money to fund his profligacy, the consequences didn't bear thinking about.

So it was with considerable trepidation that Olivia cracked open the door to her bedroom at a quarter to five in the morning. Just after midnight, the rain had stopped, and now a pale wash of moonlight spilled in through an uncurtained window above the main stairs. Although the light was dim, she ascertained the gallery was deserted. Indeed, all was still and silent except for the wild drumming of her heart, the harsh whisper of her rapid breathing.

The servants would rise by six o'clock, so she needed to be certain she wouldn't bump into anyone at all. After making sure her leghorn bonnet was secured tightly beneath her chin, she tucked Peridot's empty cat basket beneath her arm and hoisted up her tightly packed valise. Her door closed behind her with a gentle snick, and then she was scurrying down the hallway as quietly as she could, wincing whenever she encountered a creaking floorboard, inwardly praying all would go well.

By the time she reached the main hall, her spirits were buoyed by the prospect of imminent success. She'd exit the town house via the drawing room—

The sound of a door creaking somewhere nearby made Olivia jump with fright, and she nearly tripped over her own feet as she scuttled into the dark drawing room. Within moments, she was unlatching the French doors and ducking through the velvet curtains onto the empty terrace.

She wouldn't look back. Only forward. Picking up the skirts of her woolen traveling gown, she hurtled down the stairs, then across the sodden lawn, heading for the darkest shadows.

No one called out to her, but when she reached the bottom of the garden and dared to glance back, her heart nearly stopped altogether.

Someone was in the drawing room.

A candle flame flickered in the gap between the curtains. Then the glass-paneled doors rattled. A pale oval—someone's facc—floated like a malevolent moon above the candlelight.

Bagshaw!

Oh, God. Would she be caught by that terrible woman when freedom was literally only a few feet away?

Her heart crashing against her ribs, Olivia pushed past the ivy and wrenched the hidden gate open. As soon as she was through, she rammed it shut, then flung the bolt home.

For one long minute, she sagged against the cold, damp wood. Her valise and the cat basket lay in the wet grass at her feet, but she didn't care; her knees had turned to water, and she was breathing so hard, she sounded like she'd run a mile.

And all the while, one particular thought galloped through her mind, in time with her racing heart: *I'm safe, I'm safe, I'm safe.*

Sleat House, Grosvenor Square

Coffee. He needed strong black coffee. And lots of it.

Hamish yawned, and rubbed his eye, which felt as though it were full of grit, as he summoned a footman to the drawing room.

What a hellish night he'd just spent. Who would've thought a scrap of a bairn like Tilda could create such chaos? The wee banshee had woken when Daniels tried to install her in a pallet bed in the library next door; Hamish had been working on a letter for his man of affairs, Walter Faraday, and wished to keep a watchful eye on her. The end result was that between eleven o'clock and two in the morning, he'd been trying to coax the child back to sleep.

After she'd stopped crying—around midnight—Hamish plied her with warm milk and more honeyed crumpets as Miss Morland had done. He escorted her to the water closet several times—thank goodness she seemed to be able to manage that particular business on her own—and had tasked Daniels with the job of digging out a book or two that would entertain a young child.

However, the engravings in Bewick's ornithological volumes on land birds and waterbirds, and Ehret's colorful drawings of flowering plants in *Plantae Selectae* only kept Tilda mildly entertained for a very short period of time. In the end, Peridot and the tie from his silk banyan had come to the rescue. Tilda even smiled and giggled as she ran around the library, taunting the cat with the tasseled end of the sash.

The activity had eventually tired her out, and she'd fallen fast asleep on the pallet with the cat in her chubby arms. *Thank God.*

But Hamish had stayed steadfastly awake, attending to neglected correspondence and other business matters until it was time to dress for the day ahead. He'd reasoned that there wasn't much point in sleeping when he had so much on his mind. Besides, he had days to catch up on slumber on the road to Skye.

However, his valet, Hudson, had sent him a baleful look as soon as he entered Hamish's dressing room and discovered his master had taken it upon himself to shave without assistance at four o'clock in the morning. But the man—who'd once served as Hamish's batman when he was in the military—knew from experience it was best to hold his tongue about his master's appalling sleep habits. Or lack-of-sleep habits, to be more precise.

The coffee arrived, and after Hamish poured himself a steaming cup of the black bitter brew, he wandered over to the French doors and tossed back the thick velvet curtains. The reflection in the darkened glass revealed his drawn and disgruntled expression. He sighed. He'd have to wake Tilda soon and help her to get ready for the day ahead.

At least Miss Morland would be here soon to take over those duties.

Miss Morland. What a conundrum she was. Well-spoken despite her stammer and apparently guileless. Truth be told, he also sensed she wasn't being completely honest with him about her situation. The last thing he wanted was a wealthy family breathing down his neck because he'd taken the girl from the family bosom, even if she was a penniless relation.

However, given his situation, he really couldn't afford to harbor any second thoughts. He needed Miss Morland. It was as simple as that. It wasn't the first time in his life that he'd been ruthless in his decision making. And he was certain it wouldn't be the last.

A movement on the lawn caught his attention. Someone was outside.

Miss Morland? Yes, he recognized her slight figure even though it was partially obscured by a voluminous cloak and weighed down with luggage.

Hamish put down his coffee and threw open the doors. "What the devil are you doing here so early?" he said, hastening forward to help her with her valise and basket. "It's pitch black and colder than a witch's ti—I mean, it's freezing," he amended, ushering her inside. "I said we'd depart at six, not five."

"I . . . I know," she said, removing her bonnet and cloak as she crossed to the fireplace. "But I thought it would be better to arrive well beforehand. I can . . . I can help with Tilda. She'll need to wash and get dressed."

Hamish couldn't argue with that. Closing the door with a booted foot, he put down her luggage, then offered her coffee, which she agreed to with alacrity.

"Are your family early risers?" asked Hamish mildly as he picked up the silver coffeepot.

"Oh, no. N-not at all," said Miss Morland. She dipped her head and focused on the intricate pattern of the Turkish rug beneath her neatly booted feet, but she couldn't hide the blush rising above the collar of her plum-hued traveling gown. "I bid them all adieu last night as I didn't want to disturb them this morning."

"And they don't mind that you're leaving without a last goodbye?" Hamish handed her a china cup filled to the brim with coffee.

Miss Morland blew on the hot liquid before she took a small, dainty sip. "Per . . . perhaps a little. But I don't expect them to m-miss me for long. In fact, even though it wasn't expressly stated, I'm certain they'll be glad to see the back of me."

As Hamish studied her, he decided Miss Lavinia Morland was a terrible liar. But again, he pushed aside his reservations. After all, it wasn't really any of his business. He recalled the lass stating she was almost twenty-one, and if she was but a poor relative, she might not have an officially appointed guardian. In any case, he was of the opinion that she was old enough to make her own decisions. Aloud he said, "Well, your family sounds very foolish to me."

Another delightful pink blush colored her cheeks. "That's kind of you to say so, my lord."

His mouth quirked with a wry smile. "As I informed you the other day, Miss Morland, I'm not generally regarded as 'kind' by those who know me."

"Well, I'm grateful all the same," she rejoined softly, and Hamish suddenly experienced a flash of heat across his cheekbones. Good God. Was he actually blushing?

To hide his discomfiture, he hastily turned away to refill his cup. Never in all his life had a woman—indeed anyone at all, for that matter—put him to the blush. And he really didn't wish to examine the reason why. Especially not now.

When Tilda stirred, Miss Morland hurried into the library to help the little girl get ready for the journey ahead. After they repaired to an upstairs bedroom, Hamish added a note to the letter for his man of affairs. Despite his resolve to secure Miss Lavinia Morland's services as a nursemaid come what may, he wanted to know more about her and her situation. The inquiry agent he was employing to search for Tilda's mother could quite easily check into the young woman's background and verify her claim that she was indeed a poor relative who would not be missed. Then he could dismiss this niggling sense that something wasn't quite right with Miss Morland's story.

The longcase clock in the grand entry hall of Sleat House was striking six o'clock when Olivia reluctantly bid farewell to Peridot with a final cuddle. Tilda's bottom lip wobbled ominously as she helped to place the puss in her wicker basket; fortunately, the child seemed to accept Olivia's word that there would be more cats for her to pat—

or perhaps a dog—at Lord Sleat's castle on the Isle of Skye. At least, Olivia trusted there would be. The marquess was absent from the hall at the time so she couldn't confirm if her pronouncement was indeed true.

After one of Lord Sleat's footmen had promised to deliver Peridot to the Berkeley Square address Olivia provided—along with a note for Lord Westhampton's housekeeper briefly explaining her need to return Lady Charlotte's cat—she took Tilda's small hand in hers and followed MacAlister, the butler, out the front door.

Even though there was only the faintest flush of dawn in the east, a nearby gas lamp and the light spilling from the open doorway revealed not one but two very fine four-in-hand carriages in front of Sleat House. Numerous male servants were assembled outside—half a dozen footmen, two drivers, and a pair of mounted outriders, but it was Lord Sleat himself who stood by the open door of the second carriage, apparently waiting to hand her and Tilda in.

Olivia's gaze darted nervously to the entrance of her uncle and aunt's town house as she descended the stairs with Tilda, but nothing and no one stirred, thank the Lord. In any case, her bonnet, her voluminous cloak, and the darkness should conceal her identity sufficiently. At least she prayed it would be so.

"I thought it would be best if you and Tilda traveled separately," said the marquess as his large, warm hand enveloped her gloved fingers.

"Oh, y-yes. Quite," replied Olivia, trying to ignore the jittery race of her pulse and the sinking feeling in her heart as she negotiated the carriage steps and took a seat beside Tilda. Given the terrible way her parents had died, Olivia didn't relish the idea of undertaking a long journey by any means, but she really had no choice. And while *she* enjoyed the marquess's company—and no doubt she would find his presence reassuring—it was only natural that he would want a carriage to himself. She was only a lower servant after all. Aside from that, she was a single young woman. Lord Sleat might be her employer, but he was wise to maintain a veneer of respectability. Not that it *was* a veneer. While the marquess flirted with her a little during their first unconventional meeting, he'd behaved exactly as a gentleman ought to on each subsequent occasion.

"There are warm bricks for your feet, plenty of blankets, and a basket of food," added Lord Sleat. "It's stashed beneath the seat opposite you along with a few books to keep you and the bairn entertained."

Olivia smiled. "That's . . . that's very considerate of you. Thank you, my lord."

"It's the least I can do, Miss Morland," said the marquess, with a slight tilt of his head. "As I mentioned last night, we shall be setting a cracking pace, but if you need anything at all—even if Tilda needs a comfort break—just alert the driver."

"Yes, my lord."

The door closed, and Olivia helped settle Tilda into a corner of the carriage, wrapping a large tartan blanket about the tiny child to keep her warm. Tilda's stuff gown, flannel petticoats, nankeen shoes, and velveteen cape were of decent quality, but the morning was chill, and Olivia didn't want the girl to catch cold. Even by the feeble light of the exterior carriage lamps, Olivia could see her breath misting within the close confines of the coach.

Leaning back against the squabs, Olivia cast a last look at the front of her family's town house as the carriage pulled away. What would Aunt Edith, Uncle Reginald, and Prudence and Patience make of her abrupt departure? How would Felix react?

No doubt there would be a good deal of anger and outraged consternation. She'd left a note upon her dressing table, explaining her desire for independence, the burning need to strike out on her own, even if it was without the blessing of her uncle and aunt. She'd urged her family not to worry about her. And, of course, they wouldn't be concerned for her welfare. No, they only cared about her money. She supposed Uncle Reginald would assume she'd eloped with some ne'er-do-well fortune hunter. Felix would suspect she'd decamped out of fear—which would be an entirely correct assumption. Aunt Edith would suggest she'd run off to Gloucestershire, seeking sanctuary with Charlie, Sophie, or Lady Chelmsford. As soon as it was practicable, Olivia would write to her friends to assure them she was safe and well.

Olivia didn't believe her family would make an enormous to-do about her escapade. Uncle Reginald might be moved to employ an inquiry agent or two to undertake a discreet search rather than making a hue and cry on the Bow Street Runners' doorstep. Aunt Edith in particular would be leery of creating any public scandal, especially after the "academy incident"—she wouldn't want it to have an impact upon her daughters' chances of securing advantageous matches next Season.

Felix—after Olivia's discovery yesterday—had the most to lose and would no doubt be dogged in tracking down her whereabouts. But she was counting on the fact that no one would be able to establish a link between her and Lord Sleat. If she could just stay hidden at Muircliff Castle on Skye until she turned twenty-one in mid-October, then she would be free in a legal, if not a financial, sense. Her uncle couldn't dictate where she lived or whom she could see. She would not need his permission to wed. Of course, both Uncle Reginald and her trustee, Mr. Thackery, might not release her fortune if they deemed her choice of husband unsuitable, but she would deal with that if and when such an eventuality arose.

Olivia's conscience pricked more sharply than a bramble hedge whenever she contemplated the fact that she was lying to Lord Sleat about who she really was and why she'd jumped at the chance to offer her services as a nursemaid. Despite the marquess's forbidding appearance and roguish reputation, Charlie had been correct; Lord Sleat really was a noble gentleman. He definitely deserved to be on the list of eligible bachelors, entitled "Rakes of Interest," a list that had been compiled by the Society for Enlightened Young Women at the beginning of this year's Season. Charlie had surmised that rakehells might be the only men in London willing to overlook all of their scandal-stained pasts. And so far, she had been correct in that regard: shy Sophie had well and truly ensnared the affections of the wicked rake Viscount Malverne, and bluestocking-to-her-very-bones Arabella was happily wed to the former libertine but now thoroughly besotted Earl of Langdale.

At long last, Olivia would be spending an inordinate amount of time in the company of the marquess she'd mooned over from afar.

Charlie had long ago suggested that the best way to snare a rake's attention—and then perhaps win his love—was to infiltrate his natural habitats and study his interests. Indeed, Olivia suspected the main reason Charlie had asked her to look after Peridot was that her friend knew the cat would stray into her neighbor's back garden at some point. And yes, Charlie's plan had worked even better than expected. Olivia now had ample opportunities to learn all about Lord Sleat.

Not that it would really do her any good. Not when she was pretending to be someone else.

Olivia sighed as she drew a sleepy Tilda against her side. As she studied the streets of London, already bustling with activity in the gray early-morning light, her eyelids began to droop with weariness too. Daydreams about happily-ever-afters were all well and good, but Lord Sleat wasn't a suitor at a ton ball and she wasn't a debutante with an impeccable pedigree and an unblemished reputation. He was her employer, and she was practicing a terrible deceit. Leaden guilt weighed heavily upon her heart.

At some point, Olivia knew she would have to confess all to Lord Sleat. She just prayed that when the moment came, he would understand why she'd resorted to subterfuge, and forgive her. Because if the man she'd dreamed of for so long ended up despising her, she really didn't think she could bear it.

CHAPTER 5

Lavender's blue, dilly dilly,
  Rosemary's green.
When I am king, dilly dilly,
You shall be queen.
      "Lavender's Blue," eighteenth-century folk song

The Hart and Hare Inn, Kendal, Cumberland

September 17, 1818

A dismal twilight was cloaking the hills in a chill gray mist as Hamish directed his driver to pull into the Hart and Hare coaching inn on the outskirts of Kendal. After traveling solidly for two days and an entire night with only the briefest of breaks to change horses and attend to the call of nature, everyone deserved a decent rest before they continued north.

Not only had Miss Morland dealt with the furious pace he'd set with a stoicism that he couldn't help but admire, she'd also been assiduous in caring for Tilda. Even though they'd traveled in separate carriages, he'd observed that the little girl seemed content enough whenever they'd stopped to stretch their legs in an inn yard or snatch a quick meal in a taproom. There'd been no more tears—not that he'd seen, at any rate—and he was nothing but relieved that things had worked out so well given the complexity of the situation.

Of course, alone in his carriage, he'd had ample time to sift through all the names of his past paramours—at least the ones he could remember. For once in his life, he was almost ashamed of how long the list actually was. However, in the end, the exercise proved to be futile. He still had no idea if Tilda was really his. And if she was, who the hell her mother might be.

He'd also had hours and hours to catch up on slumber. But again, that proved to be a fruitless endeavor. He was a restless sleeper at the best of times, and his insomnia had worsened because he was plagued by a surfeit of entirely inappropriate and entirely carnal thoughts about the lovely Miss Morland.

Never in his life had he lusted after a female in his household staff. Nor a lass so young. Good God, he was a decade older than the wee chit. It was most unsettling that certain aspects of her figure—the shape of her long, slender legs when a gust of wind pressed her skirts against them, or the delicious swell of her hips and fulsome breasts beneath an entirely sedate traveling gown—were enough to heat his blood and accelerate his pulse; the sensation was not dissimilar to downing half a dozen drams of whisky in quick succession.

More than once he'd caught members of his own staff and male travelers at other inns casting Miss Morland sly, lascivious glances. He couldn't really blame them, not when he was guilty of the very same behavior. But still, it gave him a peculiar sense of unease, a sharp, stabbing feeling of resentment that he suspected was jealousy, an emotion he'd hitherto been unaccustomed to.

Indeed, he was presently being assailed by the inconvenient and most unwanted feeling as he alighted from his coach and saw that his footman, Daniels, was in the process of handing Miss Morland down. The cheeky young buck even cast her a thoroughly teasing, lopsided smile and a wink before he relinquished her gloved hand and turned to pick up Tilda. As Miss Morland lifted her skirts to keep them out of the muck of the yard, Hamish approached and offered his arm. Was that a telltale flush of pleasure across her cheeks?

He gave an inward sigh. He shouldn't behave like an aggrieved suitor. He had no claim on Miss Morland whatsoever. As long as she did what she'd been employed to do, he couldn't really complain about a wee bit of harmless flirting. Still, he'd keep a watchful eye on Daniels and his other footmen. He'd not tolerate things going further.

Miss Morland readily tucked her hand into the crook of his elbow. However, the brim of her bonnet shielded her expression from him as she murmured, "Th-thank you, my lord. How long do we have before we depart again?"

Hamish steered her around a rather unsavory-looking puddle. "Why, we have all night, Miss Morland. I've decided we all need a decent night's rest. We still have a long way to travel."

"Oh . . . oh, that's wonderful," she replied. "Our carriage is very well sprung, but all the same, it will be lovely to sleep in a bed tonight. I'm sure Tilda will appreciate it."

"Aye. Indeed." They'd gained the covered portico of the inn, and Hamish held open the door for her as he would do for any well-bred young lady. Although Miss Lavinia Morland claimed she was from a genteel yet impoverished background, he was also aware she had very wealthy relatives. And if he didn't look out for her, who would?

Once inside, Hamish got caught up in securing suitable sleeping quarters for everyone. He also hired a private dining room. "Miss Morland, I expect you and Tilda to join me for dinner at seven o'clock sharp," he said after he'd made the arrangements.

"Of course, my lord." Miss Morland had taken Tilda from Daniels and had settled the little girl on her hip as naturally as any mother. The child snuggled into her nurse's shoulder, and Hamish marveled at how quickly the two seemed to have formed an affectionate bond.

If Miss Morland thought it odd that he'd asked her to dine with him, she didn't show it by way of expression. Perhaps she simply thought her employer wished to spend a little more time with a child who might very well be his daughter.

As Hamish watched her follow one of the inn's chambermaids up the stairs to the upper floor where the bedrooms lay, he couldn't help but wonder if that really was the true motive underlying his invitation.

O livia cast aside the *Times* onto the small pile of other London newspapers the young chambermaid had supplied at her request along with a pitcher of piping-hot water for washing. Alone in her room, Olivia had taken the opportunity—her first in the last two days—to quickly flip through all the pages from front to back, scanning every article in each paper, but she came across nothing related to her disappearance. *Thank God.*

It seemed she'd been correct in her assumption that her family would be leery of causing a great kerfuffle. Though that didn't mean Uncle Reginald and Felix weren't still looking for her.

The small mantel clock above the fireplace chimed the hour—six o'clock—and Olivia stirred. She needed to get herself ready. She had anticipated that she would order a tray for both her and Tilda, so it was a surprise indeed when the marquess requested their presence at dinner. It seemed highly irregular. She was certain that men like Lord Sleat didn't routinely seek out the company of their child's nursemaid. Indeed, if it weren't for Tilda's presence, Olivia and the marquess would ostensibly be alone.

Olivia's cheeks were feverishly hot and blooming with bright color as she quickly splashed fresh warm water into a chipped ewer and washed her face and hands. She'd already helped Tilda to bathe and change into fresh clothes; Olivia also tied a pale blue satin ribbon in the child's toffee brown curls to match the sash on her fine muslin dress. Even though Tilda's mother had given her daughter up, it appeared she'd had sufficient funds to provide good-quality clothing for her child.

Tilda was presently curled up in an armchair before the fire, studying one of the illustrated books on flora and fauna that Lord Sleat had stowed away in their carriage to keep her entertained. To think a man like the marquess had been so thoughtful—especially given the fact that he had so much else on his mind—touched Olivia deeply.

It seemed the silly tendre she'd been harboring for a man she knew virtually nothing about—bar his wicked reputation—was beginning to grow and deepen, despite her best efforts to quash it.

Telling herself the only reason she was taking trouble with her appearance was to make herself presentable—she was dining with a marquess, after all—she spent a few minutes repinning her hair into a low and becoming chignon at her nape. Then she dug through her valise and selected a fresh gown of mulberry-colored wool. The small looking glass by the washstand revealed that her cheeks were still pink, so there was no need for her to pinch them.

Tilda appeared beside her and tugged on her skirts. "You look pretty, Miss Devinia," she said softly. "A bit like my mama."

If Tilda had suddenly sprouted cherub's wings and flown about the room, Olivia would have been less surprised. For the past two days, she'd said little more than yes or no in response to any of Olivia's questions. And now that the little girl had attempted to say her name—well, her assumed name—meant a lot to Olivia. Even more astounding was the fact that Tilda had disclosed something about her mother. Would she be able to tell her anything else?

Olivia knelt down and took the child's tiny hands in hers. "Why, thank you, Tilda," she said gently. "Does your mama look a little like me then?"

Tilda nodded, her blue gray eyes solemn, but she didn't offer anything further.

"Does . . . does she have hair like mine?" Olivia touched one of the tendrils by her temple. "Is it dark brown?"

Tilda shook her head this time. "No, it's this color." She pointed to her own hair. "And curly."

"Oh. And does she wear papers to bed to curl it? Or use curling tongs?"

Tilda shook her head. "No. It's just curly."

It wasn't a revelation by any means, but at least it was a start. At any rate, Olivia would be sure to share this new detail with the marquess. Aloud she said, "Well, she must be very pretty indeed if her hair is like yours."

Tilda offered a shy smile, but then tears brimmed in her eyes. "I miss Mama."

Olivia's heart cramped with sadness as she drew the child close for a hug. "I know, dear one," she whispered against Tilda's hair. "Lord Sleat and I will find out where your mama is and take you b-back to her. But first we are going on a grand adventure."

"That's what my mama said."

"See, there you are." Olivia sat back on her heels and gently wiped the tears from Tilda's cheeks. "Everything will b-be all right."

A small crease appeared between Tilda's fine eyebrows. "Why is your talking so bumpy, Miss Devinia?"

Olivia smiled. She wasn't offended at all by the child's question. "To be perfectly honest, I'm not really sure. Talking can be tricky sometimes. And it has always been for me. Ever since I was a little girl just like you."

Tilda nodded sagely. "It's tricky for me too. I can never say"—her forehead wrinkled with concentration—"efe . . . efelent."

"I know exactly what you mean," agreed Olivia. "Though, sometimes I find it helps to break big words into smaller bits. Like this: ella . . ."

Tilda dutifully copied. "Ella . . ."

"Then you add 'funt.' Ella . . . funt."

"Ella . . . funt." Tilda smiled. "Elephant."

"Perfect." Olivia smiled back. "Do you think you're ready for dinner?"

Tilda nodded. "Oh, yes please, Miss Devinia."

Miss Devinia. Olivia didn't have the heart to correct Tilda's pronunciation of her name at the moment. Especially since it wasn't even her real name to begin with. Perhaps that could be a lesson for another day.

The Hart and Hare's private dining room was a cozy, perhaps even intimate room; the flickering light generated by the blazing fire and numerous clusters of fat beeswax candles danced about the wooden wainscoting and the low-beamed ceiling. The curtains of burgundy red velvet were drawn against the cold, drear night. The weather had deteriorated; the wind had picked up and squalls of rain hit the windowpanes, making them rattle intermittently. Thunder growled in the distance.

Hamish congratulated himself on making the decision to spend the night here as he dropped into a sturdy Jacobean-style chair of blackened oak at the dining table already set for dinner and poured himself a glass of claret. While there was a pressing need to get to Skye as soon as possible, there was no sense putting everyone in danger by continuing on through the darkness, doing battle with the elements.

He was particularly aware that he now had a duty of care toward not only Tilda but also Miss Morland. What a dashed nuisance it was that he couldn't seem to stop thinking about the young woman in wholly inappropriate ways. The fact that he'd had been obliged to install Miss Morland and Tilda in the chamber adjacent to his wasn't helping matters—the inn was full to its bursting point, no doubt due to the onset of the inclement weather. Of course, the presence of the child would assuredly have a dampening effect upon his unseemly desire, but just the thought of Miss Lavinia Morland next door to him in any state of dishabille was still damnably arousing.

To ensure he had any chance of sleeping tonight, it was best he get well and truly soused. To that end, Hamish promptly downed his claret and refilled his glass . . . and then there was a knock at the door. Daniels, who stood on duty, opened it to reveal Miss Morland and Tilda.

Even though Miss Morland was one of his staff, he rose as any gentleman would and bowed as she entered. "You're early," he remarked as she and Tilda approached the table. The clock on the wooden mantel revealed the time to be ten minutes to seven.

"And so are you, my lord," she replied with a shy smile. The candlelight lent her dark brown eyes a mysterious, luminous quality he found most appealing. "In any case, it would be poor f-form indeed to keep my employer waiting."

"Indeed."

The footman drew close, perhaps to seat the new arrivals at the table, but Hamish waved him away, yet again unaccountably disgruntled by the young man's eagerness to court the nursemaid's attention. "Daniels, make yourself useful and chase up our meal," he instructed, pulling out a nearby chair for Miss Morland instead. "And then consider yourself dismissed for the evening. We shall dine *à la française*."

"Aye, my lord." Daniels's face fell, but nevertheless he complied. However, Hamish didn't miss the longing look he threw the nursemaid before the door closed behind him. The lad would be better off chasing the barmaids in the taproom.

Miss Morland hovered by her seat. A slight frown pleated her brow. "I suspect Tilda will need to sit upon a cushion or two to reach the table, my lord."

"Yes. You're quite right." He snagged two cushions from a damask-upholstered sofa by the fireside and stacked them on another chair before lifting the light-as-a-feather child and placing her on top. "Will that do, Miss Tilda?" he asked, pushing the chair in carefully so the cushions wouldn't wobble too much. He didn't want her to fall.

The child stared wide-eyed at him for several seconds before nodding. "Thank you, sir," she murmured.

An unexpected warmth spread inside Hamish's chest. It pleased him that the bairn didn't find him quite so frightening anymore. Perhaps she might eventually be coaxed into talking to him more about her mysterious mama. "You're very welcome, wee one."

"Yes, thank you, my lord." Miss Morland sat gracefully, and once again Hamish wondered about her background. The deep purple gown she wore was of fine wool and well cut even if it was far too spinsterish for his liking—the neckline was high, concealing the lass's lovely décolletage. Miss Morland might claim she was a poor relative of the de Veres, but her family hadn't scrimped on providing her with a decent, albeit sedate, wardrobe.

Come to think of it, Tilda's gown seemed to be of a superior quality too. Hamish studied the little girl's white muslin gown with its bright blue sash as he reclaimed his seat at the table. Not that he was an authority on children's clothing, by any means, but Tilda certainly wasn't dressed in patched, soiled, or ragged garments. It made him even more curious about her mother's circumstances. She must have had money at some point. He'd seek Miss Morland's opinion on it later when Tilda was out of earshot.

He was just pouring Miss Morland a glass of claret when a trio of female servants—the innkeeper's wife and two daughters, no doubt—arrived with their dinner. An array of domed platters and china dishes were deposited in the center of the oak table, and then he, Miss Morland, and Tilda were left alone once more.

Hamish played servant, carving up the roast chicken, while Miss Morland uncovered the other dishes and served up vegetables for them all—crunchy golden potatoes, roasted carrots and parsnips, and steamed buttered beans and sprouts.

"Goodness, you've thought of everything, my lord," remarked Miss Morland when she discovered the pitcher of warmed milk he'd requested for Tilda.

"I didn't think claret would be to Tilda's taste," he replied, helping himself to a thick slice of fresh bread and slathering it with butter. "I trust it is to yours . . ."

"Oh . . ." Miss Morland picked up her glass and examined the deep ruby red contents. "To be p-perfectly honest, I've never had claret before."

"Please don't feel obliged to drink it on my account. I can easily send for something else. Whatever you'd like, in fact. Sherry, perhaps. Small beer or cider. Tea . . ."

"No, it's quite all right. I'd like to try it." She took a tentative sip, and he watched her pink tongue swipe across her fulsome lower lip, leaving a slight sheen. He had to bite his own lip to stifle a groan. God's teeth, what the hell was wrong with him?

He forced himself to speak to break the odd spell she'd effortlessly cast over him. "So, what do you think, Miss Morland?"

"It's rather nice," she replied, and took another sip as if to demonstrate she spoke the truth. "Not quite as pleasant as champagne. I had that once at Lord and Lady Mal . . . I mean, at a f-friend's wedding. I most certainly prefer it to brandy."

Hamish cocked a brow in surprise. "You've tried brandy?"

"Yes. Al-although it was some time ago. Awful stuff, if you ask me." Miss Morland picked up her knife and fork and proceeded to slice the chicken breast on Tilda's plate into smaller pieces. Bright color had stained her cheeks, making Hamish suspect there was more to the brandy story than she wished to admit.

"I prefer whisky myself," said Hamish, "but if brandy isn't to your taste, I'm sure you wouldn't like that either. It's evil stuff. And illegal, so hard to come by too"—he winked—"unless you know where to find it."

Miss Morland's gaze returned to his. A small frown puckered her brow. "Then why do you drink it?"

Because it's the only alcohol strong enough to knock me unconscious so I'm not constantly plagued by nightmares. But Hamish couldn't admit that. Instead, he simply shrugged and threw her a devilish grin. "Och, I'm a High-lander, lassie. Whisky, the *uisge beatha*—that's Scots Gaelic for the water of life—it runs through my veins."

Miss Morland blushed again, and she turned her attention to her own dinner. "I'm looking forward to seeing the Isle of

Skye, my lord. I've never journeyed to Scotland before. I hear the Highlands are beautiful."

"Aye, they are indeed," agreed Hamish. "Although Muircliff Castle, my home, is at the northern end of the island in quite an isolated, some might even say desolate, spot. In fact, it sits upon a cliff overlooking the Little Minch, a channel separating Skye from the Isles of the Outer Hebrides. I hope you like the sea, Miss Morland. It's a constant companion, along with the wind and the gulls."

"It sounds wonderful. And yes, I do like the sea. Very much." Miss Morland's mouth lifted into a smile, and another delightful petal pink blush bloomed across her cheeks. "This summer, I had the op . . . the opportunity to go sea bathing in Brighton. In a bathing machine, of course. It was most refreshing."

The sudden image of Miss Morland's pale and slender naked form rising from the sea sprang into Hamish's mind, and he nearly choked on his mouthful of chicken. He took a quick swig of claret and then cleared his throat before speaking. "I'm afraid sea bathing is out of the question around Muircliff. The waters of the channel are treacherous, even in calm weather. And freezing cold. You'd turn into a block of ice within a few minutes."

"Oh, I didn't expect to . . . I mean to say . . ." Miss Morland closed her eyes momentarily, then took a deep breath. "I'm sure I will love Muircliff Castle, my lord."

At least one of us will, thought Hamish grimly. They continued to eat in polite but strained silence until Hamish could bear it no longer. It was his fault the mood in the room had changed. Keen to avoid further conversation about his own home, he asked Miss Morland where she originally hailed from.

When Miss Morland put down her cutlery and took a slow sip of wine, Hamish studied her face. Was she prevaricating? Again he was struck by the notion that Tilda's pretty nursemaid was hiding something. He had begun to suspect she wouldn't answer at all when she cleared her throat and responded in a voice so soft, he had to lean forward to catch her words. "I was . . . I was raised in Warwickshire, an only child, n-not far from Birmingham . . ." A sigh shivered through her as she added, "Unfortunately, both of my p-parents passed away some time ago in a terrible carriage accident, and I have been f-forced to rely upon the goodwill of my extended family ever since."

Dear God. Guilt, sharper than a bayonet blade, pierced Hamish's heart. What a king-sized dolt he was for forcing her to talk about such a distressing topic. Of course she was an orphan. Why else would she be living as a companion with relatives who had little regard for her? Swallowing past the lump of remorse in his throat, he said, "I'm very sorry to hear of your loss, Miss Morland. It was thoughtless of me to ask you to speak about things that must pain you. Please accept my sincerest apology."

"No, it's quite all right, my lord," she replied. The expression in her large brown eyes was melancholy but her gaze steady as she regarded him over the candlelit table. "It's understandable that you'd be curious. After all, I've not been terribly forthcoming about my personal history up until now."

Hamish waved a dismissive hand and leaned back in his chair. "I suspect we all have particular topics we'd rather not talk about at length, Miss Morland."

"Yes . . ."

An ominous roll of thunder reverberated around the inn, shaking the windows, and Tilda clutched at her nurse's sleeve, her eyes wide with fear. Miss Morland bent low, and the child whispered in her ear.

Miss Morland caught Hamish's eye. "Would you m-mind if we dispensed with the usual formalities at the dinner table? Tilda is terribly frightened of storms and would like to sit upon my lap." Her brow wrinkled with a grimace. "I'm afraid she's also requested a lullaby. Which might not be a pleasant experience for you, my lord, as I'm not an accomplished singer by any means. Although, I'm less prone to stam . . . to stuttering when I sing. So there's that at least."

"Of course I don't mind. I don't want the bairn to be afraid. And I would be delighted to hear you sing, Miss Morland. Why don't you take a seat by the fire, where you'll both be far more comfortable?"

Miss Morland gave him a grateful smile. "Thank you."

She repaired to the damask sofa with Tilda, and the little girl promptly clambered onto her lap, snuggling into her nurse's arms. Glass of claret still in hand, Hamish joined them at the fireside, claiming the chair on the opposite side of the hearth. Truth to tell, he was intrigued. Despite her stammer, Miss Morland had a lovely voice; there was a velvet softness about it, an appealing husky quality that was strangely seductive. He was certain she was underestimating her ability.

Indeed, he was beginning to notice she lacked self-confidence, and he wondered if it was because of her stammer. The thought of anyone teasing her about her speech impediment, or treating her like an afterthought as her family seemed to have done, bothered him more than he could say. Which reminded him, she still hadn't told him how much she'd like to be paid for her services. He'd mention it in the morning.

"This . . . this is a lullaby my own mama sang to me when I was young," murmured Miss Morland as she gathered Tilda closer. Her slender shoulders rose as she took a deep breath. And then the voice of an angel emerged from her sweet mouth, drowning out the howl of the tempest, the crackling of the fire, and every other sound save for the wild thrumming of Hamish's own blood through his veins.

> *Lavender's blue, dilly dilly,*
> *Rosemary's green.*
> *When I am king, dilly dilly,*
> *You shall be queen.*

Call up my maids, dilly dilly,
At four o'clock,
Some to the wheel, dilly dilly,
Some to the rock.

Some to make hay, dilly dilly,
Some to shear corn,
Whilst you and I, dilly dilly,
Keep the bed warm.

By the time Miss Morland had finished her beguiling, perfectly sung lullaby, Tilda's eyelids were drooping, and Hamish was completely enthralled.

Damn, now his mind was filled with images of Miss Lavinia Morland warming his bed upstairs. How her slender legs would entwine with his. The silken slide of her rich dark tresses over his bare chest. She would raise her head and press those full, berry-sweet lips to his, and then he'd flip her onto her back and plunder her—

Miss Morland cleared her throat. "My lord," she whispered. "I think it might be time to put Tilda to bed."

"Aye . . . yes. Quite." Hamish swallowed, and adjusted the fall of his waistcoat and jacket to hide a telltale swell at the front of his buckskin breeches. This attraction was getting out of hand. His life was complicated enough, and dallying with the nursemaid was a distraction he could do without. Miss Morland was here to make his life easier, not harder (his current state notwithstanding). And as soon as he found Tilda's mother, he would either return Miss Morland to her family or help her to find another situation—the choice would be hers entirely.

The fire in his blood now subsiding, Hamish put aside his claret and stood. "Let me escort you upstairs. The inn is busy, and you shouldn't have to fend off the advances of drunken louts."

"Oh, I'm sure that won't be necessary—"

"But I'm sure that it is." Hamish crossed to the door and

held it open for her. A burst of raucous male laughter sounded above the general hubbub of the storm, and he raised an eyebrow. "You're not going to argue with your employer, are you, Miss Morland?"

"No, my lord. Of course not," she murmured, slipping past him into the hall outside.

Hamish followed, stalwartly studying the chignon at the back of Miss Morland's head, rather than the elegant length of her neck or the tantalizing sway of her hips beneath her dark purple skirts. When they reached the bottom of the main stairs, he took a sleeping Tilda from her. The child nestled against his shoulder, and when she slipped her thumb into her mouth, Hamish felt an unfamiliar wave of protectiveness wash over him.

Is this what it feels like to be a father? he thought as he climbed the stairs, still following Miss Morland. Hamish doubted his own father, Torquil MacQueen, had ever experienced such a tender emotion. Not for him, his eldest son and heir, nor for his other offspring, Angus and Isobel. Not even for his wife, Margaret.

Hamish barely suppressed a violent shudder and tried to bury all thoughts of a man he despised. A brutish man who'd tormented those he was supposed to love and brought untold anguish into all their lives. Hamish was sorry about many things, but he'd never be sorry his father was dead.

Christ, what he wouldn't do for a bottle of whisky right now. He paused outside Miss Morland's bedchamber door as she unlocked it, and took a moment to calm his riotous thoughts. The wild thudding of his heart. It was a good thing he had a sleeping child in his arms because if he didn't, he might just be tempted to throw all his scruples out the window and take Lavinia Morland to bed after all, just so he could lose himself for a while.

But he wouldn't. Because in the morning he'd be tortured by guilt for ruining an innocent girl for reasons that were utterly selfish.

Instead, he carefully tucked Tilda into her pallet bed by the fire. After muttering a cursory good night to Miss Morland, he headed for the door, intending to visit the taproom downstairs. But then the cursed woman followed him and touched his arm, staying him.

"My lord, might I have a quick word?"

Hamish swallowed, again fighting the overwhelming urge to drag Lavinia Morland into his arms as he turned to face her. The fragrance she favored—something sweet and floral like violets with an underlying note that was entirely feminine, vanilla perhaps—teased him, making his nostrils flare like a stag scenting a hind. Did she realize she was in danger of being ravaged? His voice, when it emerged, was rougher than he'd intended it to be. "What is it? I hope it won't take too long."

Color flooded Miss Morland's cheeks, and she immediately took a step back. She pleated her fingers tightly together at her waist. "No. No, it w-won't," she murmured in a breathless rush. "It's about Tilda. Well, her mother, at least. A small clue, perhaps?"

Curiosity spiked inside Hamish. "Yes? Did the child tell you something useful?"

Miss Morland nodded, then shared what she'd learned about Tilda's mother's appearance. "Although she's young, Tilda's manner of speech also suggests to me that her mother is well-spoken. And all her clothes are of good quality too. She was well cared for."

"Aye, I agree," remarked Hamish. He sighed. Tilda's mother—who might have light brown, naturally curly hair—probably hailed from the middle classes. And aside from being literate, at some stage she'd been in possession of an adequate amount of money. It still wasn't a lot to go on, but he supposed it was better than nothing. In the morning, he'd dash off a letter to his man of affairs and ask him to pass on the additional information to the inquiry agent.

"If . . . if Tilda tells me anything else," said Miss Morland softly, "I'll be sure to inform you straightaway, my lord."

Hamish inclined his head. "Thank you. And in case I haven't said it before, I appreciate everything you're doing.

For me and for Tilda. So . . ." He opened the door and forced himself to step into the hallway. "I bid you good night again, Miss Morland. Be sure to lock your door after I leave. And I hope you sleep well. On the morrow, we'll depart at eight o'clock."

"Yes, my lord. And I hope you sleep well too."

Now, that would be a bloody miracle. Hamish turned on his heel and all but raced for the stairs before he could change his mind about seducing Miss Morland. If the innkeeper didn't have an illicit stash of whisky somewhere, he was sure to have brandy or port.

Maybe when he'd emptied a bottle or two, he'd at last reach that much-sought-after state of total oblivion he so badly needed yet rarely found.

CHAPTER 6

❧

> The wind roared down the chimney, the rain beat
> in torrents against the windows, and everything
> seemed to speak the awfulness of her situation.
>
> *Jane Austen*, Northanger Abbey

The Hart and Hare Inn, Kendal, Cumberland

September 18, 1818

Even though Olivia was exhausted from traveling—and pretending to be someone she wasn't, much to her shame—her sleep was fitful. The unfamiliar bed was lumpy. She was alternately too hot and then too cold, so she kept tossing her covers off or dragging them back on. And most annoyingly of all, strange noises kept jolting her awake whenever she did manage to slip into a doze. The wind wailed about the eaves, and rain hurled itself at the bedchamber window until well past midnight. Fellow guests stomped down the hall, laughing and chatting and slamming doors, and in the inn yard below, departing patrons called out to each other.

So when an anguished, unearthly cry shattered the relative quiet of the early hours—the storm had at last abated—Olivia immediately sat bolt upright in her bed.

Her heart pounding, she held her breath, listening. Had the sound come from Lord Sleat's chamber? Surely not. But when a strangled moan filtered into her room again, Olivia knew it was coming from the corner suite next door.

Good Lord. Was the marquess hurt? In any case, something was terribly wrong. Her gaze darted to Tilda, but she was still sound asleep and tucked up snugly in her pallet.

Another cry, rather like an agonized sob, penetrated the stillness, and Olivia slid from her bed. Where on earth was Hudson, the marquess's valet? Shouldn't he be attending to his master? Unless Lord Sleat had dismissed him for the night . . .

The fire had died down, but the lingering glow of the coals helped Olivia to locate her woolen shawl on the cold, bare floorboards by the end of her bed. Wrapping it about herself to cover at least some of her flannel night rail, she tiptoed quickly to the door in her bare feet and peered into the hallway. It was dark and deserted and utterly quiet except for the intermittent sounds of distress emanating from Lord Sleat's room.

After carefully closing and locking her own bedchamber door behind her to make sure Tilda would be safe, she hastened to the marquess's door and rapped. "Lord Sleat," she called in a hushed but urgent tone. "Are . . . are you all right?"

The moaning stopped abruptly, but then there was a loud thump and a smashing sound like glass breaking. Panic flared anew inside Olivia.

"Lord Sleat!" She hammered on the oak door again, not caring if she disturbed anyone else now. "If you can hear me, p-please let me in—"

At that moment, the door flew open, and she was dragged inside by a dark looming figure. *Lord Sleat?*

Oh, thank God, it was. Even though the marquess's face was in deep shadow, a branch of candles on the mantelpiece and a low fire in the grate gave off just enough light for Olivia to discern that it was indeed her employer.

As the door shut behind her, she sagged against the wooden panels. The relief flooding her body turned her knees to water and made her head spin. "M-my lord," she breathed. "I . . . I thought . . . I was worried . . ."

Lord Sleat's long fingers were still wrapped tightly around her upper arm. His grip loosened, but instead of dropping his hold, he slid his hand up to her shoulder. His touch was hot, burning her flesh through her night rail, making her shiver. Beneath the flannel fabric covering her chest, her nipples pebbled in the most alarming way.

"Miss Morland. What in the devil's name are you doing here?" The marquess's voice was low and hoarse, roughened by sleep and perhaps those awful cries he'd made.

Olivia swallowed. "I . . . I came to see if you n-needed assistance. You woke me, and then I heard something smash—"

"My apologies." Lord Sleat spoke with such deliberate slowness, Olivia wondered if he was more than a little foxed. "I have bad dreams sometimes . . ." With his free hand, the one that wasn't resting upon her person, he pointed to the scarred side of his face. It was then that Olivia realized the marquess wasn't wearing his eye patch. However, the fall of his tousled, overly long hair and the shadows shielded the worst of the damage.

"Oh . . . oh, I'm so sorry." Olivia's heart clenched with sympathy. The marquess was such a powerful, confident, vital man, one wouldn't suspect that he'd suffer from any sort of mental or emotional affliction. Clearly the injuries he'd sustained during his time in Wellington's army weren't just physical.

Lord Sleat sighed heavily and swayed closer. "It's no matter," he murmured, his warm breath fanning across her cheek. "And I'm sorry for disturbing you." He gestured to a patch of the floor beside his bed where shards of broken glass and a pool of liquid glittered in the dying firelight. "It seems I thrashed about a bit and knocked over a bottle."

Oh, my goodness. She'd been right. The marquess *was* foxed. Olivia could hear that his speech was slightly slurred. Smell the alcohol on his breath. And there were other scents—cigar or wood smoke, perhaps, and exotic spices like clove and sandalwood and musk. A heady blend of masculine fragrances.

Olivia clutched her shawl more tightly about her shoulders as her awareness of Lord Sleat's inherent maleness flickered to life. She was in a scandalous state of dishabille, and when her gaze fluttered downward, her breath quickened. The marquess was barely dressed as well.

Indeed, he wore nothing but a pair of snug buckskin breeches and a dark blue velvet banyan. It hung open, revealing a wide expanse of muscular chest scattered with dark hair and, below that, an intriguingly ridged torso.

The marquess was breathing heavily too. His large hand, which had remained on her shoulder all this time, skated up the side of her neck. Curled around her nape beneath her braid. And then his strong fingers speared into her hair, cradling the back of her skull, angling her head. Holding her steady. All his attention seemed to be focused on her mouth . . .

The air caught in Olivia's lungs, yet her heart bolted clean away.

Was Lord Sleat going to kiss her?

While a wholly feminine part of Olivia yearned to succumb, to simply close her eyes and give in to wicked temptation—just as she'd done countless times in her dreams—a sane part of her mind asserted this was a very bad idea. For so many reasons. She listed them in her head.

Lord Sleat was inebriated and not making sound decisions.

He was her employer.

She was deceiving him.

If he kissed her, she might not want him to stop . . .

Swallowing past a throat tight with nerves and longing, Olivia forced herself to speak. "F-forgive me for saying so, b-but I think you're a little drunk, my lord, and—"

Lord Sleat's wide, chiseled mouth tilted into a smirk. "Aye, I am indeed, lass," he said, his voice as rough as gravel. "Actually, it might surprise you to know, I'm not drunk enough."

Not drunk enough? Olivia's mouth dropped open. The

man was as drunk as a wheelbarrow. Or three sheets to the wind, as her father used to say.

"Now, now, now, Miss Morland. Don't go all mish . . . I mean missish on me. I can see by your expression that you've already passed judgment on my character. On my insalubrious ways and ungentlemanly conduct. If I were your guardian . . . well, if you *had* a guardian," he amended, "I'd tell you to run a mile."

"I'm . . . I'm not being missish," she protested, crossing her arms over her chest.

Lord Sleat continued as if she hadn't spoken. "Not that I would blame you if you did decide to run a mile. I mean, look at me. I'm an utter disaster. Inside and out." All at once he stepped away and raked his hair back from his brow, revealing the full extent of his damaged face; his left eye was still intact but clearly sightless, the orb glowing a strange milky white in the lambent light of the candles and dying fire. The jagged scar that bisected his eyebrow also pulled down the corner of his eyelid before taking a slashing turn across the crest of his cheek.

Olivia tried to but failed to suppress a gasp; she wasn't horrified or revolted by the sight of his injuries, just shocked. Unbidden tears brimmed in her own eyes. To think of the terrible pain Lord Sleat must have endured. No wonder he suffered from nightmares.

The marquess's mouth twisted into a sneer of a smile as he dropped his hand and his hair tumbled back into place. "So, my bonnie wee lassie, now that you've seen this particular beast in his true natural state, unfettered and unhinged, I suspect you'd like to go."

Olivia frowned. "I'm not frightened, if that's what you're thinking, my lord. And I won't leave, not until I know you *are* all right. Can I get you anything? Summon Hudson? Help clean up the broken glass?"

Lord Sleat waved a dismissive hand. A scowl replaced his smile. "There's no help for me I'm afraid, Miss Morland. And as for the glass, don't worry about it. You should go back to bed. Get some sleep." He suddenly yawned and scratched the dark stubble on his jaw. "Christ knows I need some," he muttered.

Olivia worried at her lower lip, not at all convinced the marquess didn't need some kind of assistance. But what could she do if he was going to reject any and all offers of help? So she released a defeated huff and said, "Well, if you're sure then . . ."

"I am." Lord Sleat leaned past her and opened the door. "Good night once more, Lavinia Morland. I wish you nothing but sweet dreams."

Back in her own room, Olivia stoked the fire to life. Tilda stirred a little, then rolled over and began to suck her thumb.

A wistful sigh escaped Olivia. If only she could sleep so soundly. But that wasn't likely now that she'd learned something truly shocking. Despite the marquess's intemperate tendencies, mercurial moods, and deeply wounded spirit, she couldn't deny that she wanted him even more than she had before.

Because in those tense moments when she'd been pressed against the door with the marquess only inches from her, her fingers had itched to push aside his robe and explore every inch of his muscular body. Her lips had tingled at the thought of him kissing her. In fact, they still did.

Olivia touched her mouth with trembling fingers and stared into the bright, dancing flames of the fire. How she'd summoned the strength to resist Lord Sleat when he'd held her in his handsome grip, she really had no idea.

Yes, if the marquess had thought to scare her off by revealing his "beastly self" to her, he'd been sadly mistaken. Because the only thing truly frightening about that whole encounter had been how much she truly desired Lord Sleat.

Good morning, Miss Morland. I trust you slept well."
Standing beneath the Hart and Hare's portico, Tilda's hand in hers while she waited for the carriage to be

brought around, Olivia turned away from her examination of the muddy inn yard and the teeming rain, and dipped into a curtsy. "Lord Sleat. I did, thank you." What did one more lie matter when she'd told a countless number already?

"I'm very pleased to hear it," Lord Sleat replied smoothly as he adjusted the angle of his beaver hat and then tugged on black leather gloves.

From beneath her eyelashes, Olivia studied the marquess's appearance. By rights, the man should be bed-bound with a frightful megrim, considering the amount of alcohol he'd imbibed last night. But then again, perhaps he was practiced at hiding how unwell he felt. He'd all but admitted to her that he habitually overindulged.

However, aside from a slight tightening of the skin across his cheekbones and a deepening of the grooves around his mouth, he seemed perfectly hale and hearty. He certainly wasn't pasty or green about the gills.

Thanks to Hudson, his valet, he was freshly shaven, and above the collar of his great coat, she could see a glimpse of a starched snowy white cravat. While his leather eye patch was in place again, his right eye was a clear gray and his gaze steady as he finished adjusting his attire and turned to regard her face.

Drat, he'd caught her examining him with unseemly interest. Embarrassed, Olivia looked quickly away and began to fuss with the ribbon ties on Tilda's dimity cap.

But she needn't have worried that the marquess might tease her with a flirtatious remark or a smile. It seemed the wild, hot-blooded Highlander of last night had vanished and the nobleman with the practiced manners was back. "We've a fair way to travel today," he said in a matter-of-fact yet perfectly polite tone of voice. "I'd like to cross the border into Scotland and spend the night at Gretna Green if at all possible." His gaze returned to the rainy aspect. "Weather permitting of course."

For some reason she couldn't quite explain, Olivia was irked. "Yes, of course."

The carriages rolled into the yard, and Lord Sleat beckoned over one of the footmen holding an umbrella. As the young man approached, the marquess tilted into a slight bow and gave her another perfunctory smile. "Daniels will assist you and Tilda from here, Miss Morland."

When the footman handed her into the carriage, Olivia realized why she was so annoyed. It was almost as though she and Lord Sleat were distant acquaintances—perhaps even strangers—exchanging inconsequential pleasantries. Perhaps he'd been so deep in his cups last night, he'd forgotten about her visit to his room. Or maybe he recalled everything that had occurred but had decided it was best to dismiss the whole incident and pretend it hadn't happened. That he hadn't tried to kiss her.

Olivia sighed as the carriage door closed. In any event, she supposed it was better this way. She was used to being disregarded most of the time. After all, she was nothing but a lowly nursemaid. Someone of little consequence. An employer should keep his distance.

Oh, but why did Lord Sleat's sudden indifference hurt so much?

Because you might just be starting to fall in love with the real man—with all of his flaws, and all of his scars— not just the make-believe hero of your daydreams.

To think she might be genuinely developing true feelings for Lord Sleat, after only a very short span of time, was sobering indeed.

To keep Tilda amused, and to take her own mind off the marquess and the long journey ahead, Olivia dug out several illustrated volumes from the concealed compartment beneath the opposite seat. The one Tilda chose to look at featured the fauna of Scotland, and Olivia proceeded to spin fanciful tales about all manner of creatures: eagles and stags, badgers and seals, wildcats and mountain hares. Tilda particularly liked it when she made up funny voices for each of the characters—a squawk for the eagle, a snuffling sound for the badger, a deep cultured voice like Lord

Sleat's for the stag, and a honking tone for the seal. To hear the child giggling warmed Olivia's heart.

When her ideas for storytelling ran dry, she sang songs and recited nursery rhymes until she heard Tilda's tummy grumble. Then she opened up the basket of food that Lord Sleat always had stowed in the carriage, and they both dined on cheese and gammon sandwiches, crisp apples, and sticky jam tarts.

Eventually, Tilda began to yawn and to rub her eyes; wrapped up in a tartan blanket, she curled up on the bench and fell asleep with her head resting in Olivia's lap. Olivia stroked her bright curls and watched the raindrops sliding down the glass panes of the carriage windows.

They'd been traveling for hours but the bad weather hadn't abated, and their progress along the muddy country roads was slow. She felt sorry for the coach drivers, attendant footmen, and outriders. Being constantly lashed by the chill wind and persistent heavy showers would not be comfortable by any means. It seemed Lord Sleat really was determined to reach Skye as soon as possible.

Not for the first time, Olivia ruminated about the nature of the urgent matter Lord Sleat needed to attend to at Muircliff. He never spoke of it, and it wasn't her place to question him, but she did wonder if it might have something to do with his family. Because surely an estate matter could be handled by his steward or a man of affairs.

She supposed she would soon find out.

Lulled by the rocking of the cab and the sound of the rain drumming on the roof, Olivia soon felt her eyelids begin to droop as well. It wasn't until the carriage was drawing to a stop at a busy coaching inn that she was jolted awake. Lord Sleat appeared at the slightly fogged window with his wide umbrella.

"Where are we, if you don't m-mind my asking?" said Olivia in a voice croaky with sleep when he opened the door and admitted a rush of cold air. "I've been dozing . . ." Indeed, the side of her face had been squashed against the leather squabs, and she had a horrible feeling there were crease marks on her cheek and that her hair was a frightful mess.

But then again, the marquess had hitherto seen her in worse states of dishevelment and undress. *Stuck on a wall with torn skirts and soiled stockings. Barefoot and wearing nothing but a nightgown and shawl . . .*

Lord Sleat's gaze traced over her blushing countenance, but he replied to her question matter-of-factly enough. "We're in Carlisle. We'll change horses here even though we only have an hour or so to go until we reach Gretna Green. I'm concerned there might be flooding that will prevent our traveling farther if we don't press on. I also thought you and Tilda might like a break."

Within a half hour, they were back on the road again, and the rain seemed to grow heavier with every passing mile. The windows kept fogging up, and Olivia had to wipe the glass clean periodically so she could take in the passing scenery. When they rumbled across a stone bridge and Olivia glanced downward, she was alarmed to see how swollen the river rushing below it had become; the brown, turbulent waters were flowing so swiftly, one would surely be swept away within seconds if one fell in.

Somehow, she also felt reassured. They were almost in Scotland, and no one knew where she was. She would be hidden.

She would be safe.

The carriage's progress slowed to a snail's pace whenever they forded a section of low-lying road that lay underwater or if the muddy surface was particularly churned up. Lord Sleat had told Olivia before they'd quit Carlisle that she'd know they were very close to Gretna Green when they crossed a russet-bricked bridge spanning the river Sark.

So when the horses picked up their pace and Olivia spied the Sark Bridge through her window, she leaned forward in her seat, eager to see her first glimpse of Scotland. Lord Sleat had also informed her that they'd be staying at

Graitney Hall, a well-appointed inn on the northern edge of Gretna Green. She couldn't wait to sit before a toasty fire, warming her stiff, cold fingers about a hot cup of tea—

The carriage suddenly gave a violent pitch forward as though the horses had bolted, and then slid sideways through the mud before hitting a grassy embankment.

Tilda squealed with terror, and Olivia clutched frantically at the little girl to stop her from flying off the seat. But it was to no avail. The carriage bounced and skidded back onto the road before careening off the opposite bank . . . and then the whole cab listed sideways and began to topple over. Someone screamed, glass shattered, and Olivia hurtled headlong into a deep black void . . .

Chapter 7

☙☙

Receiving no answer, he went to the carriage, and
found her sunk on the seat in a fainting fit.
  Ann Radcliffe, The Mysteries of Udolpho

The English-Scottish Border, Cumberland . . .

A frantic series of shouts followed by the scream of a
horse and a resounding crash made Hamish start, tearing him out of the self-inflicted, self-pitying doldrums he'd
been wallowing in for most of the day.

What the bloody, blazing hell had just happened?

Terror gripped his gut, but before Hamish could look
back through the rear window—the horrendous sounds had
come from behind—or direct his driver to stop, his carriage lurched to an abrupt halt.

In the next instant, Hamish was flinging open the door
and leaping onto the muddy ground. Racing down the road
through the rain to where a nightmarish scene was laid out
before him.

Oh, no. God, no.

Miss Morland's carriage lay on its side. A wheel had
splintered, and a valise or portmanteau had ruptured, spew-
ing its contents far and wide. One horse was down and, to
Hamish's horror and sorrow, not moving. Hudson was attempting to calm the two wild-eyed, snorting, and stamp-
ing beasts still trapped in the broken traces. The fourth
animal appeared to have bolted.

One of the footmen, MacSwain, was in the process of helping the coachman over to the grassy verge, and Daniels was on top of the overturned cab, attempting to wrest the door open.

Hamish vaulted up to join him. The side of the carriage was slick with rain, and he almost lost his footing.

"I can't budge it, my lord." The footman kicked at the edge of the door with the toe of his shoe. "It's stuck. Miss Morland and the bairn are trapped."

Hamish swore beneath his breath. The windowpane was still intact, but the door handle had snapped off.

Dropping to his knees, he peered through the fogged-up glass. Tilda was crying, but it was difficult to make out anything much in the dim interior. The child seemed to be huddled up against a slender form that was partly shrouded by a tartan blanket.

Lavinia.

Had she been knocked unconscious or worse?

Hamish pushed his sodden hair away from his face and tried to tamp down a wave of rising panic. He didn't want to break the window and send shards of glass showering down on the child and Miss Morland, both of whom might be injured already, but he might just have to.

Unless the nursemaid could be roused and then she could open the door from the inside. "Miss Morland. Lavinia, lass." He rapped sharply on the glass with his knuckles. "Can you hear me?"

There was no response, and Hamish cursed profusely, not caring who heard him this time. He examined the door and its broken handle more closely. "We'll need something to lever it open."

"Aye, my lord," said Daniels. "I think there's a spade stored with the tools in the other carriage."

"Good thinking, lad."

While Daniels fetched the spade, Hamish tried to calm Tilda with soothing words and reassurances that everything would be fine. However, trying to provoke a response from Miss Morland proved to be futile. Aside from the sound of Tilda's weeping and the pattering of the rain, there was utter silence.

Hamish wasn't in the habit of sending up prayers to heaven, but in this instance, he did.

If anything happens to Lavinia . . .

No, he couldn't think like that. She would be all right. And so would Tilda.

Daniels reappeared and threw the spade to Hamish. Straightaway, he rose and jammed the narrow metal edge of the blade between the doorframe and the latch. With his foot on the edge of the spade, he then used all of his not-inconsiderable weight and whatever strength he possessed to try to prize the door open.

The worst curse word he knew of was hovering on the tip of his tongue at the precise moment the obstinate door at last gave way. Wrenching it open, Hamish fell to his knees. Little Tilda reached up to him, and he plucked her out and handed her to Daniels.

A terrible sense of foreboding settled over him as he turned back to the gaping doorway. Miss Morland still hadn't responded to a goddamned thing going on around her. But even though she was curled up in a corner of the cab, Hamish sensed she was alive. Still breathing. The tartan blanket had fallen away, so he could see that her arms were wrapped about her drawn-up knees, her head bent as though she was trying to make herself as small as possible. He carefully eased himself into the space, his booted feet crunching on the broken glass pane of the other window, which had now become the floor, and then knelt down beside the immobilized girl.

Christ, the poor lass was shivering, her whole body trembling. Her breathing came in short, shallow pants. There was a small cut upon her pale forehead oozing blood, but other than that, Hamish couldn't discern any other obvious injuries.

"Lavinia. Can you hear me? Does anything hurt?" Hamish tugged off a damp glove and laid a hand upon her shoulder. He squeezed gently.

At his touch, the lass looked up and began to shake her head. "No, no, no," she whispered hoarsely. Her expression was wild. Distraught. Her gaze skittered to his and then away again, seeking out a dark corner of the cab. "No, no, no. Don't be dead. Don't be dead. Don't be dead."

Hamish frowned. "Tilda's safe, if that's who you're worried about, lass."

"No." Lavinia began to rock back and forth. Tears streamed down her face. Her words tumbled out between her frantic gasps for air. "No, they're not . . . they're not safe. They're d-dead. I . . . I can see them . . . there . . . over there . . . Mama and Papa . . . There's too much blood. I can't, can't stop it. Can't help."

Realization hit Hamish like a facer to the jaw. What a prize idiot he was. Lavinia wasn't here with him. Not really. She was caught up in some other horrendous memory. A living nightmare from her past. He'd seen it before in men he'd served with in battle.

He experienced it far too often himself . . .

He needed to bring her back to the present.

"Lavinia, look at me, lass." He carefully grasped her chin and turned her head toward him. "It's me. Lord Sleat. I'm here with you now. I'm just going to check you're not injured, and then I'm going to get you out of this carriage. Do you think we can manage to do that?"

Her gaze connected with his, and even in the gloom, he could see she recognized him at last. That she wasn't mired in her terrifying memories any longer. She nodded. "Yes."

"Good, lass. Tell me if anything hurts." Hamish tugged off his other glove and then quickly and lightly ran his hands over her skull, along her arms and collarbones, then over her legs and down to her booted ankles. She still shivered, but her breathing was beginning to slow. "Everything seems fine. Do you think you can stand?"

Again she nodded. "I . . . I think so."

"Here we go." Hamish slid an arm about Lavinia's slender frame and helped her to rise.

She leaned against him, her head on his chest, and he

tightened his hold when she swayed on her feet. "I f-feel a b-bit giddy," she murmured through chattering teeth. "And c-c-c-cold."

"You've had a bit of a knock to the head, I'm afraid." The rain had turned to mizzle, and Lavinia's dark brown hair was covered with a gauzelike veil of tiny droplets. "We need to get you somewhere warm and dry."

"I'd like th-th-that." Her fingers curled into the lapels of his greatcoat as though seeking the warmth of his chest beneath the damp wool. "A c-cup of tea would be n-nice."

"You can have whatever you like, lass. But first let's get you into my carriage. I'm sure Tilda is anxious to see you."

As Hamish lifted Lavinia out of the ruined cab, she looked down at him and gave him a tremulous smile, then an earnest, whispered thank-you that lit her lovely deep brown eyes. And even though the day was gray and miserable and filled with terrible, heartrending things, Hamish suddenly felt as though there were a break in the clouds and the sun had come out.

But only for a few fleeting seconds. The space between one breath to the next. Because in the midst of that dizzying, glorious moment, Hamish was also struck by a lightning bolt, a horrifying epiphany that made his blood run colder than the sea crashing against the rocks below Muircliff in the depths of winter.

For the very first time in his misbegotten life, he might be in danger of feeling something beyond lust for a woman. Emotions he'd never thought could exist within his granite-hewn heart threatened to stir: warmth and tenderness and something akin to affection.

And he'd never been more terrified.

Graitney Hall, Gretna Green

Graitney Hall was the loveliest inn Olivia had ever come across. As Lord Sleat's carriage rolled down the tree-lined avenue toward the elegant whitewashed manse, the marquess informed her that the Earl of Hopetoun had lately had the house converted into a coaching inn. "Probably to take advantage of the trade in clandestine marriages," he remarked with a wink as they drew to a stop outside the front door. "The man certainly seems canny when it comes to matters of business."

Olivia offered him a small smile. She appreciated the marquess's attempt at levity. However, she suspected it would take a little more than congenial conversation to pull her out of her deeply unsettled state. Even though Tilda sat upon her lap, periodically offering her gentle hugs about the neck and, at one point, a sweet kiss upon the cheek, and Lord Sleat was nothing but consideration personified, Olivia still couldn't shake how odd she felt. Disconnected from what was happening around her. She had to keep reminding herself that she wasn't trapped in an overturned carriage.

That her parents' bodies—broken and lifeless—weren't beside her. That this time, she could do the impossible and somehow save them.

Indeed, the strange feeling of detachment and disquiet persisted even after she'd installed herself upon a silk-upholstered sofa before a roaring fire in a small but well-appointed sitting room located between her bedchamber and Lord Sleat's. The interconnecting doors between their rooms stood wide open, and if Olivia hadn't been so addled, she might have remarked upon it. As it was, such a scandalous breach of decorum hardly seemed important at the moment.

The cup of tea she'd been craving before disaster struck sat untasted on a finely carved mahogany occasional table by her elbow. Tilda snuggled up against her beneath a cashmere blanket. And Lord Sleat sat close by in a leather wingback chair.

He frowned at her, his gaze shadowed with concern. "How is your head, lass?" he asked. In his long fingers, he held a tumbler of whisky; the amber liquid caught the firelight as he raised the glass to his lips and took a sizable sip.

Olivia raised her fingers to carefully probe the egg on her

forehead. The cut had been cleaned and had stopped bleeding some time ago, but the flesh surrounding it was bruised and tender. "I have a slight headache," she admitted. "But I also feel . . ." She trailed off, not sure what to say.

"Like you're not really here?" asked Lord Sleat gently.

"Yes. How . . ." She frowned and winced. Even the slightest movement hurt. "How did you know?"

"Because I've experienced the same feeling, shall we say? And I've seen many a soldier—even those who are battle hardened—suffer a similar reaction. It's as though you're stuck in a terrible moment from your past and you can't break free from it. Your mind keeps showing you the event, over and over, until you think you'll go—" He broke off and looked away. Swallowed another mouthful of his drink.

"I know you probably won't like it, lass," he said at length, "but I can highly recommend a dram or two of whisky to help you feel better, at least for a wee while. I know it's not a healthy habit"—his lips twitched with a ghost of a smile—"but it's more effective than tea."

"All . . . all right." At this point in time, Olivia was willing to try just about anything to alleviate the unease still holding her captive. Feeling this way was disconcerting, to say the least.

Lord Sleat poured her a glass of the strong liquor from the bottle he'd apparently procured from the innkeeper's secret stash, and she took a tentative sip. The liquid blazed down her throat, stealing her breath and making her cough. But after she swallowed a second and then a third mouthful, a pleasant warmth began to spread through her body. Her limbs felt heavier, and the knot of tension inside her belly loosened.

"You're right," she said. "It does help."

"Of course I'm right," he said with a trace of his roguish grin. "And I'm glad you're feeling a little better." He refilled his glass, then leaned forward in his chair, aiming a direct stare her way. "At the risk of opening old wounds, I wanted to let you know that if you ever want to talk about your parents and what happened, I'm always here to listen."

Olivia dropped her gaze to her whisky glass. She was simultaneously touched and terrified. She could barely recall what she'd said or done in the minutes following the carriage crash near the Sark Bridge. It was all a horrible blur—this accident had somehow melded with the accident that had claimed the lives of her parents five years ago. Until Lord Sleat had climbed into the cab and had spoken ever so gently to her, she hadn't known what was real and what was a memory. It was as though she'd lost her mind.

She could sense that the marquess still watched her, assessing her reaction to his invitation to share something about her past. Had he ever come across the newspaper accounts of how the wealthy arms manufacturer Edmund de Vere and his wife, Grace, had been tragically killed when their coach overturned along a treacherous stretch of road outside Birmingham? But, by some miracle, their daughter, Olivia, had survived? And if that were the case, had he already guessed that she wasn't Lavinia Morland, but really Olivia, Edmund de Vere's only child, who stood to inherit her father's vast fortune on her twenty-fifth birthday?

Olivia really wished she could remember what she might have said to the marquess in those fraught minutes after the accident.

She was faced with a conundrum. Her conscience compelled her to confess her true identity to Lord Sleat and attempt to explain why she'd been lying to him for the last few days. But that might put her in unnecessary jeopardy if he hadn't put the puzzle pieces together by himself. Because surely he would want to wash his hands of a troublesome runaway once he learned the truth; he had enough problems of his own to deal with.

And then she'd be packed off to London and placed under her uncle's care again in the blink of an eye.

Olivia took another sip of whisky and glanced down at Tilda. The little girl, clearly exhausted by the whole ordeal of the crash, had fallen fast asleep.

A wave of tenderness washed over Olivia. She'd grown inordinately fond of the sweet-natured child and would be

loath to leave her just now. If Lord Sleat discovered her
secret, she prayed she would be able to convince him to
keep her on as a nursemaid at least until they reached Skye.
Then she could seek another situation. She needed to stay
hidden for only a few more weeks.

Then again, she might be getting ahead of herself. The
marquess hadn't yet challenged her identity. If she shared
some small, nonspecific details about her past, he might be
satisfied enough to let the subject go.

"I . . . I appreciate your offer to lend a sympathetic ear,
my lord," she began. "The truth is . . . my memories of the
crash that took my parents are fragmented. I was later told
that one of the axles on the coach snapped and be-because
we were traveling at a considerable speed . . ." She shook
her head as her vision blurred. "I don't know how I wasn't
killed too. And to be in another crash, and survive . . . At
this point, I'm not sure if I'm the unluckiest or luckiest
young woman alive."

Lord Sleat's gaze was filled with compassion as he said,
"Your coach driver informed me that one of the traces
snapped and spooked one of the horses. When the beast
bolted, he couldn't control the carriage on the wet, muddy
road. I'm saddened that one of the horses perished today,
but I'm also extremely grateful everyone else escaped relatively unscathed. Especially wee Tilda. And of course you,
Miss Morland."

Olivia wiped a tear from her cheek. "I need to thank
you, my lord, for . . . for everything you did. As you saw, I
wasn't in my right mind. I've never experienced anything
like it before."

"Your reaction was perfectly understandable given the
situation. Old memories we think are long buried often
have a way of resurfacing when we least expect them to."
His mouth tilted into a sardonic smile. "Believe me, I
should know, lass. Now . . ." The marquess put down his
glass and stood. "I'm afraid I have some matters to chase
up. If your carriage can't be repaired within a day, I'll have
to hire another conveyance. And as I'm sure you would like

to change into fresh clothes, I'll also check on the where-abouts of your luggage. I asked Daniels and MacSwain to retrieve everything, but they seem to be taking a while."

"Thank you, my lord." Apparently the contents of her valise had been strewn across the road when the carriage overturned. Olivia suspected most of her garments would need to be laundered if that were the case, but she appreciated Lord Sleat's thoughtfulness all the same.

Lord Sleat departed, and Olivia nursed her whisky, staring into the leaping flames of the fire.

The marquess hadn't pushed her for too much information about her past, thank goodness. But Olivia's guilty conscience was still a persistent worm that niggled away at her. She wanted to be honest with him, to lay all her secrets bare, but the risk was too great.

Because they were staying here in Gretna Green another day, at least she'd have the opportunity to write to Charlie—and even Sophie and Arabella—to let them all know about her situation and current whereabouts. If Uncle Reginald did decide to go to the newspapers and report that she was missing, Olivia didn't want her friends to worry about her.

And after she turned twenty-one, she might be able to stay with one of her friends—at least for a little while—until she found a way to support herself . . . or a good man who would happily take her to wife. Her heart still longed for a love match. Surely it wasn't an impossible dream. Her parents had been happily wed for seventeen years before tragedy struck. And, by all accounts, Sophie and Arabella were blissfully content with their new husbands.

Olivia sighed wearily. Would that Lord Sleat cared for her in a romantic way—she'd already dismissed the "al-most kiss" they'd shared the night before as nothing more than a momentary lapse in Lord Sleat's judgment because he'd been befuddled by sleep, bad dreams, and too much alcohol. And even though the marquess exercised a considerable degree of consideration following the accident this afternoon, she shouldn't misinterpret his acts of kindness.

Yes, she needed to be realistic about her situation. She

needed to firmly put aside these persistent, starry-eyed thoughts that Lord Sleat might actually be developing tender feelings for someone like her—an unqualified nursemaid who could barely get a word out most of the time, including her name, real or otherwise. And when he did eventually learn the truth about her—as he was bound to— he'd surely view her as a troublesome chit. An encumbrance or, worse still, someone who couldn't be trusted.

Someone not worthy of love.

A tear slipped onto Olivia's cheek, and she brushed it away with an impatient swipe of her fingers. Her parents had loved her, and her friends did too. She shouldn't be so maudlin and self-defeating.

She *did* deserve love. And one day, God willing, she would find a man who truly cared for her and her alone. A man who didn't give a fig about her stammer or her money.

Despite Olivia's best efforts to quash the thought, her foolish heart whispered: *If only that someone could be Lord Sleat.*

This is everything, my lord."

"Thank you, Daniels." Hamish frowned as he regarded the items spread out on the oak table in his bedchamber: Miss Morland's ruined valise and a pile of damp, muddy belongings beside it. "I'll need you to send up one of the chambermaids to attend to the laundry. Miss Morland will need something fresh to wear."

"Aye, my lord. I'll do it straightaway."

Daniels took his leave, and Hamish propped a hip on the edge of the table. There was also an array of miscellaneous items that had apparently been retrieved from the interior of the coach: the books he'd selected from his library at Sleat House to keep Tilda entertained; Miss Morland's crushed straw bonnet and her soiled traveling cloak; and a small stack of leather-bound volumes with various titles— *Northanger Abbey: and Persuasion. The Mysteries of*

Udolpho. Frankenstein; or, The Modern Prometheus. Marmion: A Tale of Flodden Field.

Hamish picked up Walter Scott's book, the only one he'd read. Of course, he'd heard of the other titles, particularly *Frankenstein*. It seemed Miss Morland preferred romantic and gothic literature. He'd never have suspected that this quiet, sweet-natured young woman might have a taste for things that were dark and passionate. What an intriguing lass she was.

Hamish flipped open *Northanger Abbey: and Persuasion* and perused the first page. And then he blinked in astonishment. The heroine's name jumped out at him from the very first line. Catherine Morland.

Morland.

How odd. Of course, it could just be a coincidence that his nursemaid and the heroine of the book she was currently reading shared the same surname. Morland was a perfectly ordinary last name. And probably not all that uncommon.

But still . . .

Hamish frowned. From the very beginning he'd harbored suspicions about Lavinia Morland's background. And this discovery only compounded them.

On the table, there was one other item that intrigued him as well—a slim, rectangular box fashioned from satinwood. It was an exquisite piece of marquetry. The glossy lid was inlaid with tortoiseshell, ivory, and various types of wood veneer to create a delicate pattern of flowers, dragonflies, and butterflies. Hamish picked it up to examine the design . . . and that's when the brass clasp came apart and the box's contents spilled out.

Damn. Hamish didn't want to invade Miss Morland's privacy—he already felt bad enough that his footmen, Daniels and MacSwain, had been handling all her clothes. But Miss Morland had suffered a shock and a knock to the head, so in all good conscience, he couldn't have asked her to pick up her own garments off the roadway in the drizzling rain.

Even if he hadn't meant to look at Miss Morland's personal effects—at first glance the items all appeared to be keepsakes—it was too late now. All manner of odds and ends were scattered across the table or had fallen onto the floor: a fan-shaped shell, a neatly folded bill of fare from Gunter's Tea Shop in London, a scarlet ribbon, a comb inlaid with mother-of-pearl, a scrap of pink muslin (that seemed vaguely familiar, but he wasn't sure why), a silver locket, and a kerchief. The last two items were marked with the initials GdeV.

If Hamish hadn't been intrigued before, he certainly was now. The locket and the very feminine scrap of fabric—a confection of fine linen and lace that smelled faintly of violets—clearly belonged to a woman whom Lavinia Morland was fond of. Someone from the de Vere family.

Hamish suddenly wished he'd paid more attention to what MacAlister, his butler, had told him about his wealthy Grosvenor Square neighbors before he'd left London.

Blowing out a sigh, Hamish carefully placed all of Miss Morland's mementos back inside the box and refastened the clasp. While he'd like to find out more about the lass and her family, now clearly wouldn't be a good time, considering the ordeal she'd just endured. It was definitely a conversation for another day.

Although, when all was said and done, Miss Morland was doing an admirable job as a nursemaid; he couldn't fault her dedication to Tilda. So what did it really matter if the lass was less than forthcoming about her past? She'd witnessed the loss of her parents in a tragic accident, had been forced to rely on the charity of her extended family, and was now striking out on her own. There was nothing wrong with any of that.

Hamish's mouth twisted in a sardonic smile. No, not everyone had a past as shameful as that of Hamish Torquil MacQueen, the Marquess of Sleat, the Earl of Eyre, Chief of Clan MacQueen of Skye, and last but not least, the most befitting title of them all..

Inveterate sinner.

CHAPTER 8

A sudden scud of rain, driving full in her face,
made it impossible for her to observe anything
further, and fixed all her thoughts on the welfare of
her new straw bonnet.

Jane Austen, Northanger Abbey

Gretna Green, Scotland

September 19, 1818

The sky was a solid iron gray, and the wind tugging at
her straw bonnet was chill as Olivia set out for the village of Gretna Green on foot.

She was grateful for several things this afternoon. Lord
Sleat had quite unexpectedly presented her with a brand-
new hat this morning because her leghorn bonnet had been
ruined in the crash and she hadn't another. To think he'd
gone into the village and chosen something himself touched
her deeply. Again she told herself that the gesture was nothing more than *noblesse oblige*, but she was quite certain
most masters wouldn't go out of their way to replenish the
wardrobes of their nursemaids.

The marquess had also given her a few hours off so that
she might finish her letters and post them. Tilda was currently being looked after by Marjorie, one of the inn's
young chambermaids, and Lord Sleat's footman, Daniels.
He'd offered to take Tilda for a pony ride around the

grounds of Graitney Hall to keep her amused, and when the
little girl's face lit up, Lord Sleat hadn't had the heart to
say no.

The marquess had also offered to use a private courier to
deliver Olivia's letters, but she was concerned he would become suspicious of her identity when he read the names and
addresses of the recipients: Deerhurst Park in Gloucestershire belonged to his good friend Nate Hastings, Lord Malverne, and Hawksfell Hall in Cumberland was the ancestral
seat of Gabriel Holmes-Fitzgerald, the Earl of Langdale.
And he would surely know Lord Malverne's younger sister,
Charlie, who was currently residing at her father's estate,
Elmstone Hall, also in Gloucestershire. As soon as he read
the names of her friends—Lady Charlotte Hastings, Lady
Malverne, and Lady Langdale—she'd be questioned and
summarily dismissed. She hated being dishonest, but she
just couldn't afford to jeopardize her own safety.

Graitney Hall's innkeeper had kindly informed her that
the proprietor of Gretna Green's general store also served
as the village postmaster. The village was small, so it would
be easy enough to find. And as the rain was holding off,
Olivia reasoned the fresh air and the walk would do her
good. The lump on her forehead was still sore to the touch
and a horrid purple bruise had flowered, but she trusted the
arrangement of her hair and her new bonnet would hide the
worst of it. Not that she was vain by any means. She did,
however, wish to avoid stares and any inconvenient questions from complete strangers about what had happened to
her. She'd barely be able to get a word out, and there was
nothing worse than being stared at as though one were a
spectacle at a fair.

She gained the village in good time, and once her letters
were posted—she trusted that Charlie, Sophie, and Arabella wouldn't mind paying for the postage on their end—
she decided to continue her walk. Gretna Green was famous
after all.

There was the blacksmith's forge to see, the place where
so many "over the anvil" weddings took place. The Graitney

Hall innkeeper, Mr. Marchbank, had also informed her that a little farther on was the hamlet of Springfield and the King's Head Inn, where other couples sometimes opted to get married.

Indeed, the village was a hive of activity, and on one occasion, Olivia needed to step out of the way of a carriage hurtling down the main street lest she get splashed with muddy water or, worse, run over. It drew to an abrupt halt before the blacksmith's forge, and the young couple who alighted and hastened inside was clearly eloping. There was something wholly romantic about the idea of running away with the one you loved that made Olivia's heart ache with longing. Imagine being so in love that nothing else mattered. That you'd risk everything to be with that one person you had a perfect affinity with. That special someone you adored with your entire being and who felt exactly the same way about you.

Olivia continued her excursion, following a quieter country lane toward Springfield and the King's Head. When Daniels had visited her sitting room to fetch Tilda, he'd mentioned that Lord Sleat had some business in the village related to organizing the carriage repairs. Olivia wondered if she might cross paths with the marquess during her walk, but so far she hadn't seen hide or hair of him.

By the time Olivia reached the hamlet of Springfield— there were but a few cottages and the whitewashed, two-story hostelry scattered along the main street—she was dismayed to see the weather had taken a turn for the worse. A light rain started to fall, and because she'd quite foolishly neglected to bring an umbrella, she was bound to get wet. A most annoying circumstance indeed considering her new bonnet was at risk of getting ruined and she was still waiting for Graitney Hall's laundress to return the majority of her clothes.

Dare she take shelter in the public taproom of the King's Head until the shower passed? She had only a few coins in her purse, but she might have enough to purchase a cup of tea or a glass of small beer. There really was nowhere else to go. But it was the middle of the afternoon and surely the few patrons frequenting the establishment wouldn't be too deep in their cups yet. She trusted that she wouldn't be accosted by any unsavory characters and would be relatively safe.

Decision made, Olivia pushed through the heavy black oak door into the poorly lit interior. The taproom smelled of hops, woodsmoke, and something flavorsome, like a meaty soup or stew. It wasn't at all unpleasant. In fact, it made her mouth water.

The middle-aged publican behind the bar looked her up and down as she approached him across the sticky wooden floor, as did a craggy-faced gentleman who was enjoying an ale and a bowl of soup at a small table by one of the sash windows. There was only one other patron—another fair-haired, younger gentleman seated by the fire who still wore his well-cut garrick coat and beaver hat. His face was in shadow, but she could see he nursed a glass of spirits. When he took a sip, the contents of his glass glowed like sunlit amber in the firelight.

"What'll it be, lass?" the publican asked, claiming her attention. His hooded dark eyes were hard with suspicion. "Ye canna stay here unless ye intend to purchase something."

"Of . . . of c-course," replied Olivia as she dug out her coin purse from her reticule. "How . . . how much is a glass of small b-beer?"

The publican smirked and gave her another appraising glance. Even though her stammer was an endless source of amusement for many people, and she should be used to such reactions from strangers, she still never failed to feel a hot blast of mortification; her whole face burned, and she knew that her stutter would only grow progressively worse.

"It's on the house fer you as I havna seen a tangle-tongued lassie who's quite so bonnie." The publican gave her a wink and then pulled her beer from a keg behind the bar. "Here ye go. Take a seat wherever ye'd like."

Olivia picked up her drink with a murmured thanks and

headed toward one of the vacant tables by another window. While part of her was irked at the publican's condescension—she would prefer to pay for her own beer—she was also grateful she wouldn't have to head out into the rain. It had grown heavier in the last few minutes and lashed against the windowpanes in driving sheets. With any luck, by the time she finished her small beer, the downpour would have eased.

She removed her bonnet and gloves and placed them carefully upon the vacant seat beside the window. And that's when a long, dark shadow fell across the table, making her start.

Had the publican changed his mind and decided to charge her for the beer after all?

Olivia frowned and glanced up. And then her heart all but stopped.

It wasn't the publican.

It was Felix de Vere.

"Hello, dear c-c-cuz," he murmured as he claimed the remaining vacant seat by her left elbow. His hand slid onto her thigh beneath the table and squeezed. His blue eyes gleamed with malice. "Fancy meeting you here."

Olivia opened her mouth to speak, but nothing came out. Her tongue had ceased to function at all, and her breath froze in her lungs. Terror like she'd never known snaked its way down her spine and curled through her belly. Dark spots began to dance before her eyes.

She gripped the edge of the table so tightly, the wood cut into her palms. *Hold on, Olivia de Vere. Because if you do faint, all will be lost.*

Felix leaned closer, his grip tightening on her leg, and whispered in her ear, "You've led me a merry dance, haven't you, you sly little bitch? But that's all about to end. I'm taking you back to London."

Olivia swallowed past the boulder-sized lump of fear in her throat and forced her mouth to work. "How . . . how did you f-find me?" Her voice was little more than a hoarse whisper, but Felix understood her all the same.

"When it was discovered you'd absconded, Bagshaw mentioned she thought she'd seen someone at the bottom of the garden in the hour or so before dawn. I found the gate you must have used to gain entrance to Lord Sleat's residence. Bagshaw also mentioned your friend's bloody cat had gone, so when I questioned one of the scullery maids at Hastings House, she reported that one of the marquess's liveried footmen had dropped the cat off that very morning. One of Lord Sleat's grooms also confirmed that his master had just departed for Skye with his newly employed nursemaid and that he would likely take the toll road passing through Gretna Green. I don't know how you managed to persuade someone like Lord Sleat to spirit you away, Olivia, but I'll concede it was a fine feat." Felix's mouth twisted into a knowing smile. "But then again, perhaps the marquess thinks you are a bonnie lassie like the publican here." He pinched the inside of her thigh through her gown and petticoats, and Olivia gasped at the pain. "I've never heard the term 'nursemaid' used as a euphemism for 'whore' before, but I can well imagine you might spread your legs in exchange for a carriage ride all the way to—"

"I . . . I did no such thing," hissed Olivia, enraged that her cousin thought she would stoop so low as to prostitute herself.

"Now, now. There's no need to get so upset, Livvie. I don't see a ring on your finger, so I'll still marry you even if you're no longer as pure as the driven snow. Hell, I'll still marry you even if you're carrying the marquess's bastard. It would save me the chore of having to fuck you myself."

Olivia gaped in horror at Felix's foul words. She'd rather die than marry this detestable, cruel man. "Fe-Felix. If you don't take your hand off me this instant, I'll—"

"Scream? Cry? Throw your beer at me?" His lips curved with a sneer. "Please, spare me the theatrics. I already paid the publican a few extra sovereigns to turn a blind eye while you were choosing your seat. He thinks I'm rescuing my runaway sister from the clutches of an unscrupulous lover. And that old man over there"—Felix gestured with his chin—"he won't lift a goddamned arthritic finger to help you either."

Despair crashed over Olivia in a great smothering wave. Felix was right. The elderly gentleman wasn't likely to challenge someone as young and strong as her cousin. And she'd already sensed the publican was a mercenary type of man.

But if she went with Felix now, perhaps there would be other opportunities to escape along the way. She also didn't want to risk raising his ire, because then his cruel streak was sure to show itself. No, it was best that she comply. And try to keep her wits about her.

Actually, she might just have a plan.

"I'll go with you, F-Felix," she murmured. "Only, might I use the privy before we leave?"

Felix laughed and pinched her leg again. "Do you really think I'm that stupid, Livvie? While we're waiting for my carriage to be readied, you can lift your skirts in the alley out the back."

Damn and blast. This might be harder than she thought. Fighting to quell another surge of despair, Olivia donned her bonnet and gloves at Felix's urging, and then he dragged her out of the front door into the street.

The heavy shower hadn't abated in the least, and within moments, Olivia was blinking stinging rain out of her eyes. Felix's hand was clamped around her upper arm like a vise, but if she twisted away . . . His leather gloves were wet, so she might be able to slip from his grasp. Dare she make a break for it and seek shelter at one of the nearby cottages?

But Felix would probably just throw money at the occupants and tell them the same story he'd told the publican.

In the distance, she could hear the clop of horses' hooves on the road. Perhaps when they reached the main street of Gretna Green she could take a chance and jump out of Felix's carriage if it wasn't traveling too fast. Once they reached the toll road, she'd have less chance of escaping when it sped up.

They reached the corner of the inn, and Felix roughly

tugged her around the side, heading for the back of the building, where Olivia assumed the stable yard lay. Could one of the stable hands or the head ostler be persuaded to offer assistance? If she summoned a scream . . .

When she splashed through a particularly deep puddle, she tripped and bumped into Felix. He immediately swore and clipped the side of her bonnet with his hand. "Watch where you're going, Livvie," he sniped. "You clumsy cow—"

All at once, his cruel hold on her arm fell away as he was hurled backward. Indeed, the suddenness of the attack set Olivia stumbling again, and she nearly fell a second time. But when she regained her footing and discovered who her rescuer was, she almost cried with relief.

For it was none other than Lord Sleat.

The marquess was a picture of towering, blistering anger as he threw Felix up against the wall of the pub, anchoring him there with his iron-hard forearm. As Lord Sleat leaned forward, pressing into her cousin's throat, Felix frantically clawed at the marquess's sleeve, but his efforts to free himself proved futile. Lord Sleat was far too strong.

"What the hell are you doing?" The marquess's voice shook with murderous, pulsating, thunderous rage. "How dare you lay a hand on Miss Morland."

Felix's eyes bulged. His face had turned an alarming shade of puce. When he opened his mouth and nothing but a hoarse gasp emerged, Lord Sleat eased off the pressure a fraction. "Answer me, you bastard."

"She's not . . . Her name . . . Killing me . . ."

Panic had Olivia in its grip again. Everything was about to come unstuck. She couldn't let Felix reveal her secret. Nor did she want Lord Sleat to murder her cousin. But perhaps if she tried to explain first . . .

"Lord Sleat." She stepped forward and laid a hand on the marquess's rigid shoulder. "There's, there's something I m-must t-tell you—"

At that moment, Felix somehow broke free and shot off around the corner of the inn faster than the quarry at a fox hunt.

Lord Sleat cursed and made to bolt after him, but Olivia caught his arm, staying him. "Let him . . . let him go, my lord. I beseech you."

The marquess's black brows crashed together. "What on earth for?" he demanded. "The cur is lucky I didn't snap his neck."

A sharp cry suddenly rang out, and when Lord Sleat glanced around the back of the building, he smirked. "Not to worry, the dog's tripped and almost broken his own neck."

"Is he . . . is he all right?" Olivia stepped closer to Lord Sleat and peered around the corner too. It appeared that Felix had slipped in the mud and fallen heavily with his arm outstretched.

Lord Sleat shrugged as he continued to watch. "Judging by the way he landed and the snap I heard, I suspect he's probably fractured his collarbone. Oh, look. One of the stable hands has taken pity on him and has come to lend a hand, which is more than the blackguard deserves."

"Yes . . ." Olivia drew back and turned to face the marquess. "My lord . . ." She was pressed between the wall and Lord Sleat's body, and her thoughts were in a terrible scramble. What should she tell him about what had just happened? Felix had fled before he'd mentioned her real name. Perhaps there was a way to preserve her identity.

Lord Sleat captured her chin between gentle fingers. His gaze was steely as he said, "You mentioned you had to tell me something, Miss Morland. You know that man, don't you? And he knows you. Is that why you urged me to let him go? I insist you tell me what's really going on."

Oh, no. It seemed the cat was at least halfway out of the bag. Judging by the determined glint in Lord Sleat's eyes, this was one catastrophe Olivia had no hope of escaping.

CHAPTER 9

❧

Every young lady may feel for my heroine in this critical moment, for every young lady has at some time or other known the same agitation. All have been, or at least all have believed themselves to be, in danger from the pursuit of someone whom they wished to avoid; and all have been anxious for the attentions of some one whom they wished to please.

Jane Austen, Northanger Abbey

Gretna Green

We'll be back at Graitney Hall in no time at all," said Hamish after he'd installed Miss Morland on his horse and leapt up behind her. Lashing an arm about the lass's slender waist to keep her steady in the saddle, he then urged his mount into a gentle trot. The sooner they were away from the King's Head, and out of this infernal rain, the better.

Because if he stayed, he was likely to tear the blackguard who'd assaulted Miss Morland limb from limb. Indeed, he might have done just that if Miss Morland hadn't entreated him to let the bastard go. That was the one thing he could never abide, the violent treatment of a woman. When Hamish thought of all the times his father had beaten his wife, and Hamish, a powerless, helpless lad, had been forced to listen to his mother's cries . . .

His lip curled, and his gut clenched. It made him see red even now, all these years later.

Miss Morland leaned back against him, and Hamish was conscious of how slight she was. How her slender body trembled against his. This was the second afternoon in a row she'd been through a terrible experience, and it bothered him more than he could say. Not only that, she'd been soaked to the skin again. It was a wonder the lass hadn't caught a chill.

"How . . . how did you f-find me, m-my lord?" Miss Morland asked as he directed his horse onto the main road that would take them back to Gretna Green.

"As it happens, it was quite by chance," Hamish admitted. "When I was at the forge in the village, the blacksmith suggested the stables behind the King's Head might have a spare conveyance available for hire if I didn't want to wait another two days for him to complete the repairs to your carriage. He offered to send his apprentice over to Springfield, but as I was already out and about, and it was only a short ride . . ." He shrugged. "It just seemed easier to chase it up myself."

"W-w-well, I'm v-very grateful that you d-did."

Hamish could well imagine, considering the scene he'd stumbled upon. A near kidnapping. No wonder Miss Morland was still shivering in his arms. The sodden brim of her bonnet—the one he'd purchased for her this morning on a whim—hid her face so he couldn't read her expression. However, the lass's stammer had worsened, and he knew from experience that such a thing tended to happen whenever she was particularly nervous or unsettled. As well she might be.

She had some explaining to do.

Miss Morland. Was that the lass's actual name? More than ever, Hamish was convinced that Lavinia Morland was not who she claimed to be. Her assailant clearly knew her and had called her Livvie, which in Hamish's mind was usually a diminutive form of Olivia, rather than Lavinia. Of course, he could be wrong. Needless to say, there would be no putting off the conversation they needed to have once they reached Graitney Hall.

S o, lass, would you care to explain what happened outside the King's Head?" asked Lord Sleat as soon as the door to Olivia's sitting room closed behind Daniels and Tilda. After the marquess had taken the footman aside for a quiet word, he'd offered to take Tilda downstairs to Graitney Hall's kitchen in search of hot chocolate, cake, and the resident cat. "You said you had something to tell me . . ."

He stalked across the carpet, all power and grace. He'd discarded his coat and was wearing only shirtsleeves, a plain wool waistcoat, form-fitting breeches, and his muddy Hessians.

Olivia moved closer to the fire and stirred the logs, hoping to marshal her riotous thoughts into some semblance of order. On the way back from Springfield, and while she'd been changing into her only fresh gown, one of pale lavender wool, her mind was awhirl as she contemplated how Lord Sleat would react when he learned the truth—and in each imagined set of circumstances, not one of them ended well for her.

Now that the moment for her to confess had finally arrived, Olivia found she'd never been more nervous in her entire life.

If the marquess tried to send her back to her uncle and thus into Felix's clutches . . . She wasn't able to suppress a violent shudder of fear.

"My lord, might . . . might I have a whisky?" Olivia knew he kept some in his room, and although it was presumptuous of her to ask such a thing, she really needed something to help her calm down.

The marquess frowned, but nevertheless he fulfilled her request. When he joined her at the fireside and passed her a glass, his gaze was filled with concern. "Miss Morland, I might resemble a brutish ogre in a physical sense, but I assure you, I won't bite your head off." He drew closer to the fire. The flickering light of the flames danced over his stern but handsome countenance, lending him an otherworldly appearance. "But I do want you to tell me the truth. I sense you are in some kind of trouble, and I cannot help you unless you tell me exactly what it is we are dealing with here."

What we *are dealing with.* Olivia liked the sound of that. But would Lord Sleat feel that way once he realized how much of a nuisance she was?

Olivia took a fortifying sip of the whisky, welcoming the fiery warmth that spread over her tongue, down her throat, and then into her belly. "Thank you. I needed that," she said as she carefully placed her glass on the mantelpiece. "And thank you for your reassurances. However, you might not feel so magnanimous or kindly disposed toward me in a moment."

Lord Sleat's mouth kicked into a small grin. "What, are you about to confess you're a thief or a murderess on the run, lass?"

"Nothing quite so dramatic as that, my lord." She drew a bracing breath, then met his gaze directly. "Actually, I'm an heiress on the run. And . . . and as you might have already guessed, my name isn't Lavinia Morland. It's Oliv . . . Olivia de Vere."

Lord Sleat's brows sank into a puzzled frown. "Olivia de Vere. I've heard your name somewhere before, but God knows why I know it. Wait a moment . . ." He studied her face. "Are you telling me your father was Edmund de Vere, the arms manufacturer? Good Lord, my regiment used his weaponry—de Vere bullets and rifles—when we were fighting Old Boney." He rubbed his forehead as though his head hurt. "*Olivia* de Vere you say?"

"Yes, my lord. After my parents died, I was sent to live with my father's brother and his wife, Edith, as my mother had no family to speak of. Reginald de Vere is my appointed legal guardian until I turn twenty-one on the fifteenth of October. But I won't gain access to my fortune until I turn twenty-five. Or my uncle and trustee both agree to assign control to my husband if I wed before then. Such are the terms of my father's will."

"So, Miss de Vere, tell me why you took it upon yourself to abscond from London. Your aunt and uncle must be frantic with worry . . . unless . . . I take it that the man who accosted you at the King's Head is someone from your family?"

"Yes . . ." Olivia was relieved beyond measure that Lord Sleat seemed to be taking this so well. "He's my cousin. Uncle Reginald's son, Felix de Vere. And . . ." This was the difficult part she had to get out. "And my uncle and aunt want us to wed to keep my fortune in the family. But I do not."

Lord Sleat's gaze hardened. "That man who hauled you down the street, hit you, and insulted you is your cousin?"

"Yes, my lord."

"By God. You should have let me throttle the bastard."

Olivia swallowed another mouthful of whisky. "I'm afraid it's worse than that," she said. "You see, I know things about Felix that my uncle and aunt don't. And that knowledge puts me in grave danger."

And then she poured out everything to Lord Sleat. How she'd come across Felix embezzling her inheritance money and how he'd threatened her, if she told his father about the theft. That her aunt and uncle controlled every aspect of her life and how her cousins Prudence and Patience despised her. How she would have sought sanctuary with her friends Lady Charlotte, Lady Malverne, Lady Langdale, or perhaps even Lady Chelmsford, but they wouldn't be able to protect her, not when the law was on her uncle's side.

And so, when the opportunity to become Tilda's nursemaid and quit London altogether had presented itself, she hadn't hesitated to take that chance. "I was so terrified, my lord. And I could think of no other way to protect myself. I reasoned that if I became someone else, Lavinia Morland, and stayed hidden until I turned twenty-one, then I could seek support from my friends. And they wouldn't get into trouble either. My uncle cannot force me to live beneath his roof, or do anything at all, once I am legally of age."

Lord Sleat rubbed his jaw. The bloodred ruby in his gold signet ring flashed in the firelight. "Lass, that is quite a story."

"I assure you it's entirely true."

"I believe you. That's not the problem."

Olivia swallowed. The marquess's expression was as hard as granite, his mouth a flat line. "I know I have deceived you terribly, my lord. I've . . . I've misrepresented who I am and done nothing but lie to you over and over again. But I was desperate and knew not whom to turn to."

"Aye. That alone is a terrible thing, Miss Mor . . . I mean, Miss de Vere. That you had no one to ask for help. At least, no one who could make a real difference. You are right when you say the law is on your uncle's side. I only wish . . ." He scrubbed a hand through his thick sable hair, ruffling it into wild spikes. "I only wish you had come to me sooner."

"You're not . . . you're not angry with me? I would understand if you were. I'm not a good person."

Lord Sleat threw back his head and laughed at that. "Lass, you have no idea what you're saying. Not a good person? So you've told a few white lies in order to save yourself from marriage to a despicable dog. It hardly signifies."

"But I've also brought trouble to your door. Trouble you don't need given everything else you have to contend with."

He grimaced. "Aye, you've done that."

"And believe me, I feel terrible about it. The reason I didn't tell you the truth sooner was that I feared you would terminate my employment and throw me out. Or, worse, return me to my uncle's care. And to Felix."

A muscle flickered in Lord Sleat's jaw. "You can rest assured, that's not going to happen. If I ever see your cousin again, he'll rue the day he was born."

"Then . . . you'll let me stay on as Tilda's nurse?"

"I didn't say that, lass."

Olivia frowned. "I don't understand."

"Miss de Vere. Even though your cousin Felix might be temporarily incapacitated with a broken collarbone, do you think he's just going to let you walk away now that he's discovered your whereabouts?"

"I . . . I hadn't thought that far ahead." Indeed she hadn't. What a wigeon she'd become. She'd been so preoccupied with what Lord Sleat might do, she hadn't even thought about the threat Felix still presented.

"Well, I have." Lord Sleat's expression was grim.

Apprehension flared inside Olivia. "What . . . what are you suggesting then, my lord? I'm confused."

"There's only one sure way to protect you and your fortune, lass." Lord Sleat took a step closer and captured her hand. Fire lit his gaze from within as he stated with the solemnity of a man upon the gallows, uttering his last words to the crowd below, "Olivia de Vere, I'm going to make you my wife."

O livia de Vere gaped in openmouthed horror even as she simultaneously blushed. "Surely you're jesting, my lord."

"Indeed, I'm not." It was the only way Hamish could think to save her. And it might just benefit him too. A plan began to take shape in his mind.

"But why?" Olivia shook her head. "Why would you do this?"

"I assure you I don't need your money, if that's what you're worried about."

"No, I didn't think that." Olivia's brow wrinkled in confusion. "It's just . . . I don't understand."

"You're a gentle, sweet-natured lass, and it would be a travesty indeed to see you wed to a self-serving blackguard like your cousin. And all because of greed. I won't stand for it." His mother, Margaret, had been forced to wed a terrible man, and he couldn't let that happen to Miss Olivia de Vere.

"Besides, as I understand it, we have a fair few mutual friends," he continued. "Lord Malverne and Lord Langdale would surely have my guts for garters if I simply washed my hands of you in your hour of need. I'm certain their wives and Lady Charlotte Hastings would make mincemeat of whatever remained too."

"But . . ." Olivia's dark eyes were filled with dismay as she murmured more to herself than to him, "It . . . it's not supposed to be like this." Raising her chin, she added, "You might call my dreams foolish and girlish, Lord Sleat, but I've always wanted to marry a man who loved me. Truly loved me. Not just the contents of my bank account. Never once did I entertain the idea that a man might propose to me out of a sense of obligation."

"It's true this will be a marriage of convenience, Miss de Vere. Or may I call you Olivia now? In any case, there's every chance that a love match could be in your future."

A scarlet blush marched up Olivia's neck and across her face. "With . . . with you? I mean, I know we've only just met—"

"While it is true I am attracted to you in a physical sense, Olivia, and you certainly have many other qualities I admire, I'm afraid I'm not the sort of man who falls in love."

"You're a rakehell," she said flatly.

"Aye. And a wicked one at that. But that's not all." Hamish blew out a sigh. How could he warn this young lass that he not only was inherently sinful but also constantly struggled to keep a dark and dangerous streak in check? He didn't want to scare her, not when he was essentially offering to marry her to protect her from her predatory cousin.

"Suffice it to say, I'm not good husband material. But I have a proposition for you."

Her eyes narrowed with suspicion. "And what are the terms?"

"I've already told you I'm rushing home to Muircliff Castle for family reasons. You see, I have a younger sister, Isobel. And she's become entangled with a ne'er-do-well.

The younger brother of the local minister in the village of Dunmuir. According to my younger brother, Lord Angus, Isobel fancies herself in love with this fellow. But I suspect he's nothing but a fortune hunter. As head of the family and her guardian, I believe she could do far better. And that's part of the problem. She's nineteen, and she's never had a Season. She's never seen that there are far better men out in the world. And it's just occurred to me that you, Olivia, might be able to help introduce her to society. You and your friends."

"What? Me? But I'm . . . I've never been introduced to society. I may be an heiress, but in some circles, I'm known for my disgraceful conduct more than anything else. I'm sure I would be a hindrance, not a help."

"Disgraceful conduct? Whatever do you mean?"

"A little over three years ago, I was expelled from a well-to-do and rather exclusive young ladies' academy in London."

"Ah, yes. I do recall that now. Lord Malverne's sister, Charlie, was also caught up in the scandal."

"Yes, along with my friends Sophie and Arabella."

"Who've since wed Malverne and Langdale."

"Yes."

Lord Sleat waved a dismissive hand. "And so now you'll be Olivia, Lady Sleat. A marchioness. Why should you care about the opinion of polite society anymore?"

"I suppose you're right," she conceded. "I've never thought of it like that before."

"But I haven't finished stating my case yet," said Hamish, pleased that he might be winning her over. "As my wife, Olivia, I would ask you to help Isobel with her debut and to assist her in finding a suitable husband. But when you turn twenty-five and inherit your father's fortune in a little over four years' time—if not sooner, if I have anything to do with it—I propose that you and I part ways. Then you will be free to marry whomever you choose. You'll have your love match and your money."

Olivia's fine brows descended into a deep frown. "You're

saying we'll get divorced. But I thought that hardly ever happened."

"It's true it's a rare occurrence in England, but under Scots law, it's a much easier process. A woman can sue for divorce on the basis that her husband has committed adultery. And as we'll be wed according to Scots law, and I will agree to the divorce, I don't anticipate that there'll be any problem at all with terminating our union when the time comes."

"But what . . . ?" Olivia blushed bright red. "But what if we should have children in that time period? If I'm your wife . . . and if we . . . if you . . . if you and I . . . You're a marquess, so I'm sure you'll want an heir. And when we divorce, won't the children stay with you? I don't think I could bear that, being separated from my children."

Hamish shook his head. "I don't want an heir. I'm happy for the title to go to my younger brother, Angus."

"Oh . . ." Olivia frowned again. "You really are suggesting a pure business arrangement, my lord. Nothing more."

"Aye. Nothing more."

"I . . ." Olivia pressed a hand to her belly. "This is a lot to think on. It's not what I would have chosen. But it seems I have little choice."

"I'm a marquess, Olivia. And a ruthless one at that. You won't just have the protection of my name, but my body as well. Because if your uncle or your cousin tries to steal you away, or even lay one of their dirty little fingers on you, I'll crush them to dust."

Olivia's countenance paled, and Hamish felt a twinge of guilt for scaring the poor lass with his ferocious declaration. "I believe you, my lord," she whispered.

"My name is Hamish," he said in a gentler tone. "If we are to be wed, you may call me that."

"Very well." She inclined her head. "Hamish."

"So it's settled, then? You'll say yes to my proposal?"

A pretty rose pink blush flared across Olivia's cheeks. "I will."

"Excellent." Hamish picked up his fiancée's hand and

laid a gentle kiss upon her slender fingers. He'd never planned on getting married, so he was surprised that he should suddenly feel so inordinately pleased about it, despite the added complications it would bring to his life. "I'll go downstairs and speak to Mr. Marchbank, the innkeeper, and ask him to make the arrangements for the ceremony. By nightfall, you'll be Lady Sleat."

By nightfall, you'll be Lady Sleat.
Olivia's free hand—the one Lord Sleat wasn't holding—fluttered to her throat. "Wh-what? What did you say, my lord? I m-mean, Hamish?" Surely she'd mishcard. "You mean to marry me this afternoon? Now?"

The marquess frowned. "Aye, of course I do. We're in Gretna Green, the veritable capital of clandestine marriages. We'll say our vows before a few witnesses, sign a certificate, and the deed will be done."

"And it will be legal." Olivia wasn't certain if she was asking a question or making a statement.

"It certainly will be." Lord Sleat crossed his arms over his chest. "We're not in England anymore, lass, so Hardwicke's Marriage Act doesn't apply. You don't need your guardian's permission to wed if you're under the age of twenty-one. And the banns don't need to be called for three consecutive Sundays, not unless you wish to wed in a kirk. Why do you think so many English couples elope to Scotland?"

That was all well and good, but Olivia had another question. One that made her heart beat wildly. "But . . . but what about tonight? Our wedding night?" she asked. She couldn't hide the quiver in her voice. "You said you don't want an heir. But don't we need to . . . to . . ." A hot blush stung her cheeks, and she dropped her gaze to the hearthrug. Even though her body thrummed at the idea of sharing a bed with Lord Sleat, her husband-to-be, another part of her was so nervous, she could barely speak. Especially when he was standing so close to her and regarding her so intently. Why, they hadn't even shared a kiss yet.

"Och, dinna fash yourself, lassie." Hamish grinned at her and patted her hand. "I won't come near you tonight or any night. Besides, you certainly won't be able to act as Isobel's chaperone next Season if you're increasing. That's reason enough to keep my distance." He placed a large hand upon his chest. "I give you my word as a gentleman, a peer of the realm, the Chief of Clan MacQueen of Skye, and a former officer in His Majesty's army that this marriage will never be consummated."

Olivia frowned with confusion. "I'm sorry to keep belaboring the point. But don't we need to consummate our union for it to be considered valid?"

"Aye, 'tis true. But who would dare question the Marquess of Sleat? I can ruin a woman just by being alone in the same room with her. I'm a rakehell, and you are a bonnie lass, Olivia. Everyone will believe I've claimed my conjugal rights, even if I haven't." He squeezed her hand. "I aim to have everything ready within the hour. Will that be enough time for you to prepare?"

Olivia bit her lip and nodded. Lord Sleat spoke sense. Yet his offer—while practical and fair—was also as cold as arctic ice. And it cut her to the bone. She knew Lord Sleat hadn't intended to hurt her—indeed, he was doing everything within his power to protect her by marrying her—but all the same, he had.

It was clear that all the little things that meant so much to her, the special moments she'd hidden away in her heart like precious keepsakes—the flirting that had taken place when they first met, the "almost kiss" incident at the Hart and Hare, the care he'd shown her after the carriage accident—they meant nothing to him.

It's a business transaction, nothing more.

The whole idea of it was enough to make Olivia want to hurl things and cry at the same time. A childish reaction no doubt. But damn it, her heart was cracking. Her dream was

fracturing before her eyes. As she'd told the marquess only
a few moments ago, it wasn't supposed to be like this.

Was it unreasonable of her to seek the marital bliss her
parents had? Or the joy Sophie and Arabella had found
with their respective husbands?

Of course, love took time to grow. However, she didn't
think she was asking for the impossible.

Olivia kept up a brave face until Lord Sleat took his
leave. Then she sank onto the padded stool before the small
oak dressing table in her bedchamber and steadfastly
crushed down the urge to dissolve into a fit of self-indulgent
weeping. She didn't have time for tears. Tilda would be
back soon, and Olivia needed to make herself presentable.
And somehow, she had to marshal the nerve to go through
with the wedding ceremony.

But first things first. Olivia had to attend to the bird's
nest atop her head; she hadn't had time to repair her damp,
disheveled hair after she returned from Springfield, and
when she took her vows, she didn't want to look like something Peridot had just dragged in.

She grimaced at her reflection as she tugged a hairpin
from a particularly stubborn snarl. Her tongue might be
perpetually tangled, but her hair didn't need to be.

As she teased each knot loose with her comb, Olivia
wondered if she could work through her messy, jumbled
thoughts just as easily. For one thing, perhaps it would help
if she forced herself to look on the bright side rather than
dwell on all the negative aspects of Lord Sleat's proposal.

She'd only just met the marquess—Hamish, she mentally amended—but she was certain there was a spark between them. She could feel it whenever they were together.
If she could just nurture that tiny spark, gently coax it and
breathe life into it, perhaps it would eventually burst into
flame and they'd share a grand passion that would never die.

Hamish wasn't a coldhearted man by nature—she'd witnessed his softer side on many occasions. And he was certainly hot-blooded with a rake's carnal appetite—or so the

rumors went. So why was he so insistent that their marriage should be in name only?

It didn't make sense.

Olivia tried to hide the cut and bruise upon her forehead by rearranging her part before repinning her hair into another simple chignon, a style she thought flattered her face.

She knew she wasn't unattractive in a physical sense; her hair and eyes might have been an ordinary brown, but she'd always believed her complexion, physiognomy, and figure were pleasing enough. Indeed, Hamish had said as much to her. And he never remarked upon her stammer.

Olivia frowned at herself as she adjusted the Vandyke lace collar on her lavender-hued gown. So what was the problem? Why didn't Hamish want to consummate their marriage? Why wouldn't he want their union to bear fruit? Wasn't that what all noblemen wanted? An heir and at least half a dozen spares?

Well, he might not want to bed her, but Olivia certainly wanted to bed him. She wanted a real marriage with lots of healthy, happy babies.

She wanted her husband's love.

Somehow, she had to show Lord Sleat that he might want those things too . . . with her.

CHAPTER 10

৵৯

With this ring I thee wed, with my body I thee
worship, and with all my worldly goods I thee
endow.

The Scottish Book of Common Prayer, 1637

Graitney Hall, Gretna Green

Nightfall

When Olivia ventured downstairs an hour later, her
heart was racing so fast, she thought she might ex-
pire before she even reached Lord Sleat's side.

Tilda, on the other hand, was absolutely thrilled. Indeed,
her eyes were alight with excitement as Tilda and Olivia
negotiated the oak staircase together. Despite Olivia's nervous agitation, she was touched to see how delighted the
little girl was to be "Miss Devinia's bridesmaid." In honor
of the occasion, she'd changed into her freshly laundered
white muslin gown with the blue sash. Another blue ribbon
and sprigs of lilac heather adorned her light brown curls.
She really was the prettiest, sweetest child.

"Miss de Vere?" One of the Graitney Hall maids stepped
forward from the shadows and dipped into a curtsy. Her
bright red hair stood out like a flame in the gloomy vestibule. "My name is Marjorie Marchbank, and my da will be
marrying ye and Lord Sleat today. And if it pleases ye"—
she presented Olivia with a small bunch of purple, lilac,

and white heather sprigs—"this bouquet is fer you to carry. Fer luck."

Olivia murmured a heartfelt thanks, and then the maid escorted her and Tilda to the private parlor where the wedding ceremonies at Graitney Hall were conducted.

Hudson, Lord Sleat's valet, waited by the heavy oak door. As Olivia drew close, he bowed. "Are ye ready, lass?"

Olivia drew a deep breath and nodded. "I . . . I think so." In a matter of minutes, she would be wed to a powerful nobleman. A man she was willing to admit she desired and was beginning to fall in love with. A man she believed she could find happiness with.

But only until he divorces you.

What a quelling thought *that* was, when what she yearned for was forever.

It's not what you'd hoped for, but at least you will be safe, Olivia reminded herself. *Be grateful for that if nothing else.*

And who knows, maybe Lord Sleat will fall in love with you. In time . . .

The middle-aged servant gave her an encouraging smile. His blue eyes were kind beneath the sweep of his freshly combed, graying hair. "Ye ken, I've served Lord Sleat for many years, as his valet and as his batman. And I can attest he's as decent as they come." A frown creased his brow. "So dinna ye go believing any rumors ye hear. He'll make ye a verra fine husband, lass. There's no need to be nervous."

Olivia scraped together a small smile. She was well aware of Hamish's rakish history, but she appreciated the valet's attempt to reassure her. "Thank you, Hudson. I'll remember that."

She touched the silver locket resting just below her throat. It had once belonged to her mother—her initials were engraved upon the back. There was no need to hide the treasured piece of jewelry anymore, but oh, how she wished her mother were here. And her father and, of course, all her dear friends—bold-as-you-please Charlie, sweet Sophie, and clever Arabella.

But they aren't, and Lord Sleat is waiting.

She nodded at Hudson, and he opened the door. And then Olivia's breath caught when her gaze met her groom's on the other side of the candlelit parlor.

Oh, my goodness. Lord Sleat had certainly dressed for the occasion.

Rather than wearing the usual attire of a gentleman, the marquess had donned his traditional clan garb. And the sight was magnificent.

Instead of breeches or pantaloons, Hamish wore a kilt of deep red and black tartan with a touch of yellow running through it. Over his white cambric shirt and black silk waistcoat, he wore a well-cut coat of black superfine that was perfectly molded to his wide shoulders. A black leather pouch hung from a belt at his waist, and below the hem of his kilt, Olivia caught a glimpse of his bare knees before his plaid-patterned hose began. Silver-buckled shoes of black leather and a sheathed but still-lethal-looking short sword, also at his waist, completed the ensemble.

Olivia swallowed. From the top of his tousled sable locks to the bottom of his thickly muscled calves, her husband-to-be was every inch the formidable Highlander. Indeed, she was certain she'd never seen such a handsome devil in all her life.

Even the flame-haired maid who'd joined her equally redheaded father by the fireside looked like she was about to swoon at the marquess's feet.

Tilda tugged at her sleeve, and Olivia bent down. "Why is Lord Sleat wearing a skirt, Miss Devinia?" she whispered in her ear.

"It's called a kilt. It's what men from Scotland wear sometimes," she whispered back. "I like it."

Tilda nodded. "I do too."

Hudson, who'd also joined his master, the maid, and the beaming marriage-celebrant-cum-innkeeper by the stone fireplace, crouched down and beckoned to Tilda. She let go of Olivia's sleeve and skipped across the polished wooden floor to the hearthrug.

And now it was Olivia's turn to cross the room. Rain drummed against the lead-paned windows, matching the drumming of her pulse. Smoothing her lavender wool skirts with a damp palm, she started forward, clutching the bunch of fresh-smelling heather to her chest, her steps slow and measured even if her heartbeat wasn't, until she reached Hamish's side.

His large hand engulfed hers, and then he brought her fingers to his lips. "You look lovely, Olivia," he said in that deep, low voice of his that reminded her of a lion's purr.

"So . . . so do you," she whispered back. "No . . . I mean . . ." She blew out an exasperated breath. "You look very handsome in your kilt."

His wide mouth curved into a roguish, lopsided smile. "Och, thank you, lass."

Mr. Marchbank cleared his throat. His face had turned bright red. It seemed that Lord Sleat had the power to make even *him* blush. "Shall we begin, my lord? Miss de Vere?"

"Aye," Hamish said, his gaze never leaving Olivia's. She simply nodded, transfixed by the intentness of her bridegroom's regard.

"Weel then," continued Mr. Marchbank. "I have some questions for both of ye before we begin." He turned to Olivia. "Miss de Vere, are ye of marriageable age and free to wed?"

"Y-yes," she murmured. Hamish hadn't relinquished his hold, and his thumb was caressing the top of her hand, distracting her.

"And are ye, my lord?" asked Marchbank.

Hamish's attention flicked to the celebrant, and he smirked. "Aye."

"Verra good. And do ye have a ring for yer bride, Lord Sleat?"

Hamish's gaze returned to Olivia. "Aye. I do." He released her hand and tugged the ruby-and-gold signet ring off his little finger.

Olivia shook her head. "Oh . . . oh, you don't have to—"

"Lass, I want to." Without the celebrant's prompting,

Hamish continued in a solemn yet smooth-as-velvet voice as he slid his ring onto Olivia's left ring finger, "With this ring I thee wed, with my body I thee worship, and with all my worldly goods I thee endow."

Olivia had to force herself to breathe again. The ring was warm and heavy on her finger, and the dark red ruby glinted in the firelight. For a man who'd asserted this was to be a marriage of convenience, the intensity of Hamish's expression, the gravity of his tone, suggested otherwise. He might not love her, but he was taking this commitment very seriously. And perhaps he was simply trying to reassure her that he'd honor the deal they'd both agreed to. That he would protect her until she could claim her own independence.

Mr. Marchbank nodded and smiled. "Verra good. Now it's time for the handfasting."

Handfasting? Olivia's interest was piqued as Marjorie stepped forward to relieve her of her heather bouquet, and the ruddy-faced celebrant pulled a long tartan sash from somewhere inside his coat. "Take yer bride's hand, my lord," he instructed. "And hold it between ye so that I might bind ye together."

Hamish immediately entwined his fingers with hers in an intimate clasp. His skin was hot, his palm calloused, and Olivia's flesh tingled.

If this were a real marriage in every sense, Hamish would be touching her in the most intimate of ways with those large hands of his. Worshipping her with his body as he'd just stated when he'd placed his ring upon her finger.

Regret pooled in her chest. She really shouldn't have stopped him from kissing her that night at the Hart and Hare.

If he had kissed her, would their arrangement be any different now?

Mr. Marchbank wrapped the tartan sash securely about their joined hands. "Ye need to make yer promises to each other now," he said, then turned his attention to Olivia.

Olivia drew a deep breath and dutifully repeated her vows as best she could. "I, Olivia Grace de Vere, here-hereby take thee, Hamish Torquil MacQueen, to b-be my husband. And thereto I plight . . . I plight thee my troth."

Beneath the tartan sash, Hamish gave her fingers a light squeeze. His voice was sure and strong as he declared, "And I, Hamish Torquil MacQueen, hereby take thee, Olivia Grace de Vere, to be my wife. And thereto I plight thee my troth."

Mr. Marchbank beamed his approval. His chest puffed out as he announced in a suitably officious tone to the small gathering, "Forasmuch as Hamish MacQueen and Olivia de Vere have consented to be wed, and have witnessed the same before God and this company, and thereto have given and pledged their troth either to other, and have declared the same by the giving and receiving of a ring, and by the fasting of hands, I pronounce that they be man and wife. Those whom God hath joined together, let no man put asunder."

Leaning forward, he winked at Hamish. "And as we like to say here at Graitney Hall, ye may now kiss yer bonnie bride, my lord."

Olivia's breath quickened, and her pulse fluttered like butterfly wings against her throat. A kiss wasn't usually part of a traditional marriage ceremony as far as she knew. But this wasn't a regular wedding, and they weren't in a church.

If this was to be a marriage of convenience, this might be her only chance to share a kiss with Lord Sleat. And she'd wanted to do this for the longest time. She would be mad to pass up the opportunity.

Olivia raised her eyes to Hamish's face. "Well . . . well, if it's customary, my lord," she murmured huskily.

His mouth twitched with a smile. "Who am I to stand in the way of a local tradition?"

He raised his free hand and gently cupped her jaw. As the pad of his thumb stroked along her cheek, his gaze fell to her mouth, and when he began to lower his head, Olivia closed her eyes.

The press of his lips against hers was warm and firm. A

light silken brush. A tantalizing taste. Desire beckoned, and she leaned closer, curling her fingers against the silk of his waistcoat. Eager for more, her lips moved beneath his. Parted in silent invitation . . .

And then it was over.

Hamish pulled back, and Olivia frowned in confusion while everyone around them clapped.

That was it? Her first and perhaps only kiss, and that's all there was to it?

While the kiss had been lovely, it certainly hadn't been breath stealing. The world hadn't tipped on its axis, and her heart hadn't melted.

Disappointment and frustration welled, and to hide the sudden rush of tears in her eyes, Olivia focused her gaze on Hamish's hand still bound to hers. Hamish's kiss had felt perfunctory. There'd been no passion behind it. Of course, others were in the room, watching, including Tilda. But wasn't he supposed to kiss her, his bride, like he meant it? Even just for the sake of appearances?

Apparently not.

As Hudson offered his congratulations and Tilda claimed her attention with a hug about the legs, it suddenly occurred to Olivia that for some unfathomable reason, Hamish MacQueen, the Marquess of Sleat, the Chief of Clan MacQueen of Skye, and a former officer in His Majesty's army, was reluctant to be intimate with her. He was deliberately holding himself back.

It just wouldn't do, and if they were to have any chance of forming a lasting bond, she needed to not only weaken his defenses . . . she needed to find out why he was determined to keep such a tight rein on his passions.

"What did you find out, Daniels?" Hamish finished pouring himself a whisky and then lounged back in the leather wingback chair by the fire in his bedchamber.

The young footman ran a hand through his damp hair. He'd just returned from running a few errands in Springfield, and because of the nature of one of those errands, Hamish hadn't wanted the lad to wear his livery. Evidently it was still raining outside. "It was just as you'd predicted, my lord," he said. "Miss Morland's. No, I mean Miss de Vere's . . . I'm sorry, Lady Sleat's cousin is currently indisposed with a broken collarbone. The innkeeper at the King's Head confirmed that a physician paid him a visit late this afternoon. And apparently Mr. de Vere has rented a room for at least another two days."

Excellent. It looked like Felix de Vere would be receiving a visit from his cousin's new husband in the morning. Aloud Hamish said, "Very good, lad. And what of the carriage for hire at the King's Head? Is it suitable?"

Daniels grimaced. "I'm afraid not, my lord. From what I saw, it was in a poor condition both inside and out. I'm not unconvinced that there wasn't an infestation of mice under one of the seats."

Damn. It looked like Hamish would have to employ an alternative plan if they were to depart on the morrow. "Why don't you go downstairs and order yourself some dinner, Daniels. And make sure you have an ale or two. I'm sure Hudson and the others are still downstairs in the taproom celebrating."

The footman smiled. "Aye, my lord. And may I extend my congratulations to you on your nuptials? I've always thought Miss . . . I mean Lady Sleat is a bonnie—" The flustered young man blushed beet red. "I'm sorry. I shouldna have said that, my lord. I simply mean to say that I wish you both well."

Hamish wasn't able to suppress his own smile. "Thank you, Daniels. I shall pass your congratulations on to her."

As the door closed behind the footman, Hamish sighed. The young man spoke the truth. His wife was indeed bonnie. He'd even go so far as to say she was beautiful. He hadn't failed to notice the disappointment in Olivia's brown eyes after he'd given her the most superficial of kisses at the end of the wedding ceremony. Or how her smiles seemed forced rather than natural.

And no doubt it was all his fault. He grimaced and tossed back his whisky. If he weren't such a monstrous mess, he'd be with her right now, making slow, sweet love to her, learning all the ways he could bring her pleasure, rather than spending his wedding night alone in his room with only a bottle of whisky for company.

But things were better this way. He needed to ruthlessly crush this wave of desire and tender concern that kept threatening to rise up and swamp him. The lass was far safer if he stayed away.

Steadfastly ignoring the fact that their rooms were connected, and only separated by a tiny sitting room, he picked up the whisky bottle and topped up his glass. Far better to focus on the good things he could do for Olivia.

He dragged his chair closer to his traveling desk and pulled out parchment, ink, and a quill. He had several letters to write before he was too far gone in his cups. First of all, he needed to inform Olivia's uncle that his niece was now legally wed to the Marquess of Sleat (that should get the scoundrel's attention). And then he was going to ask his man of affairs to investigate a few matters related to Olivia's inheritance. He'd been honest when he told her he didn't need her money. But he wanted to ensure that Reginald de Vere and Olivia's trustee had been managing the funds appropriately. Well, up until the time Felix de Vere and Giles Thackery had begun to siphon money off. At any rate, he wanted a full accounting of every penny spent.

Once he'd attended to those matters, Hamish planned on getting rip-roaringly drunk. Maybe then he'd stop thinking about the young woman next door and how much he wanted her.

CHAPTER 11

For if it be true, as a celebrated writer has maintained,
that no young lady can be justified in falling in love
before the gentleman's love is declared, it must be
very improper that a young lady should dream of a
gentleman before the gentleman is first known to
have dreamt of her.

Jane Austen, Northanger Abbey

Graitney Hall, Gretna Green

Ten o'clock

Tucked up snugly in her pallet bed, Tilda gave a sigh and
a murmur as she rolled over. The little girl had succumbed to the pull of slumber several hours ago. Unlike
Olivia . . .

Frustrated beyond measure that she couldn't fall asleep
no matter how hard she tried, Olivia threw back the covers
from her tester bed and padded over to the dying fire to stir
it to life. Her mind wouldn't rest as she kept trying to work
out the best strategy to employ to get closer to Hamish. To
stop him from pushing her away.

But she felt like she was floundering in the dark. She had
no experience to call on. Right at this moment, she missed
her friends more than ever. What would Sophie and Arabella advise her to do? They had won their husbands'

hearts. And Charlie was always full of good ideas—albeit unconventional ones. After all, she was the one who'd founded their Society for Enlightened Young Women to help them snare husbands who were love matches. Except Olivia didn't feel enlightened at all.

The rain still battered the hall, and the room was growing cold. After prodding the coals with the poker, Olivia threw another log into the grate, then plopped disconsolately into an armchair. Her makeshift wedding band—Hamish's signet ring—felt odd on her finger, like it didn't belong there. When she lifted her hand to examine it, the bloodred ruby caught the light of the fire and winked as though mocking her.

As Olivia idly twisted the ring back and forth, her stomach growled noisily; she'd been so out of sorts this evening, she'd barely touched any of her dinner, which had turned out to be a sad affair indeed. After the ceremony, she'd dined in her room with only Tilda for company as Hamish had informed her he had "business to attend to." He hadn't even bid her good night.

Olivia's stomach protested again, and she plucked an uneaten bread roll from her dinner tray to appease her hunger. All evidence to the contrary, she wasn't really hungry for food though.

She craved her husband's company. He might be in the next room, yet the distance between them felt so great, he may as well be in the antipodes, or even on the moon.

Was he still awake? About an hour ago, she'd heard a knock on his door and a male voice. It could have been Hudson, attending his master. If so, she wondered if the valet would think it odd that the marquess wasn't spending the night with his bride.

Olivia tore a chunk off her roll and chewed it without enthusiasm. It just wasn't fair. Shouldn't a bridegroom want to bed his wife? Even the kiss Hamish had given her was lackluster. If it weren't for Charlie's claims that the Marquess of Sleat was a wicked rake, or the occasional reports in the *Beau Monde Mirror* that attested the same, Olivia could well believe she'd just married a monk. It wasn't as though Hamish *wasn't* attracted to her. She'd recognized a certain gleam in his eye when he looked her way. A gleam that made her blush and stammer all the more. It had been like that from the very first moment they met.

And then inspiration struck. Instead of alternately fretting and moping by the fireside, Olivia had a plan. A way to bridge this distance between her and Hamish using logic, a little bit of cunning, and a great deal of spirit.

Mustering her courage, Olivia discarded her half-eaten roll and slid on her only pair of soft kid slippers. She picked up a cashmere shawl to wrap about her flannel night rail, then dropped it on the end of her bed again. No, she wouldn't need it. Hamish was her husband. He could see her without a stitch on and there'd be nothing wrong with it.

Instead, Olivia untied the ribbon at the neckline of her nightgown, thus exposing her collarbones and a glimpse of cleavage. Then she loosened her braid and freed her hair.

It fell in thick dark waves about her shoulders and down her back. She'd heard somewhere that men liked it when women left their hair unbound, and as she didn't have any scandalous, flimsy night attire, she'd have to rely on whatever she had at her disposal to break down Hamish's resistance. To tweak his male interest.

She didn't need to pinch color into her cheeks because when she glanced in the dressing table mirror, she could see they were already stained pink with excitement. Indeed, Olivia hardly recognized the brazen young woman staring back at her with fire in her dark eyes.

After dabbing scent on her wrists and behind each ear, she was ready. Or as ready as she'd ever be. She'd best go now and knock on Hamish's door and say what she needed to before she lost her nerve.

It was time to deal head-on with her bridegroom's inexplicable reluctance to be intimate with her.

* * *

When there was a light rapping on the door connecting the sitting room to his bedchamber, Hamish let out a groan before lifting his head from the table that he'd been slumped over.

God damn it. Logic dictated there was only one person that could possibly be. The one person he both wanted and feared in equal measure.

Olivia. His wife.

Hamish yawned, scrubbing a hand down his face. His night beard scraped his palm. Dressed only in his kilt and a cambric shirt, open at the neck with the sleeves rolled up to his elbows, he didn't much care that he was in a shambolic, inebriated state. And perhaps his dishevelment might work in his favor. If Olivia had any sense at all, she'd go scampering back to her room as soon as she laid eyes on him.

He squinted at the mantel clock and yawned again. It wasn't that late, so he hadn't been asleep for long. Although he had managed to down half a bottle of whisky in a relatively short amount of time before he drifted off.

As he rose from his chair, the world swam for a brief moment before righting itself. He had a sudden premonition this exchange wasn't going to end well. He hoped the interaction would be brief.

The knock came again, and Hamish padded to the door in bare feet. "I'm coming, lass," he called. He turned the key in the lock and opened the door. "What's wrong?"

And then his breath froze in his chest as his gaze dragged over his wife. Damn, Olivia would have to be wearing her night attire. Despite his best efforts to suppress his desire, interest stirred below Hamish's kilt.

Her dark gaze flitted over him, too, taking in his state of undress. A blush colored her cheeks. "Nothing's . . . nothing's wrong, Hamish," she murmured in a voice that was noticeably husky. She cleared her throat and added, "I mean, not exactly. In . . . in any event, I do need to speak with you."

He frowned and leaned an arm against the doorframe,

filling the doorway with his wide shoulders, barring her entrance. "Can't it wait until morning then?"

She lifted her determined little chin and crossed her arms over her chest. "No it can't."

Hell. Couldn't the lass take a hint? The whisky in Hamish's veins was unraveling his good intentions, and his self-control was hanging by a gossamer-thin thread. The scent of her wafted about him—warm female and that damnably appealing vanilla and violet perfume she wore— and his nostrils flared. His mouth watered. If she came any closer, stayed any longer . . .

Hamish gritted his teeth. He just needed to ignore the hardening in his loins and harden his resolve instead. "Very well then," he grated out, and stepped back from the door, away from her.

He wouldn't seduce her. He wouldn't ruin her. He'd married her to protect her—he couldn't bear the idea of a woman being mistreated. And he sincerely wanted her to be able to walk away from him in four years' time—or less, all going well—an unsullied, unencumbered woman.

Such a sweet lass deserved more than what a damaged bastard like him could ever offer.

And it would be far easier for him to resist temptation if he put some distance between them. Curling his hands into fists—a reminder to himself not to succumb to the overwhelming urge to touch her—Hamish stalked over to the fireplace and planted his feet on the hearthrug and attempted to fix her with a glowering stare.

His efforts were all for naught, though, as Olivia followed him and, exasperating minx that she was, took up a position by the end of his four-poster bed.

Alarm bells began clanging in his head. Good God, was Olivia trying to seduce him?

If she sat on the mattress and patted the counterpane, he was done for.

However, she simply laced her fingers together in front of her waist, the prim gesture entirely at odds with her state of dishabille.

"Hamish," she began. "From the very first moment I met you, I cannot deny that I've felt an overwhelming attraction to you, and not just in a physical sense. And although I expect you're going to deny it, I think you feel it too."

Hamish frowned. "I know where this conversation is headed, but whatever you say, it's not going to sway me. We agreed this is going to be a marriage of convenience. One in name only."

"Yes, but it *is* still a marriage. So shouldn't we at least pretend it's real and we care for one another just a little? Otherwise, what will your family think when we arrive at Muircliff? Indeed, what will all our friends think—Lord and Lady Malverne, Lord and Lady Langdale, and Lady Charlotte—if we appear estranged from the outset? It won't make a lick of sense considering we've just thrown caution to the wind and been married at Gretna Green.

"Furthermore, if my uncle and Felix hear even a whisper of a rumor that our marriage is a sham, they'll be sure to challenge its validity and try to have it dissolved. And yes, I know you're a marquess, but they're desperate to control my money, and they won't be put off if they think for a moment they can succeed."

She took a few steps closer. Her eyes held a determined light. "To that end, I think it's particularly important that we look as though we're smitten with each other even if we're not." She shrugged a shoulder. "Unless you do want everyone to believe you married me for my inheritance. And that I mean nothing to you at all."

Hamish scrubbed a hand through his hair in frustration. Damn it, she had a point. "No, I don't want it to appear that way. Nothing could be further from the truth. I do care about your well-being, Olivia."

In fact, he was probably beginning to care too much, and that's what he was afraid of. But he couldn't admit that. There wasn't any point in giving the lass false hope. In the end, he'd never be able to give her what she wanted. He was broken. His soul was irrevocably stained. If she learned what he was really like—and of the terrible things he'd done, the things he was capable of—she'd be horrified. Even his friends—Nate, Gabriel, and Max, the Duke of Exmoor—didn't know the half of it.

Olivia crossed the hearthrug until she stood but an arm's length away from him. "I know that you mean well, Hamish. Why else would you have offered to m-marry me?" she said gravely. "Be that as it may, the only way that I will be able to convince others that we've been physically intimate—even if we don't actually consummate this marriage—is if I stop behaving like a nervous maid. Which is exactly what I am. At the moment, I'm constantly blushing and jumping out of my skin every time you come near me. I . . . I must get used to being near you.

"So . . ." Olivia drew so close, she had to lift her chin in order for her gaze to connect with his. "I have a suggestion. I . . . I think you should k-kiss me until I become accustomed to it."

Now they were moving into exceedingly dangerous territory. Hamish composed his features into a hard stare, the kind he would have used when disciplining a subordinate in his military days. "I've already kissed you."

To his astonishment and begrudging amusement, it had no effect whatsoever. Olivia waved a dismissive hand. "Pfft. The kiss you bestowed this afternoon was pleasant, b-but on the whole, it really wasn't good enough."

He knew exactly what she meant; it had been his intention to keep the kiss light. But that brief bussing of lips hadn't been enough for him either. Nevertheless, he felt compelled to defend himself. Casting her a wry smile, he said, "I've never had that complaint before, lass."

Olivia narrowed her gaze. "You can joke all you like, but I'm serious. Remember, two of my dearest friends are married to reformed rakes, so I know what to expect. And by all accounts, you're a rakehell too. Yet you kissed me as though I were a porcelain doll. As if I would break." She laid a hand upon his arm. "But we're married now, Hamish, and I want you to kiss me as if you mean it. Kiss me how you meant to kiss me in your room at the Hart and Hare.

Kiss me as you would a lover. Don't be all missish about it as you were at the handfasting ceremony."

He couldn't help but smile at the fact that she was throwing his own words back at him. "Missish? I've been accused of being a lot of things before, but never that."

"Well, prove to me that you're not. It's our wedding night, for heaven's sake, and I demand that you give me a proper kiss."

"Proper," he repeated, strangely amused despite the fact that a battle royal was taking place inside him—a sudden surge of lust waged war with his conscience. "It sounds as if the sort of kiss you want is entirely improper."

"Proper. Improper. C-call it whatever you like." A lock of Olivia's lustrous brown hair brushed against his bare forearm, and he cursed beneath his breath. For an inexperienced maid, she seemed to know exactly what she was doing. Her cheeks were bright with color, and challenge flashed in her deep brown eyes as she sought his gaze. "Kiss me with unabashed passion," she urged, her voice soft and husky yet commanding at the same time. "I'm your wife, and I deserve nothing less than your b-best effort."

The gossamer-thin thread snapped, and the hungry beast within was unleashed. Hamish gripped Olivia by the shoulders and pulled her flush against his chest. She gasped and pressed her palms against the hard swells of his pectoral muscles. An emotion he couldn't quite identify—desire, excitement, or perhaps it was fear—sparked in her eyes.

"Well, here it is, my Lady Sleat," he murmured as he pushed his fingers into the tumbling silken mass of her hair, clasping the back of her head. "You'd best brace yourself for my best effort."

He intended to claim her mouth in a bruising, ravaging kiss. A kiss that wasn't just improper but so fierce and bold, it would rattle this naive, presumptuous maiden. To warn her she was courting danger, not a chivalrous knight of old. That there was a reason to keep her distance.

But as soon as his mouth came down on hers, something

happened he couldn't explain. Some elemental force, some strange alchemy, swept through his blood, and instead of kissing Olivia like a mindless, lust-bitten brute in full rut, he kissed her with passionate tenderness, with an ardor that bordered on reverence.

His mouth melded with hers, and even though her response was unschooled, there was no doubting her eagerness to learn. To please him. Her lips were as soft and pliant and sweet as ripe summer berries, and they parted for him without hesitation when he sought to enter her with his tongue. Cradling her jaw, he thrust deeply, gently plundering every inch of that delicious honeyed recess. Savored the silken slide of her tongue as it shyly caressed and teased him in return. Had a kiss ever been so exhilarating? So all-consuming?

Hamish doubted it. This kiss was different from any other he'd hitherto shared with a woman. And he had no idea why. All he knew was that he needed more.

Desperate for a taste of Olivia's skin, he grazed his lips along her jaw, then down her throat. Pushed aside the shoulder of her night rail and set hot, sucking kisses upon the sensitive juncture between her neck and shoulder. The taste of her, the smell of her, was heady. More intoxicating than the strongest whisky.

And it seemed Olivia was more than willing to give in to his every demand. She swept aside the curtain of her hair so he could ravish her with greater ease. She arched her neck. Tangled her fingers in the locks at his nape and melted against him when he returned to feast upon her mouth again. Everything she did, every sound she made—the tiny moans and sensual little gasps that spilled from her lips—set his pulse racing madly. Triggered a sweet ache in his chest, a longing that went beyond physical craving. It was a bone-deep yearning that shocked him to the core.

What the bloody hell was wrong with him?

Hamish tore his mouth away. His chest rose and fell as he sucked in air and struggled to regain some semblance of control. To quell the desire urging his body to claim her. To cast out the raw tenderness threatening to undo him. "That's enough, lass," he panted.

Olivia's eyes fluttered open, and she frowned up at him. "Why?" she demanded huskily. Confusion clouded her gaze. "We're both attracted to each other. Desire each other." Her fingertips stroked along the line of his jaw, raising shivers of awareness all over his fevered flesh. "Why shouldn't we have a real marriage in every sense—"

"I said it was enough." Hamish pulled Olivia's hands away and clasped them against his chest. He couldn't think when she caressed him. "We need to stop, and you need to go. For your own good."

"I don't want to." Reproach laced her tone. "I'm not accustomed to your kisses yet."

"Well, that's all you're going to get from me, Olivia."

"I'm not leaving."

"Aye. You are."

She raised her chin. "Make me."

"Very well," Hamish growled.

He bent low and tossed Olivia over one shoulder, her arse in the air.

She gave a short, sharp shriek of surprise. "What are you doing?" she hissed as he strode out of his room and across the sitting room, heading toward her bedchamber. Her slippers fell off, but he didn't care.

"Putting you to bed," he replied.

"I'm not a child."

No she wasn't. Hamish could feel the press of her breasts against his back. The plump swell of her delectable buttocks beneath the palm of his hand as he held her steady. The taste of her sweet mouth still lingered on his tongue.

"Put me down," she demanded as he approached her bed.

"Hush, you'll wake Tilda," he admonished in a harsh whisper before tipping her onto the mattress. She bounced against the pillows, and he forced himself to step away so he wouldn't follow her onto the bed. Wouldn't bury himself in her abundant feminine softness and warmth. Even now, her body called to him like a blazing fire on a freezing Highland midwinter night. "Good night, Olivia."

She pushed herself up and scowled at him. "Why are you being so . . . so difficult?"

"It's in my nature," he said, trying to ignore the sight of her aroused nipples poking against the fabric of her nightgown. The way her hem had ridden up, exposing an elegant foot and a good deal of one very bare, very shapely leg. "And it seems I've just discovered you are similarly inclined."

"Gah, you're im-impossibly stubborn, Hamish MacQueen." Her pretty pink lips, still swollen from his kisses, dipped into a pout. But Hamish wouldn't let himself be pushed to the brink of madness again.

"Aye," he said gruffly, heading for the door. "And the sooner you come to terms with that, the better, my lady wife. We'll depart tomorrow morning at ten o'clock. I'll meet you downstairs."

As the door shut behind Hamish, Olivia decided she was going to be impossibly stubborn too.

She relaxed back against the pillows and pulled the bedcovers up to her chin. If Hamish MacQueen thought that this battle of wills was over, he was sorely mistaken.

Never in her life had Olivia felt so alive. Her whole body hummed with excitement. Her lips tingled with the memory of Hamish's glorious kisses—they'd felt wild and desperate. Needy but also worshipful. She'd demanded that he kiss her as he would a lover, and that's exactly what she'd got.

And it wasn't enough. Not by far. She'd been given a taste of bliss, a glimpse of what love felt like, and she wouldn't give up until she had it all.

One thing she'd been thrilled to discover: Hamish did indeed want her. She'd felt the unmistakable evidence of his arousal pressing against her own body. So clearly a lack

of desire wasn't the reason behind her husband's reluctance
to bed her and sire an heir.

And she didn't think his reluctance to have children
stemmed from a fundamental dislike of them. Even though
he might not be Tilda's father, he was nothing but wonderful with her.

Olivia sighed and turned over, hugging a pillow to her
chest. His words leapt into her mind. *We need to stop, and
you need to go. For your own good.*

What did he really mean by that?

He was shielding her from Felix and her avaricious family, yet he also seemed to think she was in some sort of
danger when she was with him, her husband. Her reputation was no longer at risk. And she'd happily give up her
virginity to him in a heartbeat.

She'd seen flashes of temper—he'd certainly looked as
if he could murder Felix today—but even when Hamish
had been a tad exasperated with her, she never felt in any
danger. Most of the time, she felt his glowering stares and
occasional cynical quips were all for show. And surely
Charlie wouldn't have suggested the Marquess of Sleat appear on their list of eligible bachelors if there was anything
truly wrong with his character.

He was hiding something, not just from her, but from his
friends.

None of it made any sense otherwise.

As Olivia watched the log she'd thrown into the grate
crumble into ashes, she decided she might just find the an-
swers she was looking for on the Isle of Skye.

CHAPTER 12

❧❧

> I wished sometimes to shake off all thought and feeling; but I learned that there was but one means to overcome the sensation of pain, and that was death.
>
> *Mary Shelley*, Frankenstein; or, The Modern Prometheus

The King's Head Inn, Springfield, Scotland

September 20, 1818

The early morning was foggy, but Hamish's mind was clear as he pushed into the King's Head Inn and sought out the innkeeper.

"Here you are, my lord." The shifty-eyed Lowlander passed Hamish the key to Felix de Vere's room along with a sly wink. "It's the third bedchamber to yer left at the top of the stairs. And if ye need anythin' else at all, dinna hesitate to ask. I am at yer disposal."

Hamish gave a curt nod. "I thank you, but that will be all." He wasn't impressed with the man's fawning demeanor. However, Hamish did appreciate the publican's lack of integrity insofar as he'd got what he wanted—easy access to de Vere's room—and for the price of only a few guineas. He suspected the publican would probably sell his grandmother's soul to the devil for the right price.

When Hamish opened the door to Felix's room a short

time later, he was greeted by snoring. It was still early, and as he expected, the bastard was still abed. Even though the light was dim, Hamish could see Felix was propped up awkwardly against the bedhead with a heavily bandaged shoulder. A dark bottle of Kendal's Black Drop, an opium tincture, stood on the scarred wooden bedside table beside a bottle of wine and a half-empty glass.

Marching over to the window, Hamish threw open the dusty, moth-bitten curtains. Felix immediately stirred, then moaned and threw an arm up to cover his eyes. "What the bloody—?" he mumbled. And then he saw who'd invaded his room. "Oh, fuck . . ."

Hamish moved to the end of the bed and crossed his arms over his chest as he scowled down at Olivia's good-for-nothing cousin. He'd worn his full clan regalia, complete with a dirk and short sword at his waist. There was nothing quite like the sight of an armed, savage-looking Highlander in an equally savage mood to put the fear of God into one's enemies. At least Hamish thought so.

"You'd best listen carefully, de Vere," he said in the precise tone of voice that always brought even the most recalcitrant of soldiers to heel, "if you know what's good for you."

Felix winced and let out an agonized groan as he attempted to sit up. "How the hell did you get in here?" he ground out between clenched teeth. The weak sunlight drifting in through the grimy window illuminated the lines of strain around his frost blue eyes and the sweat-soaked strands of dark blond hair plastered across his pale forehead.

Hamish ignored his question. "Although we met briefly yesterday, allow me to formally introduce myself. I'm the Marquess of Sleat . . . Olivia's husband."

If Hamish had thought Felix looked pale before, he was wrong. The cur's face took on the same washed-out hue as the threadbare sheets tangled around the lower half of his body.

Felix's throat convulsed in an audible gulp. "You must be joking," he rasped. "Unless of course"—his expression changed, his top lip curling into a sneer—"you need her money. Because why else would you marry such a half-witted chit?"

Pure anger flashed through Hamish hotter and swifter than a lightning bolt. It was time to put this dog in his place. "It's a love match, de Vere." Of course, that was a lie, but Olivia made a good point last night. And Felix wasn't to know it wasn't true.

Leaning forward, Hamish was gratified to watch Felix visibly shrink into the pillows at his back as he added, "Why else do you think we raced for the border? She's Lady Sleat now, and I'll go to any lengths to protect that which is mine. And . . ." He cocked a brow and smirked. "I also know every single thing about you, including how you and Giles Thackery have been embezzling my wife's money to cover your gaming debts and generally dissolute way of life. So unless you want me to take legal action against you, I suggest you return to whatever hole you crawled out of and stay there." Even though it would create a massive scandal, Hamish wasn't above using the threat of publicly exposing the man's crimes if it meant keeping Olivia and her fortune safe. A well-honed warning could be just as effective as the actual blow.

Felix's eyes widened, and he gripped the sheets with his fisted hands.

Good, the sniveling, grasping bastard was scared for once. It was time to twist the knife. "And if you ever come near my wife again, or even try to communicate with her in any way, you will be relieved of several vital body parts." Hamish grasped the handle of his short sword. "Do I make myself clear?"

Felix's eyes gleamed with an odd, feral light, reminding Hamish of a cornered weasel. Nevertheless, he bit out an answer. "Crystal."

"Excellent. Good lad." Hamish bared his teeth in a ferocious grin. "And while I have your undivided attention, don't even think about trying to get this marriage dissolved. It's perfectly legal under Scots law, and I have powerful friends in very high places. I could make your life a living hell, so you'd best take heed, Felix de Vere. This is your one and only warning. There will be no second chances."

Felix's face twisted with hatred. "Fuck you," he spat.

"Thank you for the offer, de Vere," Hamish said drily, "but considering the fact I'm now happily wed, I'm afraid that's never going to happen." And with that, he quit the room.

The early-autumn morning was crisp and fair when Olivia took Tilda down to Graitney Hall's vestibule for a ten o'clock departure. However, her husband's expression was darker than a thundercloud. He waited in the open doorway, the collar of his greatcoat pulled up and the brim of his hat pulled down. In one hand he gripped his leather gloves, which he slapped against his buckskin-clad thigh as though he were displeased about something.

"Is . . . is everything all right?" A frisson of apprehension slid down Olivia's spine as she drew closer to Hamish. The longcase clock in the hall hadn't even struck ten, so he couldn't possibly be cross that she was tardy.

Surely he wasn't in a temper because she'd pressed him for a kiss last night. She couldn't imagine he'd be so petty.

He straightened and tilted into a bow when she reached his side. "Good morning, my lady wife. And wee Tilda." He stroked his hand over the child's hair before returning his attention to Olivia. "I'm afraid we're down to one coach. The village blacksmith is taking too long to fix yours, and there's no other suitable conveyance for hire in the immediate vicinity. I'll leave one of my drivers and a footman behind to oversee the remaining repairs. All going well, we'll reach Glasgow tonight. I should be able to hire another coach there."

"Oh . . ." Olivia frowned in confusion. Now that she had

an unfettered view of the drive, she could see that there was indeed only one coach. She couldn't disguise the note of disappointment in her voice as she continued, "But . . . we're married now, so surely it won't matter if Tilda and I travel with you."

"No, it won't. However, I've decided to ride," said Hamish. His tone was firm, his manner unyielding. "I'm sure you and Tilda would prefer to have more room—"

"No. No, that doesn't matter." Truth to tell, after the accident outside of Gretna Green, Olivia was feeling more than a little jittery this morning. Indeed, she had rather hoped that Hamish would join her and Tilda for the remainder of the journey to Skye. Not only would his solid presence be reassuring, his company would be a most welcome distraction. At the risk of sounding querulous, she added, "Honestly, I'd be happy to share—"

But Hamish shook his head. "And I'd prefer to ride. Ah . . ." He gestured outside. "Here's my mount. I could use the exercise anyway, lass. My sleep is always sounder after a good bout of physical activity."

That might be true, but Olivia could see Hamish's right eye was shadowed with fatigue. As concern for *his* safety obliterated her own misgivings, she touched his arm in an effort to sway him. "But . . . but won't it look odd?" She knew her argument was weak, but it was the only one that sprang to mind. "Surely newlyweds should travel together."

Was that a flicker of remorse that crossed Hamish's face? He raised a hand to his eye patch and adjusted it slightly, effectively avoiding her gaze. "Most newlyweds don't have company," he said, nodding at Tilda. "Honestly, you'll be glad I'm not cluttering up the cab. Especially if I fall asleep. According to Hudson, I snore, and believe me, lass"—his mouth twitched with a smile—"neither you nor Tilda wants to hear that. The bairn really will think I'm some sort of beast. Now . . ." Hamish pulled on his gloves, then offered his arm to escort her down the flight of stairs to the drive below. "Let us away, my lady. We've a great deal of ground to cover before we reach Skye."

What else could she do but acquiesce? Once she and Tilda were settled in the carriage, she watched Hamish mount his horse in one fluid movement. Yet again, he was steadfastly avoiding her. It was more than a little frustrating and lowering. How could they possibly get to know each other better if he kept doing this?

He maintained he snored, but Olivia sensed that was another convenient excuse to keep her at a distance. She also sensed that if she made a fuss, he'd dig his heels in even more.

One thing was certain: her husband seemed to be plagued by poor sleep. Before he'd closed the door to the carriage, she'd noticed again how exhausted he looked, the deep lines of strain bracketing his mouth, and the bruise-like shadow of weariness beneath his good eye. He really should be resting rather than spending a whole day in the saddle.

Olivia frowned as the carriage pulled away from Graitney Hall. At the Hart and Hare, Hamish had admitted that he sometimes experienced bad dreams. But what if he was plagued by nightmares on a regular basis? That would explain his exhaustion. And perhaps that was the real reason he didn't wish to share a carriage with her and Tilda. Was he afraid they'd witness him having a nightmare, so he thought to spare them?

How touching and sad if that were the case; the whole notion made Olivia's heart twist in the strangest way. If only she knew how to make a decent sleeping draft. Charlie had a good recipe, but she was hundreds of miles away. Laudanum induced sleep, but Arabella—who could have been a physician if women were allowed to practice—always advised that it must be used with caution. Then, of course, there was chamomile tea and warm milk. Perhaps even lavender-scented linen. Such measures might not cure Hamish's bad dreams, but if he could achieve better sleep, surely that would provide him with some sort of relief.

If only she could summon the courage to broach such a

difficult subject with a husband who seemed determined to push her away.

The Village of Abington, Lanarkshire, Scotland

"Damn it," cursed Hamish beneath his breath as he strode out of the stable yard of the Abington Arms, heading toward the public taproom. His horse was lame.

Even though they'd all changed horses at the Black Bull Inn in Moffat two hours ago, it seemed his poor beast had picked up a stone. Unfortunately, the hostelry here in Abington was so small, they'd barely been able to change over the outriders' mounts and the carriage's team of four. And they still had over three hours to go to reach Glasgow.

Hamish sighed heavily as he ordered a tankard of ale at the bar. The coach already had too many bloody footmen perched on the outside of the vehicle, so there was no room for him there. He could scout farther afield for another horse—the ostler at the Abington Arms believed the inn in the nearby village of Crawfordjohn might have a suitable mount. But because they'd have to travel an additional five miles to the west and then back again, it meant another hour or more would be added to their trip. It seemed there was simply no avoiding it: Hamish was going to have to travel the rest of the way to Glasgow with Olivia and Tilda.

Three hours wasn't so long. Even though Hamish's good eye felt as gritty as hell, and his body ached like an old man's—it had been a while since he'd spent such a long stretch in the saddle—it wasn't likely that he'd fall asleep in the carriage in such a short span of time.

You better bloody not, he told himself as he glanced over to where Olivia sat with Tilda; he'd escorted them inside as soon as they arrived at the Abington Arms, and the pair were presently sharing a plate of scones smothered in jam and cream at a small table by one of the windows. Perhaps sensing his gaze on her, his new wife looked up at him and smiled.

Jesus Christ and all his saints, she was lovely.

Hamish's chest suddenly felt too tight, and something deep inside him began to ache with a feeling he really didn't want to put a name to. The afternoon sun filtering through the leaded glass pane wandered over Olivia's face, illuminating her smooth-as-cream complexion and the long lashes fringing her large brown eyes, picking out the strands of copper and mahogany in the lustrous waves of her dark hair that she'd somehow tamed into a sedate arrangement at the back of her shapely head.

Her traveling gown of dark purple wool was well cut but far too plain for his liking. And it covered far too much. To think she'd been in his room last night wearing nothing but a thin nightgown, with all that gorgeous hair tumbling about her shoulders. And the memory of her demanding that he kiss her properly, like a lover . . . Hamish had never been so aroused in all his life. Even now he could feel his blood stirring.

Olivia was fearless and passionate, and he wanted her so badly, it scared the hell out of him. Thank God Tilda would be in the carriage with them; otherwise he'd be hard-pressed to keep his hands off his delectable wife.

Something in his expression must have given away the less-than-gentlemanly direction of his thoughts, as a becoming blush pinkened Olivia's cheeks.

But instead of looking away as she might have done when they'd first met, she pressed her even white teeth into her full lower lip, and her soft-as-velvet gaze strayed to Hamish's mouth. Even across the room, there was no mistaking what she was thinking about.

The ruby on his signet ring—now Olivia's wedding ring—glowed a deep claret red in the sunlight. It proclaimed Olivia to be his, and by rights, he could take her to bed whenever he wanted to. Considering the knowing look she was casting him, he knew she'd be more than willing to acquiesce.

But he wouldn't. He hadn't married her for any other reason than to protect her and her fortune, and for what she could do for him in return—act as a chaperone and facilitate the coming-out of his foolish, lovesick sister. Knowing they had mutual friends only made him more determined to play the noble gentleman. It would be unconscionable if he were to take advantage of Olivia's budding desire—which in her naivety, she'd probably convinced herself was love—just so he could slake his lust.

Yes, no matter how many come-hither looks his new wife threw his way, or how many beseeching speeches she gave about needing to be kissed "properly" so she wouldn't be so jumpy about him, he would ignore the lust simmering in his blood.

As he'd stated at the outset, this was a temporary marriage of convenience, nothing more.

D o the story about the wolf and the deer and the wicked witch again, Lady Livvie," said Tilda, pulling the volume *The Fauna of Scotland and Its Isles: An Illustrated History* from the small stack of books on the carriage seat beside her.

Olivia smiled at Tilda. Since her real name had been disclosed, and because she'd wed Hamish, Olivia had helped the little girl pick another name for her that was relatively easy to say and not as formal as Lady Sleat. Lady Livvie seemed to work just nicely. "I'd be happy to, Tilda," she whispered. "Only, I won't be able to do the wolf's voice too loudly." She nodded at her husband on the opposite bench. "I . . . I don't want to wake Lord Sleat."

Tilda nodded. "That's all right," she whispered back. "I don't mind." Her forehead creased into a small frown. "He sounds like a wolf though. Or maybe a bear."

Olivia had to bite her cheek to stop herself from laughing. Hamish did sound rather like a bear at the moment. After he'd joined them in the carriage at the Abington Arms, Olivia had watched him struggle against the pull of sleep for at least an hour before he'd eventually succumbed. He was presently sprawled on the opposite bench in a semi-reclined position, with his head thrown back against the leather squabs, his wide mouth relaxed and slightly open. His long legs were canted across the space between the seats in such a way that his booted toe kept brushing her ankle. Not that she minded. Indeed, if Tilda weren't here, Olivia would be tempted to curl up beside Hamish, using his wide chest as a pillow.

Not only had he removed his hat, gloves, greatcoat, and riding jacket, he'd also loosened his cravat, revealing the strong line of his neck. What would it be like to press a kiss to that neck, to inhale her husband's potent, spicy scent? To feel the comforting rumble of his snores beneath her ear as she smoothed her hand over his sleek waistcoat? To slide open a button or two and push her fingers inside? To trace the intriguing hardness of muscle and sinew and bone beneath . . .

Tilda pushed the book into Olivia's hands, pulling Olivia away from her delicious but entirely wistful musings. The page before her featured an intricate rendering of a shaggy, gray-haired wolf with pale golden eyes.

"Tell me about the wolf's castle," murmured Tilda, pressing against Olivia's side so she could get closer to the book, "and how the deer gets trapped inside."

"Of course." And so Olivia began to respin her tale about the wolf who was really a handsome Scottish laird but had been turned into a savage beast by Morag, an evil witch living in the nearby woods. And the red deer was really a pretty young woman named Fenella from the local village. "You see, Fenella, who had lovely red hair, caught the laird's eye when he was riding through the village one day on his way back to the castle. And Morag, who'd loved the laird from afar for many years, was so jealous, she cast a spell on her too—"

Hamish mumbled in his sleep and shifted restlessly. Olivia glanced up and then frowned—a deep line had appeared between his slashing black brows, and his mouth had twisted as though he were in pain.

Tilda gripped Olivia's sleeve. "Is he all right?" she whispered. "Does he have a bellyache?" Her eyes were wide with worry.

Olivia offered a reassuring smile. "I think he's just having a bad dream." She turned over a few pages of the book, hoping to distract Tilda. "Let's see if we can find that picture of Fenella—"

Hamish let out a whimper, then an agonized moan. "Too late. Can't go back," he muttered through clenched teeth. His hands had curled into fists, and the cords of his neck stood out starkly. "Christ. I can't . . . Don't want to . . ."

"Livvie, I'm frightened."

Olivia put the book aside, and Tilda immediately climbed onto her lap. "Hush. There's nothing to be scared of," she murmured against Tilda's ear. "Lord Sleat will wake up soon—"

"Oh, God help me . . ." Hamish bolted into an upright position, then slid to the floor of the rocking carriage. His knees were drawn up to his chest, and he covered his face with his hands as he sobbed, "Oh, God . . . I can't. I won't . . ."

Oh, dear heaven above. Olivia had no idea what to do. Should she wake Hamish? The nightmare that held him in its grip must be horrendous. Her own vision blurred as tears filled her eyes. What on earth had happened to this man? Did he dream about the time he was injured at Waterloo? Or of all the terrible things he must have witnessed during battle?

"Must die . . ."

The carriage bounced over a particularly deep rut in the road, and Hamish lurched to the side, bumping his head against the carriage door. He cried out, but the jolt was enough to wake him.

He shook his head, and although he'd just come to, his groggy gaze sought out Olivia. "Sweet Jesus. Are you and the bairn all right?" His face was paler than his cambric shirt as he pushed himself up and then collapsed onto the opposite seat. Chest heaving as though he'd run a mile, he rasped, "Please tell me you're both all right." His gaze, wild and desperate, locked with hers.

"Yes, we're f-fine." Olivia wasn't quite sure if that was actually the case. Her heart was racing, and Tilda was still trembling in her arms. But she didn't want to alarm Hamish when he was so clearly rattled already.

Hamish dragged a shaking hand down his face, then pushed his tangled hair back from a sweat-sheened brow. "I can't believe I fell asleep," he said, his voice laced with deep remorse. "I'm so, so sorry, lass. Such a stupid thing to do."

He rapped on the carriage roof above his head, attracting the attention of the driver. "Pull up," he called. "At once."

The carriage immediately slowed, and as soon as it drew to a halt, Hamish threw open the door and bolted from the cab. The sound of violent retching reached Olivia's ears.

"I was right, Lady Livvie," whispered Tilda. "He does have a sore belly."

"Yes," agreed Olivia. She gave Tilda a gentle squeeze. "I think I should go and help him. Would you stay here in the carriage while I do?"

Tilda nodded and climbed off her lap. "Yes, Lady Livvie," she said solemnly. "And when you come back, let's tell Lord Sleat a story to make him feel better."

Olivia smiled. "I like that idea very much."

She retrieved two flasks from the basket stowed beneath Hamish's seat—a leather one containing water and a pewter one of whisky—then clambered down from the carriage. Hamish stood beneath an oak tree at the side of the road, hunched over with his hands on his thighs. He was breathing heavily, but the fit of vomiting appeared to have passed. Hudson waited nearby, concern creasing his brow.

When the valet looked up and saw her approaching, he gave her a small nod and then retreated to a discreet distance. Olivia cast him a grateful smile in return.

"Hamish?" she murmured. She hovered a few feet away, unsure how any offer of assistance would be received.

He straightened and leaned a shaking hand against the oak's trunk. "I'll be all right. No need to worry."

"I . . . I fished out the flasks of water and whisky," she said, taking another few steps forward.

Hamish wiped his forearm across his brow before turning to face her. "Thank you. I must confess, I wouldn't mind a sip or two of water." He took the leather flask and, after rinsing out his mouth, swallowed a long draft.

"How's wee Tilda?" he asked as he handed back the water.

"She's concerned you have a bell . . . bellyache," replied Olivia. "And she'd like to tell you a story when you return—"

But Hamish shook his head. "No, I don't think that would be a good idea. I need fresh air. Hudson can sit with you and Tilda. I'll sit up with the driver."

"Oh . . ." Olivia blinked in surprise. "Well, if you're sure . . ."

"I am." Hamish's voice had a steel-like edge to it. "We'll be in Glasgow in an hour or so. And by tomorrow, I'll have secured another carriage. This won't happen again."

"Hamish, it . . . it really wasn't a prob—"

He took a step closer and grasped her arm. "I'd appreciate it if you didn't argue with me. Please . . ." His tone softened as he added, "I feel bad enough already that you had to witness that . . . Just do as I ask."

"Of course, my lord."

The corner of his mouth quirked with a weak smile. "Thank you. You're too good for me, Olivia."

"I'm really not."

He cocked a dark brow. "Are you arguing with me again?"

Olivia couldn't help but smile back. "It . . . it would seem so. But it shouldn't really come as a surprise to you after last night. Didn't you agree that I can be 'difficult' after you unceremoniously carted me back to my room?"

A spark of genuine amusement lit Hamish's gaze. "Aye, I did, didn't I? Well, off you go, my difficult-but-undeniably-kindhearted wife. Don't make me unceremoniously cart you back to the carriage."

If only you would. That was the thought uppermost in Olivia's mind as she retraced her steps and Hudson handed her in. *And would that I could somehow ease your pain.*

An impossible feat considering Hamish appeared to be determined to keep her at arm's length, no matter what.

CHAPTER 13

❧

> While they waited till the servant within should
> come to open the gates, she anxiously surveyed the
> edifice: but the gloom, that overspread it, allowed
> her to distinguish little more than a part of its
> outline, with the massy walls of the ramparts, and
> to know, that it was vast, ancient and dreary.
>
> *Ann Radcliffe*, The Mysteries of Udolpho

Isle of Skye, Scotland

September 24, 1818

The next four days passed in a blur for Olivia. Seemingly endless hours spent alone in Hamish's carriage with only Tilda for company—and then on horseback after they crossed by ferry from Glenelg over to the village of Kylerhea on the Isle of Skye—left her exhausted and aching. Poor Tilda was so tired, she slept for most of the final leg, rugged up in blankets in the back of the dogcart that Hudson drove over the vast tracts of rough moorland between Kylerhea and Muircliff Castle.

By the time their small traveling party reached the tiny village of Dunmuir on the very northwestern edge of the island, the afternoon had turned cold and dark. Sullen clouds threatened rain, and a chill, brine-laden wind tore at Olivia's bonnet, traveling gown, and woolen cloak. When

Hamish informed her they only had three miles left to travel, she was thankful the journey was almost over.

However, her relief was short-lived. The approach to Muircliff was along a narrow stony track, high above the hissing, roiling sea. Waves hurled themselves at the basalt cliffs and jagged black rocks below, sending plumes of spray and foam into the air. Olivia had learned to ride when she was a girl and felt comfortable in the saddle, but not at the present moment. Her stomach was a mass of tangled knots, and she kept a tight grip on the reins of her small gray mare as she followed Hamish. He rode his fine black gelding with practiced ease even though the cutting wind whipped his sable hair and the cape of his greatcoat all about.

Olivia wanted to glance back over her shoulder to see how Hudson was managing to steer the dogcart along the path, but she dared not in case she lost her seat. Daniels now sat with Tilda—he'd hopped into the back of the cart at Dunmuir—so she trusted the footman was taking care of her.

Some hours ago, as they'd clattered over a stone bridge spanning the shallow Sligachan River with the rugged Cuillin mountain range rising above the surrounding heather-covered moors, Hamish had explained to Olivia that Muircliff had been built by the MacQueens of Skye several centuries ago. "Even though various ancestors have added improvements over the years, it's still a hulking pile of stone and essentially inhospitable," he'd remarked without enthusiasm. "At least I think so. Although, you might disagree."

As they gained the top of the headland and Muircliff loomed ahead, Olivia decided Hamish's assessment was quite accurate: the medieval fortress was entirely unwelcoming. Its dark brooding mass, complete with sawtooth battlements and mismatched towers, crouched upon the cliff top like a great fossilized beast. A slain dragon, perhaps. Nothing relieved its bleak, menacing bulk. Not a tree, nor a trace of shrubbery. Every window Olivia could see was devoid of light.

There even appeared to be a ruined tower; the turret roof and part of the wall had collapsed, leaving a wide, misshapen scar along its side. Toppled brickwork and boulders lay like scattered, ancient bones among the clumps of wind-ravaged grass.

The castle's and indeed the whole landscape's forbidding air only worsened when a freezing rain blew in; sharpened by buffeting gusts straight off the sea, the icy needles pricked at any exposed skin, and within a few minutes, Olivia was shivering.

Hamish slowed his horse as he neared the gatehouse so Olivia could draw alongside him. "Welcome home, my lady wife." He had to raise his voice to be heard over the howl of the wind and the crash of the waves.

Olivia nodded and attempted a smile—although she feared it might have been more of a squint-eyed grimace—and then she followed her husband beneath the raised portcullis and into the shadowy barbican passage, the dogcart and the remainder of the mounted staff trundling behind them.

Once inside the main courtyard—a massive, cobblestoned area—the elemental assault lessened considerably. The sound of the sea had reduced to a dull roar, and the wind no longer battered Olivia from all sides. Additional staff appeared as if from nowhere to take care of the horses and luggage, but it was Hamish who lifted Olivia down from her saddle.

"Let's get you and the bairn inside," he said as Daniels approached with Tilda in his arms. She was bundled up in several woolen blankets, her small thumb planted firmly in her mouth as she gazed in wide-eyed wonder at the towering walls and ramparts surrounding them, but she seemed happy enough to stay with the footman.

Considering she was half-frozen—and Tilda must be too—Olivia wasn't about to disagree with Hamish's suggestion. To her surprise, her husband slid an arm about her waist, and she had to quell the urge to nuzzle into him, to get closer to that invitingly hard, warm body lurking beneath his greatcoat. Such moments had been few and far between since the carriage incident just outside of Glasgow, so this small display of affection was welcome indeed.

A pair of massive iron-studded wooden doors in an arched recess, clearly the entrance to the main keep, stood wide open. As Hamish led Olivia up a wide set of worn stone stairs, a young man, dark of hair and well dressed in tonnish attire, appeared in the doorway. A large, shaggy deerhound stood at his side.

"Hamish, you came," cried the gentleman, rushing forward to envelop the marquess in a hug. But when he saw Olivia, he stopped abruptly and simply reached out a hand to grip Hamish by the shoulder.

"Angus." Hamish's face split with a genuine smile. "Of course I came. But let's continue the greetings and introductions inside, shall we? Out of this infernal rain."

Olivia was so flabbergasted by the sheer size of the great hall Hamish ushered her into, she started when a young footman stepped forward to relieve her of her bonnet, cloak, and gloves.

Tilda tugged at her skirts. "Is this a castle, Lady Livvie?" she whispered, staring up into the shadows of the impossibly high ceiling. Dark beams arched overhead, and an enormous and somewhat wicked-looking chandelier—apparently constructed from antlers—was suspended from the very center.

"Yes, it is indeed," Olivia returned as she bent down to help remove the little girl's damp bonnet and coat.

"It's so big . . . Is Lord Sleat a prince?"

"No, Lord Sleat is a marquess."

Tilda nodded sagely, as though she understood what that meant. "It's dark in here. And a bit scary. I hope there aren't any ghosts."

Olivia gave her a quick hug. "I'm sure there are none at all," she murmured. Although, she couldn't disagree with Tilda's initial observations. The great hall was rather dark and more than a little sinister. The flagstone floor was bare, and the gray stone walls were covered in gruesome-looking weaponry—swords, axes, shields, and maces—as well as the mounted heads of glassy-eyed stags and tapestries of hunting scenes. The only welcoming feature Olivia could see was the huge fire blazing in the ornately carved black marble fireplace at the other end of the hall.

But then she'd discounted the amiable smile of the young man standing before her as she straightened.

Placing his hand in the middle of Olivia's back—another unexpected yet entirely welcome gesture—Hamish made the required introductions. "Angus, may I present my lovely new wife, Olivia. And Olivia"—Hamish caught her eye—"this is my brother, Lord Angus MacQueen."

"Oh . . ." Angus's blue eyes widened with surprise as his gaze traveled over Olivia; no doubt she looked like a disheveled wreck in her rumpled, damp, travel-stained clothes, and not marchioness material at all. "I . . ." Bright color flooded his face as he affected a courtly bow. "My Lady Sleat," he said with scrupulous politeness. "Welcome to Muircliff."

"Th-thank you," she replied with a small inclination of her head. "It's a pleasure to meet you, Lord Angus. But please, call me O-Olivia." Her smile slipped a fraction, and her gaze darted between and Hamish and her new brother-in-law. "If th-that's all right with you, of course. We've only just met, and I d-don't want things to be aw-aw-awkward . . ."

She blushed. She was flustered and stammering, and the whole exchange was as awkward as could be. She suddenly wished she could fade into one of the tapestries on the nearby wall.

But Lord Angus was charm personified. "I would be delighted to call you Olivia as long as you call me Angus," he said with a kind smile.

Hamish held his hand out to Tilda. She stepped out from behind Olivia's skirts, and his fingers all but swallowed hers as she placed her small hand in his. "Angus, allow me to introduce my ward," he said. "Miss Tilda. And, Tilda, this is my brother, Lord Angus."

To Olivia's surprise—and Hamish's, judging by his

startled expression—Tilda dipped into a small curtsy without prompting. "How do you do, Lord Angus," she said quite clearly. The child had obviously been schooled in the etiquette surrounding formal introductions.

"I'm very well, Miss Tilda," replied Angus. "And it's a great pleasure to meet you too." He tilted into another gentlemanly bow. "And this is my dog"—he gestured at the deerhound—"Shadow."

"He's not a wolf?" asked Tilda, her eyes wide and fearful.

"No, he's just a dog. And a friendly one at that. You may pat him if you like." He clicked his fingers, and the hound loped over to Tilda. She reached out a tiny hand and stroked one of the dog's ears.

The younger MacQueen then threw Hamish a quizzical look. "It seems your life has been rather eventful of late, dear brother," he observed. There was no mistaking the speculative twinkle in his eye.

The corner of Hamish's mouth quirked. "Indeed. And it seems life at Muircliff has been rather eventful too." His brow descended into a deep frown. "I quit London as soon as your letter arrived. I trust everything is all right at the moment . . . with Isobel . . ."

"Aye." Lord Angus sighed. "All things considered, I would say the situation is now . . . Well, things are tolerable." His gaze darted to Olivia and then back to Hamish. "Isobel is safe, even if she's not entirely happy with me for sending for you. I imagine you'll soon see for yourself."

"Olivia knows about Isobel," said Hamish in a low voice. "In fact, she's here to help."

"Oh . . ." Lord Angus gave an astonished blink. "That's marvelous, then."

When Angus smiled at Olivia, she shifted uncomfortably beneath his gaze. Of course she'd attempt to uphold her end of the bargain, but so many things were beyond her control. What if Isobel didn't like her? And how was she to help the poor girl overcome her heartbreak? Not only that, how could she facilitate Isobel's debut into polite society when she'd never even attended a ton ball or set foot in Almack's herself? The task suddenly seemed too over-whelming. An impossible feat.

These were the questions and anxious thoughts that tumbled about in Olivia's mind as Hamish introduced her to Muircliff's servants. A small group had assembled in the hall—the butler, housekeeper, cook, steward, several foot-men and chambermaids—to greet their master and his guests. When it was announced that she, Olivia, was Lord Sleat's bride—and thus the new mistress of Muircliff Castle—there was more than one eyebrow raised.

Olivia tried not to mind and endeavored to present a brave face—she was certain Hamish wouldn't permit his staff to be insubordinate—but after years of being put down by Agnes Bagshaw, she found it difficult to believe she'd have any authority or be treated with respect, despite the fact that she was now Lady Sleat.

The formalities over, Hamish offered to escort her and Tilda upstairs to the north wing where the bedchambers lay. The housekeeper, Mrs. Boyd, accompanied them.

"Lady Sleat shall have the use of my chamber until the adjoining room has been suitably made up and aired," he instructed the silver-haired housekeeper as they climbed an enormous oak staircase to the second floor. Portraits of Hamish's ancestors—the men sporting plaids and the women garbed in stiffly boned gowns and powdered wigs—glowered down at Olivia, and she tried to banish her fanciful and entirely unhelpful thoughts that they were judging her too.

"Verra good, my lord," replied Mrs. Boyd. Her expres-sion was dour, her manner brusque. The woman was clearly all business and Olivia wondered how working with her would be. "And shall I have the nursery prepared for Miss Tilda?"

"Aye . . ." He caught Olivia's eye. "If that's all right with you, my lady wife. And Tilda. We haven't really discussed the arrangements for the bairn, but my old nursemaid, El-len Swan, still resides here at Muircliff. I believe she'll do a wonderful job taking care of Tilda. I'll arrange a meeting after we've all had a chance to freshen up."

"Yes. Of course." A pang of sadness penetrated Olivia's heart. Now that she was Hamish's wife, she understood that she could no longer act as Tilda's nursemaid. But after spending over a week in the little girl's company, caring for her every need, she knew she would miss doing so. And she was certain Tilda would miss her company too. Even though she needed to spend time building some kind of rapport with her new sister-in-law Lady Isobel MacQueen, while simultaneously settling into her new role as mistress of Muircliff, Olivia determined that she would visit the nursery whenever she could.

Hamish's bedchamber, situated in the north wing, was both magnificent and sumptuously appointed. A series of arched, diamond-paned windows commanded stunning views of the turbulent sea and the lowering sky. A massive bed with carved posts and a headboard of dark oak dominated the room, while the curtains, bed linen, upholstery, and thick carpets were a study in various shades of muted blue, soft gray, and ivory. All of the walls were bare stone except for one—the panels flanking the fireplace had been adorned with toile de Jouy silk wallpaper.

As Mrs. Boyd was pointing out the dressing room, the main bedchamber became a veritable hive of activity. Hudson and several footmen arrived with all their luggage, while another footman began to light all the candles and the fire in the gray marble fireplace. A pair of chambermaids also appeared bearing fresh towels and hot water for washing. Olivia had never seen so many staff in one bedroom in all her life.

When Mrs. Boyd was the only servant left in the room, the housekeeper addressed Hamish. "My lord, I imagine you'd like the jib door between your room and Lady Sleat's to be unlocked . . ." She pulled a large set of keys from a pocket in her gown of black stuff and looked expectantly at her employer.

Hamish's gaze met Olivia's for a brief moment before

returning to the housekeeper. "Aye. Thank you." To Olivia he said, "This bedchamber and the adjoining one, which will be yours, are the only two that are connected at Muir-cliff. The jib door is rather small, but I imagine it will suffice."

"I see," replied Olivia carefully, when she really wanted to demand, "How will it suffice, Hamish? What purpose will it serve other than to give others the impression that we share a bed on the odd occasion?"

But no matter how much Olivia wanted to vent her frustration, she knew a public display of temper wouldn't help. With an effort, she pushed away her uncharacteristically sour thoughts and watched Mrs. Boyd cross to one of the panels beside the fireplace and push a key into a lock that was almost impossible to discern; it was neatly camouflaged by the intricate pastoral scenes depicted on the silk wallpaper. When the housekeeper turned a small handle the same blue gray hue as the fabric, the well-hidden door opened soundlessly into the next room. The sounds of activity—the rustle of linen, the muted murmur of female voices—filtered into Hamish's bedchamber.

"Yer room should be ready within a half hour, my lady," said Mrs. Boyd. "If there's anything I can do fer ye in the meantime, just ring." She nodded toward the bellpull beside Hamish's bed. "For instance, if ye need a maid to help ye . . ." The housekeeper raised a sparse eyebrow, and Olivia knew by the hard look in the woman's eyes that she wasn't being helpful. She was clearly judging her new mistress for not having brought her own maid to Muircliff.

Olivia blushed hotly. "I . . . no, that w-won't be nec-necessary," she stammered.

Hamish didn't miss the slight either. "Mrs. Boyd," he began in such a noticeably sharp tone, the housekeeper visibly paled. "No doubt my wife will expect you to select a number of candidates for her to interview for the esteemed position of lady's maid. I'm sure there's someone already employed here at Muircliff who will fit the bill. So I suggest you begin thinking about who might be suitable.

Her ladyship will call on you when she is ready to discuss the matter further with you." He smiled at Olivia. "Won't you, my dear lady wife?"

Touched beyond words at Hamish's unexpected show of support, Olivia took a moment to find her voice. "Yes . . . I will."

Mrs. Boyd curtsied with due deference. "Verra good, my lady. My lord."

"Excellent," said Hamish. "That will be all."

The chastened housekeeper quit the room, and then Hamish began to take his leave as well.

"You're not going to use your own dressing room?" Olivia asked his retreating back.

Hamish paused on the threshold with one arm braced against the doorjamb. The line of his broad shoulders was tight, his back ramrod straight. He curled his fingers into a tightly clenched fist. "It's better if I use Angus's room," he said without turning around. "I thought you and wee Tilda might like some privacy."

"Yes. Of course," replied Olivia. He was right. But all the same, his continued refusal to spend time alone with her stung.

"I'll be back in half an hour to escort you and Tilda to the nursery to meet Nurse Swan."

"We'll . . . we'll be ready . . . Only . . ." Olivia's gaze darted to the hidden door that would never be used by her husband. She watched Tilda slip through it into the next room to observe the maids at work. She couldn't bear this ongoing estrangement. Each rejection felt like another little chip into her self-esteem. A chiseling away of her dream to build a lasting, loving relationship.

Without thinking, Olivia moved to the door and reached out toward her seemingly implacable husband. Dared to place a hand on his shoulder. Tense muscle flexed beneath her palm. Shifted.

All at once, Hamish moved, and Olivia found she was trapped between a cold stone wall and a granite-hard body.

"Christ, Olivia," he grated out, and captured her face in his hands. "Forgive me."

And then he kissed her.

He couldn't bear it any longer. He couldn't resist his worst impulses.

He might wish himself to be as unfeeling as stone, but he wasn't.

As soon as Olivia reached out to him, Hamish knew he was lost. Her tentative touch seared through his clothes. Branded him.

He wanted. He burned. Hot lust shot through his veins, and Hamish knew he had to kiss Olivia. Claim her in the most basic of ways.

His kiss was ravaging. Plundering. Hard, bruising, demanding, and desperate. There was no way to contain this pent-up desire. It was overwhelming. *Incendiary.* And the taste of Olivia's sweeter-than-honey lips, her tongue, the sound of her moans, the feel of her soft, silken flesh beneath his hands, were the only things that would quench the insatiable need roaring through his veins like wildfire.

The last few days had been hellish. Not only had Hamish been in a constant lather of thwarted lust—because he refused to give in to his base male urges—but he'd also been plagued by bouts of self-loathing. He never should have joined Olivia in the carriage on the final leg to Glasgow. Not when he'd been so exhausted.

When he was in the throes of a nightmare, he had no idea what he was doing. If he'd lashed out . . . the danger to anyone nearby was real. When he'd woken on the floor of the carriage and realized what had happened, he was physically ill at the thought of what he could have done to wee Tilda or Olivia.

He'd endeavored to keep his distance from Olivia for as long as possible. But as soon as he'd set foot on Skye, it was as if the savage blood of his ancestors began to thunder through him. His hunger for Olivia had grown keener. Hotter. And at the very first opportunity, the mindless ravening beast who wanted to take, take, take everything this lovely gentle lass had to offer had been unleashed.

Yet it seemed he wasn't the only one who wanted. Olivia was in no way a reluctant participant. Her hands kneaded his chest. She brazenly pushed her hips against his growing erection as she kissed him back with a fervor that astounded him. And it only made Hamish that much madder for her.

Yes, he'd succumbed to madness. He didn't care that Tilda might be nearby. Or that half a dozen maids might be in the next room.

Nothing mattered to him except this woman and this abandoned, completely addictive kiss. And deep down, he knew this wouldn't be enough.

He wanted Olivia in every conceivable way. To show her pleasure beyond her wildest dreams. He wanted to strip her bare. To take her up against this stone wall. On his bed. On the hearthrug before the fire. In his library downstairs. In the great hall. On the ramparts. On the desolate moorland, among the spent heather. On the sand in the cove below Muircliff . . .

Olivia whimpered, and Hamish pulled away as a sliver of sanity at last penetrated the fog of his rising lust.

"I'm sorry," he rasped in between panted breaths.

"Don't be." Olivia was smiling.

Was she mad too?

He attempted to gather the will to move away but failed. "I was too rough." Remorse laced his voice.

"No you weren't. I liked it. No . . . I loved it." She stroked his cheek with gentle fingers. "I won't break, Hamish."

Hamish leaned his forehead against Olivia's. "Aye." She was strong and fearless, and he didn't know whether to rejoice or despair at her confession. The promise of a heaven he could never have taunted him when he looked into the dark velvet softness of Olivia's doe eyes. Caught her delicious scent. Felt the rise and fall of her breasts against his chest.

God, he sounded like a lovestruck boy, not a hardened, scarred-to-the-soul scoundrel of the first order.

Forcing himself to unwind Olivia's hands from his neck, he stepped away at last. "I still have to wash and change. And I'm sure you'd like to do the same. You'd best make use of that warm water in the dressing room before it gets cold."

"Yes . . . Hamish . . ." Olivia pushed a disheveled lock of her hair behind her ear, an endearingly nervous gesture, then offered a shy smile. "I'm afraid I'm not . . . I'm not accustomed to your kisses yet. I might need a few more."

"Hmm. We'll see," he said, trying to ignore the discomfort of his erection as it strained in vain against the fall front of his buckskin breeches. "You might break *me*, Olivia."

And with that, he quit the room, heading for Angus's chamber.

Olivia might welcome his kisses, but her judgment was clouded. She didn't know the shameful truth about him. If she ever found out how beastly, damaged, and dangerous he really was, she'd surely shun him. Reject his every touch.

And rightly so.

The problem was, he was too ashamed—nay, too cowardly—to reveal the worst of himself to her.

The best he could do was promise himself that he wouldn't succumb to temptation and lose control again. They could never, ever share a bed.

One thing was certain: unlocking the jib door between their bedchambers now seemed like the worst idea Hamish had ever had. Because if Olivia entered his room during the night, anything could happen. And he'd only have himself to blame.

CHAPTER 14

My temper was sometimes violent, and my passions vehement.

Mary Shelley, Frankenstein; or, The Modern Prometheus

Muircliff Castle, Isle of Skye

So how iş Isobel?" Hamish called from his brother's dressing room. "Now's the time for plain speaking, Angus." He selected a fresh cambric shirt from the few Hudson had set out for him and threw it over his head.

"She's . . . when she's not with Mother, she keeps to herself quite a lot," said Angus, his voice floating in from the bedchamber. He was currently ensconced on a sofa before the fireside, his deerhound, Shadow, at his feet. "But you know what she's like. So that's nothing out of the ordinary."

"But how are her spirits?" Hamish fastened his cuffs and then his collar. He'd dismissed Hudson, opting to dress himself. After such a long journey, his valet needed time to refresh too. "You mentioned she wasn't eating."

"Well, she's less upset than she was initially . . ." said Angus. "When I first discovered what was going on between her and Brodie MacDonald—"

"And how did that happen, exactly?" Hamish fished out a linen cravat. "You didn't really say in your letter."

"I caught them kissing . . . in the library after my Latin

and mathematics lessons with MacDonald had ended. And after I'd sent him packing, Isobel confessed all to me. About how they'd fallen in love and wanted to marry in Dunmuir Kirk. But because you would probably be against the match, they were also thinking about eloping and marrying over the anvil."

They're damn right about that. Anger flashed through Hamish, and he nearly choked himself as he tied the knot on his cravat with rough movements.

Good God. Brodie MacDonald is a brazen scoundrel. He's lucky I don't call him out. Have him flayed. Castrated. Gutted. Minced into worm's meat—

"Honestly, I was so shocked, I didn't know what to do, so I wrote to you," continued Angus. "Of course, poor Mother was alarmed, too when she first found out what Isobel had been planning. However, while she agrees that it's not an ideal match given MacDonald's inferior birth, I'm afraid . . ."

"Go on." Hamish frowned at his reflection in the looking glass as he undid the neckcloth and started again. "How is Mother, by the way?"

"She's well enough . . . only . . . the problem is, Isobel has managed to persuade her that this match isn't entirely unsuitable."

Hamish's hands stilled. "What did you just say?"

He marched into the main bedchamber and pinned his younger brother with a hard-as-steel stare. Angus's vagueness about Isobel and the whole situation was making him very uneasy. "Stop equivocating. I asked you to speak plainly. What the hell is going on?"

Angus immediately leapt to his feet. "Now, now there's no need to get upset. If you'd just speak with Mama and Isobel, I think that you—"

Incredulity blasted through Hamish. "Don't tell me you have changed your mind too!"

Angus blushed redder than a lobster that had just been plunged into a cauldron of boiling water. He shifted uneasily from one booted foot to the other. "Look, you need to talk to

Isobel. And Mother. I've done all I can. I wrote to you. I dismissed MacDonald. I put every measure I could think of in place to ensure Isobel didn't run off and make the worst mistake of her life. Now it's up to you to sort out the rest."

With that, he gave a great harrumph and deposited himself on the sofa again.

Hamish crossed his arms and stared down at his younger brother. Guilt shredded his guts. Angus was right. It wasn't up to him to clear this mess up. Hamish sometimes forgot the lad was only seventeen.

Hamish softened his tone. "Of course. You've done well, Angus. And I will speak with Isobel and Mother. I just need to make sure Tilda's settled into the nursery first. It's been over a decade since Ellen Swan had any young charges in her care. If I need to arrange for one of the other younger maids to assist her, I'd rather know now. The last thing I need is more discord in my life."

Angus arched a brow. "I know it's not really any of my business and I shouldn't pry into your affairs, but I must say, I was more than a little surprised to see you arrive home with a ward and a wife. It all seems rather sudden."

Hamish sighed heavily and walked over to the mirror above the mantelpiece to finish tying his cravat. "Aye. It is." He glanced at Angus's reflection and caught his eye. "And just in case you're wondering, Tilda is not my wife's daughter."

"Oh . . . I never thought . . ." Angus blushed bright red all over again. "Olivia seems too young . . . Not that I mean anything by that. Although, I did wonder if—"

"Tilda might be mine?" finished Hamish. "To be perfectly honest, I don't know." And he described how the child had been dumped on his London doorstep and the contents of the note that accompanied her. "I tell you all this in strict confidence, though, Angus. I'd rather Mother and Isobel didn't know that poor wee Tilda might be my by-blow and that I have no idea who her mother is."

Angus nodded, his expression grave. "Does . . . does Olivia know?"

His cravat now tied, albeit sloppily, Hamish turned around to face his brother. "Aye. She does. Everything."

"And she doesn't mind?"

"No. Surprisingly she doesn't."

"She sounds like a very understanding young woman, then."

"Aye . . ." Hamish focused on adjusting one of his cuffs to avoid Angus's curious gaze. He wasn't ready to divulge how he'd met Olivia or how their marriage had come about. Because half of it would be lies.

The worst part was that most of the lies careening through his mind were ones he needed to tell himself. The litany crashed about in his head.

You don't care for Olivia.

You're not falling in love with her.

You feel nothing but lust.

And then there were the cold, harsh, altogether inconvenient but immutable truths.

When she inherits her fortune, it will be better if you set her free.

You could never be the husband she deserves.

She'll be happier without you.

However, it seemed that Angus would not be put off that easily in his quest to find out more about his new sister-in-law. "So, did you meet her in London?"

"Aye." Hamish retreated to the dressing room to dig out a waistcoat and jacket. He'd already donned his kilt and boots. "We have mutual friends." At least that wasn't a lie.

"Hamish, you know that Isobel and Mother will have even more questions for you. Particularly when you tell them both that Olivia is here to help Isobel in some capacity. They'll wonder what you mean. Even I'm wondering what you mean."

"I know." Hamish emerged from the dressing room. "I'm hoping that Olivia can help introduce Isobel to polite society next Season. In London."

Angus gave a snort. "I'm sorry," he said. "But poor Olivia is going to have a hard time of it then. You know Isobel would rather jump off Muircliff's battlements into the Minch than have a Season. Especially now she fancies herself in love with Brodie MacDonald."

Hamish arched a brow. "And I'd rather throw Brodie MacDonald into the Minch than see him marry our sister."

Angus grimaced. "Why is it that I think you're only half-joking, Hamish?"

"I don't make half jokes, lad. If Isobel doesn't heed my advice and look farther afield for a husband, she'd better hope that Mr. Brodie MacDonald can swim."

O livia discovered the nursery was conveniently located on the floor directly above her bedroom and Hamish's. The spacious chamber featured a pair of comfortable-looking beds made up with fresh linen and an abundance of fat pillows, thick carpets, several stuffed armchairs, windows with wonderful views of the sea, and, most importantly, lots of books and toys to keep Tilda amused. There was even a child-sized dining setting—a small round table and four matching chairs—set before the fireside.

Ellen Swan turned out to be a delightful woman of middling years with a warm disposition and a jolly, apple-cheeked smile. And Tilda took to her immediately. When Olivia and Hamish eventually bid the child farewell, she barely looked up from the doll's house she was playing with. Nurse Swan informed them that she would take good care of her; she'd order a dinner tray for Tilda and make sure she said her prayers before bed. Olivia also promised to return to bid Tilda good night.

"How strange to think Nurse Swan was once your nurse-maid, Hamish," observed Olivia as they began to descend the stairs to the floor below. "I can't quite imagine you as a little boy."

"I was an unholy terror, even back then," remarked Hamish, with a roguish grin.

Olivia smiled back. "Surely not."

"Aye. Ask Nurse Swan to tell you about the time I put frog spawn in her sago pudding."

Olivia gasped. "Hamish. That's terrible."

"Aye. And I deserved every one of those whacks she gave me with Cook's wooden spoon. I had the pinkest arse—I mean behind—for days."

Olivia bit her lip to suppress a laugh, and Hamish stopped on the landing, his hand on her arm.

"You shouldn't do that, you know," he said in a low voice.

"I'm sorry. What shouldn't I do?"

"Bite your lip."

Olivia's pulse rate kicked up a notch. "Why?"

"Because it makes me think sinful thoughts about you, lass." They commenced walking again, Hamish's hand at her elbow. "Indeed, the ever-present unholy terror lurking inside me might return and subject you to another one of my wholly wicked kisses."

A dark thrill flared inside Olivia. When she'd bitten her lip in the taproom of the Abington Arms, she hadn't failed to notice the smoldering heat in Hamish's gaze. "Well, if you're trying to discourage such behavior, my lord, I'm afraid your warning has failed miserably. Because I happen to like your wholly wicked kisses, I will be sure to bite my lip frequently."

There was a quicksilver flash in Hamish's eye, but she wasn't quite sure if the emotion was amusement. "Are you flirting with me, my lady?"

Even though a blush heated her cheeks, Olivia cast him a coquettish look from beneath her lashes. "Perhaps."

Hamish halted at the bottom of the stairs and turned to face her, his hands on his lean, kilted hips. His expression changed. Grew serious. "You know you're playing with fire, don't you?"

Pausing on the bottom step, Olivia gripped the newel-post and raised her chin. "Perhaps . . ."

"It's dangerous, Olivia. And I don't want to burn you."

"But what if I'm willing to take that risk?" she challenged. "You can't deny there's a spark between us. I can see the fire in your gaze every time you look at me. What if . . . what if I want this to be a real marriage? You can have me—"

"Believe me, you don't want that, Olivia. I'm simply not worth it." And with that he turned on his heel and marched down the hall with floor-eating strides, leaving her alone and confused and frustrated once more.

Evening was descending like a dismal and dark shroud as Hamish charged downstairs to Muircliff's library; it was the only space in the whole castle he felt somewhat at peace.

But then, perhaps it was because that's where he kept a stash of his favorite types of spirits. Once he reached the enormous chamber with its towering bookcases full of ancient, leather-clad tomes, he opened the glass-fronted cupboard beside his mahogany desk and reached for the decanter of whisky.

He really should seek out Isobel and pay his respects to their mother. But devil take him, before he did that, he also needed to down a dram or two to douse the fire searing through his veins. To try to banish the overwhelming urge to take his wife up on her invitation and have her over and over again, until she was crying his name to the heavens.

Driving rain lashed the diamond-paned windows, and the sea hurled itself against the cliffs below the castle with such force, Hamish didn't hear the door to the library snick open and his sister's approach until she called his name. Midway through pouring his first drink into a cut-crystal tumbler, he started and sloshed whisky over the oxblood leather blotter of his desk.

Damn. Wiping his hand on his kilt, he turned to face Isobel.

She hovered on the hearthrug, a picture of uncertainty as she pushed a lock of dark auburn hair behind her ear.

"Hamish . . . Angus told me you'd returned . . . that he'd written to you . . ." Her soft gray eyes traced over his face, and then her brow knit into a frown. "I'm sorry for upsetting you. It's such a long way to come, and I know how much you hate this place."

"Isobel, lass . . ." Now that his sister was here, the anger that had been simmering inside Hamish dissipated. "I had to come," he continued, his voice thick with emotion. "You and Angus and Mother mean the world to me. You know I'd do anything for you." He firmed his voice. "Even if that means I must be cruel in order to be kind. You deserve to wed a better man than Brodie MacDonald."

Isobel lifted her chin. "You don't know him. I love him, and he loves me—"

Hamish shook his head. "My dear sister. How can you know what true love really is? Just because an attractive young man pays you a wee bit of attention, it doesn't mean he's in love with you. You're nineteen years old, lass. You've hardly seen anything of the world. You've never had a Season. Your entire life has been spent here on Skye. Why throw away a chance at true, lasting happiness because some ne'er-do-well pays you pretty but meaningless compliments and pretends to make calf's eyes at you? And all the while he's probably got his sights set on your dowry?"

Anger flared in Isobel's eyes. "How dare you! Brodie's not pretending. He does love me. In any case, I don't see how you can pass judgment on whether the feelings we share are real or not. What do you know of love, Hamish MacQueen? Angus tells me you've suddenly wed some poor girl over the anvil who's barely older than me. You can't tell me that's a love match, can you? Angus thinks you must have compromised her—or got her pregnant—and your sense of honor compelled you to do the right thing."

Hamish bristled. "No, I didn't compromise her. And no, she's not with child. Olivia is an heiress. Her father, who was a wealthy arms manufacturer, passed away five years ago, and when she turns twenty-five she stands to inherit an absolute fortune."

"So you're telling me you married her for her money?" Isobel arched a delicate brow. "Unless you've suddenly developed some terrible gambling habit no one knows about, I don't believe that either."

Dear God. What could he possibly say that would make any sense? He'd have to resort to half-truths and being a bombastic ass. "I care for Olivia," he said. "And what I do is none of your business, Isobel. Or anyone else's."

"You care for her," Isobel said in a flat tone that spoke of her skepticism. "What an entirely prosaic, lukewarm declaration. I also care about my mare, Epona, my new capote bonnet, and whether my cup of tea is hot. You're not half-hearted about anything that you do, Hamish. Something's going on, and I want to know what it is."

Hamish forced himself to unclench his back teeth. "Olivia is a lovely young woman who's well connected. She can assist you with making your debut next Season. It will be an opportunity for you to meet—"

Isobel gave a derisive, completely unladylike snort of laughter. "My debut? Now I know what the problem is. You've gone mad." She took a few ungainly steps toward him, her left foot dragging across the Turkish hearthrug. "Look at me, Hamish. I mean *really* look at me. You know I don't want a debut. I never have and never will. I could think of nothing worse than limping through the ton's ballrooms and Almack's. Being stared at, and whispered about, and laughed at. Or, worse, looked upon with pity."

"It wouldn't be like that. Look at me, for God's sake." Hamish pointed at the mangled side of his face. "This has never stopped me from entering a ton ballroom. You're my sister and—"

"Now you're the one who's being naive, Hamish. Of course it would be like that. I may be Lady Isobel Mac-Queen, but that will hardly signify when all anyone will notice is my clubfoot. Aside from that, I love Muircliff. I love the Isle of Skye. I don't want to live somewhere else. And I don't want to leave Mama."

"Ha! So that's the real reason you're settling for someone like MacDonald." Cynicism sharpened Hamish's tone. "And I'm sure he's more than happy to set up home with you here at Muircliff."

"No! That's not . . . just stop it, Hamish." Isobel pressed a hand to her forehead and closed her eyes for a moment. "Stop twisting everything I say. Look . . . I don't want to argue with you anymore. Not tonight when you've just arrived home with your new bride. Oh, and your ward whom you've said nothing about as well. But I suppose that's a discussion for another time." She huffed out an exasperated sigh. "I just wish you would think on all I've said. And that you'll consider meeting with Brodie. Hear what he has to say."

Hamish hardened his gaze. "You can give me reproachful looks and sigh all you like, Isobel. I won't change my mind about this."

A steely light entered Isobel's eyes. "And neither will I. You're lucky Brodie and I didn't decide to wed over the anvil weeks and weeks ago. But both of us wanted a regular church wedding. Brodie's brother is Dunmuir Kirk's minister after all."

Damn her and her stubbornness. Hamish could feel a megrim beginning to penetrate the base of his skull. Why was his life suddenly dominated by females giving him boundless grief all at once?

Despite his headache, he had the sudden urge to get soused. If he were in London, he could visit the Pandora Club and try to forget all his woes by losing himself in all manner of nefarious activities—drinking, gaming, and whoring, and not necessarily in that order.

His marriage was one of convenience only, and men in his position took mistresses to bed all the time. He'd kept mistresses in the past. Four years was a long time to forgo sexual congress until he and Olivia parted ways. Except, could he do that to the lass? Go behind her back and swive other women? Would he even find it satisfying?

Oh, dear God. Could it be that he didn't actually want to bed anyone else *but* his wife?

Pushing the disturbing thought away, Hamish picked up his glass and swallowed a large, soothing gulp of whisky. "How is Mama? Angus says she's well at the moment."

"She is . . ." Isobel's brow pleated into a frown. "Will you visit her this evening? She'll dine in her rooms as usual, but she'd very much like to see you and hear all about your news."

Hamish nodded. "Aye. I will." He wasn't relishing the idea of having to describe how he'd suddenly come by a wife and a ward. He hoped his mother would take his explanations at face value even if Isobel and Angus hadn't.

And then, of course, he'd have to tackle the difficult subject of Isobel's ill-advised love affair. He'd have to tread carefully though. He was loath to shock or worry their mother and cause her undue emotional stress.

God knew, she'd endured enough of that to last a lifetime.

CHAPTER 15

Almost fainting with terror, she had yet sufficient command over herself, to check the shriek, that was escaping from her lips, and, letting the curtain drop from her hand, continued to observe in silence the motions of the mysterious form she saw. It seemed to glide along the remote obscurity of the apartment, then paused, and, as it approached the hearth, she perceived, in the stronger light, what appeared to be a human figure.

Ann Radcliffe, The Mysteries of Udolpho

Muircliff Castle, Isle of Skye

September 25, 1818

Olivia woke to the sound of the wind and waves battering the castle and flames licking the logs in the gray marble fireplace in her room. A chambermaid had obviously slipped in while she was sleeping to relight the fire, and she was glad of it. Muircliff—perhaps because of its exposed aspect atop a cliff, and the fact that they were so far north—was a cold residence indeed.

Pushing herself up against the pillows of her enormous tester bed, Olivia yawned and brushed her tangled hair from her eyes. She had no idea what time it was, but she suspected she'd slept late. Despite the fact that the long journey north had been exhausting, her mind wouldn't rest,

and she'd tossed and turned most of the night until fatigue
eventually claimed her sometime in the small hours. Even
then she'd been troubled by odd dreams.

One in particular stood out in her mind. It had seemed
so very real and was altogether unsettling. At one point,
Olivia could have sworn there was someone in her bedchamber.

Although the fire had all but died and the room was
poorly lit, a dark ghostly figure—a female wearing a black
mourning gown and heavy lace veil—drifted across the
carpeted floor toward her bed. As the figure hovered by the
carved oak footboard in watchful silence, Olivia's throat
had constricted in terror. But before she could scream, the
mysterious wraith seemed to melt completely into the dark
shadows cast by the bed canopy and its heavy velvet
hangings.

Now Olivia didn't know what to make of her nightmare.
The vision she'd seen couldn't have been real . . . although
the lingering feeling of uneasiness inside her certainly was.

The rosy glow of the fire and a gray shaft of morning
light penetrating a chink in the curtains revealed that everything in her room appeared to be in its place. No
figure—real or imagined—lurked in any of the shadowy
corners as far as she could see. The jib door between her
room and Hamish's was firmly shut. She supposed all of
the gothic novels she'd been reading of late, such as *The
Mysteries of Udolpho*, had made her as fanciful as Catherine Morland in *Northanger Abbey*. Or perhaps it had been
Tilda's comment on their arrival about ghosts that had put
the idea in her head.

Olivia rose, and after ringing for a maid, she wrapped
herself in her cashmere shawl, then crossed to the nearest
window. Drawing back the dusky blue damask curtains,
she then lowered herself onto the window seat to take in the
magnificent view. However, her mind was as troubled as
the wind-tossed sea stretching toward the pewter gray
clouds on the horizon.

Just like last night when she'd tried in vain to fall asleep, thoughts of Hamish and the disastrous state of their marriage had tumbled about in her mind. After he'd stormed away from her following their visit to the nursery, she hadn't seen him at all. And she was partly to blame. When Mrs. Boyd appeared to help settle her into her new bedroom, she'd informed Olivia that dinner would be served at seven o'clock should she care to join Lord Sleat and Lord Angus in the downstairs dining room.

But Olivia, in a fit of pique, decided she wouldn't go. She was so very tired of being rebuffed by Hamish. The fact that Mrs. Boyd had delivered his invitation to dinner spoke volumes. So she'd politely but firmly declined, opting instead to visit the nursery and share Tilda's meal of coddled eggs, toast, cock-a-leekie soup, and poached pears in custard.

If her husband wanted to spend time with her, she'd reasoned, he could jolly well issue his invitation in person. And if he didn't believe the message she had asked Mrs. Boyd to relay back to him—that she was concerned about how Tilda was settling in at the castle so she wanted to spend the evening in the nursery—well, too bad for him.

However, this morning, sadness suffused Olivia's heart. How lowering that she and Hamish had been married less than a week, yet her husband eschewed her company both in and out of bed. In all her life, she'd never felt lonelier than she did right at this moment.

Her gaze strayed to the elegantly papered wall panel beside the fireplace and its well-concealed door. Last night she hadn't even bothered to check whether it was still unlocked. Hamish wouldn't visit her chamber, and she was too miffed to visit him.

Although, in the end, before she retired for the evening, she softened a little and asked Hudson to organize a few small things that she thought might improve the quality of Hamish's sleep. It was an olive branch of sorts, an apology for snubbing him.

But had Hamish even noticed her absence? Perhaps he was relieved she hadn't come to dinner.

Olivia sighed. Moping about in her room all day, lamenting the fact that she'd been a crosspatch last night, worrying about what Hamish may or may not be thinking, none of these things would do her any good. She could visit Tilda in the nursery, or pen letters to her friends, and although she was a little nervous about how she would be received, she was looking forward to meeting Hamish's sister, Isobel. And at some point, she needed to speak with Mrs. Boyd about selecting a lady's maid. She had more than enough things to do to keep her from dwelling on the widening gulf between her and Hamish.

When Hudson pulled back the curtains in his master's bedchamber, Hamish turned his head away from the window and groaned. He really didn't want to face the day. For once he'd managed to sleep like a log, and it hadn't been because he'd consumed a wine cellar's worth of alcohol.

He didn't like to think the chamomile tea Olivia had suggested he drink before bed might have helped, because it made him feel foolish that he hadn't tried such a simple remedy before. In fact, he had been dubious as hell when Hudson had first produced a pot of the pale yellow brew that smelled like something a woman would use to scent the flimsy undergarments in her armoire. Of course, he'd also been weary to the bone from traveling for days and days with little to no sleep, so in the end, perhaps it was just pure exhaustion that had won out.

In any event, Hamish couldn't recall waking during the night, a rare occurrence indeed. Or having a nightmare. Although he did have one particularly vivid, very erotic dream about Olivia. He'd been making love to her in this very bed. He'd undressed her slowly, revealing her luscious hips, those slender legs, her satiny skin, her round-as-pomegranate breasts . . .

Hamish groaned again. Just recalling the dream was producing a rampant, throbbing cockstand. He rolled over and then swore beneath his breath when he encountered a damp patch on the bedsheets. What the bloody hell? Had he come in the night like a sexually frustrated adolescent boy?

It would seem so. He supposed it had been weeks since he'd had a woman or even come off by his own hand. It was bound to happen sooner or later. Especially given the fact that he was in lust with Olivia but refused to take her to bed. He wouldn't risk getting her pregnant. If she produced a male heir, or a daughter, she wouldn't want to leave; she'd stay for the sake of the child. She'd be stuck with him—a deeply flawed man—in an unfulfilling marriage forever. He couldn't think of anything worse for a starry-eyed young woman who desired a love match.

Of course there were measures Hamish could take to prevent conception if he bedded his wife. Indeed, he used French letters whenever he had casual sexual intercourse with prostitutes or even wealthy women from the ranks of the ton. Only a fool would risk contracting some horrific disease like the pox. But he didn't want to cheapen the sexual act by using a condom with his wife. And withdrawal was not always a reliable method to prevent pregnancy. So abstinence was the only solution.

It seemed that being sexually frustrated would be his lot in life for some time to come.

Hudson started making noises in the dressing room, so Hamish supposed he should rise and get dressed. He needed to meet with his steward, go through a massive pile of correspondence, deal with his recalcitrant sister and his entirely too-tempting wife, who suddenly seemed set on avoiding him. Not that he could blame her. He'd been so contrary of late—behaving like a lustful brute one minute and then a cantankerous killjoy the next—even he was starting to become annoyed with himself.

Once he'd hauled himself out of bed, he snagged a banyan off the bedside chair and then wrapped it around his naked body. And that's when something caught his eye. Something peeking out from beneath his pillow. Reaching for it, Hamish pulled out a small nosegay of dried lavender tied with a purple ribbon.

"Hudson," he called. "What's this? Why do I have flowers under my pillow?"

His valet emerged from the dressing room. "Oh." His cheeks reddened, and Hamish cocked an eyebrow. Hudson had once been a sergeant in His Majesty's army. He never blushed.

"Well?" Hamish prompted.

"Yer wife asked me to place it there, my lord. She thought the scent of lavender might help ye sleep. And as I didna think it would do any harm . . ." Hudson shrugged a shoulder.

"Hmph. Right." Hamish rather thought he'd prefer to be lulled to sleep by the scent of violets and vanilla and sexually pleasured woman. But as that would never happen, lavender would have to do.

The words of the lullaby Olivia had sung to Tilda floated into his mind.

Lavender's blue, dilly dilly. Rosemary's green . . .

What a beautiful voice the lass had. He'd missed her company at dinner last night. But he understood her need to mother Tilda. It was within her nature to care for others. Even in London when they'd first met, she'd gone out of her way to rescue that persistently mischievous cat she was minding.

And last night, she'd sent him tea. No one had ever thought to do that for him before, and he was immeasurably touched. That sweet ache in the vicinity of his chest had started up again.

Was this what Nate and Gabriel had experienced when they fell in love? This terrifying tenderness that threatened to unman a fellow? To overthrow any and all convictions one had to remain indifferent and invulnerable?

Once attired in his preferred garb of kilt, boots, cambric shirt, and simply tied cravat, Hamish tucked the lavender posy into the pocket of his waistcoat before sliding on his coat of navy blue wool. Just on a whim. Not because it meant anything. It wasn't a precious keepsake like the ones Olivia kept in her memento box. To think a hard-as-flint, battle-scarred Highlander like him would do anything that was remotely romantic or sentimental was ludicrous.

Examining his reflection in the mirror to check that his leather eye patch was properly in place, Hamish looked himself in his one good eye and grimaced.

It seemed the lies he was determined to tell himself were becoming more preposterous by the day.

As soon as Olivia set foot in the nursery, Tilda squealed with excitement, dropped her honeyed crumpet onto her fine china plate, and rushed over to throw her chubby arms about Olivia's legs.

"Och, Tilda, lassie. You'll make her ladyship's skirts all mucky wi' yer sticky fingers," admonished Nurse Swan.

Olivia ruffled Tilda's curls. "It's quite all right. I don't mind."

Nurse Swan smiled. "Verra well. Would ye like to sit a wee while and take tea? I can ring down to the kitchen fer a pot of oolong. The mistress willna mind."

The mistress? Did Nurse Swan mean Lady Isobel? Of course, even though Hamish's younger sister was only nineteen, it was only natural that she would have assumed the role of mistress at Muircliff. She would let the nurse's slip of the tongue slide. "That would b-be just lovely," she replied with an inclination of her head.

Taking Tilda by the hand, Olivia returned to the table by the fire. It was a small setting of polished cherrywood with four dainty chairs, just perfect for a younger child like Tilda. Olivia carefully lowered herself onto a seat opposite her former charge. In a chair to Olivia's left sat a lovely china doll with big blue eyes and blond ringlets. The doll was perched upon several cushions, and the skirts of her elegant lace gown had been arranged very carefully.

"Her name is Mia," Tilda said gravely. Addressing the doll, Tilda continued, "And, Mia, this is Lady Livvie. Now you must use your manners and curtsy." She lifted the doll and made her perform a little dip upon the tabletop among a miniature china tea set, a jug of milk, and a plate of crumpets. "Just like that."

Olivia smiled and tilted her head in greeting. "I'm very pleased to meet you, Miss Mia." She caught Nurse Swan's attention. The woman had settled in one of the window seats and had picked up a needle and thread to mend one of Tilda's dresses. "I trust everything is going well?"

"Aye, my lady. After ye left, Tilda went to sleep straightaway and I heard no' a peep out of her. She is a verra well-behaved lassie. Bright as a button too. Just like my Lady Isobel used to be."

"I'm pleased to hear it." Olivia was tempted to ask her about Hamish's childish escapades after yesterday's disclosure, but perhaps tales of sago pudding laced with frog spawn and other similar instances of tomfoolery weren't fitting for Tilda's innocent young ears.

Tilda tugged on her sleeve and beckoned Olivia closer. "Does Lady Isobel like black dresses, Lady Livvie?" she whispered.

The hair at the back of Olivia's neck prickled. "I . . . I don't know," she replied softly. She glanced over at Nurse Swan, but her attention was focused on repairing the hem of Tilda's gown. "I haven't met her yet."

Tilda nodded. A small crease appeared between her brows. "There was a lady who came to visit last night. After Nurse Swan fell 'sleep." She lowered her voice to a whisper. "She snores like Lord Sleat . . . I mean Nurse Swan, not the lady in black." Tilda's bottom lip wobbled. "I didn't like the strange lady, Livvie. I couldn't see her face. I wondered if she might be Morag, the witch from the woods in your story."

Oh, my goodness. Tilda had seen the strange figure too. So it hadn't been a dream. Not prone to flights of fancy, Olivia doubted it was a ghost. Hamish had mentioned that his sister was very upset when Lord Angus had driven her suitor away. Had Lady Isobel taken to wearing black? But how very peculiar and unnerving that she should creep into Olivia's bedroom and Tilda's while they were sleeping. An icy shiver trickled its way down Olivia's spine.

But she didn't want to alarm Tilda, so she smiled gently and said, "It was probably just Lady Isobel who'd come to say hello but she discovered that you were asleep. I'll make sure that both of us meet her this afternoon. Do you think that would be all right?"

Tilda nodded and smiled. "Yes. I'd like that."

There was a light rap at the door, and Nurse Swan looked up from her sewing. "'Tis aboot time someone came to see wha' I wanted," she grumbled. "There isna tha' many stairs to climb to the nursery." Her shoulders rose and fell on an irritated sigh before she tersely uttered, "Weel, come in then."

But instead of a maid or a footman, it was Hamish who appeared in the doorway.

Olivia's breath caught. She hadn't expected to see him at all this morning. When her breakfast tray had arrived in her room, the maid informed her that Lord Sleat was in the library, meeting with his steward about estate business and attending to correspondence.

"My lord." Nurse Swan rose and curtsied. Her plump cheeks had turned as rosy as apples. "I didna ken it was you. If I did, I wouldna have been so rude. What can I do for ye?"

"I came to see how wee Tilda is faring this morning," he said, approaching the small table. His gaze connected with Olivia's. "And my wife."

"Och, weel . . ." The flustered nursemaid bobbed into another curtsy. "If ye will excuse me, my lord, I need to chase up a pot o' tea fer her ladyship."

"Of course," replied Hamish. "Tea sounds perfect."

As the door shut behind Nurse Swan, Hamish gestured at the empty chair at the table. "Do you mind if I join you, my fair ladies?"

"I . . . I mean we would be most delighted. Wouldn't we, Tilda?" said Olivia. "Only . . ." She nodded toward another larger chair by the fireside. "Perhaps you might be more comfortable if you chose a different seat, my lord."

"Och, no. There's no need."

To Olivia's utter astonishment, Hamish pulled out the remaining tiny chair, flipped out his coat, and then lowered his substantial yet lean frame onto the silk-upholstered seat. Because his muscular legs were so long, his kilt rode up a little and his bare knees bumped the table.

Tilda giggled, and Olivia had to bite back a laugh too.

"Good heavens, what on earth is so amusing?" asked Hamish, cocking an eyebrow.

"You're too big." Tilda's eyes sparkled with mirth.

"Ah, but I'm also strong. And that's because I drink all my milk." With that Hamish picked up the jug and carefully poured a small amount into one of the miniature china teacups. "Would you care for some, Miss Tilda?" He glanced at Olivia. "My lady?"

Tilda nodded and giggled again. "And some for Miss Mia, too, please." She pushed forward a cup for the doll.

"Of course."

After they were all armed with tiny cups of milk, Hamish took a dainty sip and declared it was delicious.

"You seem in good spirits this morning, my lord," remarked Olivia as they watched Tilda reach for her half-eaten crumpet.

"Aye." Hamish's wide mouth lifted in a rare genuine smile. "And I believe I have you to thank for that, lass. The chamomile tea worked wonders, and I had the best sleep I've had in Lord knows how long."

"Oh . . ." Olivia felt a flush of pleasure warm her cheeks. "I'm so very pleased to hear that."

"And I trust you slept well too . . ."

Olivia fiddled with the tiny handle of her teacup. "To be honest, not really." She offered a weak smile. "I had a restless night. I suppose I'm not used to the sound of the sea yet." She didn't want to admit she'd been fretting about their marriage. Or that she'd had an odd visitation in the night, lest Hamish think she'd gone mad.

Hamish nodded. "I'm sure you will grow accustomed to it." He paused and took another sip of milk. "Actually, now that I've found you up here in the nursery, I'd like to speak with you about a particular matter or two. Nothing too serious."

Olivia's curiosity stirred. "Yes?"

"I'd like to introduce you to my sister, if I may. You and Tilda. She would like to meet you both. Very much. And I'm pleased to report she's in much better spirits than she was when Angus first wrote to me."

Olivia smiled. "I'm glad to hear it. I would love to meet Lady Isobel too."

"Excellent. I think Isobel is arranging an afternoon tea in the drawing room for us all at three o'clock."

"I look forward to it. And is there anything else you wish to discuss?"

"Aye. There is . . ." Hamish cast a look Tilda's way before his gaze returned to Olivia's. "I just received a letter via a courier this morning. I'm afraid the inquiry agent my man of affairs employed in London has not had any luck whatsoever in finding out about a certain someone's parentage. Of course, the agent has only just begun his search, so it's early days yet. But I'd rather hoped that because you've been spending so much time with Tilda of late, you might pick up another clue or two that would help. As I've said before, even the tiniest crumb of information could help."

Olivia nodded. "I haven't heard anything new," she said. "But I will keep my ears open."

Hamish smiled. "Thank you."

Nurse Swan returned with Daniels bearing a tray containing all the trappings required for tea making, and Olivia was soon busy dispensing grown-up-sized cups for Hamish and herself.

The oolong tea was lovely and Hamish's company lively. As Olivia watched him push Tilda on the old painted rocking horse by one of the windows, she marveled at how different he seemed today. Cheerful and playful rather than brooding. His ready smiles and deep chuckles were a soothing balm for her own spirits.

Had a simple cup of chamomile tea and a good night's sleep wrought such a change?

Olivia had no idea, but it gave her a glimmer of hope for the future. Hamish maintained he didn't want sexual relations with her because he didn't want to get her with child—that he never wanted children, not even a male heir—but seeing how wonderful he was with Tilda, Olivia was more than a little curious and doubly perplexed.

And still more than a little determined to find out why his conviction to remain fatherless was so steadfastly set in stone. Olivia could only hope that Lady Isobel might give her greater insight into the inner workings of Hamish's mercurial mind.

CHAPTER 16

Even broken in spirit as he is, no one can feel more deeply than he does the beauties of nature. The starry sky, the sea, and every sight afforded by these wonderful regions, seem still to have the power of elevating his soul from earth.

Mary Shelley, Frankenstein; or, The Modern
Prometheus

When Hamish came to escort Olivia down to Muircliff's drawing room, she felt as if her stomach was churning even more than the constantly roiling sea below her bedroom window. How would the sister of a marquess look upon her—a shy, stammering interloper, the daughter of an erstwhile army captain turned arms manufacturer? She might be an heiress, but she really was someone of little consequence within the eyes of the ton. At least that's what her aunt Edith always told her. Charlie, Arabella, and Sophie wouldn't agree, of course, but they knew and loved her.

She just prayed Lady Isobel would be inclined to get to know her rather than dismissing her outright. Because if she didn't establish a rapport with Hamish's sister, how on earth was she, Olivia, to fulfill her promise to Hamish? It would be difficult indeed to help Isobel overcome her heartache and assist with her debut next Season if they didn't form some kind of amicable if not affectionate bond.

"H-how do I look?" Olivia observed Hamish's face

anxiously. She hadn't had time to meet with Mrs. Boyd about selecting a lady's maid, so she'd dressed and styled her hair herself. She supposed she could have rung for a chambermaid to help, but when she had gone to her room to prepare, it had all seemed like too much bother.

Now, as she fiddled with the lackluster curls framing her face and fretted over whether her mulberry wool gown was stylish enough and not too crumpled, she decided she really should have called for assistance.

However, as Hamish's gaze raked over her and she detected an appreciative gleam in his eye, she knew that her husband approved of what he saw at least. "You look very well, lass. But then you always do."

"Thank you," she replied. "I'm not usually one to fish for compliments. I just want to make a good impression."

"Olivia." Hamish drew close and lifted her chin with gentle fingers. "You are a beautiful young woman with the warmest smile and the kindest heart. Of course you are going to make a good impression. In fact, I predict Isobel is going to adore you."

"I hope so."

He touched his chest. "I'm more than a wee bit hurt that you doubt me."

Olivia frowned. "I can't help it. For such a long time I've b-been looked down upon. Well, except for those few people who are close to me. It's hard for strangers to see beyond my halting speech. I see the pity or disdain in their eyes whenever my tongue gets tied in knots and I can't get the words out."

"You're not stammering much now."

She smiled shyly. "That's because I'm getting to know you. The more time I spend with someone, the less likely it is that I'll stammer."

Understanding lit Hamish's gaze. "It might help you to know that Isobel feels a little like you when she first meets someone new."

Olivia gave him a quizzical look. "Does she have a stammer as well?"

Hamish shook his head. "No. She has a pronounced limp. You see . . . she was born with a clubfoot."

"Oh . . ." Olivia frowned. "Is it . . . is the condition painful?"

"No, I don't believe so. But, like you, Isobel thinks others will judge her and find her wanting. That's part of the reason why she's reluctant to have a London Season. But, just like you, she's pretty and accomplished and has a loyal, sweet nature. Any man would be lucky to have her as his wife."

Yet you don't feel lucky to have me. Olivia dropped her gaze away from Hamish's as the self-indulgent, bitter thought entered her mind. Aloud she said, "Yes. It certainly sounds that way. I only hope that I convince her that's the case too."

M uircliff's drawing room was located on the first floor, not far from Hamish's library. Like most of the main rooms at the castle, lead-paned windows afforded one with spectacular views of the ever-changing sea and sky. This afternoon, bruise-colored clouds had rolled in, obliterating what little sunshine there had been earlier in the day. The turbulent sea had turned a sullen shade of dark gray.

But it wasn't the seascape that Olivia noticed. It was the elegant young woman sitting before the fire upon a burgundy damask settee. A lavish afternoon tea was laid out upon the low oak table before her—an array of tiny cakes, pastries, and delicate sandwiches sat upon fine Wedgwood china plates, and a silver urn and teapot gleamed in the bright firelight.

Attired in a lovely peacock blue gown that was the perfect foil for her perfectly styled dark red hair, Lady Isobel MacQueen lifted her wide mouth into a welcoming smile as Hamish escorted Olivia over to the fireside.

Rising to her feet, she took both of Olivia's hands in hers and gave them a gentle squeeze as Hamish conducted the introductions.

"I must confess, I've been dying to meet you, my lady,"

Lady Isobel remarked, gesturing to Olivia and Hamish to take a seat on the settee near hers. She reclaimed her own seat and smoothed out her skirts with pale, slender fingers. "Ever since you arrived late yesterday and our other brother, Angus, told me Hamish had arrived with a wife."

Olivia drew a bracing breath, praying she wouldn't stutter too badly. "Please, c-call me, O-Olivia," she said, mentally wincing at her less-than-smooth speech. "As we are now sis-sisters, I would like nothing m-more." She couldn't detect any shock or derision in the younger woman's clear gray eyes. Not for the moment, anyway.

Isobel's answering smile was warm. "I would be most honored," she said, reaching out to lay a hand on Olivia's arm. "And please, you must call me Isobel. I'm not one for using titles to address dear friends and family. I eschew stuffiness of any kind."

"I'm pleased to hear it."

As Isobel dispensed tea according to everyone's preferences, Olivia studied her. Surely this lovely young woman wasn't the person who'd entered her room and Tilda's last night. And then she recalled what Hamish had told her. Isobel limped. But the figure Olivia had seen drifted across the floor like a ghost.

She was just taking her first sip of tea when Nurse Swan arrived with Tilda. Hamish introduced his ward to his sister, and Tilda, as she'd done with Angus, dipped into a neat little curtsy, which earned an exclamation of delight from Isobel. Once Tilda had carefully selected a small plate of treats, and Nurse Swan had installed her in a nearby armchair, Isobel turned to Olivia and said, "I hope you don't mind my asking, Olivia, but I'd love to hear more about how you and my brother came to meet. And marry."

Olivia caught her husband shooting a not-so-subtle scowl at his sister for being so nosy, but she was ready with an answer. Fortunately, as she and Hamish had made their way to the drawing room, they'd discussed what their story would be should Isobel ask. It lay somewhere between the truth and fiction.

"We . . . we were Grosvenor Square neighbors. My guardian and uncle, Reginald de Vere, leases the town house next door to Sleat House. And we also have several mutual friends." Olivia briefly explained the connections between Charlie, Sophie, and Arabella, and Hamish's friends Lord Malverne and Lord Langdale.

Isobel replenished her cup of tea. "And so you two wed in Gretna Green?"

"Yes . . ." Olivia forced herself to smile and took another calming breath. Given that Hamish's feet had been hitherto firmly planted in the not-of-the-marrying-kind bachelors' camp, it was only natural and inevitable that his family would be curious about the circumstances surrounding their unexpected union. "You see, I'm not quite twenty-one and my uncle and aunt wished me to wed a man of their choosing, a man I hold no affection for and did not want to marry. But as I knew of . . . I mean knew Hamish through our shared acquaintances, well, he stepped in and offered for my hand instead. However, as I'm not of age, we decided to wed in Gretna Green on the way here."

Isobel clapped her hands together. "Oh, how romantic. My brother was your knight in shining armor." She pinned Hamish with a knowing look. "Now, why doesn't that surprise me?"

Hamish shifted uncomfortably in his seat. "I'm not sure if that's the most apt description, Isobel. If you read the scandal rags, I'm generally not known for my chivalry, especially where the fairer sex is concerned."

His sister waved away his comment. "Oh, pooh. You don't give yourself enough credit, Hamish." She turned her attention to Olivia. "I could tell you about half a dozen instances—at the very least—when my brother has leapt into the fray to save someone. Why, even his rush back to Muircliff on this occasion, misguided though it is, is another perfect example—"

"Now, Isobel . . ." Hamish warned. "You know why I had to come back. Brodie MacDonald is not—"

At that moment, the heavy oak door to the drawing

room opened, admitting Lord Angus. "So sorry to interrupt, everyone."

Hamish turned in his seat. "What is it, Angus? Have you come to pilfer some afternoon tea?"

"Actually, Hamish, I can pinch your share because Mr. MacArthur and the stonemason, Mr. Isaacson, need to speak with you about some of the more urgent repairs on the south tower before the rain sets in again. They're waiting in the courtyard."

Hamish sighed and got to his feet. "Och, it seems there's no rest for the wicked. My apologies, ladies." Turning to Olivia, he added, "Mr. MacArthur is my steward, and unfortunately the repairs can't wait. One of the walls is in danger of crumbling."

Olivia frowned. "That doesn't sound very safe." She recalled the scarred wall she'd glimpsed on their approach to the castle yesterday. "You'll be careful, won't you?"

Hamish shrugged. "The tower fell into disrepair some years ago. It's just the elements here"—he nodded at the windows—"have wrought havoc on the remains, and I've neglected to do anything about it until now."

"Hamish will be fine," said Isobel.

"Aye," agreed Angus, taking the seat his brother had just vacated. His deerhound, Shadow, perhaps sensing Tilda might drop something, took up a position by her chair. "And, Hamish, we'll look after Olivia and Tilda in your absence, won't we, dear sister?"

Hamish pointed an admonitory finger at his siblings, but there was a gleam of amusement in his eye. "Please be on your best behavior, you two. I'll not have you offending my wife, or worse, scaring her off by asking her too many questions or telling her terrible tales about me." He winked at Olivia. "I'll be back as soon as I can."

Hamish needn't have worried, as Olivia soon discovered that Isobel and Angus were delightful company. They both seemed to go out of their way to make Olivia and Tilda feel welcome. When everyone had had their fill of afternoon tea, Isobel suggested they teach Tilda how to play spillikins. The child had drifted down to the hearthrug and was currently lavishing Shadow with pats and cuddles.

"Ordinarily I'd propose we all go for a walk outside rather than play parlor games. There's a courtyard with a lovely knot garden on the east side of the castle, but the weather has taken a turn for the worse." Isobel scowled at the view beyond the windows. "Just look at that rain. It's simply coming down in sheets."

"Spillikins?" Angus pulled a face. "Where's the fun in that?" He rubbed his hands together. "I think it would be far more exciting if we played hide-and-seek. What say you, Miss Tilda?"

Tilda nodded eagerly. "Can Shadow play too?"

"If you can get him to move away from the fire, he can help you and Nurse Swan find everyone when it's your turn to look," suggested Angus.

Tilda clapped her hands. "Hooray!"

Olivia smiled. "I think it sounds like a marvelous idea. Will we keep to this floor of the castle though? I'm afraid I might get lost otherwise."

"Yes, I think that's a good idea," said Isobel. "We'll be hunting each other for hours if we can hide anywhere at all."

Nurse Swan approached Tilda and held out her hand. "If ye dinna mind, Miss Tilda and I might do the seeking first. This morning I was teaching the wee one to count, so this will be a verra good opportunity to practice." She smiled down at her charge. "Do ye think ye can count to ten with me?"

Tilda nodded. "Can I use my fingers to help?"

"Aye."

Angus stood. "Good heavens. You mean I have to find a place to hide before you reach the number ten, Miss Tilda?"

She nodded. "Yes."

Nurse Swan winked. "We'll practice a few times before we start searching fer you, Lord Angus. I ken ye are starting to get a wee bit slow in yer old age."

Angus grinned. "Perfect. I'm ready if everyone else is."

At Nurse Swan's prompting, Tilda began to count to ten on her fingers, "One . . . two . . ." and Isobel, Angus, and Olivia all headed for the drawing room door.

Upon reaching the gallery outside, Angus bolted off. "Good luck, you two," he called over his shoulder.

Isobel rolled her eyes. "Good heavens. Anyone would think he's seven years old, not seventeen." Turning back to Olivia she said, "You might have noticed that I have a limp. So, unlike my brother, I'm not going far." She nodded at the next oak-paneled doorway only a little farther along the gallery. "In fact, I think I might hide in the dining room next door." She moved off and then, like Angus, called over her shoulder, "Good luck, Olivia," before disappearing.

Left alone in the gloomy gallery—the servants hadn't yet lit the candles in the wall sconces—Olivia looked this way and that. She hadn't been on a tour of the castle yet, so she really had no idea where any of the halls led to or what was behind any of the doors, even on this floor.

Tilda's high voice floated through the ajar drawing room door. She was on her second recitation of counting to ten. "Five . . . six . . ."

Olivia smiled. She wanted to stay and listen to Tilda. But in the spirit of the game, she really needed to find a hidey-hole, and quickly.

Deciding to head in the opposite direction of Angus, she lifted up her mulberry wool skirts and rushed down the gallery. But as soon as she turned a corner into another hallway, she barreled straight into a hard, muscular wall that emitted a rather human-sounding "oof."

Hamish.

He grasped her by the shoulders and held her away from him. "Oh, God. Olivia. Is everything all right?" Concern was etched into his every feature as his gaze traced over her face.

Pausing to draw breath, she nodded. She'd been winded a little too. "Yes . . . I'm . . . I mean, we're playing hide-and-seek. And I'm looking for somewhere to hide." She frowned, taking in her husband's disheveled appearance; he was coatless, his cambric shirt and satin waistcoat were damp and clinging to his skin, and his hair dripped in his eyes. "You're wet. And why do you smell like lavender?"

"I got caught in the rain," he said as if that explained everything. "But that doesn't matter." Hamish laced his fingers through hers and grinned. "I know the perfect place to hide. This way."

A bit farther along the hall, there was another wide set of oak doors, which he tugged her through . . . into a magnificent library. But Olivia barely had any time to take in the beauty and majesty of the bookcases or the massive stone fireplace at one end, as Hamish was leading her across the thick Turkish rug toward an ornate mahogany desk.

"We could hide behind the curtains. In the window seat," she suggested as they swept past a tall arched window, the type one might see in a cathedral.

"No . . . I know somewhere better."

They rounded the desk, pausing before a triptych of hunting tapestries on the wall behind it. Hamish reached out to touch the oak wainscoting between two of the hangings and pressed something. And then a jib door in the paneling snicked open.

"In here," murmured Hamish, drawing her into a round turret room. Light filtered into the stone chamber through a pair of narrow, curtainless windows.

"Oh, it's wonderful," whispered Olivia. The chamber itself contained little more than a few slender bookcases, a glass-fronted cabinet, and a compact oak desk piled high with papers and leather-bound volumes. But it was the spectacular scenery beyond the windows that caught her attention the most. Even though the aspect was rainy, she had an uninterrupted view of the dramatic coastline. The pounding waves exploded against piles of jagged black rocks and stony beaches, sending giant plumes of spray into the air.

Hamish closed the door. "It's my private study," he said, moving closer to Olivia. "Who's looking for you?"

His hands came to rest upon her shoulders, and his breath coasted along her ear, sending a delicious shiver across her skin. Beneath her stays and chemise, her nipples hardened, and Olivia's pulse began to thunder harder than the wild sea outside. "Tilda and Nurse Swan."

"Well, they'll be searching for a while then."

Suddenly breathless with anticipation, Olivia had trouble summoning her voice. "Why?" she whispered. Confusion and desire fogged her mind.

"Because I have need of you, my lovely wife." He brushed one of her drooping, poorly styled curls aside and pressed his firm warm lips against her neck, just below her ear. His damp hair felt cool and silken against her suddenly feverish flesh.

"You'll catch cold if you don't dry off," Olivia murmured, closing her eyes, drinking in the delicious sensations her husband was effortlessly stirring. After all this time, was Hamish really trying to seduce her? Was she dreaming?

And why on earth was she trying to put him off?

He chuckled against her ear, his breath a warm, pleasant gust. "I'm a braw Highlander, lassie." His voice was a soft, low growl. "A wee bit of rain willna hurt me."

She turned in his arms and captured his scarred, beautiful face between her hands. "Why are you doing this, Hamish? Why now? You could have had me days ago. Last night. Anytime at all. What's changed?"

"To be honest, I don't rightly know, lass. All I know is that when I bumped into you in the hall, I needed a taste of you more than I needed my next breath. Must there be any other reason than that for me to kiss you?" The corner of his mouth quirked with a smile as his large hands slid around her waist and pulled her flush against him. "As you keep reminding me, you're my wife."

She shook her head, bemused and thrilled yet also disappointed. She dropped her hands to his impossibly wide shoulders. He only wanted kisses.

But kisses can lead to other things, Olivia. Remember that salacious book Charlie lent you once, Memoirs of a

Woman of Pleasure? If she could tempt Hamish to let go of his tightly reined-in control, even just a little, things might go further than kisses . . .

Olivia looked up through her lashes at her ruggedly handsome, stubborn-as-a-rock husband, and her fingers flirted with the unruly locks caressing his damp collar. "No, there doesn't need to be any other reason . . . only, Tilda and Nurse Swan might miss me . . ." And then she quite deliberately snagged her bottom lip with her teeth.

Lust transformed Hamish's gaze from storm-cloud gray to a hotter, smokier hue. "With any luck, they won't find you, lass. Because right now, I want you all to myself."

And with that, he trapped her face between his large hands and claimed her mouth in an unbearably sweet, yet undeniably passionate kiss.

His lips were gentle yet demanding, their slide against hers agonizingly slow and searingly tender. When she kissed him back, his thumbs dragged upon her lower lip, coaxing her to open wider for him. She did so willingly, and his tongue swept inside, plunging deeply with bold, sure strokes.

This breath-stealing, bone-melting, worshipful kiss was everything a kiss should be. Everything she'd ever dreamed of and more.

Hamish groaned against her mouth. Pulled away to drag in a breath before capturing her lips again for another heavenly incursion. Then another.

Her husband kissed her with all the lingering reverence he'd employed during their very first "proper" kiss. He kissed her with desperate hunger as though this were his last day on earth and he'd never have this chance again.

He kissed her as though he loved her. As though he wanted to make love to her . . .

Yes. Oh, please yes . . . Could he hear her silent entreaty? Moaning, rendered helpless by desire, Olivia clung to Hamish's massive biceps, brazenly arching her body, pushing her suddenly too-sensitive breasts against his chest. She was so very impatient for more than kisses.

Through the damp cambric of Hamish's shirt, she felt his muscles tense and flex under her palms; she'd do anything to run her fingers over the hot, powerful flesh beneath his clothes. Explore the intriguing, iron-hard shaft eagerly pressing against her body through the barrier of her gown and his kilt.

Lust pulsed low in her belly. Slick heat gathered between her feminine folds.

If Hamish didn't take things further, she thought she might go mad.

All at once, he backed her toward the desk and hoisted her onto the leather blotter. Ledgers and papers and inkwells went flying, but she didn't care.

Neither did Hamish.

His large, calloused hands rucked up her skirts with shocking swiftness, and then he pushed his lean hips between her legs, parting her thighs. But even though she was spread wide and aching for his touch, he didn't caress her down there. Instead, he transferred his attention to her neck.

Swooping down, his teeth scraped along a tendon. His hot mouth seared the bare flesh where her shoulder met her gown. Raising a hand, he massaged one of her breasts through her clothes. His thumb found her already taut nipple and rubbed and rubbed until she didn't think she could bear it a moment longer.

"Hamish," she whispered hoarsely, gripping the back of his head. "For the love of God, touch me. Take me."

He raised his head and cradled her face. Looked deeply into her eyes and searched her gaze. His brows plunged into a frown. "Olivia, lass. If we do this, I won't spend inside you. I'll have to pull—"

He broke off as a high-pitched scream pierced the turret room.

Chapter 17

Suddenly I heard a shrill and dreadful scream.
Mary Shelley, Frankenstein; or, The Modern Prometheus

What on earth?

Olivia's heart froze, and Hamish swore beneath his breath.

"That sounded like Tilda." He stepped back, adjusting the fit of his kilt and waistcoat, and Olivia slipped off the desk.

Apprehension, colder than a dousing with seawater from the Minch, sluiced over her, dampening all desire. "Something's wrong. Dear God, I hope she's not hurt."

"Aye." Hamish strode to the jib door and threw it open. Tilda's wails grew louder. "Come, lass, we'd best see what's happened."

Olivia followed him into the library. And then she stopped dead in her tracks.

Lady Isobel stood by the main door with Nurse Swan, who was holding a distraught Tilda in her arms. The child's face was buried in the older woman's shoulder as she clung like a muslin-clad, curly-haired limpet to her neck.

But that's not why Olivia froze or why her breath caught in her chest. No, she was startled to stillness because there was someone else in the room. The exact same figure who'd visited her bedchamber and the nursery last night.

The woman in black.

"I'm so sorry. I'm so sorry, wee child," the strange woman cried, wringing her gloved hands in front of her black bombazine skirts. "I did not mean to frighten you. Look, I'm wearing my veil again." She raised a visibly trembling hand to the heavy lace concealing her face. "See . . ."

"Mother." Hamish advanced across the floor and laid a hand on the woman's shoulder. "It will be all right."

Mother? This mysterious, extremely anxious individual was Hamish's mother?

To say Olivia was shocked would be an understatement.

As Olivia slowly made her way toward the fireplace on the other side of the room, her gaze riveted to the visibly agitated woman, Hamish crossed over to Tilda and took the child from the nurse's arms.

"Hush, *mo chridhe*, hush," he crooned, gently stroking her hair. "There's no need to be afraid. This is my mama. Isobel's and Angus's too. She won't hurt you. I promise."

"Yes," agreed Isobel. "She's kind and lovely and very sweet. Don't be scared."

Tilda's sobs began to subside, and she lifted her head to glance at Hamish's mother. Her face was red and tearstained, her gaze suspicious. "Is . . . is that really your mama?" she whispered to Hamish.

"Aye. Her name is Margaret, Lady Sleat." His gaze darted to Olivia for the first time since they'd reentered the library. "Or should I say, Margaret, the dowager Marchioness of Sleat?"

Hamish's mother turned to face Olivia where she still waited uncertainly on the edge of the hearthrug. Even though the woman's heavy black veil concealed her countenance, it was clear she had dark red hair just like her daughter. Besides the fact that she was tall and slender, nothing else about her appearance could be easily discerned.

"Lady Sleat." The dowager marchioness's voice quivered. "I did not mean for us to meet this way. Believe me, it was never my intention to alarm the bairn, or you, my new daughter-in-law. Olivia, isn't it? I must apologize for creating such a fuss."

"I . . . I . . ." Olivia had no idea what to say or do. Should she curtsy to the woman who'd visited her bedchamber and the nursery like a ghostly sneak thief in the middle of the night? Confusion assailed her. Hamish had introduced her to his brother and sister. Why would he keep his mother's existence a secret? Not once had he spoken of her. Was the woman eccentric? Or perhaps even mad?

But Hamish told Tilda there was no need to be afraid.

Before she could dredge up some sort of response that wouldn't be a tangled mess, Hamish spoke. "Aye, I'm sorry it has come about this way too," he said gravely. He passed a much calmer Tilda back to Nurse Swan, then joined Olivia on the hearthrug. He took her hand and pressed it between his own. "I should have introduced you to my mother sooner."

"I d-don't understand," murmured Olivia. "You never said a word . . ."

Hamish's brow creased. "There's a reason for that . . . but first things first." He tucked Olivia's hand into the crook of his elbow and led her closer to the other Lady Sleat of Muircliff Castle. "As I said, this is my dear mama, Margaret."

"My lady . . ." Olivia bowed her head and dropped into a curtsy. "I'm . . . it's such a pleasure and . . . and an honor to m-meet you."

"Likewise, dear child." The dowager marchioness tilted her head. Her hands were still clasped at her slender waist but she no longer seemed to be trembling like an autumn leaf in a gale. "Hamish has told me so many wonderful things about you."

"He has?" Olivia aimed a puzzled look at her husband, who seemed to have more secrets than she'd hitherto realized.

"Oh, yes. Angus has too. And Isobel told me that she was most eager to meet you this afternoon." Margaret gestured toward her daughter with a gloved hand. "Didn't you, my dear?"

Isobel inclined her head and smiled warmly at Olivia. "I did indeed."

While Olivia felt at a disadvantage—it seemed the entire MacQueen family had been discussing her behind her back—she was also wildly curious about this woman who'd given birth to Hamish. She suddenly wanted to know about so many things. What was he really like as a little boy? Was he always a rapscallion? Did she think he was noble and kindhearted too? What was he like before he was injured at Waterloo and began to suffer from terrible dreams?

Why doesn't he want an heir when it's clear he would be a wonderful father?

"Speaking of Angus . . ." Hamish frowned at the library door. "You'd think he would have emerged by now given all the kerfuffle. Could you not find him, Nurse Swan?"

"Nae, my lord. And Tilda and I couldna get Shadow to help, could we, my bonnie lassie?"

Tilda shook her head. "But I did count to ten, didn't I?" she said solemnly.

"Aye, you did. Several times." Nurse Swan gave her a kiss on the cheek. "You're a clever thing. Ye take after yer fa—" The nursemaid broke off and blushed beet red. Her panicked gaze darted from Hamish to the dowager marchioness to Olivia and then back to her master again. "Och, my lord. I dinna mean to suggest tha' you . . ."

Hamish held up a hand. "It's all right, Nurse Swan. A slip of the tongue, I expect."

"Hamish, is there something you're not telling me about the situation with your ward?" asked Lady Sleat in a querulous tone.

Hamish traded a glance with Olivia before he answered. "You know about as much as I do, Mama," he said with a heavy sigh, "which is very little, all things considered. As I explained yesterday evening, it's a highly unusual situation. But I hope to get to the bottom of the mystery soon." He cocked an eyebrow. "I think, for the bairn's sake, we should talk about this later . . ."

His gaze connected with Olivia's again, and she offered

him a smile. She'd try to glean further details about Tilda's mother by spending more time in the nursery. Other than that, there wasn't much else she could do.

As they all began to troop out of the library, Lady Sleat drew close to Olivia. The scent of her rose perfume was as thick and heavy as her veil. "I won't dine with you tonight, my dear, as it is my custom to have a tray in my suite," she said as they entered the hallway. "However, I'd be most honored if you would accept my invitation to take tea with me in my sitting room tomorrow afternoon. I'm sure you're abuzz with questions just like I am."

"I-I would like that." She noted Hamish was conversing with Isobel and out of earshot before she added, "And yes, I do have quite a few things I'd like to talk to you about. So thank you. Very much."

At that moment, Angus appeared around the corner, yawning and rubbing his eyes. "So the party moved to the library, did it? Oh, and Mama has joined in on all the fun and games too." He approached Tilda and gave her a gentle chuck on the chin. "You took so long to find me, I drifted off."

She giggled. "You're a sleepyhead."

"Guilty as charged," Angus said. "I hope dinner won't be too late tonight, as I fear I won't be able to stay awake past eight."

"You want dinner after all the cakes and pastries you just ate?" asked Isobel. Her expression was aghast. "No wonder you fell asleep. Your body went into hibernation to digest everything."

Olivia smiled. How wonderful to be part of a family who played games and teased each other in a good-natured way. They might have their differences of opinion— Hamish was still against the idea of his sister marrying Brodie MacDonald—but at the end of the day, it was obviously they all held a great deal of affection for one another. Even Lady Sleat, despite her forbidding garb and eccentricities, seemed like a lovely woman.

Olivia had another burning question to add to the list she would put to her mother-in-law when they took tea on the morrow. . . . Why did Hamish dread Muircliff when he had such a caring family? After living for five years with an extended family who despised her, Olivia missed her parents so much, it hurt. She'd do anything to be part of a loving family again.

She'd do anything to create a loving family with Hamish. If only he would give their marriage a chance.

H amish, why didn't you tell me about your mother?" asked Olivia, her gentle tone laced with quiet reproach. Perched on the edge of a settee in the drawing room, she put down her postprandial cup of tea and regarded him with dark, solemn eyes. "I mean, when you asked me to be Isobel's chaperone, I assumed she must have passed away . . . And even though she resides here, we hadn't been introduced. In fact, no one's spoken a word about her. It's almost as if you've been hiding her away. And I'm wondering why."

Hamish grimaced inwardly. "No, I didn't say anything," he admitted, thanking God they were alone. He didn't need Isobel or Angus to weigh in on any of this. "And I'm sorry for that," he added. "But there is a reason for all of the subterfuge."

Actually, there were many reasons. However, he needed to arm himself with a drink—something stronger than tea—before he could muster his courage to venture into the fraught territory of his family history. His heart drumming, his mouth dry, he was as skittish as a soldier before his first battle. He also needed to keep his wits about him so he could answer Olivia without betraying too much. It was a blasted conundrum. Just like his entire life.

Stalling for time to gather his thoughts, Hamish crossed to the oak sideboard where several crystal decanters sat upon a silver tray, and reached for the cognac. All through dinner, he'd been waiting for Olivia to ask him this particular question. In fact, he'd been so preoccupied with turning over various ways to respond, all the food tasted like dust and he'd only half listened to the conversation going on around him.

Isobel and Angus both accused him of being as staid as a maiden aunt, but he didn't much care.

Returning to the fireside, he claimed a wingback chair of oxblood leather.

Olivia watched him as he sipped his drink, a frown creasing her brow. Her fingers toyed with the silver locket resting below her delicate collarbones. "Your mother came to my bedchamber, you know . . . in the middle of the night. I thought it was a strange dream or a ghostly visitation until Tilda told me she'd seen a similar figure in the nursery as well."

Hamish took another sip of his cognac. He wasn't altogether surprised. Although he was surprised Olivia hadn't said anything to him this morning, and he said as much.

Her mouth twitched with a wry smile. "I thought you might think I was being fanciful or, worse, going m-mad."

Sadness weighed heavily upon Hamish's heart. His new wife didn't trust him with her confidences, and he supposed he couldn't blame her. He'd done everything he could to discourage this growing intimacy between them. Although, considering what had taken place in the turret room earlier, it seemed he was fighting a losing battle.

Aloud he said, "I would never think that. And I'm sorry if you or Tilda was alarmed. And I do owe you an explanation about why my mother is the way she is. And why I kept her existence from you . . ." He expelled a shaky sigh. "You may have noticed this afternoon that my mother is an anxious, flighty woman. She keeps to herself a great deal. In fact she, rarely leaves her suite of rooms. And she never ventures outside of the castle. She seems to be possessed by a mortal fear of open spaces. She once told me that she's terrified the earth will open up and swallow her whole, or she'll somehow fall into the sky and disappear." He shrugged. "I know that probably doesn't make much sense, but for my mother, these fears are all too real and they govern every aspect of her life."

Concern was etched into Olivia's every feature. "My goodness, how awful," she murmured. "I can't even imagine feeling that way."

Hamish was relieved Olivia seemed to understand. "My mother is also quite fearful about encountering new people and avoids all social gatherings unless they are of an intimate nature with those she knows well. Mariah MacDonald, the local reverend's wife, is one of the few women she will receive. And I imagine that's why she paid a nocturnal visit to your room and the nursery. She wanted to see you and Tilda before she met you. Like me, she often has trouble sleeping and is prone to wandering the halls of Muircliff at night."

"That's . . . that's so sad . . ." Olivia's frown deepened. "So is that why she wears a veil? To shield herself from the eyes of others?"

Hamish was impressed by Olivia's compassion. "Not exactly. She does wish to shield herself from scrutiny, but not because of her timidity . . ." He blew out a sigh and caught Olivia's gaze. "When I went to meet with my steward and the stonemason this afternoon, I mentioned that the south tower had been damaged."

Olivia nodded. "Yes . . ." A shadow of apprehension—or was it foreboding?—passed across her face. "Wh-what happened, Hamish?"

"My parents once shared a suite of rooms in that tower. But one night, ten years ago, there was a terrible fire. It started in my mother's room and spread quickly, engulfing their whole floor. Indeed, if it weren't for a change in the weather—a storm blew in from the sea and with it came a heavy deluge—the whole castle could have burned to the ground. My mother only just survived. But my father—his name was Torquil—died."

"Oh, dear God. How tragic." Olivia blinked away tears. "I'm . . . I have no words."

Hamish swallowed past a hard, boulder-sized lump in his throat. "Aye," he said, his voice hoarse with emotion. "It was tragic. Sadly, my mother sustained burns to one side of her face, her neck, and her hands. That's why she wears a veil and gloves. To hide the scarring."

Olivia shook her head. "I can't even begin to comprehend what she must have been through." Her voice was thick as she wiped her eyes with trembling fingers. "And how this terrible tragedy must have affected all of you. Isobel and Angus. And you, Hamish."

"I'll admit it hasn't been easy for any of us. But it's my poor mother who's suffered the most. She's not the woman she used to be." Hamish's fingers tightened around his glass. "If it weren't for my fa—" He snapped his mouth shut. He'd almost said too much. "I hope you can see why Isobel will need your help when she makes her debut in London. Our mother's fears are so debilitating, she cannot leave the castle."

"But, Hamish . . . are you sure Isobel really wants a Season? If it means leaving your mother here, I could understand her not wanting to wed and move away—"

Hamish stood abruptly, and Olivia broke off.

Curse all these women trying to talk him out of doing what was right. Isobel was the sister of a marquess, for Christ's sake. She deserved to marry an upstanding gentleman of rank. Someone from her own class, not some good-for-nothing, fortune-hunting scoundrel who had pretensions of grandeur.

When he'd spoken to his mother yesterday evening, she'd all but changed her mind and given her blessing to the match between Isobel and Brodie, which irked Hamish no end. She'd argued that Brodie MacDonald came from a fine family and had studied at the University of Edinburgh. Apparently, he'd also begun assisting MacArthur with duties about the estate. The elderly steward, who'd been in the family's employ for years, had become forgetful of late and had begun making mistakes, so she'd asked Brodie to step in and help. By all accounts, he was doing a very good job.

But then, their mother had an ulterior motive in singing Brodie's praises. She didn't want her daughter to leave Muircliff.

"Even though you've only just met Isobel, you seem to be set on taking her side too," Hamish said with such gruffness, Olivia winced. Guilt made him temper his tone as he added, "Isobel needs to see the world. Meet other people. It's not fair that she feels she has to stay here, trapped by obligation. While I have the utmost sympathy for my mother and her situation, Isobel should have a chance at finding true happiness."

He refilled his glass with cognac, and when he returned to his chair by the hearth, Olivia was staring into the fire, watching the tongues of flame licking at the logs. Her fingers toyed with her locket again.

"We cannot help whom we love, Hamish," she said sadly. "At the risk of provoking your ire again, may I ask, what if you're wrong about Isobel and Brodie?"

"I'm not," he said, sounding mulish even to his own ears. "Isobel's young. She's simply suffering from a bout of calf-love. That's all." He waved a dismissive hand. "She'll soon get over her infatuation for this boy when she sees all the ton bucks at her first ball."

Olivia shook her head. "She's not wrong to be worried about society's cruelty. That's one thing I've experienced f-firsthand. It doesn't matter if you're well connected, pretty, or accomplished, or even possess a fortune. If you are deemed to be lacking in some other fundamental way, you will be gossiped about and ridiculed behind fans and closed parlor doors. The humiliation can be crushing, and I can appreciate why Isobel would want to avoid putting herself in such a vulnerable position." All at once, she stood. "I find I'm rather weary, Hamish. I hope you'll forgive me if I bid you good night."

"Of course." Hamish rose too. "We'll talk more about it tomorrow."

"Yes . . ." She gave him a weak smile. "I hope you sleep well. I can arrange another pot of chamomile tea to be sent up to your room if you'd like . . ."

"Aye, I'd like that. Good night, Olivia."

As he watched his lovely wife depart, Hamish gave a

weary sigh and deposited himself back in his chair to stop himself from chasing after her. Christ, he was a mess.

He rubbed his forehead, hoping beyond hope he could sort himself out. After their passionate tryst in his private study, he'd been alternately champing at the bit to drag Olivia into his arms again versus feeling angry with himself for giving in to temptation. If things had gone too far this afternoon, the lass might have lost her innocence on his bloody desk. And she deserved better than a quick, rough tup, especially for her first time.

Her first time should be with a man who truly loved her. Who would make her feel treasured and adored. A man who would be willing to give her children.

But alas, he was not that man. He knew it to his very bones.

As Hamish finished his cognac, his thoughts strayed to Isobel again. One thing he could sort out was this business with Brodie MacDonald.

His mouth quirked with a sardonic grin. Tomorrow, a visit to Dunmuir might just be in order.

CHAPTER 18

Was I then a monster, a blot upon the earth, from
which all men fled, and whom all men disowned?
Mary Shelley, Frankenstein; or, The Modern
Prometheus

Dunmuir Village, Isle of Skye

September 26, 1818

The air was crisp and the vast sky above a bright clear
blue as Hamish directed his horse onto the narrow
road leading to Dunmuir. With the ragged coastline to his
right, open fields, low hills, and rolling moorland stretched
out before him in every other direction as far as the eye
could see. Urging his mount into a canter, he relished the
feel of the brine-laden wind in his face and the glare of
reflected sunlight dancing upon the indigo blue sea. In the
distance, an eagle soared toward the sun.

At times like this, he loved his home. Its majesty and
raw natural beauty. Given the change in the weather, he'd
been tempted to invite Olivia to join him when he'd first
looked outside his bedchamber window this morning—he
knew she enjoyed riding—but unfortunately, this excursion
was all about business, not pleasure.

During breakfast, he'd quizzed Angus about Brodie
MacDonald's whereabouts and confirmed he was still

residing at the manse with his brother, the Reverend Hugh MacDonald. Angus also confirmed what his mother had told him—that Brodie had been helping the steward with maintaining the estate's books and even occasionally sorting out issues with some of the tenants.

The fact Hamish had been kept in the dark about Mac-Arthur's decline bothered him no end. Partly because he should have noticed it himself, and also because his mother had made the decision to employ Brodie MacDonald without consulting him, the laird of Muircliff and the Mac-Queen of Skye's entire estate, first.

So to say he was in a filthy, resentful mood when he rode through Dunmuir and arrived at the village kirk would be an understatement. The manse—a single-story stone building with a slate-tiled roof—stood atop a small grassy knoll behind the church and the small cemetery. All was quiet save for the plaintive call of the gulls wheeling overhead and the rustle of the sea breeze through the bracken and a small copse of pines.

As Hamish dismounted and secured his mount's reins to a rusted iron ring in a low stone wall bordering the cemetery, the door to the manse opened and a lean man in his late thirties with a shock of red hair emerged. Reverend MacDonald.

The minister called a greeting as Hamish followed a path of roughly hewn flagstones up the rise. "Good morning to ye, Lord Sleat. I wasna expecting to see ye until Christmastide."

"Aye," Hamish replied, reminding himself to keep his tone civil. "I wasn't expecting to come home in September either."

"And I hear ye have a bonnie wife." An uncertain smile played about the reverend's lips. "Congratulations, my lord."

"Thank you. But I didn't drop by to chat about my bride." Hamish halted in front of the manse and planted his fisted hands on his kilted hips. "I came here to address a matter of grave importance involving my sister and your brother."

"Oh . . . I see." Reverend MacDonald made a show of hefting several books that were tucked under his arm. "I was aboot to head to the vestry. My wife is visiting some of the crofters' wives, so I thought I'd take the opportunity to finish writing tomorrow's sermon." He gestured at the kirk with his free hand. "Would ye mind if we moved our chat— I mean our discussion—down there?"

Hamish narrowed his gaze. The fact that the good reverend was trying to steer him away from the manse was telling indeed. Especially after one of the curtains in the sash window twitched. "While I always value your counsel, I'm sure you know it is not you whom I came to see." Impatience and ill-humor sharpened his tone. "Where's Brodie?"

Reverend MacDonald's Adam's apple bobbed above his starched minister's collar. "I . . . er . . . he's . . ." His eyes darted toward the manse. "He's . . . ah . . . he's on his way to Portree to run an errand—"

Hamish shook his head at the minister. "Really, Reverend MacDonald? You of all people are going to lie about his whereabouts?" Taking a step back, he called out, "Brodie MacDonald! Stop hiding behind your brother's cassock and get your cowardly arse out here right now."

The kirkman's countenance grew so pale, Hamish thought the man might faint. "Don't worry, Reverend," he said. "I only came here to talk to your brother. Not tear him to pieces. I'm not that uncivilized."

"Oh. Good . . ." Reverend MacDonald braced an arm against the doorjamb as if his knees were still too weak to support his weight. "That's verra reassuring. Although, when ye use a word like arse—"

Hamish cocked a brow. "You're going to lecture me about my manners right now? When it's your scoundrel of a brother who's taken liberties with my sister? He's lucky I didn't come here to castrate him."

"Quite . . . Indeed . . ." The minister stepped away from the door. "Why don't you come inside then? You ken where the parlor is. I'll have my housekeeper prepare a pot of tea."

Hamish pushed his way inside the manse. The lintel was so low, he had to duck his head. "I don't need tea, Reverend. Just a word with Brodie."

Hamish didn't have to wait long. No sooner had he taken up a position by the sash window, which commanded a view of a grassy slope running down to a black stony beach and the Little Minch, than he heard a man clear his throat behind him.

"Lord Sleat, I understand ye wish to speak with me."

Hands clasped behind his back to stop himself from planting a fist in the face of the dog who'd been doing God knew what with his sister, Hamish turned around slowly. "Aye. I do."

Brodie MacDonald was a tall, broad-shouldered young man with a strong jaw and piercing blue eyes. From beneath a tousled sweep of bright red hair, his intelligent gaze met Hamish's directly. Even though he'd always thought Brodie quick-witted and affable—and eminently suitable for the role of Angus's tutor—Hamish now looked at him with new eyes. How profoundly disappointing that the cur had decided to take advantage of Isobel's naivety and inveigle his way into her heart.

But not for much longer.

Brodie swallowed audibly before he spoke again. "My lord, I ken ye are no' here to listen to me beat aboot the bush. So let me begin by saying, I am deeply in love with Lady Isobel and there's no' a day that goes by that I dinna regret that Lord Angus walked in on us before I got the chance—"

"So you only regret the fact you were caught, not the fact you've been dallying with my sister?"

"No. Tha's no' what I mean at all, my lord." Brodie inhaled a deep breath as though he was trying to harness his own fraying temper. "Look, I ken we've got off to a bad start, but I'm sure we can work this out."

"There's nothing *to* work out." Hamish reached into the pocket of his coat and withdrew a blank banknote. "This madness ends now. Today. Name your price. How much do you want to stay away from Isobel? Ten thousand pounds? Will that do?"

Bright color flagged the crests of Brodie's sharply cut cheekbones. "I dinna want yer money, my lord. I want to marry yer sister. We're both in love. It's that simple."

"Twenty thousand, then? Do you have a pen or a quill somewhere?"

Brodie shook his head. "My lord—"

"Name. Your. Price."

But Brodie would not be cowed, even by a snarling, six-foot-three Highlander with a half-mangled visage and death in his glare. The young man crossed his arms over his wide chest and thrust out his jaw. "I willna. Lady Isobel and I will wed. She is of age, and we have the blessing of yer mother, Lady Sleat, even if we dinna have yours. Indeed, we could have been married weeks ago if we'd exchanged vows of handfasting. But we both wanted to wait and wed in a kirk."

Hamish ground his back teeth together hard enough to crush gravel. He had to give the lad credit, he had balls. "It doesn't matter what you want—"

"The only thing that matters"—Brodie punctuated his point with a jab of his finger—"is Isobel's happiness. And I intend to make it my life's work to give her whatever her heart desires. Unless ye intend to strike me down, there's no' a goddamned thing ye can do about it. The banns have already been called for two consecutive Sundays. And tomorrow will be the third."

Hamish took a step forward. "What did you just say?" His voice was a low, menacing growl.

Fear flashed like quicksilver in Brodie's eyes, but the young man didn't budge an inch. "You heard me. After I was banished from Muircliff, yer sister explained the whole situation to Lady Sleat, and she now understands my intentions are true. And after I had a word with my brother, he agreed to read the banns. Isobel and I can marry tomorrow if we so choose."

"Are you telling me that everyone in Dunmuir, indeed, everyone far and wide, knows about this?"

"Aye."

Hellfire and bloody brimstone. Hamish wheeled around and faced the window. Leaning forward, he slammed his fists onto the sill and stared out at the sea. The banknote crumpled in his grip. He felt gutted. Duped.

There was no way he could force his sister to throw over Brodie MacDonald if the whole community knew of the impending nuptials. *Well, everyone but me,* he thought bitterly. No wonder Isobel had been as blithe as a bird in spring. It was a fait accompli.

What stung the most was the deceit. His mother, Isobel, and even Angus had lied to him about what had been going on behind his back as he'd raced pell-mell to Skye.

At least bloody Brodie MacDonald had been honest.

"I ken it's a lot to take in, my lord," continued Brodie. "But I want to reassure you that I'm no' a fortune hunter. I am no' without means or connections or aspirations. My uncle Sir Archibald MacDonald has offered to support me should I choose to pursue further studies at the University of Edinburgh with the view to becoming a solicitor. He'll even provide us with a town house to reside in. But I willna move away if Isobel wishes to remain here. I would do anything at all fer her, my lord. She means everything to me."

"Yet you won't give her up." Hamish turned around and sat back on the sill with his arms crossed.

"Nae, that I will no' do. And ye ken as well as I, tha' canna happen now the banns have been called."

Hamish scowled. "Aye . . . all I can say is well played, Brodie MacDonald. You've certainly got me over a barrel." He shoved the crushed banknote back in his pocket. It was true, there was no way out of this. Isobel's reputation would be ruined if Brodie jilted her, even for honorable reasons.

It was too late.

"So I take it ye willna oppose our union?"

Hamish snorted as he pushed away from the window.

"As much as I hate to say it, no, I won't. I cannot. But mark my words"—he closed the distance between himself and his sister's husband-to-be, and looked him straight in the eye—"if you ever break Isobel's heart, I will hunt you down and kill you. Slowly. Then feed you to the sharks in the Minch. Do you understand?"

Brodie didn't flinch. "Aye, my lord. But I promise you, I willna do such a thing. Ever."

"You'd better not." Hamish clapped him on the back on his way out the door. "I expect to see you and your brother and his wife at Muircliff tonight," he called over his shoulder. "Dinner is at seven o'clock sharp. Don't be late."

Muircliff Castle, Isle of Skye

"How do you take your tea, Olivia?" Lady Sleat reached for a rose-patterned cup and saucer of fine bone china. Even though the dowager marchioness's face was shrouded by her heavy black veil, Olivia sensed the woman's gaze on her. "I hope you don't mind if I call you Olivia."

Olivia smiled. "Of c-course not. I would be honored, my lady. And I like my tea with just a little milk. N-no sugar."

"Lovely. And you must call me Margaret. It will be rather confusing if we insist on calling each other Lady Sleat." With sure movements, Hamish's mother dispensed tea from the engraved silver teapot. Unlike yesterday, she didn't seem at all nervous. Perhaps she felt far more comfortable in her own rooms with only Olivia for company.

The marchioness's suite was beautifully appointed. This particular parlor was full of delicate rosewood and cherrywood furniture. The brocade curtains and upholstery and cushions on the chairs were all in shades of deep rose and scarlet with touches of yellow and gold. The thick Aubusson rug was a riot of roses in similar bright hues, and large vases of freshly cut flowers graced every tabletop and sideboard as well as the white marble mantelpiece. One set of windows looked out upon the sea, whereas another pair, directly opposite Olivia, afforded her a view of the knot garden that Isobel mentioned yesterday.

Olivia's gaze dropped to the marchioness's hands as she passed Olivia her cup of tea. Today her gloves were of lace rather than leather, and the thin fabric did little to conceal the angry red weals marring the backs of her hands. Olivia's heart clenched in sympathy. Her mother-in-law's scars must be dreadful indeed.

"And how are you settling in, dear?" Lady Sleat asked as she poured a cup of tea for herself. "I imagine Mrs. Boyd has been a bit prickly. I'm afraid she's rather protective of me, so it will be hard for her to see you as the new mistress of Muircliff."

"Oh, I have no intention of usurping your role here, my lady . . . I mean, Margaret."

"I know that, dear child. But you are the new Marchioness of Sleat and should be afforded all due respect. And I'm happy to step back from some of my duties." She reached out and patted Olivia's hand. "But it is not my intention to throw you in at the deep end either. I'm sure we can come to a mutually suitable arrangement about how the household should be managed."

"Thank you, I would be most grateful. Perhaps you might even be able to help me choose a lady's maid. I don't have one, and Mrs. Boyd mentioned she would think about who might be suitable for the role. But when I asked her about it this morning, I'm afraid she was . . . a little vague about it all. And I must admit, I'm all at sea." No doubt her past history with Bagshaw had something to do with the reason she was so intimidated by the dour housekeeper. She might have the title of marchioness, but she didn't feel like one at all. "I don't wish to create d-discord," she continued, "but if you could have a quiet word with her, I do believe it would help."

Margaret patted her hand again. "Of course. I will make sure you have a suitable maid at your disposal by this evening. Now . . . if you don't mind, Olivia. I need to lift my veil in order to drink my cup of tea."

"Oh yes. Please do. Don't worry on my account."

"Thank you. I thought I should warn you though. I did shock Tilda yesterday, and I should hate to frighten you."

"I'm sure you won't."

"I wouldn't be so sure about that."

Despite the warning from the dowager marchioness, when she raised the lace that had concealed her face and smoothed it back over her auburn hair, Olivia had to press her lips together to stifle a gasp.

Oh, my goodness. Hamish's mother was a beautiful woman, and the sight of the terrible scarring across her right cheek and jaw and down one side of her neck made Olivia want to weep. What pain she must have endured. And no wonder she hid herself away. Even though she tried to keep calm, tears pricked Olivia's eyes. She blinked quickly to clear them.

Margaret's mouth trembled with a smile. "Don't be sad for me, dear child. Terrible things happen sometimes. I thank God every day that I'm still here and can be a part of my children's lives. To see them grow up, and marry, and achieve wonderful things is a blessing indeed."

Olivia nodded. Her thoughts strayed to Tilda and how her mother had felt compelled to give her up. She must have been in an impossible situation to do such a thing. And then Olivia thought of her own mother and how much she missed her. Dropping her gaze, she picked up her tea and took a sip to conceal her own sadness.

Margaret offered a plate of delicate cucumber and salmon sandwiches to Olivia. When she politely declined, the dowager marchioness continued, "It goes without saying that I'm looking forward to becoming a grandmother, too, one day." Sliding off one of her gloves, she selected a sandwich for her own plate. "It's lovely having Tilda here in the nursery, but I do long to hold my own wee grandchild in my arms." She caught Olivia's gaze. "Not that I mean to put undue pressure on you and Hamish, of course. I know you've only just wed. There's plenty of time."

Olivia felt herself blushing. What could she possibly

say? "Your son doesn't want to have children with me"? "In a few short years, if not sooner, we are going to get divorced"? She needed to steer the conversation in another direction, and quickly. "Actually, I've been wondering what Hamish was like as a boy," she ventured. "Yesterday he admitted to me that he was rather mischievous."

Margaret laughed. "Oh, yes. He was indeed a scamp. And a rumbustious and willful adolescent too. But he's grown into a noble man. A man I'm proud of." Her expression changed. A shadow passed across her gray eyes. "Unlike his father . . ." Her gaze met Olivia's directly. "I thought you should know that, in case you hear any rumors. Which you are sure to."

"Oh . . ." Olivia put her tea down and folded her hands in her lap. "Hamish hasn't told me all that much other than his father perished in . . . in the fire here. I gather it's a topic that is difficult to revisit . . . for both of you."

Her mother-in-law nodded. Her scarred hand fluttered to the high neck of her black wool gown. "Yes. But I'd prefer you hear the details from me rather than anyone else, especially the servants. You see, Torquil—I suppose Hamish had told you his name—was not a good man. In fact, one might even venture to say he was cruel." Her mouth twisted with bitterness. "He had a bad temper, and the worst thing was, I never quite knew when he might have an outburst. He would just . . . explode over the smallest things that displeased him, and I could never tell what it would be that would trigger his anger. I was always walking on eggshells around him. Needless to say, we did not have an amicable relationship. He was not a good father either . . ."

Her fingers touched the scars on her neck, and her gaze grew distant. "In fact, the night of the fire, we fought. Most viciously. For the life of me, I can't even recall what it was about. But Torquil did come to my rooms and—" She swallowed, and when she spoke next, her voice trembled. "I'm afraid my recollection is somewhat hazy, but what I do know for certain is that if it weren't for Hamish, I would have died that night. I'm told that Hamish risked his own life to save mine. That he carried me out of the conflagration with only moments to spare before the tower collapsed."

"Oh, heavens. I had no idea," breathed Olivia. "Hamish didn't share those details with me. But your disclosure doesn't surprise me. I've already seen how loyal and protective he is of those he cares about. He truly is a brave man."

Margaret smiled. Tears glazed her gray eyes. "Yes, he is. And I can see how much he cares for you, Olivia, just by the way he looks at you. I never thought my braw, fearless lad would fall in love but—"

At a knock on the door, Margaret broke off. "Ah, that might be Isobel. She mentioned she might join us."

But it wasn't Isobel. It was Hamish who entered. Olivia's pulse sped at the sight of him in his kilt, just as it always did.

"Mother, I apologize for interrupting." His gaze skipped to Olivia before returning to the marchioness. "But I need to have a word with you."

"Of course," she replied. "Why don't you join us for afternoon tea?"

Olivia, still astonished by Margaret's pronouncement that Hamish cared for her, gave herself a mental shake. Hamish's expression was so serious, she wondered if he would prefer to speak with his mother alone. "I'd be happy to leave if you'd like some privacy," she murmured as he settled into a dainty shepherdess chair beside her.

"No, it's quite all right," he replied in a somber tone. "You should hear this too."

Well, that sounded ominous. Indeed, as Olivia studied her husband, she sensed he was quite agitated. Beneath his kilt, his muscled leg jiggled with impatience as he watched his mother reach for another cup off the silver tea tray.

As Margaret began to pour the tea, he said in a low voice, "So, dear Mama, when were you planning on telling me that Isobel and Brodie were betrothed and that Reverend MacDonald has already begun calling the banns?"

"Oh . . ." Margaret's panicked gaze flew to Hamish's face, and she almost dropped the teapot. "Yes . . . did . . . did Isobel tell you? Or Angus . . . ?"

Oh, dear. Olivia's fingers curled into her navy wool skirts. The tension in the room was palpable.

"No. It was Brodie himself," continued Hamish, depositing two lumps of sugar in his cup. "I've just returned from a visit to Dunmuir Kirk."

Margaret's countenance paled. "Oh, I see."

"I must say, I'm more than a wee bit hurt that you, Isobel, and Angus kept me in the dark about all this." Hamish stirred his tea carefully, then placed the silver spoon upon his saucer. "When Brodie told me what was going on, I felt like the biggest fool on Skye."

"I'm so, so sorry, Hamish," Margaret said in a breathless rush. "But Isobel and I have been so nervous about telling you . . . we . . . we kept putting it off. Because we knew you'd be angry."

"I might look like an ogre, Mama, but it seems you thought I might behave like one too." Remorse tightened Hamish's features. "As I rode back to Muircliff, I couldn't stop going over my own role in all of this. And it crushes me to think you were all so afraid of my reaction that you couldn't tell me the truth. And that's what cuts the deepest. In my pigheaded pursuit of trying to do what I thought what was best for Isobel—by believing my opinion was the only one that mattered—I've become that which I despise. A tyrant. A man to be feared. Someone like my father."

"Oh, my sweet lad." Margaret rose from her seat and enveloped Hamish in a warm embrace. "Nothing could be further from the truth. You were motivated by love to protect Isobel. Nothing else. You're not like your father. Never, ever think that."

Hamish's strong arms came around his mother's frail, slender frame as he hugged her back. And this time as Olivia watched, there was simply no way on earth that she could keep her own tears at bay.

CHAPTER 19

❧❧

Drink to me only with thine eyes,
  And I will pledge with mine.
                    Ben Jonson, "Song to Celia"

What a merry party it is, thought Olivia glumly as she
glanced around Muircliff's dining room. She could
still hardly fathom Hamish's complete change of heart
where Isobel and Brodie were concerned. But she was glad
for Isobel's sake that he had come around. The clearly besotted pair had decided they would wed without delay in
two days' time.

*If only Hamish would have a change of heart about our
marriage,* Olivia thought despondently.

Seeing Isobel and Brodie together made her own situation feel that much worse. She, Olivia, was hopelessly in
love with a man who steadfastly refused to take her to bed
even though he clearly desired her. Who only yesterday
professed that he needed to taste her more than he needed
his next breath.

Yet he maintained he would never give her children.

And she was only just beginning to understand why.

For some reason, Hamish feared he might take after his
wicked, brutish father. The things he'd said two days ago
when they first arrived at Muircliff—that he'd burn her, that
he wasn't worth it—suddenly made sense. And the words
he'd said to his mother this afternoon were also telling.

I've become that which I despise.

A tyrant. A man to be feared.

But he wasn't. Anyone could see it. But how could she convince him otherwise?

Conversation ebbed and flowed around Olivia like a babbling burn as she took a sip of champagne, hoping the fizz of the alcohol through her bloodstream would quell her altogether disorderly and disconsolate thoughts. Isobel chatted animatedly with Angus and her handsome fiancé, Brodie; Lady Sleat spoke with Reverend MacDonald's wife, Mariah, at Olivia's end of the grand oak table; and at the other end, Hamish conversed with the good reverend himself.

Although, there were moments when her husband's attention wandered down the table and she sensed his gaze upon her, hot and heavy like a physical touch. She wondered if it was because she'd taken extra care with her appearance tonight. Lady Sleat had been true to her word. After Margaret spoke with Mrs. Boyd, the housekeeper had procured a young maid named Eliza to assist Olivia. The girl had apparently worked alongside Isobel's lady's maid on the odd occasion, and it showed; Olivia discovered Eliza had a deft hand when it came to arranging hair.

Olivia also wore one of Isobel's fine evening gowns for the occasion. When her sister-in-law discovered Olivia had but a meager wardrobe, she'd loaded her up with a pile of clothes—gowns, a riding habit, and undergarments she professed she never wore—and Olivia was most grateful.

Although the scooped neckline of her borrowed gown was quite low and revealed a good deal of the tops of her breasts, the silk was a lovely deep rose color, and Olivia felt quite the princess with her hair curled and piled atop her head. Every time she glanced in her husband's direction and she discovered him watching her, awareness shivered along Olivia's skin, and longing whispered through her veins. But then, at other times, it seemed he barely noticed her at all. It was most disconcerting. And exceedingly frustrating.

Her confusion about Hamish's hot-and-cold demeanor persisted when they all repaired to the drawing room after dinner. He'd escorted her to the fireside, and his hands had caressed her all-but-bare shoulders as she sat, but then he removed himself to the other side of the room, where he stood in the shadows armed with a glass of whisky. Isobel played the pianoforte, and then Angus regaled them with several tunes. The lad possessed a handsome voice—not quite as deep as Hamish's, it had a pleasing timbre nonetheless—and Olivia enjoyed his performance greatly in between sneaking looks at her husband.

At the end of Angus's third song after the applause died away, Hamish spoke. "I think my lady wife should sing for us."

Olivia jumped in her seat and then blushed as all eyes focused on her. "I-I couldn't."

"Yes you could," said Hamish. "I've heard you sing before. You have a beautiful voice."

Olivia's cheeks felt as if they were ablaze. He must be referring to that time at the Hart and Hare when she'd sung Tilda a lullaby.

"Yes, please do sing for us, Olivia," entreated Isobel. "I'm tired of Angus's tuneless droning in my ear. Do you know 'Drink to Me Only with Thine Eyes'?"

Olivia would be lying if she said she didn't. "Y-yes."

Isobel smiled. "Wonderful."

Angus claimed a seat beside Brodie, and it seemed Olivia had no choice but to take his place at Isobel's side at the pianoforte. She cleared her throat several times and made herself draw a deep, calming breath. She would do this for Hamish because he'd asked her to. At least she knew she probably wouldn't stammer.

Fixing her gaze on the dancing flames of the fire and nothing else, she sang the familiar, terribly romantic air.

> *Drink to me only with thine eyes,*
> *And I will pledge with mine;*
> *Or leave a kiss within the cup.*
> *And I'll not ask for wine.*

It wasn't until she finished the last verse that she dared herself to steal a glance at Hamish. And the sight of him watching her stole her breath away. His hot, smoky gaze fairly smoldered, burning her, even across the room.

Hamish wasn't just drinking to her with his eyes. He had the look of a man who was desperate to devour her. In that moment, it was as if everyone else in the room faded into the shadows and only she and Hamish remained.

Olivia's heart began to pound wildly with equal amounts of trepidation and anticipation.

Tonight she wouldn't be put off. Tonight she would go to Hamish's room and entreat him to make love to her. He'd almost done so in the turret room.

Even if they didn't consummate their union tonight, there were other things they could do. Things she'd once read about in an erotic set of memoirs. Things she'd glimpsed in salacious pictures three years ago at a young ladies' academy.

Things her married friends Sophie and Arabella had whispered about in quiet moments and hinted at in their letters.

She might be a novice when it came to bed sport, but somehow, some way, she would seduce her husband. And perhaps, just maybe, he might admit that he'd fallen in love with her.

An hour later, after the party had dissolved, Olivia sat at her dressing table and closed her eyes as her new maid Eliza pulled a brush through her unbound hair. Her stomach was awhirl with butterflies, but she wouldn't let a bout of nerves sway her from her purpose. Even Hamish's perfunctory good-night kiss a short time ago—a mere brush of his lips against her temple before he disappeared into his own room—wouldn't deter her.

Because she knew he wanted her.

Eliza spoke, pulling Olivia away from her musings

about what she would say and do when she crept next door. "Would you like me to braid yer hair before bed, my lady?"

Olivia caught the girl's eye in the gilt-edged dressing table mirror. "No, I shall do it myself," she said. "You may go now, Eliza. I won't need you until morning. Thank you."

The maid couldn't quite suppress her knowing smile before she turned away. "Aye, my lady. And good night."

Of course, it was obvious what the newly married Marchioness of Sleat's objective was tonight. Instead of putting on her plain flannel night rail, Olivia opted to don another one of Isobel's castoffs—a robe of antique gold satin with touches of frothy cream lace at the sleeves. And because seduction was on her mind, she wore nothing underneath. Well, nothing but a dab of scent. Once Eliza was gone, Olivia applied the perfume to her wrists, behind her ears, and even between her breasts.

Hamish was about to get a visit from his near-naked wife, and she wanted to make sure he knew exactly what she was about. She was a married woman, and she was so very sick and tired of being treated like a virtuous maiden. A slip of a girl who needed protecting from her husband's base urges.

Well, this virgin bride had some base urges, too, and despite the riotous fluttering in her belly, her blushes, and her stammering, she was about to vanquish her very own beast.

Rising from her seat, Olivia made sure her robe was sufficiently cinched at the waist—she didn't want to expose too much flesh until she knew for certain that Hudson had retired for the night—then with her heart in her mouth, she pushed through the jib door into her husband's bedchamber.

And she wasn't disappointed. It was as though Hamish knew she was coming.

Her magnificent husband, wearing nothing but a midnight blue banyan and his eye patch, was sprawled in a wingback chair before the fire. In one hand, he held a tumbler of whisky. In his other, he held a leather-bound book. But upon seeing her, he sat up straight and deposited both the book and glass onto a nearby table. His gaze dragged over her before connecting with her eyes.

"Olivia, lass," he said, his dark brows knitting into a frown. "What are you doing here? Is everything all right?"

Ignoring his questions, Olivia padded across the carpet, her bare toes sinking into the plush pile. "Is . . . is Hudson here?"

Hamish's gaze narrowed. "No, I dismissed him."

"Good."

She moved closer, and Hamish stiffened. "I think you should go back to your room," he said in a voice laced with warning.

"Really?" She stopped before him, and for once he had to tilt his head back to maintain eye contact with her. Lowering her voice, she continued, "Are you certain that's what you want?"

Her hands moved to the sash at her waist, and she loosened the knot. Even though she trembled inside and her knees felt weak, she could do this. She had to, for both their sakes. "Because I know exactly what I want. And I mean to have it."

Hamish's tongue darted out to swipe along his full lower lip, and his long fingers curled around the arms of his chair. "You know I want you, lass. But it's not as easy as—"

She placed a finger against his wide mouth. His lips were firm yet satiny smooth, his breath hot. "Yes it is, Hamish. I want you. You want me. We're married. We can do whatever we like." Tugging the sash loose completely, she opened it so he could see her. *All* of her. "We can strip bare and pleasure each other with nothing but our hands and mouths like lovers do," she murmured. "There's no one to naysay us."

Hamish swallowed, and his gaze grew heavy-lidded as he studied her body. Her naked breasts with their tightly furled, dusky pink nipples. The softly rounded swells of her hips and belly. The dark triangle of curls at the apex of her thighs.

At the sight of her husband's hunger, Olivia felt a dark

thrill arrow through her, straight to her sex. Her folds pulsed with longing.

"How do you know about things like that?" he whispered hoarsely.

She laughed, suddenly feeling powerful. Hamish was becoming aroused too. Already she could see his member stirring beneath the quilted satin of his banyan. He clearly liked what he saw.

"I'm not a child," she said softly, shrugging off the rest of her robe. It slithered to the floor, pooling at her feet. "And . . . and I have friends who are married to rakes, remember? Your friends. I might be inexperienced, but I'm not completely naive."

To her astonishment and delight, he laughed, a rich, throaty sound. "All right then, lass. I'll play along for the moment," he said. "Show me all these wicked things that you've heard of. Do your worst."

"I intend to do my best."

Olivia reached across Hamish and snagged a cushion from a nearby chair. Dropping it on the floor, she sank to her knees before him.

"I see you do mean business," he said, spreading his legs so she could shuffle closer.

"You doubted me?" She slid her hands along his thighs, noting how the dense muscles hardened beneath her palms.

"I certainly don't now."

"Good. By the way, you're wearing far too much."

She wanted him gloriously naked. With hands that trembled only a little, Olivia spread his banyan wide. And then she bit her lip. Not to tease Hamish, but simply because she was utterly captivated.

Her husband was a work of art. The leaping firelight played over his body, highlighting the wide span of his shoulders that all but filled the back of the wing chair. The swell of his hard pectoral muscles with their light dusting of dark hair. His ridged abdomen, the flat plane of his belly, and the intriguing crests of his lean hip bones. His heavily muscled thighs. And lastly the erect staff of his enormous manhood. Thick and long with a ruddy head, it jutted proudly from a storm of black curls as though tempting her to wrap her hands around it.

To explore every magnificent inch of him.

She looked up through her lashes at Hamish, hoping beyond hope he wasn't laughing at her.

She needn't have worried. There was no trace of a smile playing about his wide, sensual mouth. His dark gray eye glittered between half-mast lids, watching her every move. Encouraged by his look of avid attention, she reached out a hand and tentatively cupped his ballocks before curling her fingers around his shaft. He was hot and hard and silken all at the same time. When she gave him a tentative squeeze, he sucked in a sharp breath.

"Olivia . . ." Her name, spilling from his lips, was little more than an incoherent groan.

"Don't think of me as your wife," she whispered, squeezing him again. "Let me be your mistress. Your lover." Relinquishing her hold on his member, she placed her hands on his thighs again and leaned forward, raining whisper-soft kisses across his chest. She touched her tongue to his small, bronze-colored nipples and licked a trail across his abdomen, then across the ridged outline of one hip bone, then the other. Every time she moved, her own nipples brushed his body, and her excitement increased all the more. The coarse, crisp hair between his legs tickled her skin. She felt like a cat in heat, rubbing herself all over him.

Hamish's penis jerked and twitched and seemed to grow harder by the moment, especially when its hot, heavy length slid between her breasts. She liked the unexpected and illicit sensation so much, she dragged his shaft through her cleavage again.

"Sweet Jesus," Hamish panted. "Where did you learn about—"

"Hush," she murmured. "Let me play."

Olivia sat back and grasped his manhood between both her hands this time. She loved the feel of it between her palms. How it pulsed with a life of its own. How would her husband taste down there? Curious, she lapped at the pearl of moisture that had seeped from the small slit atop the swollen head. Should she do more? Encircle him with her lips, draw him into her mouth? She'd seen a picture once . . .

She licked her lips, savoring the salty taste on her tongue, and then all at once Hamish groaned. "Enough." He fisted a hand in her hair and forced her head up to look at him.

"I'm sorry," she whispered. "Did . . . did I do something wrong?"

"No, of course not, lass." His gaze softened. "I've loved everything you've done, but I don't want to come just yet. Besides"—his mouth kicked into a smile—"I'm burning with impatience to pleasure you with my hands and mouth, as you so aptly put it. I want to watch you come. It's something I've dreamed about for days."

Oh . . . Olivia swallowed. "Really?"

"Aye, God help me. Really." Hamish gently but firmly urged her back with his hands. "Lie down, *mo chridhe*," he murmured huskily, shrugging his banyan off completely. And then he followed her onto the floor, prowling up her body like a great beast until he loomed over her.

Resting on his forearms, he stared into her eyes. Stark hunger filled his gaze. "Do you know how beautiful you are, Olivia? How much I want you?"

Both enthralled and momentarily tongue-tied, she shook her head. She gripped his bulging, rock-hard biceps, and they twitched and flexed; somehow this display of barely restrained male strength aroused her even more. "No . . . no I don't," she whispered huskily.

"Then I'll have to show you." And then Hamish dipped his head and kissed her.

It was a long, languorous, searching kiss. Hot and deep and thorough. He sucked her tongue into his mouth. Nipped at her lower lip.

As he continued to kiss her, he shifted his weight, and one hand came up to cover her breast. His fingers found her nipple, hard as a pearl, and when he gave it a light, teasing pinch, Olivia gasped as pleasure blasted through her. *Oh, that feels good.*

But when Hamish lowered his head and caught her other nipple between his lips and suckled, her brain all but ceased to function. Her hands came up to grasp the back of his head. She twisted her fingers into his thick hair.

"Oh, Hamish," she moaned, and arched her back, pushing herself into his mouth. "Why have we waited so long to do this?"

His only response was to mercilessly tease her other breast with his lips and teeth and tongue.

But the exquisite torture wasn't over.

Hamish slid his hot, wicked mouth across her torso. Laved her belly button with his tongue. And then he was pressing open her thighs. Exposing her most secret part to his gaze. By rights she should be embarrassed, but she wasn't. Lust throbbed deep inside her core, and her aching sex was slick with desire, demanding attention.

Ever since she'd learned that a man could kiss a woman down there, she'd often wondered what it would feel like. It seemed her husband, the man whom she now knew she loved with her whole heart, was about to introduce her to one of life's most wicked pleasures. She simply couldn't wait.

Hamish positioned his wide shoulders between her legs, then pushed her swollen folds apart with gentle fingers. "What a pretty cunny," he murmured. "And no doubt delicious." His wicked words and the wash of his hot, humid breath against her sensitive flesh made her shiver. And then he lowered his head and flicked her sex with his tongue.

Olivia bucked. Stars burst behind her eyes. She'd never imagined . . . she'd never dreamed . . .

Her thoughts disintegrated and scattered as Hamish applied himself to the task of pleasuring her most intimate parts with his fingers and mouth. Every teasing stroke, every tiny lap, every delicate suckle and kiss drove her higher and higher. Moaning, she sank her fingers into his hair, spread her legs, and undulated her hips, a mindless, writhing creature seeking untold bliss beneath his mouth.

When Hamish shifted his weight, propping himself onto one elbow, Olivia fluttered her eyes open and glanced down the length of her body. With his dark head between her thighs, she couldn't quite see what he was doing, but she sensed he'd grasped his member with one hand. His shoulder and arm were moving, pulsing as though he'd begun to stroke himself. Oh, she wanted to do that. Work him. Pleasure him. Take him in her mouth again until he spent his seed . . .

Hamish's tongue flickered against one excruciatingly sensitive part of her sex at the apex of her folds, and Olivia cried out and clutched his head. She was so close, so very close to heaven. Hamish groaned against her, his breath a hot, teasing gust, and the thought that he was about to reach that same wonderful place, too, was her undoing. All at once she came, releasing a cry of joy as ecstasy rushed through her in a great, pulsating wave.

When she opened her eyes, it was to discover Hamish gasping and shuddering and cursing beneath his breath. She raised herself onto her elbows and watched in fascination as his seed erupted onto the folds of his discarded banyan.

Then he slumped to the floor, his abdomen and chest heaving.

Olivia slid alongside him and brushed damp tendrils of hair away from his forehead. "Thank you, Hamish," she murmured, then dropped a kiss on his brow, "for giving me my first taste of pleasure."

He cracked his eye open and stroked her face. "No. Thank *you*, lass. This encounter was everything I could have hoped for and more."

"So . . . so does that mean we can do it again?"

Hamish sat up. The firelight gilded the strong line of his powerful back. The side of his face. A muscle twitched in his stubbled jaw.

She dared to place a hand upon his shoulder. "Join me, in my bed," she whispered. "We can do more. You . . . you can put yourself inside me and take my maidenhead. Spend outside my body like you just did if you d-don't want to get me with child. Or use a sheath. Just like you do with all your other lovers—"

But Hamish was shaking his head. "No. I won't take that risk with you, Olivia. I thought I'd been careful in the past, but clearly accidents happen. Tilda could be mine."

Even though they sat by the fire, it felt as though a cold draft swept through the room. Olivia was conscious of the crackle of the fire and the ever-present crash of the sea and the winds battering Muircliff's walls. "But yesterday, you almost took me in your study. You . . . you even suggested you could withdraw," she persisted, even as her confidence began to falter.

He turned his head to catch her gaze. His whole demeanor had changed. His eye glimmered with a hard, cold light. "It was a momentary loss of reason. I can assure you it won't happen again. This, what we just did, is all I'll ever permit."

"But . . . but even if there were an accident, would it be so bad, Hamish? Isobel isn't having her Season anymore, so it doesn't matter if I'm increasing." She curled her fingers around his arm. "I . . . I would love to bear your child . . . if you chose to give me one, that is . . ."

Hamish stood abruptly and draped her discarded robe over her naked shoulders. "I've told you before, lass," he said gruffly, bending to snatch up his own soiled robe. "I don't want an heir."

"You're not like your father."

Hamish froze. Then straightened. His empty fist clenched and unclenched at his side.

Oh, no. Had she gone too far?

He stared down at her. His expression was as harsh and frigid as arctic ice. "You think you know me, but you don't."

"Hamish . . ." She caught his hand and got to her feet. She hated sounding desperate, but she was. "At least . . . at least lie with me. Hold me. Until I fall asleep."

But he shook his head. A great, shuddering sigh escaped him. He dropped his robe and turned toward her. With his free hand, he caressed her cheek, then stroked it over her hair with infinite tenderness. The anger had seeped away, only to be replaced by a great sadness. "Believe me, I want to, Olivia. But I can't. You ask the impossible."

Impossible? She shook her head. She didn't understand. "I don't care if you have a bad dream and wake me."

"But you see, I do." His expression was grave. "And I won't change my mind. Not now. Not ever. Come." He led her to the connecting door between their rooms. "Good night, my sweet lady wife. I'll see you in the morning." He brushed a kiss across her temple, then pushed the portal shut, leaving her all alone with the crushing sense that she'd done something wrong yet had no idea what.

CHAPTER 20

❧

The night passed away, and the sun rose from the ocean; my feelings became calmer, if it may be called calmness, when the violence of rage sinks into the depths of despair.

Mary Shelley, Frankenstein; or, The Modern Prometheus

Muircliff Castle, Isle of Skye

*H*amish stumbled through the smoking, steaming rubble of the south tower. The blackened bricks and broken beams. Ash swirled around him like snow. The incessant roar of the waves mingled with the mournful cries of a seagull circling overhead.

"Too late," it called. "Too late." The cries of the gull grew louder, becoming an ear-splitting shriek. Or perhaps it was the wind. Or an infant . . .

Christ, what was a wee bairn doing out here?

He tried to follow the sound, but the gale kept snatching it away. The ash cloud grew thicker, expanding into a choking, swirling, smoky miasma. Terror gripped him. What if he tripped over the edge of the cliff? But he had to find the child.

And then fire exploded in his vision, blinding him. The wail of the child merged with the agonized cries of men. He couldn't see. Couldn't move forward or backward. He was on the edge of a precipice, about to fall into a fiery pit. Blazing heat seared his face.

A sob escaped him. How could he help anyone when he couldn't even help himself?

Somewhere behind him, his father laughed and he froze, all but paralyzed. Gasping, sweating, and petrified, he struggled to crawl away. He had to move. Hide.

"Oh, God. I can't . . ."

And then a hand clutched at him . . . Someone far away called his name . . .

"Hamish . . ."

Hamish lurched upward. His heart was pounding, his breath came in harsh, ragged spurts. The linen sheets of his bed were twisted around his hips and legs, constraining him.

"Hamish," Olivia repeated, capturing his attention at last. Her eyes were huge and dark in her pale face as she hovered wraithlike in her white nightgown by his bedside. In one hand she held a branch of candles. Her other hand was at her throat. "Oh, my goodness. Are you all right? I've never heard such terrible cr—"

Hamish held up a shaking hand, cutting her off. "What are you doing here?" he ground out. Bile rose in his throat, and he closed his eyes and swallowed hard.

"You . . . you were having a nightmare, and I . . . I came to check on you."

He pushed his hair out of his face and glared at her. "Well, don't. Don't ever."

"But—"

"There are no buts, Olivia. You need to understand—" Losing his battle against the swelling nausea in his gullet, Hamish broke off and lunged out of the bed, bolting for his dressing room.

When he emerged a few minutes later, wrapped in a clean banyan and with a leather eye patch in place, it was to discover Olivia had retreated to the fireside and had installed herself in one of the leather wing chairs. She'd already restoked the fire, and the branch of lit candles flickered upon the mantelpiece.

"Hamish. We need to talk about this," she said firmly. Her brow had knit into a deep frown, and she had a decidedly determined glint in her eyes. "About your nightmares and . . . and everything else. And I won't be fobbed off anymore. I just won't."

"I know." He crossed to the oak cabinet, which he kept stocked with spirits. He needed a drink first. "Would you like a whisky?" His voice was rough as he sloshed God knew how much into a glass. His hands still shook, and his throat felt raw.

"Yes, please," she replied.

After passing Olivia her glass, Hamish dropped into the wing chair beside hers. His shoulders heaved with a weary sigh, and he rubbed his forehead. Where to begin? How much should he divulge? What should he leave out?

By the look on his wife's face, the stubborn set to her neat chin, only complete candor on his part would suffice. Perhaps it was time to confess all. And then she'd understand why he was such a mess.

Why she needed to stay away and give up this futile pursuit of him.

Yes, he needed to rip off the bandage. Expose the ugly truth. And the sooner he did so, the better.

Olivia sipped her whisky with barely a grimace. "Hamish, perhaps it would help if I told you what I learned this afternoon when I took tea with your mother," she said softly. "She told me a little about the fire here at Muircliff. How you risked your own life to rescue her. And she also told me about your father, Torquil. How he had a terrible temper and how cruel he was to you all."

Ah, so that's why Olivia mentioned that she thought he was nothing like his father. Hamish tossed back a mouthful of whisky, hoping it would give him the courage he needed to continue discussing such a harrowing subject.

"Aye. He was cruel, lass. A heartless bastard with a penchant for making his family's life hell."

"So . . . so why did you tell your mother that you feared you'd become just like him? You're not cruel or heartless.

As far as I can see, you've never done anything out of malice. Even your mother said as much. Whatever actions you've taken have been because you want to protect those you care about."

"Are you so sure of that?" he demanded. "How many times have I had sudden outbursts of temper? Until yesterday morning, didn't I plan to interfere in Isobel's life, disregarding what she truly wanted? Haven't I turned your life upside down? Made you miserable with all of my caveats about our own marriage? Denying you tonight was one of the hardest things I've ever done. It didn't matter that I knew I was hurting you. I did it anyway."

"I know that's because you're afraid that you'll get me with child. That you think you'll be a terrible father," she said. "You can't deny that's what you believe. But that's not true. I've seen how wonderful you are with Tilda. So patient and kind and generous. And you're not even sure she's your daughter."

"That's different."

"No, it's not."

"Olivia. I am not the saint you believe me to be. I'm deeply flawed and dangerous."

"We all have flaws, Hamish. And from what I've seen, the only person who was ever in any danger from you was my odious cousin Felix. And he deserved everything you meted out to him."

Hamish shook his head. "You don't know what you're talking about."

"Then enlighten me. Because I'm really struggling to understand."

Hamish tossed back half of his whisky, then put down his glass. He could down a vat of the stuff and it still wouldn't erase his pain.

"All right, lass. Let me speak plainly. And if you still think I'm a good man, don't be surprised if I think you're a fool."

Olivia swallowed, but her gaze was steady. "I'm listening."

"You already know my father was an abusive man. When I was a youth, he was fond of wielding a strap at the slightest provocation. Isobel was the only one he left alone, perhaps because she was crippled. But he also believed Isobel wasn't really his, that our mother had been unfaithful, so he barely regarded her at all. But it was our poor mother who bore the brunt of his anger. She tried to hide how bad the beatings were, but I knew. And so did the servants."

Olivia paled. "Oh . . . I . . . your mother intimated they fought . . . Oh, Hamish, I'm so dreadfully sorry to hear that. You were all living in a real nightmare."

He shrugged and leaned his forearms on his thighs. Clenched his hands together so tightly, the knuckles strained against his flesh. "When I was about fifteen, I began to fill out. Grow stronger. And my father sent me away to Eton. When I came home during the holidays, he began to leave me alone. Little did I know that when I was away he was taking his pent-up frustrations out on Mother." Hamish caught Olivia's shocked gaze. "She's endured far too much. And there isn't a day that my heart doesn't weep for her."

Olivia nodded. "She told me that she and your father had a terrible fight the night of the fire. But she doesn't recall everything."

"Aye. I was twenty at the time and home from Oxford. My bedchamber, Isobel's, and Angus's were all located in the wing adjacent to the south tower and our parents' suite. I'd retired to my own room for the evening to watch a summer storm roll in across the Minch, but when the argument began, my father's thunderous voice was so loud, I could hear him even from afar. I couldn't stand by. I couldn't stay away. I knew he'd been in a filthy mood all afternoon, brooding and stacking up his anger like the storm clouds of the oncoming tempest. But I was ready for him . . .

"You see, I'd taken up boxing and wrestling at university, and because of my size, I was getting damn good at both. My father was a tall man, too, and, like me, as muscular as an ox. But that summer, I wasn't intimidated by him anymore. And when I heard the shouts and curses floating down the gallery to my door, I was just spoiling for a fight. I was ready to take my father down a peg or two. Make him pay for all the beatings and whippings I'd taken in the past. To punish him for all the terrible things he'd done to our mother."

Hamish swallowed, his mouth suddenly dry. "And then everything changed when my mother screamed in a way I'd never heard before. It was bloodcurdling. It will stay with me until the day I die."

He glanced at Olivia, and her expression was fearful yet unwavering. "What happened, Hamish?" she asked gravely. "But tell me only if you can bear it."

He nodded, grateful that she seemed to understand how difficult this was. That he felt as though he were in the process of scourging an old, festering wound deep within his soul. "By the time I got to my mother's room, it was already on fire. I don't know what happened exactly, but the bed hangings were ablaze, and my mother was knocked unconscious. When I burst in and my father saw me taking everything in, he gave an almighty roar and charged at me. I swear there was murder in his glare, Olivia. And we fought."

Hamish wiped a shaking hand across his jaw. "It was messy and vicious, and at one point we tumbled down the spiral stairwell at the end of the gallery. Because my father took a blow to the head and seemed dazed, I seized the opportunity to rush back to my mother's room. By that stage, the room was well and truly alight, and thick with smoke. How I managed to pull her from the burning bed, I'll never know."

"But you managed to get outside," said Olivia. "To safety."

"Aye. However, the winds blowing in from the sea had fanned the flames, and when I turned to see whether my father had emerged, the tower was completely ablaze. The servants, as soon as they'd smelled the smoke, had roused Isobel and Angus and taken them outside, thank God."

"You saved your mother, Hamish." Olivia's voice was soft with compassion. "I still don't see why you think you're deeply flawed and dangerous."

This would be the hardest part to confess. Hamish drew a deep breath into his lungs. He'd never told this to anyone else, ever before. "What you don't know is that when I was carrying my mother down the stairs, my father roused as I passed him. He grabbed at my ankle, trying to trip me, I suspect. And I kicked out at him. Not just because I was desperately trying to get away, but out of spite and white-hot anger. He'd tried to kill my mother. Burn her alive."

"Oh, Hamish . . ."

"I didn't look back. Not once as I rushed down the stairs. And I knew I'd hurt him. I heard the crack clearly as my boot connected with his jaw. And I was glad of it. And when I was outside and turned around, and I saw that I couldn't go back for him, that the stairwell was clogged with thick smoke and the flames were devouring the turret walls, I was glad of that too. Because it meant that, at long last, we'd all be free of that devil of a man."

"Hamish, how can you blame yourself for being relieved your monstrous father was dead? And from what you've just told me, it is not your fault he perished in the tower. Even when you were trying to save your mother, he still interfered. Of course you had to lash out at him. If you hadn't, all of you would have died."

Hamish shook his head. "You're trying to paint me in a better light, lass. But it won't work. I know the shameful, hideous truth about how I felt in that moment when I kicked him. I know how I feel even now. I was possessed by murderous rage. I hated him. I wanted him to die. And he did."

He caught Olivia's gaze. "But if that's not enough to convince you I hide a violent streak, just wait until you hear what I have to say next."

"I know you were an officer in Wellington's army." A small line appeared between Olivia's brows. "You can't be condemned for anything that happened during battle. You were fighting for your country."

"No. I don't harbor guilt about anything I did during the three years I served."

Olivia's frown deepened with her confusion. "I'm afraid you'll have to explain why you think you are an inherently violent man then, Hamish. Just because you're physically strong and powerful, that doesn't mean you're also cruel and vicious and vindictive. And I've seen nothing to indicate that you are."

Hamish rubbed a hand down his face. There would be no skirting about the truth. The time for brutal honesty had arrived. "These nightmares I suffer from," he began, "they aren't just about the war. I've battled nightmares for years and years, and many of them are about my father and the night of the fire."

"That's perfectly understandable."

"What I'm trying to say, and quite badly it would seem, is that after I was injured"—he gestured at his ruined eye and face—"when I was convalescing in London, my nightmares grew worse. I began to have them every night rather than every now and again."

"Also perfectly understandable."

"But what you don't know, Olivia, is that they also became violent."

Her brow creased. "Wh-what do you mean?"

"One night, I was having a particularly bad nightmare, and just like you did tonight, Hudson came in to check on me. He attempted to rouse me . . . and I'm ashamed to say, I attacked him."

Olivia swallowed. "Attacked him how, exactly?"

"I didn't know what I was doing. I was deep within the dream. But apparently I went berserk. I hit him so hard, I sent him flying across the room. He struck his head and was knocked unconscious." The stab of guilt in the vicinity of Hamish's chest felt fresh and new, as if he'd just been split open. His voice was little more than a ragged whisper as he added, "I could have killed him, Olivia."

Olivia's brown eyes were wide with shock. "How terrible. You must have been horrified."

"Aye." Hamish nodded, and his mouth twisted with the effort not to cry. "I still am. And I'm absolutely petrified I'll do it again."

"But, wasn't that three years ago? Have you ever done anything like it since?"

"I've never slept near anyone since to find out. Well, except for when I fell asleep in the carriage outside of Glasgow."

"But you didn't lash out at Tilda or me."

"But the point is, I could have. Remember that night at the Hart and Hare when you knocked on my door?"

"Yes."

"And do you recall that I'd managed to knock a bottle of brandy onto the floor?"

"Yes. But, Hamish, anyone can accidentally knock things off a bedside table. I've done it before."

"It's not the same at all. I have a history of going on the attack. I feel sick to the stomach just thinking of what might have happened to you and Tilda if I'd gone berserk in that carriage. Or if I'd hurt you tonight when you woke me up."

"Is . . . is that why you were ill each time?"

He dragged a hand down his face. His belly was still churning, in fact. "Aye."

"Oh, Hamish. When you had that bad dream in our carriage, not for a minute did I think that Tilda and I were in the slightest bit of danger."

He shook his head. "That's because you didn't know about my father. Or the incident with Hudson."

"Yet Hudson still serves you," she ventured.

"Hudson knows not to disturb me, ever."

"Hamish, you are not a monster. My cousin Felix is a monster. Your father was too. As far as I can see, your only real fault is that you have a history of being a very wicked rake. Why deny yourself the gift of children—?"

"God damn it, Olivia. I'm not just a wicked rake. Why can't you see that my sins go far deeper?" Hamish snapped, frustrated that she couldn't see what he knew to be true. "I'm the son of Torquil MacQueen. My blood is tainted. My mind is scarred. My soul has stains on it that can never be washed away. I'm a devil too. A sinner to my very bones. And I don't want a male heir, indeed any children, because I won't be responsible for passing on my bad blood."

He scrubbed a hand through his hair and gentled his tone. "And I can't be with you, Olivia, not the way you want me to be. The possibility I might hurt you, albeit accidentally, is very real. If we have sexual congress, and I fall asleep beside you, I would never forgive myself if I attacked you during one of my nightmares. I can never, ever sleep beside my wife. And no amount of whisky, or chamomile tea, or lavender slipped beneath my pillow, or nights filled with sexual pleasure will ever cure that."

"But what of love?" Olivia slipped from her seat and sank to her knees before him. Caught one of his hands and kissed his battle-scarred knuckles. "Hamish MacQueen, I love you," she said with such conviction, there could be no doubting the veracity of her declaration. "And I think you care for me too. Please, for both our sakes, let's try to make this work. I believe that we can."

Dear God, she was shattering what little heart he had left into a million pieces. Hamish shook his head sadly and cupped her beautiful face. "You shouldn't love me, lass. And this will never work. I'm not the man of your dreams, or your knight in shining armor, no matter how much you wish it to be so. I can't be reformed or fixed. I'm damaged. Broken beyond repair." With his thumb, he wiped away the tear that slipped down her pale, smooth cheek. "I married you to protect you from your family's predation and because I thought you could help my family in return. Yes, we desire each other and you say that you love me. But . . ." He inhaled a bracing breath, preparing himself to inflict a wound. "I do not love you and never will. That's how heartless I really am." It was a lie. But he needed to say it if it would help Olivia to see that the dreams she harbored were hopeless.

She shook her head, and he could see that she desperately wanted to deny what he'd said. "That's not true. I can see how you feel whenever you look at me. When you kiss me. It's why you keep pushing me away. Even your mother said—"

"Olivia, you need to stop this. Pleading with me will not help." He urged her to rise, then slid a hand behind her neck. Dropped a kiss on her forehead and inhaled her sweet violet scent. "I think our relationship—such that it is—has run its course. Once Brodie and Isobel are wed, the day after tomorrow, I'll return to London with Tilda. It will be easier to continue the search for her mother if I'm there. You can stay here or accompany me or go wherever you like, for that matter. Stay with your friends, or I have a number of properties in which you could establish a household. In Edinburgh and in London and in the country too. I . . . I think it's best we live apart until the question of your inheritance is sorted out."

Olivia pressed her hands against his chest. "I can't believe you're saying this," she whispered, searching his gaze. "I thought that we were growing closer. Of course I'll return to London with you and Tilda, but do you really want us to live separate lives once we're there?"

Somehow, he hardened his heart. "Aye. I do."

"I don't want this. You're making a mistake."

"You have no choice."

More tears slipped down Olivia's cheeks, but she held her ground. Lifting her chin, she said, "All my life I've struggled to articulate anything clearly. I've lost count of the number of occasions I've been disregarded and brushed aside because of the way I am. But hear me now. I love you, Hamish MacQueen—all of you, even your flaws—and I will never give up hope that one day you'll be ready to acknowledge you feel the same way about me. And that you're willing to find a way for us to live happily together. You . . . you might not believe that you are worth it, but I do."

And with that, she retrieved her branch of candles and retreated to her room, leaving him alone with nothing but a dying fire and a half-drunk glass of whisky to ward off the cold, lonely darkness that always threatened to engulf him.

CHAPTER 21

❧

At the day appointed for Solemnization of Matrimonie, the persons to be married shall come into
the body of the Church, with their friends and
neighbours, and there the Presbyter shall say thus:
Dearly beloved friends, we are gathered together
here in the sight of God, and in the face of his
Church, to joyn together this man and this woman
in holy Matrimonie.

The Scottish Book of Common Prayer, 1637

Muircliff Castle, Isle of Skye

September 28, 1818

Olivia was grateful that the next day and a half passed
in a flurry of activity as preparations for Isobel's marriage to Brodie MacDonald went into full swing. Isobel, of
course, was simply incandescent with joy that Hamish had
accepted Brodie into the family fold. While Olivia found it
difficult to witness her sister-in-law's happiness given the
insalubrious state of her own marriage, she was nonetheless
pleased for her too.

To ensure that Margaret could attend her daughter's
wedding ceremony, Muircliff's long-disused private chapel
was opened up and cleaned from top to bottom. The flagstones were scrubbed, the stained-glass windowpanes were
washed, the altar and wooden pews were polished, and all

the carpets were beaten. Fresh bunches of pale pink heather, purple lavender, and rosemary were gathered to decorate the interior of the chapel, and once the preparations were all complete, the cool, sacred space smelled like fresh sea air, beeswax polish, and the wild moors outside.

As Olivia expected, Hamish avoided her whenever possible; he clearly wanted them to begin leading separate lives straightaway. On the odd occasion they did bump into each other, he was scrupulously polite and considerate, but the warmth had left his gaze. Whatever passion or tender emotions he'd hitherto felt for her were gone; he'd either steadfastly buried them or rooted them out completely.

He was conspicuously absent at mealtimes—he took trays in his room or the library. And because he wanted to make sure everything was in order before he departed for London, he also spent a good deal of his time either touring his estate with Brodie and Mr. MacArthur, or holed up in his study, going over the books with one or both of them. It seemed Hamish had decided to let Brodie help manage the vast MacQueen estate, which meant the newlyweds would be staying at Muircliff—a situation both Isobel and the dowager marchioness were inordinately thrilled about.

Most telling of all, the jib door between Olivia's and Hamish's bedrooms was locked once more.

It wasn't until Isobel and Brodie's wedding ceremony took place that Olivia had the opportunity to spend any length of time with her husband again. Seeing him in all his kilted finery when he first appeared in the doorway of the chapel made her foolish heart long for their estrangement to end.

Of course, Isobel made a beautiful bride; she'd chosen a gown of misty blue muslin for the occasion, and her rich auburn hair was piled high and threaded with seed pearls and delicate ivory ribbon. Tears filled Brodie's eyes as Hamish escorted her down the aisle. Beneath her lace veil, Lady Sleat dabbed at her own eyes with a delicate lawn kerchief, and Tilda whispered to Olivia that she thought "Lady Bel" looked like a princess.

Olivia agreed. Although her gaze kept slipping to her husband until he joined her on the pew. Even then, he left a careful gap between them, which might as well have been as wide as the Minch. There was no touching of hands or accidental bumping of legs. No sideways glances or brushing of shoulders. And it was his mother he escorted to the dining room for the wedding breakfast after the ceremony, not her.

Pretending that nothing was wrong between them was one of the hardest things Olivia had ever done. She wanted to entreat Hamish to change his mind about living apart from her, but she realized her pleas would likely fall on deaf ears. She'd need fresh, clever arguments to challenge her stubborn-as-an-ox husband's entrenched beliefs about himself. But for the life of her, she couldn't think of anything that would be likely to succeed.

There was a single moment during the lively wedding breakfast when Olivia caught Hamish watching her with such focused, intense regard, her insides had trembled with hope and desire. But in the next instant, his expression became shuttered, and he looked away to beckon over a footman to attend to something at the table.

At least, if nothing else, Olivia was utterly convinced he was lying when he'd told her he didn't love her. But unless he could acknowledge how he truly felt and was willing to try to make things work, their marriage was doomed to fail. She couldn't do this on her own. He had to meet her halfway.

Following the wedding breakfast, everyone descended to the great hall to bid the newlyweds farewell. Hamish had offered them the use of the estate's hunting lodge, Kilmuir House, for their honeymoon. It was but a few miles away, high up on the moors, but it would give Isobel and Brodie the opportunity to enjoy some time alone together.

Olivia tried not to be jealous as she watched the blissfully happy couple mount their horses and then ride through the barbican passage together amid shouts and whoops from the assembled guests and Muircliff's staff.

When she eventually turned to look for Hamish, he'd already gone back inside.

Tilda tugged at the skirts of Olivia's lavender gown. "Lady Livvie, will you come and play with me and Mia?"

Olivia smiled down at the little girl. "I'd love to," she replied. Tomorrow they'd all be rising early to leave for London, so Olivia needed to check how Nurse Swan was progressing with preparations for the long journey. At least this time, the nurse would be accompanying them and there would be a lot more toys on hand to keep Tilda amused. Although, strangely enough, it seemed Tilda's favorite book was *The Fauna of Scotland and Its Isles: An Illustrated History*. It touched Olivia's heart that the child had grown fond of all her hastily spun tales.

Olivia was also touched that Tilda—with Nurse Swan's help—had been practicing the pronunciation of words and names she found tricky, including Olivia's name.

"I can say it, Lady Livvie, I really can. But I have to con . . . concentrate," said Tilda gravely. They were both sitting in one of the nursery's wide window seats with Miss Mia, the porcelain doll. The rays of light slanting in through the leaded panes made Tilda's light brown curls look just like toffee.

A tiny line appeared between her brows as she carefully pronounced, "O . . . Oliv . . . Olivia." A triumphant smile brighter than the sunlight dancing on the deep blue sea lit her face. "You're Lady Olivia."

"Oh, Tilda, you are so very clever," cried Olivia, and enveloped the child in a warm hug. Sadness tugged at her heart at the thought that if they did find the little girl's mother, she would soon be bidding her farewell also.

"I can say my name too," Tilda said as they drew apart.

"Your name?" repeated Olivia. "But isn't it Tilda?"

Tilda nodded. "Yes, but that's not all of it. My mama told me I have a longer name. It's . . ." The child frowned again in concentration. "Ma . . . Matilda."

"Goodness, that is such a pretty name too. Matilda. I like it very much."

Nurse Swan drew close. "And have ye told Lady Sleat how old ye are? We've been practicing that as well, haven't we, Miss Tilda?"

"Yes." Tilda held up three fingers. "I'm this many." She pointed to each one as she counted. "One, two, three. I remembered. So on my next birthday I'll be this many. Four." She held up another small finger to illustrate her point. "See. Four."

"Heavens, I'm very impressed. With you and Nurse Swan." While Olivia couldn't wait to tell Hamish what she'd learned, she wondered if Tilda might have recalled anything else useful. "And have you learned to say anyone else's name?"

"Yes," Tilda said, nodding. "Mia's name." She picked up the pretty doll and leaned her up against the leaded windowpane. "She has the same name as my mama."

This time Olivia couldn't contain her excitement. "She does?"

Tilda's brow knit. "It's a very tricky name though."

"My lady, this is news to me too," observed Nurse Swan. To Tilda she said, "Do you think ye can say it fer us now?"

"I'll try." Tilda's frown deepened. "It has 'you' at the beginning. You . . . You-feem . . ." She wrinkled her nose. "I can't do it."

"Euphemia?" ventured Olivia.

Tilda smiled brightly. "Oh, yes. That's Mama's name. Euphemia."

"And that's a very pretty name too," said Olivia, gently brushing one of Tilda's curls away from her eyes. "I'm sure it suits your lovely mama perfectly."

Tilda's expression grew solemn again. "The baron didn't like Mama though. He'd get cross with her and shout. He scared me. Mama said he was a bad man."

"The baron?" Olivia's pulse began to race. "Does . . . does he have another name? Something else your mama called him?"

Tilda shook her head. "I don't know. Mama just said he was 'the baron.' She would make me hide in my room when he came to visit. But I could hear him sometimes. When he shouted. He made Mama cry."

Oh, the poor child. Olivia's heart cramped. It sounded as though Hamish's original suspicions had been correct. That Tilda's mother may have been a former paramour or mistress who'd found herself in a difficult situation. She wondered if this baron—whoever he was—might be her new protector. But speculating on her own wouldn't do any good.

She needed to find Hamish.

When she bumped into Daniels in the gallery below the nursery, he informed Olivia that Lord Sleat was in his private study. By the time she reached the library, she was quite breathless with rushing.

The room was quiet save for the incessant pounding of the sea and her rapid breathing. Pausing by one of the tall arched windows, she took a moment to compose herself while admiring the spectacular view. The sun was setting, blazing a fiery trail across the dark waters of the Minch. To think that tomorrow she would be leaving here filled her with a horrible, aching sadness.

She really had no idea if she would ever return to Muircliff. Hamish would undoubtedly wish to divorce her as soon as her inheritance was secured. If her uncle and the trustee agreed to sign all the money over to him before her twenty-fifth birthday, they might part ways sooner rather than later.

How depressing to think this marriage would end before it had really begun.

To make matters worse, she might also be saying good-bye to sweet little Tilda very soon . . . But the child belonged with her mother. And there was no sense putting off this conversation with Hamish. He would be extremely keen to hear Tilda's disclosures.

As Olivia turned to face the tapestries along the library's back wall where the concealed door to Hamish's study was located, it clicked open and her husband emerged.

"Olivia," he said as though taken by surprise. In his hand he carried a sheaf of papers. "It would be arrogant of me to assume you'd come to see me rather than find a book." He approached his desk and deposited the papers on the blotter. His forehead creased with a frown as he added, "But I'll ask you all the same. Do you need to speak with me?"

"Y-yes, I do," she replied, moving closer to the ornately carved desk despite his rather lukewarm greeting. She nervously smoothed her palms over the skirts of her lavender-hued gown. "But not to talk about us and our situation, if that's what you're worried about. It's about Tilda. I was in the nursery with her just now and she . . . she said some things I thought you might be interested in."

Hamish's gaze was razor sharp. "I'm all ears."

"I thought you might be." Olivia quickly recounted what she'd learned about Tilda's age and her mother's name. "Do you have any idea who this Euphemia might be?"

Hamish blew out a sigh and deposited himself in the heavy Jacobean-style chair behind his desk. "Aye. I do. It could be Euphemia Harrington. I hope you'll forgive me for alluding to an indelicate subject, but she was a mistress I once employed."

Olivia sank into the chair on the other side of the desk and laced her fingers together. Tension knotted her belly. "I promise I won't go all missish on you about this, Hamish. What you did before we wed isn't any business of mine. But I do feel the need to ask you one question: if this Euphemia Harrington is Tilda's mother, could it be that Tilda is yours?"

A shadow passed across Hamish's face. "No. She's not."

"Oh . . . I'm not sure what to say, Hamish. Only that . . . Are you certain?"

"Aye. I am." Hamish's voice was grim with resignation. "The last time I had anything to do with Euphemia

Harrington was six years ago. If Tilda is only three years old, which I believe she is, there's no possible way I could be her father. But it makes me wonder why she chose to entrust Tilda's care to me."

It was obvious to Olivia and anyone who really knew him that Hamish was noble and tenderhearted beneath all his bluff and bluster about being a blighted soul. But belaboring the point wouldn't serve any purpose right now. Instead, Olivia said, "Tilda also mentioned that her mama was afraid of a bad man whom she referred to as 'the baron.' I questioned her further, but she couldn't tell me anything else about him other than that he had a terrible temper. He'd shout and make her mother cry."

Hamish's gaze hardened, and a muscle flickered in his jaw. "It sounds like this man was abusing Euphemia. At least verbally."

"Yes, I agree. Tilda said her mother would hide her whenever he visited. But she could hear their arguments."

Hamish shook his head. "It makes me sick just thinking about it." Blowing out a sigh, he stood. The interview was clearly over. "I thank you, Olivia. I doubt I would have been able to coax such information from Tilda. If it weren't for you, I'd still be floundering around in the dark."

Olivia rose from her seat. "I cannot take all the credit. Nurse Swan helped too."

Hamish inclined his head. "Then I am indebted to you both."

"You really have no need to be." Olivia could sense that Hamish wanted to return to his study. Through the open doorway she could see the corner of the desk he'd lifted her onto, and her throat tightened. She'd give anything to return to that place in which anything seemed possible with Hamish.

Swallowing hard, she cleared the lump of emotion clogging her throat before she spoke again. "It's obvious that you're busy, but before I go, I just wanted to say I've had time to think on what you said to me the other night, about living apart. While I'd like nothing more than to stay with one of my friends when we return to London, I believe it would be better if we appear amicably wed at least for the foreseeable future, as hard as that may be. If it seems we're estranged from the outset, there will be talk, and it might embolden my uncle to challenge the validity of our marriage. And I don't think either of us wants that. Uncle Reginald and the trustee won't sign over my inheritance to you unless they give our union their seal of approval. If they don't, we shall have to wait until I turn twenty-five to inherit."

That muscle twitched in Hamish's jaw again. "Aye, you're right."

"I know this will be difficult for both of us. But I just wanted to let you know, I'll do my best to stay out of your way. I don't want you to end up regretting what you did to protect me or, even worse, resenting me."

Hamish's gaze softened. "Och, Olivia. I could never feel that way about you. Don't ever think that."

She nodded. "Thank you. I'll bid you good night now, Hamish. Given the journey ahead of us, I wish to retire early."

The corner of Hamish's wide mouth lifted into a brief smile. "Good night to you too, lass," he said before turning back to his study.

As Olivia sped from the library and through Muircliff's halls to her bedchamber, she reminded herself that, if nothing else, at least Hamish had agreed they could still live under the same roof for the time being. Which meant she still had a little more time on her side to make her husband see reason.

All was not lost yet.

CHAPTER 22

Two of the ton's finest were seen entering London's most-whispered-about house of ill repute in broad daylight. And one is rumored to have recently wed over the anvil . . .

The Beau Monde Mirror: The Society Page

Soho Square, London

October 7, 1818

Maximilian Devereux, the Duke of Exmoor, gave a low whistle as he climbed from the hackney coach with Hamish. "So this is where Euphemia Harrington is currently working," he said, looking up at the fine town house with its pillared portico, white-bricked facade, and neat brass plate proclaiming it was Birchmore House. "I must say, my friend, from what I've heard, this bawdy house is not for the faint of heart."

"Aye, I know," agreed Hamish grimly as he pushed his beaver hat firmly onto his head. It was well-known in certain circles that this was an exclusive brothel of questionable practices. "And believe me, I'm more than happy you've come along to lend your moral support, or a helping hand if need be. I don't anticipate there'll be any trouble, but one never knows. Especially in an establishment such as this."

When his inquiry agent, Mr. Kent, informed Hamish

earlier this morning that his former mistress Mia Harrington was one of the prostitutes currently on staff here, Hamish was not only surprised but dismayed for her. Hamish rather suspected Mia would not have willingly chosen this life for herself. Indeed, her heartrending act of entrusting Tilda to his care all but confirmed it.

Mr. Kent also confirmed something that Olivia had shared all those weeks ago at Gretna Green—that Birchmore House was her cousin's brothel of choice. Just thinking about Felix de Vere being anywhere near Olivia or Mia—or any female, for that matter—made his blood boil.

"Shall we go inside?" asked Max, pulling Hamish from his dark thoughts. The duke glanced up and down the square before unnecessarily adjusting the fit of his perfectly tailored coat and his own top hat. "I, for one, am not keen to be lingering out the front of Birchmore House in broad daylight. Who knows what may end up in the papers."

"I agree," replied Hamish as he mounted the stairs in a few determined strides and rapped sharply on the shiny black door. "Let's do this."

It was opened by a ham-fisted footman. After subjecting them to a brief but thorough perusal from beneath a heavy brow, he ushered them into an entry hall, which was a study in crimson and gold, and dark wood. An oversized chandelier threatened to crash down upon their heads at any moment.

The thuggish footman relieved them of their hats. "If you'd like to take a seat, my good sirs." He gestured at a nearby velvet covered settee. "I'll just ring for Madam Birchmore."

"Madam Birchmore?" murmured Max as the footman turned away. "That can't be her real name."

Hamish's mouth twitched with a wry smile. "I agree. I suppose she thinks it's good for business."

Just then, a highly polished door that was flanked by a pair of large potted palms opened to reveal a petite yet wiry woman with dark hair scraped tightly into a no-nonsense bun. Attired in a severe gown of dark green wool, she looked more like the prim headmistress of a young ladies' academy than the proprietress of a notorious brothel. "Gentlemen, do come in," she said, stepping back to admit them both. "I'm Madam Birchmore."

Once they were settled in comfortable wingback chairs before the madam's desk, her sharp gaze settled on Max and then Hamish. "So what can I do for both of you today? I'm sure you're already aware that my establishment caters to the needs of all gentlemen, whatever they may be . . ." She pushed a slim leather-bound book across the blotter toward them. "This is our bill of fare. If you'd like to take a look, then tell me what type of service whets your appetite, I'll be sure to find just the right girl for you. Oh, and as I'm sure you've heard, absolute discretion is assured."

Ignoring the "menu," Hamish cleared his throat. "Actually, I already know what I want. I'd like to see Mia." His inquiry agent had informed him that Euphemia was currently using the shortened version of her name.

Madam Birchmore arched a thin brow. "Would you now? I must say, our Mistress Mia is quite popular at the moment. But you're in luck. As it's early in the day, she's currently free."

"Excellent."

"It will cost you double if there's two of you though," she added in a steel-laced tone that brooked no argument.

"I'm just here to watch," replied Max with suitably withering ducal boredom.

Madam Birchmore laced her fingers together on the desk. "And that's your prerogative, sir. But it will still cost you double."

Once a price was settled upon for an hour-long appointment with Mistress Mia, and Hamish had paid Madam Birchmore, she led them into another hallway and up a narrow flight of wooden stairs to the first floor.

At the end of the dimly lit hallway—heavy velvet curtains concealed the windows—Madam Birchmore stopped, and knocked on the last door. "Mistress Mia," she called through the oak panels. "You have company. Two handsome-as-sin gentlemen, in fact."

"Coming." A light, feminine voice Hamish immediately recognized floated out into the hall. And then the door opened to reveal Euphemia Harrington.

At the sight of him, her blue eyes widened and she blanched. "Oh . . ." She pulled her loosely cinched silk robe about her near-naked body. "Oh . . . I don't think . . ."

Quick as a flash, she attempted to close the door with a shove, but Madam Birchmore jammed her foot in the narrow opening. She was surprisingly strong for such a tiny woman. "Mia, you'll do as you're told, girl, or you'll be out on the streets."

The madam glanced back to give Hamish a tight, apologetic smile as she continued to wrestle with Mia for control of the door. "She's relatively new here. But she's not usually this skittish." Turning back to Euphemia, she hissed, "What the bloody hell is wrong with you? Open the door at once."

"Mia, I'm only here to talk," called Hamish. "About Tilda."

All at once Euphemia gave up the battle. Letting go of the handle, she shrank back into the shadows of the bedchamber.

Madam Birchmore gave a huff of annoyance. "The next time you do that, it'll be the butcher's brush for you, my girl."

"It's all right," said Hamish. "Mistress Mia and I have met before, and I think the shock of seeing me again, so unexpectedly, rattled her a little."

The madam planted her small hands on her hips and glared fiercely at Hamish. "Here, you're not one of those gentlemen who likes to beat women, are you? We do have some rules in place here, you know."

"No. No he's not," said Euphemia. "In fact, he's just the opposite, Madam Birchmore. And what he says is quite true. I was simply a little shocked to see him after so much time."

"Hmph." The madam snorted her skepticism. She lifted a small silver pocket watch hanging from a chain pinned to her bodice. "Between the pair of you, you've just wasted five minutes of the allotted hour. I'll charge extra if you go over time."

"I assure you, we won't," said Hamish.

"See that you don't." Clearly satisfied everything was in order, Madam Birchmore tripped off down the carpeted hall.

"Won't you come in, my lord?" murmured Mia Harrington. She pushed a glossy brown curl behind her ear as her gaze darted nervously to Max. "And your friend."

"Thank you."

The bedchamber was small but well-appointed, from what Hamish could see; it was barely illuminated by a branch of candles sitting upon the mantelpiece and a single candle atop a small dressing table. Although it was early afternoon, the velvet curtains were drawn; Hamish surmised it was to promote a dark, illicit atmosphere. The heavy scent of musk, sandalwood, and something vaguely floral hung in the air.

Mia crossed to the large tester bed and sat upon the edge of the crimson damask counterpane. Her blue silk robe slid open to reveal long, pale, slender legs clad in silk stockings and ribbon garters.

"So you found me," she said on a shaky sigh. Her eyes glimmered with tears. "I don't quite know how you did, but I suppose that doesn't really matter now." She gestured at a heavy oak chair with a padded seat by the window. "I'm sorry there's only one place to sit."

"That's quite all right. I don't expect we'll be staying long," said Hamish.

"Don't mind me," added Max as he prowled to the other side of the room and propped a lean hip on the dressing table. "Pretend I'm not here."

Hamish took up a position by the door. He didn't want to draw too close to the bed; the last thing he wanted to do was intimidate his former mistress. "Let me just begin by saying that even though Tilda is missing you, she's well," he said gently.

Mia pressed her lips together and nodded. "I knew you would take good care of her," she whispered.

"I know she's not mine."

"No. She's not . . ." Mia dropped her gaze. Her fingers twisted in her robe, and her tears began to fall. "I know you'll have questions. And . . . and I know you'll want me to take her back but . . ." She shook her head and dashed impatiently at her wet cheeks. "I can't." She gestured about the room. "I mean, look what I've been reduced to. This is no place for my sweet little girl."

Hamish's gut twisted. "Mia, I don't know what happened to you since we parted ways, but I'm here to help. I firmly believe Tilda should be with you, not with me."

Again she shook her head. Her fisted hands crushed her robe. "You can't help."

"Why not?"

"You just can't."

Hamish and Max traded a glance. The young woman's distress was palpable.

"Are you in some kind of trouble, Mia?" asked Hamish gently.

A harsh laugh escaped her. "Aside from the obvious?" She shook her head again. "No."

"Are you sure? Because Tilda mentioned there was recently a man in your life that both of you were afraid of. She called him 'the baron.'"

Mia Harrington's swallow was audible. "She's a child. She doesn't know what she's talking about."

"She's a very bright child and you know it." Hamish took a step closer. "Who is he, Mia? The Duke of Exmoor and I can both take care of him if he's bothering you."

"I can't say a word," she whispered. Her blue eyes were glassy with terror. "If he finds out I gave you his name—" She broke off and drew a shuddering breath. "He'll hurt Tilda. That's why I left her with you. He wouldn't dare do anything to her while she's living under your roof. You're a marquess, whereas I . . . I'm nobody."

Anger seared through Hamish's veins. "What has he done to you already? According to my inquiry agent, up until a few weeks ago, you were living in your own fine town house, courtesy of your arrangement with the Earl of Livingstone. Is that true?"

"Yes."

"Then what happened? Answer me truthfully."

Mia nodded. "Lord Livingstone was a most generous man. And yes, he did gift me a town house. He also provided me with a carriage and the most beautiful jewels. And I had such lovely plans. I was going to sell it all and move to the seaside with Tilda after the earl and I parted ways toward the end of the Season. I was going to pretend to be a widow who'd lost her husband at Waterloo. But then . . . then I got greedy."

A shadow passed across Mia's face. "Another gentleman of the ton I met at a soiree at the end of July offered to become my next protector. He pursued me with such vigor, like a man who was smitten, that I ignored some of the whispered rumors I'd heard about him . . . But it turned out the rumors were all true and the man was the devil himself. Everything he said to me was a lie. The jewels he gave me were paste. And what's worse, he then stole everything I owned. I signed over my house and its entire contents to him. I gave him my carriage, the horses, my jewelry, and even the contents of my wardrobe, because if I didn't, he said he would take Tilda away and sell her to—" She broke off and shook her head. "I can't even say it. Suffice it to say, I was terrified, and I still am. I had to give up Tilda to save her."

"Miss Harrington, you have to tell us who this man is." Max's voice was low, the menace in his tone unmistakable. "If he's a peer of the realm, he needs to answer for his actions."

"I dare not." Mia's mouth twisted with anguish. "He'll

kill me. I know he will. You don't know what he's like. What he's capable of . . ."

Hamish's knuckles cracked as he clenched his fists. "Mia, we'll be able to work out who this man is by simply making more inquiries." *And when I find him, I'll rip him to pieces.*

All color drained from the woman's face. "No. Please don't. I beg of you. Just let it go. And I know I have no right to ask you to continue caring for Tilda, Lord Sleat, but she can't live here with me. Not in a place like this. And I truly have nowhere else to go other than the streets."

"Miss Harrington, I might have a solution for you," said Max. "You mentioned before that you wished to live by the sea. Well, I own a small seaside property in the north of Devon that requires a housekeeper. Every summer, my elderly aunt, her daughter, and a paid companion visit to take the sea air. My aunt isn't fond of the bustle of any of the other larger seaside towns, so Lynton Grange suits her perfectly. I must warn you though, the house is quite isolated, and dashed difficult to find. But if you would like to take up the position . . ."

Hamish stared at his friend in surprise. "I must say, that's awfully generous of you."

Max shrugged. "I need a housekeeper, and Miss Harrington needs a safe situation. It seems like the perfect solution. There's a caveat though, one that I'm sure Lord Sleat will insist upon too . . ." The duke's gaze settled on Mia.

She lifted her chin. "And what's that, Your Grace?"

"You must take your daughter with you." Beneath the sweep of his dark blond hair, he quirked a brow. "What do you say, *Mrs.* Harrington?"

"I . . . I think it sounds perfect," she whispered, and tears filled her eyes again. "Look at me. You've both turned me into a watering pot. Thank you, Your Grace." She wiped her cheeks with trembling fingers. "And Lord Sleat."

"Think nothing of it, Mia." Hamish fished a kerchief from his jacket pocket. "Now dry your tears. I estimate that you have about forty minutes to get dressed and pack your things before the formidable Madam Birchmore comes back and starts demanding more money or whacking someone with a butcher's brush, whatever that is. The duke and I will wait outside, and then we'll all repair to Sleat House, where Tilda awaits with my wife."

For the first time since they entered the room, Mia smiled. "I'll be ready in ten."

CHAPTER 23

❧

No fairy forms, in Yarrow's bowers,
Trip o'er the walks, or tend the flowers.
Walter Scott, Esq., Marmion: A Tale of Flodden
Field

Sleat House, Grosvenor Square, Mayfair

Olivia sat on the flagged terrace of Sleat House watching Nurse Swan play with Tilda in the enclosed garden. The pair were currently looking for fairies among the lavender bushes lining the wall, and Tilda was giggling at something the warmhearted Scots nurse had said.

How odd to think that she'd only met Hamish a few short weeks ago in this very same garden—well, while she was stuck upon that ivy-clad wall. And all because of a mischievous cat.

Her mouth curved into a small smile at the bittersweet memory.

So much had happened since then, Olivia could barely comprehend it. In some ways, it all seemed like a dream. Or she'd magically become the heroine in someone else's book.

But she was yet to find her happy ending. A sigh escaped her as she picked up her cup of tea from the wrought iron table. She and Hamish were as estranged as ever, sleeping in separate bedchambers at opposite ends of Sleat House. They'd traveled in separate carriages to London and had slept in different rooms at each inn where they'd stayed. Most of their exchanges were polite but inconsequential.

Thank goodness her family didn't know this marriage was a sham. Of course, Olivia didn't want it to be. As her dear Scots friend Arabella would say, if wishes were horses . . .

Olivia's gaze drifted to the back of the neighboring town house. It felt especially odd knowing she was now the Marchioness of Sleat and no longer beholden to Uncle Reginald, Aunt Edith, any of her cousins, or even the odious Bagshaw anymore. When she'd arrived in London two days ago, Olivia had half expected her uncle or Felix to come and pound on the front door of Sleat House, demanding her return. But no one had.

Olivia wasn't quite sure what to make of it, but she suspected Hamish had something to do with Uncle Reginald's and Felix's conspicuous absence.

She gave an involuntary shudder thinking about Felix. At some point, she would like to retrieve the remainder of her belongings from her old bedroom next door, considering her current wardrobe was limited—she still only had the clothes she'd packed in her valise and some of Isobel's castoffs in her possession. Considerate as always, Hamish had recommended she send her lady's maid, Eliza, over with Sleat House's housekeeper, Mrs. Foster, and several footmen to collect it all if she didn't want to go herself. He'd also suggested she visit a modiste or two and order an entirely new set of garments. But Olivia just didn't have the heart to go shopping yet. Perhaps when some of her friends returned to town. She rather hoped they might come back to help her celebrate her twenty-first birthday in a week's time.

She was wearing one of Isobel's castoffs now—a lovely light green gown of sprigged muslin trimmed with lilac ribbons and a matching spencer. As always, Eliza had arranged Olivia's hair beautifully. Not that Hamish ever seemed to notice his wife's efforts to look as attractive and as elegant as possible.

The sound of voices drifted onto the terrace, and Olivia turned in her seat to regard the drawing room behind her. Since their return, Hamish had been so busy—either meeting with various gentlemen in the library or quitting the town house altogether and disappearing for such long periods—she'd barely seen him. She suspected that a great deal of his time was taken up with looking for Tilda's mother, Euphemia, and she was in two minds about how she felt about that. She'd grown terribly fond of the little girl, but deep down, she understood that Tilda belonged with her own mother.

And then Olivia saw the drawing room door open, and Hamish entered in the company of the exceedingly handsome Duke of Exmoor—Olivia had met the nobleman a few months before at Lord and Lady Malverne's wedding. But it was the pretty young woman with light brown curls and bright blue eyes on the duke's arm who snagged her attention.

It had to be Euphemia Harrington. There was no mistaking the resemblance between Tilda and her mother.

Olivia rose from her seat, her pulse quickening in anticipation. "Hamish," she murmured as he stepped onto the terrace with the duke and Mia Harrington. "You found her."

"Aye." He grinned. "I did. My lady wife, allow me to introduce—"

He got no further as Tilda squealed, "Mama," and then Mia was flying down the terrace steps onto the lawn and catching her daughter in her arms. "Oh, my baby girl," she sobbed, and sank to her knees with Tilda clinging to her as if she would never let her go.

Olivia's vision blurred. What a glorious, beautiful moment. Never in her life had she been so affected. Wiping the tears from her eyes, she watched Mia smother her ecstatic daughter's face with kisses.

It seemed everyone else was similarly moved by witnessing the reunion of mother and child. Nurse Swan, her hands clasped beneath her chin, was openly crying, and when Olivia glanced at Hamish, he was brushing a tear from his cheek too. Even the Duke of Exmoor's blue eyes were suspiciously bright.

Hamish drew close, and to Olivia's surprise, he laced his long fingers through hers.

"You've done a wonderful thing today, Hamish," she murmured, her heart swelling with pride for the man she couldn't help but love.

"And I would never have found Euphemia if it weren't for you."

"And Nurse Swan."

"Perhaps . . . Olivia, I . . ."

Olivia looked up into her husband's face, and her breath caught. The longing in his gaze was unmistakable. Dare she hope that he'd say something, anything, to indicate he'd changed his mind about her and their marriage? That he wanted to have children with her?

But when he spoke next, it was clear that he hadn't.

"You'll make a wonderful mother when you wed again one day—" he began, but Olivia cut him off.

"Don't, Hamish." She couldn't hide the bitterness in her voice as she let go of his hand. "Just don't. You once said, in this very garden in fact, that I should never underestimate my true worth. Well, I'm tired of you doing exactly that whenever it comes to me."

And then she descended the stairs and crossed the lawn to introduce herself to Mia.

She was wrong. Hamish knew the precise worth of his lovely wife.

The problem was, he didn't deserve her. That's what he told himself as he watched Olivia walk away from him.

Max drew closer and clapped him on the shoulder. "I think it's time for a celebratory brandy, old chap," he said. "Or whisky if you have it."

"Aye. Whisky it is."

"And when things settle down"—Max nodded toward Mia, Tilda, Nurse Swan, and Olivia—"I'll pay my respects to your new wife. It's been a while since I met her at Nate's wedding in June."

"Oh, I didn't know that you'd already been introduced."

Max shrugged. "I'm sure I mentioned it the other day when you were telling me all about your own wedding."

"No, you didn't."

"Hmm. It must have slipped my mind."

As Hamish poured the drinks, his gaze strayed to his friend. Max slouched in that negligent way of his against the French doors, watching the women fuss over Tilda. Or was it Olivia in particular he observed?

Hamish's gaze narrowed as he joined his friend and handed him his whisky. Yes, Max was paying particular attention to Olivia. He couldn't say that he blamed him—a man would have to be blind or on his deathbed not to notice how pretty she was.

So why was he, Hamish, suddenly experiencing this un-expected flash of jealousy?

He'd already told Max an abridged version of how he'd come to wed Olivia over the anvil. Of course, for Olivia's sake, he hadn't divulged all the messy details, but Max knew their marriage was ostensibly one of convenience un-til they divorced. He trusted his devilishly handsome, silver-tongued friend didn't have designs on Olivia . . .

As if he'd fathomed what—or rather who—was on Hamish's mind, Max said in a low voice, "MacQueen, are you certain you really want to let your wife go when she eventually inherits? I know your marriage was born out of necessity . . . but from what I've seen and heard of Olivia, she's a dashed lovely girl. I think it would be a shame not to give it your best shot."

Hamish sipped his whisky, relieved he wouldn't have to maim his friend to prevent him from having an affair with his wife. While Max knew he had nightmares—his friends Nate and Gabriel did too—none of them were aware how dangerous he became when he was in the midst of one. Or that his tainted bloodline precluded him from having a child. Aloud he said, "I never thought I'd see the day when the devilish Duke of Exmoor would be dispensing marital advice."

Max bared his perfect teeth in a wide grin. "Ah, you mistake my motives, my friend. It's within my best interests that you stay happily wed. You see, now that Nate and Gabriel are also well and truly leg-shackled, there'll be less competition when I go on the prowl."

As long as you don't go prowling anywhere near my wife, thought Hamish.

But then, one day in the not-too-distant future, some other man would be prowling around Olivia. And how would he feel then?

Hamish swallowed another mouthful of whisky to hide a snarl of frustration. The lass's twenty-first birthday was but a week away, and in a few days' time, he was due to meet with his own solicitor, Olivia's uncle, and her trustee, a certain Mr. George Thackery from the law firm Norton, Lyle, and Thackery. If Hamish could secure Olivia's money for her sooner, she could be free of him within a few short months. Perhaps even weeks.

With all his heart, he wanted to give this marriage his best shot, but at what cost to Olivia?

For her sake, it was a price he wasn't willing to pay.

It was so quiet now that Tilda had gone, Olivia swore she could hear the ticking of every longcase and mantel clock throughout Sleat House. The little girl had bid her a sticky, tearful farewell along with a grateful Mia about an hour ago. Apparently, Hamish's friend Max had arranged a private carriage to ferry them to Lynton Grange, one of his properties in Devonshire, because Mia would be taking up the housekeeper's position there.

While Olivia would miss Tilda terribly, she was also profoundly happy for her and Mia. After their departure, Hamish had disclosed that Mia had been in such desperate circumstances, she'd been forced to work at Birchmore House, the same infamous brothel that Felix sometimes frequented. To think that both she and Tilda would now have a safe and happy life, thanks to Hamish and his friend, warmed Olivia's heart immeasurably.

Less heartwarming was the fact that Hamish had also quit Sleat House a short time ago. Olivia had no idea where he'd gone or when he'd be back. She assumed he might have decided to visit one of his clubs, but she couldn't be sure. Charlie had once mentioned that her father, Lord Westhampton, and her brother Nate—before he wed Sophie—often spent entire evenings in such places.

She supposed she would dine alone in her room once more with only her books for company.

As Olivia trailed up the wide mahogany staircase to head for the bedrooms, she buried her nose in the small bunch of lavender she'd just picked. Hamish had told her that he didn't think chamomile tea or scented posies could cure his poor sleep and bad dreams, and while she tended to agree, there also wasn't any harm in continuing to use them if they provided some degree of relief, no matter how small.

Once she reached Hamish's bedchamber, she knocked on the door; she assumed Hudson might be about, tidying up, or polishing Hamish's boots, or doing whatever it was valets did for their masters.

When the middle-aged servant opened the door a minute later, he greeted her with a warm smile and a courteous bow. "Lady Sleat, how are ye this evening?" His gaze fell to the posy in her hands. "And I see you've brought some lavender fer his lordship."

"I'm well," she replied. "And yes, I picked some fresh from the garden. I-I've been meaning to dry some—the smell will be stronger—but it will take a few weeks."

"Would you like to pop it under his pillow?"

Uncertainty gripped Olivia as she glanced past the valet's shoulder into Hamish's bedchamber. This was the first time she'd seen his room since they'd arrived. A fire and several lamps illuminated the enormous oak tester bed; the furnishings were all in various shades of burgundy, deep gold, and rich brown. She wanted to go in, but she also felt as though she'd be trespassing.

Heavens, what a sad, sad thought.

Returning her attention to Hudson, she summoned a smile and offered him the posy. "Perhaps you should do it."

"Of course, my lady. But I'm sure his lordship wouldn't mind." The valet stepped back so that she might enter Hamish's room. "I'll have Mrs. Foster order some chamomile tea from Fortnum and Mason's as well," he said as Olivia tucked the lavender beneath one of the plump white pillows. "They're sure to have some."

"Thank you, Hudson. I appreciate your support," she replied. Unable to resist temptation, she smoothed her fingertips over the richly embroidered silk counterpane. Was it her imagination, or could she detect a hint of Hamish's cologne? Sandalwood and musk, and exotic spices blended with the fresh scent of the lavender. If Hudson weren't in the room, she would have crawled into the bed and buried her face in the pillows.

"No, it is I who should be thanking you, my lady," the valet said gently. He stood on the other side of the bed and wiped a nonexistent speck of dust off the highly polished bedside table. "I hope you'll forgive me fer speaking candidly," he continued after a moment, "but I just wanted to say you've done wonders fer his lordship."

Olivia felt a hot blush steal across her cheeks. "I don't think I've done all that much. But thank you all the same."

"'Tis true though." The expression in the valet's blue eyes was earnest as he added, "If there's anything at all I can do to help you, my lady, please let me know."

Olivia frowned. What was Hudson really suggesting? Should she ask him about her husband's purported tendency to lash out during bad dreams? There was only one way to find out if the valet would be willing to relay his side of the story.

Inhaling a deep breath, she decided to take the plunge. "Actually, Hudson. I rather w-wondered if you could tell me a little about the night you were hurt . . . by my husband.

He told me that you once tried to wake him when he was having a particularly bad nightmare . . . and that it did not end well."

"Aye." Hudson's expression grew solemn. "I'm happy to tell you what I ken, my lady. 'Tis true his lordship injured me, but he was not in his right mind. I do not hold him accountable for what happened. Indeed, it was partly my fault . . . And in hindsight, I should have known better than to try and rouse him under the circumstances. In my defense though, I was worried he might split his stitches around his eye and worsen his wounds."

Olivia nodded. "Hamish mentioned the incident occurred after he was injured at Waterloo."

"Aye, my lady. In fact, it happened in this very room. After Lord Sleat returned to London, I helped nurse him back to health. At least in a physical sense. As you can imagine, he was in a significant amount of pain, and his physician prescribed laudanum to help him cope with the agony, which was terrible indeed. The tincture of opium was verra strong and helped his lordship fall asleep. But it also made his nightmares that much worse. In fact, I suspect the drug made him hallucinate."

"Oh, my goodness," whispered Olivia. Arabella, who possessed a singular knowledge about all manner of medical subjects, had once warned her about the dangers of taking too much laudanum. "Do you think he was hallucinating when he attacked you?"

"Aye, I do," said Hudson grimly. "I hate to say it, but it seemed as though Lord Sleat wasna in his right mind that night. When I came into the room, he was thrashing violently and shouting like a lunatic. Tearing at his bandages like a man gone mad. And when I got too close, he hit out at me. His fist connected with my face, and I don't recall much after that." Hudson gestured to the opposite side of the room. "I remember flying backward, but then I was knocked unconscious. I suspect I hit my head on that oak chest—that one behind you—on the way down as there was blood on the edge of it. But I dinna blame Lord Sleat. It was an accident, pure and simple."

Olivia was breathless as she asked, "And have you seen any behavior like that since?"

Hudson shrugged. "Of course Lord Sleat has bad dreams fairly regularly. And yes, he does call out and toss and turn a bit. But not with the same intensity as that night three years ago. Even though he made me promise never to enter the room again when he's in the throes of a nightmare, I sometimes do. To make sure he's safe. But even at his worst, I havena seen him go berserk the way he did when he took laudanum. Suffice it to say, he has no' taken the drug since. He hates the stuff, in fact."

"So you don't . . . you don't believe my husband is dangerous?"

"No, my lady," Hudson said. Sympathy lit his blue eyes. "I do no'. Not at all."

Olivia sighed heavily. "But he thinks that he is."

"Aye . . ."

There was something about the valet's expression that gave Olivia pause. It seemed that Hudson might prove to be an ally in her fight to save her marriage. However, there was only one sure way to find out. Ignoring the telltale blush currently marching its way across her entire face, Olivia drew a deep breath and said, "You would have noticed that Lord Sleat and I . . . that I've never spent the night in his bed. And he's never visited mine."

"Aye . . ." Hudson's weathered cheeks reddened, too, but he didn't look away. "I have, my lady."

"And the reason is . . . he's terrified he'll accidentally hurt me if he falls asleep beside me. I haven't quite worked out a solution to our particular problem as yet—and perhaps I might never find one that will satisfy Lord Sleat. But I wondered if . . . Do you think you could see your way to helping me? Even if it's in a small way? After hearing you say that you don't believe my husband is dangerous, I think I might be able to come up with a plan that will help

Hamish to recognize his erroneous thinking. I know I'm putting you in a very difficult position. And you are free to say no. But you see . . . I love him. And I want him to be happy."

"For what it's worth, Lady Sleat," said Hudson solemnly, "I want his lordship to be happy too. And I believe he might find that with you. Indeed, I've noticed a change in him already. He's less . . ." The valet frowned as though he was trying to find the right word. "He's far less grim and moody. He smiles more, and his expression lights up whenever you're in the room. And even though he willna readily admit it, the chamomile tea and the lavender do help him to sleep more soundly. So yes, I will do what I can."

For the first time in such a long time, Olivia felt a glimmer of hope deep within her chest. And she smiled. "Thank you." With a little help and the power of a sound, logical argument on her side, she might yet win her husband over.

CHAPTER 24

My notion of things is simple enough. Let me only
have the girl I like, say I, with a comfortable house
over my head, and what care I for all the rest?
Fortune is nothing.

Jane Austen, Northanger Abbey

Sleat House, Grosvenor Square

October 8, 1818

What do you mean, thirty thousand pounds of my
wife's fortune has been siphoned off?" Hamish
slammed his fist down on his library desk and glared at the
sheaf of papers his man of affairs, Walter Faraday, had just
handed him. "How in God's name could her trustee—who
is he again?" Hamish scoured the letterhead. "This George
Thackery. How could he have allowed such a thing? I
thought Norton, Lyle, and Thackery was a highly reputable
firm of solicitors." Of course, Olivia had told him that Felix
de Vere had been pilfering small amounts here and there.
But nothing in the vicinity of thirty thousand.

"I know, my lord. It is a most shocking state of affairs,"
said Faraday in his usual dry, unflustered fashion as he
pushed his spectacles farther up his nose. Accustomed to
Hamish's outbursts, he hadn't flinched at all at his employer's display of temper. "When I met with Mr. Thackery at
his firm's offices, he was most rattled too. It appears that his

son"—Faraday scanned his notebook and tapped at a line of spidery script—"yes, his son, Giles Thackery, who was an articled clerk at the firm, has indeed been helping your wife's cousin to embezzle her inheritance money, just as you reported. Up until recently, the sums withdrawn were trifling—also just like you said. One hundred to five hundred pounds at the most, amounting to five thousand in total. And the occasions were few and far between." Faraday referred to his notes again. "But apparently a week ago last Monday, Giles Thackery withdrew a lump sum of twenty-five thousand pounds from Coutts. Again, a banknote, presumably signed by Reginald de Vere, was presented. And Giles hasn't been seen since."

Hamish wiped a hand down his face. "Has there been any sign of Felix de Vere since the twenty-five thousand pounds went missing? I assume you've had my inquiry agent, Kent, tracking both men?"

"Yes, my lord. Mr. Kent believes they both might be headed for the Continent. It also seems several creditors have been chasing Felix de Vere and the younger Thackery. Apparently they've both accrued some rather large gambling debts of late. Perhaps they've decided to lie low for a while to escape paying up."

Hamish shook his head in disgust. "Well, I hope Kent can flush the weasels out. And"—he rose from his seat and threw on his superfine jacket—"given that my wife's inheritance has been appallingly mismanaged, it only strengthens my argument that Reginald de Vere and the senior Thackery should sign everything over to me. At once."

"Yes, I completely agree with you, my lord." Faraday closed his notebook and pushed to his feet too. "In fact, I've almost finished drawing up the contract. It should be ready tomorrow."

"Excellent. And good work, Faraday," said Hamish as he walked his highly competent and efficient man of affairs to the door. "I trust that by Lady Sleat's twenty-first birthday, the entirety of her fortune will have been deposited into my account for safekeeping."

"Yes, indeed. That's what we're aiming for, my lord."

Once Faraday had departed in a hackney coach, Hamish took a moment to adjust his cravat in the entry hall mirror. His overly long hair was nicely ruffled and his expression suitably severe for his coming interview with Reginald de Vere. There was nothing like a glowering marquess with the scarred visage of a pirate and the physique of a Highland warrior to elicit fear in a man.

At least that strategy had worked when he'd confronted Felix de Vere in the King's Head Inn in Springfield. And if Hamish encountered that particular piece of vermin again, he wouldn't think twice about eradicating him.

As Hamish descended the stairs of Sleat House with purposeful strides, he was glad that Olivia was currently out on a shopping excursion with two of her good friends—Nate's wife, Sophie, Lady Malverne, and Nate's sister, Lady Charlotte—so she wouldn't see where he was going. He'd been heartened to see a genuine smile on her face this morning before she quit Sleat House.

It was Hamish's fondest hope that after he'd made short shrift of her uncle Reginald and George Thackery, she'd have even more to be happy about in the coming days.

The stony-faced butler of 16 Grosvenor Square, Mr. Finch, eyed Hamish warily as he took his card. "The Marquess of Sleat, you say?" he said with a sniff, as if he didn't quite believe Hamish could possibly possess such an illustrious title. "And you wish to see Mr. de Vere. But you haven't an appointment . . ."

"Aye," said Hamish, pinning the officious sod with a narrow look. "I don't. But according to my wife, Olivia, Lady Sleat—who also happens to be your employer's niece—it's her money that's currently being used to pay your wages as well as the rent on this property. So I rather think Mr. de Vere will be quite amenable to seeing me at such short notice. Don't you?"

The butler paled visibly. "Quite," he said in a clipped

tone and stepped back to admit Hamish into the vestibule.
"If you'd like to wait here"—he gestured at a nearby pair of
bergères by the foot of a wide, highly polished oak
staircase—"Mr. de Vere will receive you shortly."

"Quite," replied Hamish. Flipping out his coattails, he
then sprawled with deliberate negligence in one of the
chairs as if he owned the place. Well, technically, he did.

While he'd been in Scotland, he instructed Faraday to
find out who owned the town house and to then purchase it
on his behalf. The sale went through a few days ago, so
Hamish was now officially the new landlord of 16 Grosvenor Square. Of course, that meant his wife was now technically paying him rent, but that was neither here nor there at
the moment.

· He'd sort that particular detail out when he'd secured the
rest of Olivia's money.

Finch was true to his word, and within a few minutes,
Hamish was being led into a study of some sort toward the
back of the house.

Reginald de Vere was a heavily built man of middling
age with a balding pate. When Hamish was announced,
Olivia's uncle closed the leather-bound ledger he'd been
reading with a decided snap. A thunderous scowl marred
his brow as he rose to his feet.

"Lord Sleat," de Vere intoned in a deep voice, and
puffed out his barrel chest in a display of bellicose bravado.
"So you're the cur who eloped with my niece. I'm sure
you'll understand if I don't offer you my hand."

"And I wouldn't have bothered to take it if you had,"
replied Hamish with a calculated curl of his lip. He approached de Vere's desk but didn't take a seat. "I'm sure
you know why I'm here."

Olivia's uncle snorted. "Your letter and your solicitor's
correspondence were quite clear. But if you think for one
minute that I would sign over my niece's entire fortune to a
blackguard like you—"

"Well, considering I've just learned George Thackery's
son and your son, Felix, have embezzled thirty thousand

pounds and have scarpered off to God knows where, how can I trust you or Olivia's trustee to manage her fortune? So yes, I do expect you to sign every last penny over to me." Leaning forward, Hamish added in a low voice, "I have deep pockets myself, de Vere, and I will make your life a living legal hell unless you do as I say."

Reginald de Vere blanched. "You know about all that?"

"Aye," said Hamish. "And I also know about your son's rampant gambling and that various creditors are after him."

"Oh, my God." Reginald de Vere's countenance turned a sickly green shade that brought to mind pea soup. He plopped into his chair. "Oh, my God."

Hamish folded his arms. "You obviously know about Felix's dissipation and the dire financial straits he's in too?"

Reginald de Vere ran a shaking hand through his thinning blond hair. "Are you trying to blackmail me into handing over Olivia's fortune? Is that why you're here?" he snapped.

Hamish cocked an eyebrow. "Make no mistake, I'll get my hands dirty if I have to, de Vere. I'm certainly not above spreading a rumor or two about your son. Such a salacious scandal would completely ruin your daughters' chances of securing good marriages next Season, don't you think?"

Olivia's uncle sneered. "You're bluffing. How would it look if word got out that the Marchioness of Sleat's cousin is so immoral?"

Hamish shrugged. "I live on the Isle of Skye a good deal of the time, where there's not a newspaper to be had, and most of the population speak Scots Gaelic anyway. It will hardly bother me or my wife. You, on the other hand . . ."

"Christ." De Vere dropped his head into his hands. "Felix will be the death of me. I swear to God."

"Where is he, by the way?"

"Gone," said de Vere dully. "When one of the creditors from that vile establishment Birchmore House turned up on the doorstep looking for payment . . ." A violent shudder shook the man's body. "Needless to say, I threw Felix out. Disowned him. He and George Thackery's son can go to the devil for all I care."

Hamish stroked his chin as he contemplated the man slumping in his chair. Just the threat of disclosing all these secrets should be enough to obtain de Vere's cooperation. "So your son and Giles Thackery both disappeared a week ago, as soon as creditors began dogging their heels. And just recently, they also stole an additional twenty-five thousand pounds from my wife. I'd say they've both run off to the Continent to avoid being arrested and sent to debtors' prison, wouldn't you?"

Reginald de Vere's mouth twisted. "It would seem so."

"Well, here's what's going to happen now so this appalling scandal doesn't end up in all the papers," said Hamish. "Tomorrow, my own solicitor, Mr. Walter Faraday, is going to deliver a contract to the offices of Norton, Lyle, and Thackery. And when you and Mr. George Thackery sign it, and the entirety of Olivia's inheritance has been deposited into my bank account at Drummonds, I will continue to let you live here in this town house—which I now own, by the way—free of rent until your daughters are both wed. Think of it as *noblesse oblige*."

If Hamish had thought Reginald looked ill before, it was nothing compared to how he looked now. Sweat sheened his brow, and his countenance was as green as the leather blotter on his desk. "All right," he muttered from between clenched teeth, "all bloody right."

"Excellent." Hamish grinned and tapped his leather eye patch. "I'm glad we see eye to eye. I'll see myself out."

CHAPTER 25

Rumor has it that a certain marchioness has just celebrated her twenty-first birthday. And what better way to mark one's coming of age than to share a decadent ice or two with one's closest friends at London's premier tea shop?

The Beau Monde Mirror: The Society Page

Gunter's Tea Shop, Berkeley Square, London

October 15, 1818

I . . . I can't quite believe you're all here to help me celebrate my birthday," said Olivia in a voice that was more than a little choked with happiness. Tears misted her vision as she looked upon all her darling friends—Charlie, Sophie, and Arabella—sitting around her. They'd gathered at Gunter's for tea and cake and ices. To laugh and reminisce.

"There's no place we'd rather be," said Charlie, reaching out across the table past their half-drunk cups of tea to squeeze Olivia's hand. Her topaz brown eyes were suspiciously bright too.

"Aye," declared Arabella, digging in her fashionable beaded reticule and pulling out a fine lawn kerchief for Olivia. "And you mustn't cry, because then I will too. And I don't want to fog up my glasses. You know, when one is a countess, one must keep up appearances. Stiff upper lips must be maintained at all times."

"Yes, it's mandatory, even for viscountesses," agreed Sophie with mock graveness. "And I would say it's especially the case for marchionesses."

Olivia laughed. "Oh, how I've missed you all," she said, dabbing at her eyes. "You always make me feel so much better."

"That's what friends are for," said Charlie. She sat back and smiled. "I'm especially proud that my three best friends in all the world have found the men of their dreams. If I ever wed, we'll have to rename our group the Society for Enlightened Young Married Women."

"It will be your turn next, Charlie," said Sophie. "We'll make it our mission to help you find a love match next Season, if not before."

"Well, if not, I will not despair," said Charlie. "I shall simply become a daring bluestocking, beholden to no man. I'll travel and take lovers, and when I'm home, I shall be a doting aunt to all of your lovely children." She cast a knowing smile at her sister-in-law Sophie.

Sophie promptly blushed bright red. Her cheeks matched the raspberry-hued velvet of her spencer. "Yes, I'm increasing," she whispered. "And I know you're all going to ask when the baby's due so I'll tell you straightaway that it's March."

"Oh, that's wonderful," cried Arabella softly. Despite her earlier pronouncement that she was determined not to cry, her eyes brimmed with tears of happiness. "Congratulations."

"Yes," agreed Olivia, and pressed Arabella's kerchief back into her hands. "Con-congratulations." She tried not to feel a stab of envy. She was truly happy for sweet Sophie and Nate.

"Olivia, what's wrong?" asked Charlie gently. "I thought you were a little subdued when Sophie and I took you shopping last week. Now I'm convinced something is not right."

Curse her friend's hawklike perceptiveness. Olivia forced a smile. "I assure you, nothing's wrong."

"Yes there is," said Arabella, studying her through her spectacles. "You can't fool us, Olivia. We know you too well."

"I'm . . . I'm afraid I can't tell you," murmured Olivia, capitulating a fraction under all their concerned gazes.

"But you must," declared Sophie. "How are we to help you if you don't?"

Olivia glanced about the bustling tearoom. She oh so wanted their advice. But what could she tell them without betraying Hamish's confidence? She'd already told Sophie and Charlie that she'd met Hamish while trying to retrieve Peridot and that Hamish had offered to marry her to save her from Felix. And because she'd only been twenty, they'd eloped to Gretna Green.

But she'd let them believe that it had all been romantic and wonderful. She hadn't told them her marriage to Hamish was actually supposed to be one of convenience only. That he didn't want an heir. That they hadn't even consummated their union, and once Hamish had secured her fortune for her, they'd likely divorce so she could find happiness with someone else.

But she had no one else to turn to, and if she didn't seek her friends' help, she feared her heart would surely break.

She could trust Charlie, Sophie, and Arabella. She absolutely knew she could. They'd been through thick and thin together. Weathered scandal together. Made plans together and shared all their hopes and dreams and fears.

She drew a steadying breath and, in hushed tones, confessed all.

"Lord Sleat is right about one thing," said Arabella when Olivia had finished. "Laudanum is a dangerous concoction. But he's wrong about everything else. Just because his father was a despicable tyrant, it doesn't mean he will be."

"Yes," agreed Charlie. "Everything else he believes about himself is erroneous."

"What's most important, Olivia," said Sophie, "in fact, the only thing that really matters, is that you love each other. Because if you love him and he truly loves you, you will find a way to overcome any and all obstacles."

"I'm so glad you agree." Olivia smiled at her friends. "I do love him, with all my heart. And I know he cares for me, too, even if he hasn't said so yet. I . . . I think he's afraid to."

"Yes, men often are," agreed Sophie. "Nate certainly was."

"And Gabriel was too," added Arabella.

"And now they're absolutely besotted with you both," concluded Charlie.

Olivia sighed. "I've been racking my brains for days and days, trying to come up with ways to change Hamish's mind and convince him we can be happy. But he's as stubborn as a Highland bullock."

"Well, now we're here to help you," said Arabella. "I feel a scientific and methodical approach is required. Irrefutable logic and a sound plan of attack will sway him, I'm sure of it." She reached for one of Gunter's printed menus of the day and turned it over to the blank side. "Does anyone have a pencil?"

"I do," said Charlie, reaching into her reticule.

"Excellent." Arabella fixed her intelligent gaze on Olivia. "So the first topic that needs addressing is, how can you get this stubborn-as-a-Highland-bullock husband of yours to make love to you?"

"Yes, consummating your marriage should be at the top of the agenda," agreed Sophie. "And there are ways to safeguard against conception if he's not quite ready to become a father yet."

"That's very true," agreed Arabella. "Of course he'd be well aware of those methods, so perhaps you'll just need to reassure him that you are quite fine with his taking precautions if they're necessary to maintain his peace of mind. Another point you can argue quite successfully is that sexual congress doesn't need to take place in a bed. Especially if he's worried about falling asleep all the time."

There was a knowing twinkle in Sophie's eye as she

said, "You could always suggest that you only make love during daylight hours. Or even out in the open."

"And you could always tie him to the bedposts," Charlie offered with an arch smile. "Just in case he does fall asleep."

"All good points," said Arabella. "Let's make a list."

"I can't quite believe we're having this deliciously wicked conversation in Gunter's Tea Shop," murmured Olivia as Arabella began to write.

Charlie laughed. "If anyone did overhear, wouldn't it make a wonderful article in the *Beau Monde Mirror*? I can see it now: 'Former "Disreputable Debutantes" provide expert advice on how to effectively seduce one's husband.'"

"Perhaps we should write a book," said Sophie, her blue eyes alight with mischief. "*The Diary of a Disreputable Debutante; or, The Memoirs of an Enlightened, Blissfully Happy, and Thoroughly Pleasured Married Woman*. I'm sure it would sell very well."

Sleat House, Grosvenor Square

Olivia's twenty-first-birthday gift—an enormous bunch of hothouse roses—sat on the low oak table beside Hamish's brown leather wingchair in the drawing room of Sleat House.

Hamish sighed heavily and touched one of the dark crimson, satiny petals with a fingertip. He wasn't even sure whether Olivia liked roses. Or if she did, what color she preferred. He always pictured purple blooms in his head—heather and lavender and violets—whenever he thought of her.

Tucked in among the roses was a handwritten promissory note for three hundred and fifty thousand pounds. Olivia's uncle and her trustee had made good on their promise to deposit all of the funds in his bank account. And as soon as Olivia gained her independence, he would transfer the entire amount into her very own account.

He'd been preparing what he should say to Olivia all morning. He'd risen late, and as he'd breakfasted alone in his room, Hudson informed him that his wife's friends, Lady Charlotte, Lady Langdale, and Lady Malverne, had whisked Olivia away to Gunter's Tea Shop to celebrate her birthday.

He was pleased her friends were all back in town, spoiling her. Indeed, last night he'd spent quite a few hours at White's with Nate, Gabriel, and Max, catching up on all the latest news. Of course, he'd declined Max's invitation to pay a visit to the gaming-hell-cum-brothel the Pandora Club. Like Nate and Gabriel, he headed home. But unlike Nate and Gabriel, it wasn't to join his lovely young wife in bed.

A pang of envy penetrated Hamish whenever he thought about what he was missing out on. He'd give anything to sleep beside Olivia. To wake up with her head upon his chest. To run his fingers through her dark, unbound hair and feel her naked, luscious body pressed against his.

Even worse was the gnawing feeling of jealousy that had taken up residence in his gut when Nate had announced to them all that his wife, Sophie, was with child.

Lucky bastard. Since Tilda had departed with Mia, Hamish felt the little girl's absence keenly. Her smiles and giggles. Her warm hugs. Of course she belonged with her mother, but now there was a fresh hole in his heart that he suspected could never be repaired. His gaze strayed to the sideboard where his decanters of whisky and brandy sat, and a heavy sigh escaped him. No amount of alcohol could quell this yearning deep inside him. Or the ache in his chest at the thought that Olivia would be free to find love with another man and bear his children after they went their separate ways.

But would she? At Muircliff, she'd declared that she loved him.

And then he'd rejected her.

Hamish raked his fingers through his hair, then dropped his head into his hands, his elbows resting on his buckskin-clad thighs.

Christ. She had to leave. He had to break this off. Divorcing Olivia was the right thing to do. The old, familiar litany played in his head: *You're tainted; you're dangerous; she deserves better.*

Even to his own ears, those words rang hollow.

The door snicked open. Light footfalls approached.

"Hamish?"

He lifted his head and dredged up a smile. God's teeth, Olivia was beautiful. He hadn't realized until this very moment how much he enjoyed the sheer, simple pleasure of taking in the sight of his wife. He could wallow in the feeling forever and a day.

Perhaps because it was her birthday, she'd taken extra care with her appearance—not that he cared, of course. She could wear a potato sack and she'd still look gorgeous. His gaze greedily combed over her. Her dark brown hair had been curled and gathered into some sort of fashionable pile at the back of her shapely head. Her delectable figure was displayed to perfection in a well-cut, elegant gown of purple silk—he supposed the modiste who'd fashioned it might dub it "amethyst." At her throat she wore her mother's silver locket, and below her delicate earlobes danced pearls shaped like teardrops. Contrary fool that he was, he was also inordinately pleased to see that she still wore his signet ring.

While he blatantly perused her body, Olivia's gaze settled on the bunch of roses.

"Are . . . are those for me?" she asked softly.

"Aye," he said gruffly. Picking up the bouquet, he rose to his feet. "Happy birthday, Olivia."

She drew closer, and her violet-and-vanilla scent mingled with that of the roses, making his mouth water. "Thank you," she murmured. Her fingers brushed his as she took the bunch from him, and he had to resist the familiar urge to drag her into his arms and ravage her sweet mouth.

When she plucked the promissory note from among the bloodred blooms, she frowned. And then her eyes widened. "What's this?" she breathed.

"Your inheritance. Your uncle and the trustee, Mr.

Thackery, handed the funds to me on a silver platter."
Drawing a deep breath, he plowed on with the hardest thing
he would ever have to say. "After we divorce, I'll transfer
the entire sum to you," he said through stiff lips. Each
horrid word of the prepared speech he uttered felt like a
lash to his soul. "The whole three hundred and fifty thousand pounds. We'll have to set up a bank account in your
name, of course. But before that happens, we'll need to return to Scotland. You'll then be able to sue me for divorce
on the basis of adultery, just as we discussed. I expect it
won't take long for it to all go through. I'm afraid there'll
be a dreadful scandal, but in time it will die down. You're
young and wealthy and beautiful. You'll soon find someone
else."

But Olivia shook her head and placed the roses and the
promissory note on the table. "Hamish," she said gently.
Stepping forward, she clasped his hands and looked up into
his face. Her dark, velvet-soft gaze connected with his. "I
thank you for everything you've done for me with my whole
heart. But I'll never want anyone else. You know I don't
want a divorce. And I don't think you really want one
either."

His resistance was threatening to crumble like Muircliff's burned south tower. He forced himself to adopt an
expression that would intimidate. An unyielding, hard-as-
steel glare. "Yes. I do."

"Oh, Hamish." Her lovely mouth curved with a soft
smile. "You really need to stop trying to save me."

Hamish inhaled sharply. "That's not what I'm doing."
Olivia reached up and cradled his chiseled, rock-
hard jaw. "That's exactly what you're doing. You've been
trying to save me from the moment we first met. And that's
why you keep pushing me away and denying what's in your
heart. You want to save me from the monster you mistak-
enly think you are. But I love you, Hamish MacQueen. And

I have for the longest time. I'm not going anywhere. And if you send me away"—she lifted her chin—"I'll only come back. You're not the only one who's stubborn, remember?"

A muscle flickered in Hamish's lean cheek. His throat worked in a swallow. "You don't know what you're talking about," he murmured huskily. "You're young, and just like Isobel, you only fancy yourself—"

"In love? Yes, I'm young. But this is not a passing f-fancy. I will admit, that for quite some time, I was in love with the idea of you. Charlie told me about the notorious Scottish rakehell, the Marquess of Sleat, at the beginning of the Season. And it is also true that I admired you, my handsome, mysterious neighbor, from afar for months and months. In a decidedly silly, girlish way of course.

"And then we met and desire replaced my calf-love. I burned for you, Hamish, with an intensity that frightened me. But little by little, I got to know you, and it's the *real* you, in here"—she brushed her fingertips across his temple—"whom I fell in love with. All of you. All your fears and imperfections. And all the very best parts of you too. Your kind heart. Your strength. Your willingness to go out of your way to help others. To save others without fail. Not just me, but your mother and your sister. A little girl who could very well have been your daughter. Your former mistress. Heavens, I'm sure you would have scaled that garden wall just outside and climbed that beech tree to save Charlie's cat if I'd asked you to.

"But no matter how much you try to hide from me, you can't. You might play the brutish beast, but I can see through your fearsome, gruff exterior to the man beneath. I'm not afraid of any of your scars, inside or out. And I'm certainly not afraid of what I want."

Both of her hands cradled his profoundly handsome face. How she'd love to kiss away that anguished expression. The tight lines bracketing his mouth and his eyes—one sightless and concealed by a leather patch, but the other a beautiful storm-cloud gray. But her kisses wouldn't heal.

Only her own, imperfectly formed words could do that. "I . . . I know I've said it before, but I'll say it again. I want you, Hamish, quite desperately and un-unashamedly, and I will always choose you over any other man. I want our marriage. I want to have your children. We can be happy together. I feel it in here." She touched her chest where her heart raced quite madly. "And I feel it in my soul. We—both of us—just have to be willing to make it work."

"God knows I want to, Olivia." Hamish's deeply graveled voice was almost a groan. "Only I don't see how. I'll always be deathly afraid that I can't control myself when I'm asleep. If I ever hurt you—" He broke off, his voice cracking. "I could never forgive myself."

A violent tremor vibrated through him as Olivia slid her hands to his shoulders, so taut beneath her fingertips. "Hamish, you ask too much of yourself. But I understand that you fear what you can't control. So don't try to. If we must always sleep in separate beds as many other ton couples do, so be it. Or we can have another bed installed in your room. Or mine. I don't care. A man with your sexual prowess can't deny that we can make love anywhere, anytime. You can have me on the terrace or on the stairs. Take me up against a wall or on the dining room table or on your library desk in the middle of the day. That way you don't need to fret about accidentally falling asleep beside me. In fact, we could even agree to abstain from engaging in all forms of nighttime bed sport if it makes you feel better." She smiled. "I'm willing to compromise if you are. Then we can both eat our cake and have it too.

"And if that's not enough to convince you"—she lifted one of his hands and feathered a kiss across his scarred knuckles—"I know you don't have an inherently violent streak. Hudson told me that you'd taken laudanum and were hallucinating when you struck him. And you've never done anything like that since. So I won't let you end our marriage just because you have this mistaken belief you are monstrous and sinful, when nothing could be further from the truth. I only see the good in you, Hamish. I love how noble you are. I wish you could see yourself the way I see you. I truly do."

Hamish released a great shuddering sigh and bowed his head, pressing his forehead to Olivia's. One of his hands crept along her shoulder, then clasped her elegant nape beneath the heavy fall of her dark, glossy curls.

Olivia's heartfelt declarations, her sweetness, her strength, her willingness to believe in him and stand by him, her love, all of it disarmed him. Destroyed all of his defenses.

This infinite tenderness in her touch and in her gaze. This complete acceptance of all that he was and everything that he wasn't . . . It was his undoing.

How could he resist her, his lovely wife? For her, he could be brave.

For her, he would do anything.

He lifted his head and, with his other hand, caressed her beautiful face. "Olivia. My sweet, bonnie lass. *Mo chridhe.* I love you. I cannot deny it. Indeed, I love you so much and so fiercely, I fear I will be consumed by it. I can feel the power of it with every beat of my heart. The surge of it in my blood. It resonates through my whole body, right down to my very bones. And I will love you with every fiber of my being until the moment I draw my last breath."

"I believe you, Hamish," she whispered. Her brown eyes were luminous with tears. "I feel exactly the same way." Turning her head, she kissed his palm. Then she stood on her tiptoes, reached up, and pressed her mouth to his. She kissed him with deliberate, agonizing slowness. Her silken, petal-soft lips brushed and teased. Her breath, warm and sweet, melded with his.

And Hamish melted. *Yes.* On a groan, he dragged Olivia against him and deepened the contact, tasting her thoroughly. Drinking her in.

This. This was what he wanted. These endless, perfect,

passionate, ardor-drenched kisses. He would never tire of them. They would feed his hungry soul until the end of time.

Olivia slid her mouth to his ear. "Hamish, my dearest heart," she whispered. "Love me. It's time to make me yours. I burn for you so badly, I fear I'll catch fire if you don't."

"Gladly." With a growl, he swept her into his arms.

"Where are we going?" she demanded. But her reddened, kiss-swollen lips trembled in a smile.

"To my bedroom of course," he replied as he exited the drawing room and crossed the hall with floor-eating strides. "It's only three o'clock in the afternoon, so there's plenty of daylight left. And as this is your first time, we're going to do this properly."

"I hope we're going to do rather improper things too."

"Aye." Hamish grinned. "You can be sure of that."

Kicking the bedroom door shut with his booted foot, Hamish carried Olivia to the bed and sat her on the edge of the mattress. Then, after drawing the curtains, he made sure the room was secure and valet free. There would be no interruptions. Not today.

He wanted his wife all to himself.

Olivia had already begun to let down her hair when he returned to the bed.

"Here, let me help," he murmured, feeling for combs and pins in the glorious tumbling mass.

Tipping her head back a little, she smiled up at him. "Only if I can help undress you too."

"We have a deal."

Within minutes, Olivia was wearing nothing but her chemise, and Hamish was naked from the waist up. Discarded clothes were scattered over the silk counterpane and on the Turkish rug beneath his bare feet. His swollen, aching cock strained against the fall of his breeches.

Olivia lightly raked her nails over his bare chest, making him shiver with want. "In your study at Muircliff, you told me that you were a braw Highlander, Hamish. And I

couldn't think of a more apt description. Just look at you."
Her dark eyes were heavy-lidded with longing as her gaze
traced over his body. "Such power and beauty. I can't believe you're all mine."

"Believe it, lass. Every single inch of me is yours."
Hamish rubbed his fingers lightly over one of her dusky
pink nipples and watched it pucker with arousal beneath
her shift. "And I cannot wait to claim you."

Tenderly cupping both of her full breasts, he tested the
weight and glorious feel of them. Reveled in the way her
breath caught and how she closed her eyes, her expression
dreamy.

Lowering his head, he latched onto one impudent nipple
and drew on her gently through the fine lawn. Olivia
gasped and clutched at his head, burying her fingers in his
hair.

"Oh, yes, Hamish, yes," she breathed.

"We need to get rid of this," he murmured between
suckles, tugging at her chemise.

"Gladly," she whispered, echoing him. She shifted her
weight to free the hem, and then Hamish dragged the gar-
ment off, revealing all of her beautiful curves. Her porcelain, almost translucent skin. The downy black curls
between her thighs.

Lust—hot, hard, and demanding—tore through his
veins. Only just suppressing a coarse word of heartfelt ap-
preciation, Hamish swallowed, and then he coaxed her
slender legs apart. "Lie back for me, *mo chridhe*."

"But you haven't taken off your breeches yet," she said
with a pretty pout.

"Shh," he said with a wolfish grin, pushing her down
onto the mattress with gentle hands. "All in good time. I'm
about to have my cake and eat it too."

Dropping to his knees, Hamish hooked Olivia's legs over
his bare shoulders, then diligently applied himself to devouring her delicious quim. He lapped, he suckled, and he savored Olivia's sweet nectar. Mercilessly tortured that little
pearl-hard nub where her feminine pleasure was centered

with tiny flicks and fluttering licks of his tongue until she was panting and writhing and arching off the mattress. Pulling his hair and calling his name.

When she at last tumbled into ecstasy, he rose to his feet and stripped off his breeches, then joined her on the bed. She immediately reached for him, trailing her fingertips up his engorged shaft. He sucked in a breath, and his belly contracted as she traced along a pulsating vein and explored his cock's shiny head—the ridged edge and tiny indentation on the underside. He was content to let her play until she leaned down, intending to take him in her mouth.

He hissed and caught her chin, lifting her head. "Not now, lass," he grated out. "I'll not last, and I want to spend inside you."

"You do?" she whispered, her eyes alight with delighted surprise.

"Aye." Hamish skimmed his hand across her lushly rounded hip and gently cupped her mound. The dark, feathery curls were soft beneath his fingers. "Our hearts are wed, so we'll do this the way it should be done when a man beds his wife for the very first time," he said gravely. This moment was important, and he wanted Olivia to understand he was sincere. "I won't use a sheath, and I won't withdraw. And if I plant a bairn in here"—he leaned forward and kissed the smooth-as-cream plane of her belly—"I'll be happy for it." Looking up, he captured her gaze again. "And if our child takes after you even just a wee bit, I'll be a blessed man indeed."

"Oh, my love." Olivia touched his cheek. "You say the most beautiful things."

So . . ." Hamish began to stroke the damp, warm crease between her folds. "Are you ready for me, *mo chridhe*?"

Biting her lip, Olivia nodded. Her belly had knotted with nerves. "Yes. I mean, as ready as I'll ever b-be." Sophie and Arabella had both mentioned that there'd been some degree of discomfort during sexual congress the very first time. But she knew Hamish was an experienced and skilled lover, and she believed he would make this pleasurable for her.

"Good." He rose over her and kissed her slowly and deeply with a tenderness that made her heart ache. Teased and taunted her breasts with decadent swirling licks and hot, toe-curling suckles. And then he found her slick passage and pushed one of his long, wicked fingers inside her, stroking gently. At the same time, his thumb rubbed in tiny, teasing circles over her sensitive bud at the apex of her sex.

Despite the gathering pleasure, Olivia's inner muscles clenched, and she dug her fingers into Hamish's wide shoulders.

"I know this intrusion will feel odd, even uncomfortable at first," he murmured as he pressed another finger inside her, "but it will help if you try to relax. I'll be as gentle as I can when I enter you."

She nodded. "I trust you, Hamish," she whispered. "And even if it hurts, I won't mind."

By degrees, the tension began to ebb away from Olivia's body. When a tiny thrill sparked and she began to undulate against Hamish's hand, eager for more, he nudged her knees apart and settled between her legs. His erection was hot and hard against her inner thigh.

"Oh, my love. My sweet Olivia. I can't wait to be inside you." Hamish's breathing was unsteady as he withdrew his fingers, then braced himself on one elbow. Hovering over her, he gripped his shaft in one hand and then positioned the broad, velvet-smooth head of his member against her virginal entrance. All at once he pressed forward, and Olivia bit her lip to suppress a whimper. Her whole body stiffened, and her fingernails marked his back. The burning sting of his entry took her own breath away.

"I'm sorry, my heart." Hamish's voice was low and ragged at the edges, as if this act of love pained him too. "But the worst will be over soon." He surged forward, claiming her body in a series of forceful, unrelenting plunges until he was sheathed to the hilt.

"It's done, my brave lass," he whispered, lowering his forehead to hers. "We are one. You're mine."

"Always and forever," she whispered, and grasped the back of his head, urging him to kiss her. The brush of his breath, the slide of his firm lips, the gentle caress of his tongue helped to take her mind off the fact that her most intimate flesh had been invaded. Filled and stretched in a way she never could have imagined. This joining of their bodies was strange and overwhelming yet exhilarating at the same time.

His mouth still fastened to hers, Hamish began to move, retreating and then gliding back into her, again and again, establishing a slow, steady rhythm. Very soon, and much to Olivia's surprise, pleasurable sensations replaced the pain. Each time Hamish slid in and then withdrew, his hot, hard length seemed to rub against some special place deep inside her, eliciting tremors of excitement. And then she began to move, too, lifting her hips to meet his, suddenly driven by a desperate need to find the overwhelming satisfaction she sensed that only this man could give her.

The exquisite friction began to intensify, and Hamish, perhaps compelled by the same urgent hunger, increased the pace and force of his thrusts. He shifted, changing the angle of his penetration, and plunged deeper and faster and harder. Working in and out of her body like a man possessed.

Olivia panted and gasped and clutched at Hamish's sweat-slickened shoulders. Her breasts bounced, and her nipples grazed his chest. She could feel her orgasm drawing closer, rushing toward her, and her inner muscles began to quiver. But that blissful crest she sought was frustratingly just out of reach.

Hamish's breathing was harsh and rapid too. His gaze unfocused. But somehow he sensed she needed something to push her over the edge. He reached between their bodies and thumbed her excruciatingly sensitive nub, rubbing circles over it in just the right way.

"That's it, Olivia," Hamish rasped between frantic thrusts. "Come for me, lass. Come hard."

And then all at once Olivia found heaven.

Her back arched and she cried out as euphoria engulfed her entire body. She was drowning in pure pleasure, oblivious to almost everything except the devastating sensations washing through her in great rippling waves.

Through it all, Hamish kept pumping. But then he, too, froze, and a deep, shuddering groan spilled from his throat. Olivia opened her eyes and took joy in watching her husband climax. Reveled in the sight of his ruggedly handsome face contorting in agonized ecstasy. Smiled when he swore beneath his breath. She could feel him jerking and pulsing inside her. The hot rush of his seed.

Her heart swelled, and tears of unadulterated happiness slipped from her eyes as Hamish collapsed, chest heaving, his head resting on the mattress beside hers. Her hands came up to embrace him; her fingers sifted through the thick, damp locks at his nape, then traced over the trembling muscles and taut sinews of his sleek back. He was heavy, but she didn't mind at all. Not when she felt so replete and completely cherished. If this was all a dream, she never wanted to wake up.

"I love you, Hamish," she whispered against his temple. Other declarations of undying devotion trembled on the tip of her tongue, but then she realized they didn't need to be said. Because this moment was perfect just the way it was.

He raised his head. "And I love you, Olivia," he said huskily, sincerity shining in his gaze, "with everything that I am or ever will be. My heart, such that it is, is yours and yours alone. Forever." The corner of his wide mouth suddenly kicked up into a lopsided grin. "God above, it feels so good to say that."

Olivia caressed his beloved, smiling face. "Then say it again, my darling husband."

"I love you." He turned his head and pressed his lips to her palm. "I love you." He brushed a strand of hair away from her flushed cheek. "I love you." And then he dipped his head, and words were no longer necessary as he showed her how much she truly meant to him with his kiss.

Epilogue

❧

Give me but a little cheerful company, let me only
have the company of the people I love, let me only
be where I like and with whom I like, and the devil
take the rest, say I.

Jane Austen, Northanger Abbey

16 Grosvenor Square, Mayfair

October 18, 1818

L ady Sleat to see you, ma'am."
 Olivia smoothed her snowy muslin skirts and lifted
her chin as she passed Mr. Finch and entered the drawing
room of the town house Hamish now owned—a residence
that had never, ever felt like home while she'd lived there.

She'd dressed with care for this occasion. Creamy
pearls—another birthday gift from Hamish—adorned her
throat and her ears, and her cherry red velvet spencer
brought out the auburn tints in her dark curls. At least her
lady's maid, Eliza, had told her so as she'd put the finishing
touches to Olivia's Grecian-inspired coiffure.

To her surprise, Aunt Edith, Patience, and Prudence all
curtsied with due deference when she paused on the edge
of the Persian rug. Even more astonishing was the sight of
Agnes Bagshaw, who presently lingered in a far corner of
the room, dipping into a grudging semblance of a curtsy

too. The woman's expression was sullen, but Olivia really didn't care. Not anymore.

"Oliv . . . I mean, Lady Sleat," said Aunt Edith, drawing her attention. "Welcome home."

"Yes, welcome," chimed in Prudence, and curtsied again, quite unnecessarily. When Aunt Edith jabbed her with her elbow, her cheeks grew bright with color.

"You look well," offered Patience. Her face was set in a perfectly polite expression, but her blue eyes dipped to Olivia's throat. No doubt she was coveting Olivia's pearls.

Olivia inclined her head in acknowledgment and attempted to calm her racing pulse and quickened breathing. She might be a wealthy, well-connected marchioness now, but that didn't erase the ingrained feeling of inadequacy that knotted both her tongue and her belly as she prepared to speak. It shouldn't matter that she stammered, but she knew how much her family looked down upon her because of it.

And then she remembered that Hamish and not a single one of her real friends cared a jot. They loved her all the same. They were her family and all she'd ever need.

The thought of their smiling faces lent her strength as she said with deliberate slowness, just as she'd rehearsed in front of her dressing table mirror, "Thank you for seeing me at such short notice. I . . . I won't stay long as I'm sure you're all rather busy."

"Oh," said Aunt Edith in the precise tone of one who's been taken aback. "Are you certain? I'm sure Cook can prepare afternoon tea in a jiffy. And we still have a touch of a very nice Lapsang souchong in the tea caddy."

"That all sounds lovely," said Olivia. "But I'm afraid I have another en-engagement with Lady Malverne, Lady Langdale, and Lady Charlotte Hastings. You might recall we all attended Mrs. Rathbone's Academy for Young Ladies of Good Character together?" She only felt a trifle guilty that she'd deliberately listed off the names of all her aristocratic friends.

Her aunt's brow furrowed. "Oh . . . oh, of course." She wrung her hands in apparent agitation. "So . . . so if you don't mind my asking . . . I mean, I do not wish to appear rude . . . But what is the purpose of your visit, my lady? If . . . if there's anything you need—although I believe your maid and house-keeper have removed everything from your old room—you only have to say so and I will endeavor to do my best to accommodate you. Indeed, your uncle and I are most grateful that Lord Sleat is content to let us reside here for the time being."

Olivia smiled inwardly. She'd never thought she'd see the day her aunt would be fairly groveling at her feet. But she did not wish to prolong this interview. She had other, better things to do. "Lord Sleat is a most magnanimous man, and I'm blessed indeed to have met him. I could not wish for a more loving and attentive husband. But I digress. The purpose of my visit is to simply reassure you all"—Olivia caught the eye of her aunt, and her cousins in turn—"that I bear none of you any ill will despite your ill treatment of me."

"Oh, that's a bit much," began Prudence, but Aunt Edith elbowed her again.

"Please disregard Prudence. She has no idea what she's saying," said Aunt Edith.

"I'm sure she does," returned Olivia, "but I'm going to ignore her slip of the tongue."

Prudence blushed, and Olivia continued. "Prudence and Patience, I also wish to inform you that I will sponsor your debuts next Season. But . . ." She paused, waiting for her cousins to stop squealing. "My charity will extend no further. I will not be taken advantage of."

"Of course," said Aunt Edith. "We wouldn't dream of doing such a thing. Would we, gels?" She shot meaningful looks at her daughters.

"No, no we wouldn't," agreed Patience.

"We'll be most grateful," added Prudence.

"Yes, I'm sure you will." Olivia replied with a tight smile. "Well, as pleasant as this . . . this reunion has been, I really must bid you all adieu. Until we meet again . . ." Olivia tilted her head, and her aunt and cousins curtsied once more.

"Good day, Lady Sleat," they chorused as Olivia turned and quit the room. She couldn't resist swaying her hips a little as she walked. She was married to a wicked rakehell after all, and he'd expect nothing less.

As soon as Olivia stepped across the threshold of Sleat House, Hamish emerged from the library, and despite the fact that there were servants present, he swept her up into his arms. "How did your meeting with your aunt and cousins go?" he asked after he'd finished giving her a resounding kiss.

Olivia smiled up into her devastatingly handsome husband's face. Since they'd consummated their love and affirmed their mutual and undying devotion, she'd noticed a brightness in his expression and a spark in his eye that hadn't been there before. It warmed her heart immeasurably to see that he was so happy. "It went well enough," she replied, adjusting the fall of his cravat. She'd managed to dislodge some of the artful folds during their rather amorous embrace.

"One would hope they were suitably contrite."

Olivia arched a brow. "I think we reached an understanding."

"Excellent." Hamish tucked her hand into the crook of his arm and escorted her toward the stairs rather than the drawing room, where she'd been intending to go.

"Where are you taking me?" she asked.

He grinned. "Upstairs. To our bedroom."

"But Charlie, Arabella, and Sophie will be here soon. They're going to help me plan the menu for tomorrow night's dinner party. And it needs to be perfect. Aside from the fact Nate, Gabriel, and Max will be here, Lady Chelmsford and Lord Westhampton are going to attend too."

"How soon is soon?"

"Half an hour."

"That's plenty of time for what I have in mind," Hamish murmured, dropping a whisper-soft kiss beside her ear. "I swear to you, you won't regret it."

Olivia laughed as a heady mix of joy and desire brimmed inside her. "My darling husband, if you are making such a heartfelt promise, I'm absolutely certain that I won't."

ACKNOWLEDGMENTS

An enormous thank-you must go to my brilliant editor, Kristine Swartz. I'm deeply grateful for your clear insight and patience, and for your ongoing faith in my stories. As always, I'd like to thank the dedicated staff at Berkley Romance, including my fabulous copy editor, the publicity and marketing teams, and also the design and cover art teams—my goodness, I fairly swooned when I first saw the cover for this book. Thanks to all of you from the bottom of my heart.

Of course, I also want to thank my amazing agent, Jessica Alvarez. I'm so glad I threw my hat into the #PitMad ring, and I'll be forever grateful that you took a chance on me and this series.

And finally, I must thank my wonderful family once again for listening to my endless book talk, for your understanding and unfailing support, and, of course, for all the cups of coffee, both fresh and reheated. You know I could never have accomplished any of this without you.

TURN THE PAGE FOR A LOOK AT
THE FIRST BOOK IN AMY ROSE BENNETT'S
DISREPUTABLE DEBUTANTES SERIES . . .

HOW TO CATCH A WICKED VISCOUNT

NOW AVAILABLE FROM JOVE!

Disreputable Debutantes in the making!

A shocking scandal of epic proportions at a certain London school for "Young Ladies of Good Character" shakes the ton.

Does your genteel daughter attend such a den of iniquity? Read on to discover ten things one should consider when choosing a reputable academy . . .

The Beau Monde Mirror: The Society Page

Mrs. Rathbone's Academy for Young Ladies of Good Character, Knightsbridge, London

Midnight, February 3, 1815

Heavens. Take care, Charlie." Sophie Brightwell winced as her friend entered her bedroom and carelessly pushed the door shut with her slippered foot. The resultant bang was decidedly too loud in the relative silence of the dormitory wing of the Hans Place town house. "You'll wake Mrs. Rathbone for sure. If she finds out what we're up to . . ." Sophie couldn't suppress a shiver.

Lady Charlotte Hastings—or Charlie to her friends—threw her a disarming smile as she deposited a large bandbox of contraband and a battered leather satchel on the end of the single bed. "Don't worry so, darling Sophie," she said as she untied the black satin ribbon securing the box's lid with a flourish. "I just passed her bedchamber and she was snoring like a hold full of drunken sailors."

Arabella Jardine, who was perched on the edge of a bed-side armchair, pushed her honey-gold curls behind her ears and then smoothed her robe over her night rail. "Aye, 'tis true, Sophie," she agreed in her soft Scots burr. "I suspect she's been into the sherry again."

Sophie pressed her lips together to suppress a small sigh. Even though she loved Charlie like a sister, the earl's daughter didn't have as much to lose as she did, or indeed their other two partners in crime this night—Olivia de Vere and Arabella—if they were caught flouting the young ladies' academy's strict rules. So while it was quite true that Mrs. Agatha Rathbone, the apparently upstanding, middle-aged headmistress of her eponymous boarding school, was fond of a tipple—or ten—on Friday evenings, and nothing short of an earthquake or a herd of rampaging elephants was likely to rouse her, Sophie was still anxious about the whole idea of a midnight gathering—especially because it was oc-curring in the room she shared with Olivia.

Sophie's pulse leapt once more as the door opened again, this time admitting her roommate, bearing a tray of mis-matched china teacups.

"Ah, perfect timing, Miss de Vere," Charlie remarked as she lifted two dark glass bottles from the bandbox and bran-dished them in the air. "So what poison will you choose, my lovelies?" she asked, her topaz brown eyes dancing with merriment. "French brandy or port?"

Olivia carefully placed the tray on the cherrywood bed-side table then tossed her dark braid over one slender shoul-der. "Wh-what do you r-recommend? I h-haven't tried either one." Her manner of speech was an unusual combination of the lyrical and the discordant, her tone low and melodious with an appealing smokiness. Yet it was her stammer that drew attention; Sophie knew it tended to emerge when Ol-ivia was nervous or extremely fatigued.

"My grandfather let me try a wee sherry at Christmas," added Arabella. "But I've never tasted brandy or port wine."

"Hmm. The port is probably a little smoother for unseasoned drinkers. But I've heard my brother Nate say French brandy is excellent. Perhaps we should all begin with that." Charlie turned her bright gaze on Sophie. "Wouldn't you agree?"

"Yes." A burst of curiosity overcoming her trepidation, Sophie leaned across the quilted counterpane to examine the jumbled contents of the box. "So, what else have you smuggled in here?"

An enigmatic smile tugged at the corner of Charlie's mouth. "Oh, this and that," she said as she passed the bottle of brandy to Olivia to dispense. "All will be revealed after we raise our glasses—or I should say cups?—in a toast."

"A toast to what?" Arabella asked as she took her brimming teacup from Olivia. Beneath her gold-rimmed glasses, her pretty nose wrinkled when she sniffed at the amber liquid. "You are being altogether too mysterious, Charlie."

"To us, of course. And our new society."

Sophie arched an eyebrow. "And does this society have a name?"

"It certainly does." Charlie handed a teacup to Sophie and then beamed as she added, "Right, my darling girls. From this night on, we four shall henceforth be known as the Society for Enlightened Young Women, a society that will aim to provide its members with a stimulating education in all manner of worldly matters not included in this academy's current curriculum. Such knowledge will, of course, be invaluable when each of us leaves here and is subsequently obliged to embark on a quest to secure an advantageous match during the coming Season. And as we all know how cutthroat the marriage mart can be, I, as head monitor, feel it is my incumbent duty to begin your supplementary tutelage sooner rather than later." Her gaze touched each one of them. "If we are all in agreeance . . ."

Olivia nodded, Arabella murmured yes, and Sophie's brow knit into a suspicious frown. "What worldly matters in particular?" she asked.

Charlie cast her a knowing smile. "Why, matters that all

men, young and old, know about, but we, as the fairer, weaker sex, are supposed to remain ignorant of until we are wed. But by that time, I rather suspect it is too late. To my way of thinking, it would be much better to enter into marriage with one's eyes wide open. And dare I say it, perhaps *we* might have a little fun along the way too?"

"Are . . . are you referring to sexual c-congress?" whispered Olivia, her doe brown eyes widening with shock.

"Yes, I am. Among other things. The art of flirting is also an essential skill any wise debutante should have in her arsenal, and naturally, it is a precursor to any activity of an amorous nature." Charlie turned to Sophie and raised a quizzical brow; her eyes glowed with anticipation. "What say you, my friend? You haven't responded yet."

Sophie worried at her lower lip as she considered Charlie's proposal. Even though she hailed from Suffolk and possessed a rudimentary knowledge of "sexual congress"—as it pertained to the mating rituals of farmyard animals, at least—there was still much she did not know about the ways of the world—and the male of the species—compared to Charlie.

Indeed, Lady Charlotte Hastings was the only one in their close-knit group who had several brothers—one of whom was a well-known rakehell. And she also had a blue-stocking aunt who was purported to be a "liberal thinker" and "a woman ahead of her time." For these reasons, Sophie didn't doubt for a moment that Charlie possessed unique insights into the male mind and a singular knowledge of taboo topics.

Unlike her confident, highborn friend, Sophie was not a member of the *haut ton*. But if Charlie was prepared to equip her with the skills and knowledge of a sophisticated debutante, she would be an avid pupil. She'd much rather possess a modicum of self-assurance attending ton social events when the Season began in earnest. Heaven forbid that she should come across as a naive and nervous bumpkin who blushed and stammered whenever an eligible gentleman asked her to dance or even cast a glance in her direction. "Your idea has some merit," she at last conceded with a smile. "After all, forewarned is forearmed. How often will we meet?"

"Oh, once a week, I expect," said Charlie with a wave of one elegant hand. "And only when we are certain Rathbone is as drunk as a wheelbarrow. Which always seems to be on a Friday."

Sophie inclined her head. "Then I agree too."

"Excellent." A spark of mischief lit Charlie's eyes. "Now, if we were male students, at this point we'd no doubt plight our troths by doing something dreadful like expectorating across the room or slicing open our palms to make a blood oath, or at the very least we'd all expel some kind of foul air from an orifice we shall not speak of."

A delighted bubble of laughter escaped Arabella. "Oh, Charlie. I suspect you are quite right. But I think your original suggestion of a toast will suffice."

"Yes indeed," agreed Sophie.

Charlie's smile widened as she moved to the center of the worn hearthrug. The firelight limned her unruly chestnut hair in gold, and in that moment, Sophie couldn't help but think her friend bore more than a passing resemblance to a fiery Valkyrie or Artemis, the huntress—she was a determined young woman on a mission and she would not be thwarted.

Lifting her chipped Spode china teacup, Charlie caught all of their gazes and led the toast. "Well then, without further ado, let us all raise our cups and drink to the Society for Enlightened Young Women. Long may we prosper. And may we all find happiness wherever life takes us."

Sophie, Olivia, and Arabella raised their cups and in unison proclaimed, "Hear, hear," before they each took a sip of brandy. Then Olivia coughed, Arabella gasped, Sophie's eyes watered, and Charlie laughed.

"Oh, girls. It's not all that bad, is it?" she asked, rubbing Olivia's back.

"Where did you get this . . . this firewater?" Sophie wiped her eyes with the sleeve of her flannel night rail.

Charlie took another sip before replying. "My father's study here in London. He won't miss it. And even if he does, he'll probably assume Nate took it. He's such a devil."

Nate—or Nathaniel Hastings, Viscount Malverne—was Charlie's older brother and, as the eldest son of the family, heir to the earldom of Westhampton. Sophie had met him in passing two months ago in Hyde Park while out walking with Charlie, so she could certainly attest to the fact that he was wickedly handsome—a man who could easily make females blush just by casting a sinful smile their way. Indeed, Sophie rather suspected she resembled a boiled lobster when Charlie had made the introductions.

Of course, Charlie had warned her, Olivia, and Arabella on numerous occasions that Nate was a rogue to his very bones, and exactly the sort of man they should be wary of when they made their debuts. He seduced women regularly, without care or regard for their feelings or their ruined reputations. He was definitely *not* the sort of man who wished to marry anytime soon.

But despite Charlie's warnings, a small part of Sophie had always thrilled to the idea of capturing the attention of a man like Nate, even if it was just for a little while. What was it about wicked rakes that lured her—and perhaps other women—like a candle flame lured the hapless moth? The glint of mischief in Lord Malverne's dark eyes had seemed to contain a promise as his gaze traveled over her that cold winter's day: *Come with me and I will show you sensual delights. Forbidden things both bright and burning. Secret things that are inherently dangerous yet irresistible.* No wonder she still blushed at the memory. The heat in her cheeks had nothing to do with the brandy she sipped . . .

The sound of Arabella calling her name pulled Sophie from her ruminations, and she approached her bed to examine the other illicit items Charlie had brought with her to supplement their "education." Aside from a jar of sugared almonds and one of barley sugar sweets, there were several leather-bound volumes, a slender silver box, and a folio, which Charlie had just pulled from the leather satchel.

Sophie put down her cup, picked up one of the books, and then gasped. *Memoirs of a Woman of Pleasure*, volume one.

"Charlie," she breathed. "Where on earth did you get this? You know it's banned, don't you? That the author was arrested?" She once overheard two older women at the circulating library discussing it in excited whispers behind one of the standing shelves when they'd come across another not-quite-so-scandalous book entitled *Pamela; or, Virtue Rewarded.*

"Of course, I do," replied Charlie. "And to answer your first question, I found it in my father's library, along with volume two, and these . . ." She fanned a sheaf of sketches and drawings across the counterpane that put Olivia to the blush and sent Arabella into a paroxysm of laughter.

Sophie leaned closer, and her eyebrows shot up when she saw the erotic nature of each picture. "Oh, my Lord," she whispered, picking one up with shaking fingers as heat crawled over her face. "*What*, in heaven's name, is he doing to her?"

Charlie grinned. "That, my dear Sophie, is one of the many things you'll become enlightened about."

Behind her glasses, Arabella's gaze sharpened with interest as she picked up the ornate silver box, unfastened the clasp, and lifted the lid. "Cheroots, Charlie? Are these for us to try?"

"If you like," she said, taking one of the slender, quite feminine-looking cigars from the box. "My aunt Tabitha calls them *cigarrillos*. Her tobacconist makes them especially for her using a tobacco blend from Seville."

Olivia also picked up one of the cigars and gave it a small sniff. "My g-goodness. Perhaps we should call ourselves the Society for Scandalous Young Women."

"Well, we will only be deemed scandalous if we are caught," Charlie remarked as she plucked a taper from the spill vase on the carved wooden mantelpiece. She dipped it in the flame of a candle and touched it to the end of her *cigarrillo* until the tip caught alight. Then, after inhaling a small breath, she expertly puffed out a delicate cloud of smoke. The earthy yet sweet scent of burning tobacco filled the room.

"Ha, it's clear you've done this before," declared Arabella. Following Charlie's example, she used a taper to light her *cigarrillo* before placing it between her lips. She drew a breath and then promptly burst into a fit of coughing so violent, her glasses were dislodged.

Charlie's brow dipped into a concerned frown. "Gently, gently. Don't breathe in too deeply."

"Oh . . . that's . . . that's truly awful," gasped Arabella. Her face had turned a sickly shade of green. "I'm sure my lungs will never be the same again." Wrinkling her nose, she held the smoking cigar away from her like one might hold a dead mouse by the tail. "I'm sorry, Charlie. I don't think I want any more."

"That's quite all right." Charlie took it from her, then glanced between Olivia and Sophie. "Would either of you like to try?"

Olivia shook her head and Sophie crossed to the window, drawing back the dull blue utilitarian curtains. "No thank you, Charlie. And I think we should let some fresh air in. If Mrs. Rathbone notices the smell—"

"Mrs. Rathbone *has* noticed the smell. And the raucous laughter and chatter."

Oh no. Oh no, no, no. Her heart vaulting into the vicinity of her throat, Sophie whirled around then nearly fainted. In the open doorway, her plump arms folded over her ample chest, stood a glowering Mrs. Rathbone. Even though she only wore a rumpled night rail, a coarse woolen shawl, and a linen cap that was askew, her informal attire didn't diminish her gravitas or the seriousness of the moment in the least. From beneath heavy gray brows, her pale blue eyes skewered them all in turn. Arabella's countenance was green again, Olivia was as white as the bedsheets, and Sophie wondered how she continued to remain upright when her knees felt as though they were made of blancmange.

Charlie, on the other hand, looked remarkably unperturbed. She tossed both of the *cigarrillos* into the fire and lifted her chin. "Our apologies for disturbing your sleep, Mrs. Rathbone. We shall, of course, retire immediately. If you would just give me a moment to gather my things—"

Charlie had barely taken a step across the rug when Mrs. Rathbone raised a hand. "Stop right there, my gel," she barked. Her glare swept over Sophie's bedside table and bed, and then her fleshy face turned an alarming shade of crimson when she took in the nature of the scattered sketches. "What. Are. Those?" she demanded in a shaking voice. When no one responded, she raised a quivering hand to her equally quivering jowls. "And what have you all been drinking? Brandy? Is that brandy I see in your cups? And what's that other bottle on the bed?"

"Port," replied Charlie without batting an eyelid. She started to add, "They're for medicinal pur—" but Mrs. Rathbone jabbed a finger in her direction.

"Not another word out of you, Lady Charlotte." The headmistress all but charged across the room and snatched up both bottles. Although her expression still bordered on furious, Sophie thought she detected a covetous glimmer in the woman's eyes. "This behavior is outrageous," she continued as she tucked both bottles into the crook of one arm. "Beyond the pale. Smoking? Imbibing alcohol? Studying lewd material? And all in the middle of the night! I can scarcely believe it. In all my years as the headmistress of this establishment, I have never, *ever* encountered such shocking conduct from young ladies. You should all be ashamed of yourselves. Just wait till the school's patrons and your parents hear about it!"

Charlie inclined her head. "Yes, it is shameful," she agreed in a contrite tone that *almost* sounded sincere to Sophie's ears. "And although you forbade me to speak, Mrs. Rathbone, I feel compelled to confess that everything you see on the bed—the books, the sketches, the cheroot cigars—*and* the bottles of port and brandy, all of it belongs to me. I alone bear the blame. Miss Brightwell, Miss Jardine, and Miss de Vere are innocent of any wrongdoing."

Mrs. Rathbone narrowed her eyes. "Yet all of these pro-scribed items are in Miss Brightwell's and Miss de Vere's bedchamber. And"—her gaze darted about the room—"I spy *four* teacups of brandy." She gave an inelegant sniff and looked down her flushed nose at them all. "As far as I can see, each one of you is guilty of unladylike conduct in the extreme and, subsequently, you are not fit to remain within this academy's walls. In the morning, I shall send word to your families and begin the process of having you all ex-pelled."

Arabella sucked in a startled breath, Olivia wrung her hands, and Sophie felt as though a massive weight had just crushed her chest, driving all the air from her lungs. *Oh, dear God, no. This can't be happening.* What would her family say? Her mother? Her stepfather?

The ton?

But it *was* happening. Even Charlie's face was ashen.

As Sophie struggled to drag in enough air to breathe, Mrs. Rathbone issued instructions to Charlie and Arabella to gather up all of the offending items off the bed, and Ol-ivia was ordered to tip the contents of the teacups out of the window into the frosty garden bed below.

"I'm sorry," mouthed Charlie as she picked up her band-box and followed a tearful Arabella and a righteously in-dignant Rathbone out of the room.

As soon as the door clicked shut, Sophie sank onto her bed and hugged a pillow against her chest. Hot tears of mortification and despair scalded her eyelids.

There was sure to be a scandal of monumental propor-tions. *Thrown out of a young ladies' academy.* Her reputa-tion and that of all of her friends would be ruined. There would be no invitations to Almack's. No invitations to any-where at all. Only stares and whispers, closed doors and censure wherever she went.

Her parents would be livid, her younger sisters heart-broken.

She was only eighteen, but she would be forever branded

as a woman of loose character and questionable morals. A hussy.

A slut.

Sophie swallowed, attempting to dislodge the gathering ache in her throat. How on earth was she to meet her love match now? She'd never make a socially and financially advantageous union as her family had hoped she would; indeed, without such a marriage, there was a very real chance her stepfather might lose Nettlefield Grange and the accompanying estate. How shocking that her dreams and her family's livelihood could be crushed to dust because of her folly.

The weight on her chest was back, and her heart felt as though it might crack beneath the strain.

"Do . . . do you think there's any chance Rathbone m-might try to hush things up? To preserve her own and the school's reputation?" murmured Olivia in a voice husky with tears.

Sophie dashed away her own tears with shaking fingers. "I expect she might try to, but word is bound to get out. Who doesn't love a juicy piece of gossip? And besides Charlie, none of us has any social connections that would hold sway with Rathbone. I really don't think there is anything we can do to stop our expulsion."

Olivia's eyes glimmered with fresh tears. "We'll be socially destroyed then."

Sophie's heart broke just that little bit more at witnessing her sweet friend's distress. She cast aside her pillow and crossed to the other bed. "Yes, Olivia," she whispered as she enveloped the trembling girl in a hug. "I'm afraid we will."

Ready to find
your next great read?

Let us help.

Visit prh.com/nextread

Penguin
Random
House